I0615922

Edge of Arcadia

by Kenneth Reah

First published 2014 by Fantastic Books Publishing

Cover art by Kenneth Reah
Cover design by Paula Murphy

ISBN: 978-1-909163-28-7

Dedication

To my wife, Danuta.

PROLOGUE

The undertaker was a woman. Over the years, Aidan had been to quite a few funerals, but this was the first in his experience to be conducted by a woman. No reason why not, he supposed, but distinctly unusual. She was quite young; perhaps thirtyish and attractive; neat black suit, the skirt straight, ending demurely just below the knees; shapely legs in black tights; low-heeled black shoes; and a high-necked blouse, crisply white, with some sort of black cravat at the neck. Her dark hair was combed tightly back and braided behind. The pallor of her face was relieved by the merest hint of eye shadow and lipstick. She exuded that air of calm, reverend efficiency which is the hallmark of the calling. Briefly, he pictured her in bed.

There were many more people waiting outside the chapel than he had expected. Colleagues, of course, with their spouses; the few relatives. But there were many faces he did not recognise. He had no idea she knew so many people who cared enough about her to come to her funeral. God knows, she wasn't the most gregarious of people. They were all waiting.

The back of the hearse was open. The black-suited bearers waited on either side of the partially withdrawn coffin while the undertaker stood, reassuringly capable, by the brass-handled oak doors leading to the chapel. Aidan stood, a daughter to each side, his arms about their shoulders. He looked down at Dora, the younger, squeezing her shoulder gently. She looked up at him, her eyes moist, blinking, her lips sucked in, she attempted a smile. Then he looked down at Bobby, the elder. She, unmoving, looked solemnly straight ahead.

The undertaker glanced discreetly at her watch. One of the bearers cleared his throat, the noise of it penetrating the subdued murmur of voices; greetings, as new arrivals were incorporated into the knot of waiting mourners; the trivial exchanges about the weather that served to displace temporarily the need to confront the reality of death. It was a sparkling day in early spring – the sort of day, thought Aidan, when surely nothing terrible should happen. As though in affirmation, an early blackbird in a distant tree rehearsed a hesitant note or two, while Aidan received unspoken condolences as the eyes of the late arrivals met his, responding with a nod and a wan smile.

He hated funerals. But then who loves them? He asked himself. He looked round at the assembled company. It reminded him of waiting for the second performance at the cinema, on a Saturday evening in his youth. The foyer, the closed doors guarded by the smart usherette in her brown, braided uniform, her torch at the ready. Waiting for the final crescendo of the closing music, then the national anthem, followed by the rattling of the exit doors and the chattering efflux of people. A cremation was rather like that; next in the queue, you waited outside for the last chords of the closing hymn. The doors were opened and people shuffled out – but quietly, at cremations. People very like the ones – your people – waiting to go in. People, soberly dressed, black ties, some red-eyed from weeping; all solemn and silent now, but who would later erupt, drinks in hand, into noise, even jollity, as lapsed acquaintance was renewed, news caught up on, memories revived, anecdotes exchanged. Thus were the mourners reincorporated with feasting into the community of the living and the anguish of death elided once more. Then it was your turn. The premises were now available. You had scant twenty minutes to tie up the loose ends of a life.

Aidan had seen the minister, attaché case in hand, nod to the undertaker and enter through the side door to the vestry. The undertaker glanced at her watch again. Aidan glanced at his. Two minutes to go. She had always said she wanted to be cremated. Most people seemed to these days – though Aidan rather thought that, apart from the niggling fear of being buried alive, a traditional interment was preferable; more dignified, perhaps. Perhaps less standardised, less tightly scheduled. But he didn't know … perhaps you had to queue at the graveside too these days. Well, whatever; he'd been able to grant this wish of hers.

He was thinking this when the chapel doors opened, releasing a sudden burst of music (which, with surprise, he recognised as something from Oklahoma) and discharged the preceding funeral in a slow dribble. As the last person left the chapel, the music stopped abruptly, to be replaced after a short interval by the opening bars of Mozart's 'Ave Verum'. It was now her turn, the music was what she had wanted. Not that they had ever dwelt morbidly on death and its appurtenances; It was just that they had from time to time, in the days when civilised conversation was still a possibility, discussed the music they would wish to be dispatched to – rather in the same spirit as they discussed their 'Desert Island Disc' choices – never believing for one moment that either occasion would ever actually arise. Well here was another wish whose fulfilment he'd been able to arrange.

The minister, now robed, had appeared at the open doors and at a subtle signal from the undertaker, the bearers, with practised skill, withdrew the coffin from the hearse, hoisted it onto their shoulders and, led by the minister, accompanied discreetly by the undertaker, processed slowly into the chapel. She had signalled for Aidan and his two daughters to follow, then the handful of relatives, then the rest of the congregation to tag on behind.

Arriving at the front of the chapel, Aidan organised his daughters into the first pew and slid in beside them. He forbore to bow his head in prayer as was the custom, wishing it to be clear from the start and to all and sundry, that he wanted no truck with the Almighty. He picked up the Order of Service, indicating to his daughters to do the same. As they sat, waiting, he looked at the coffin, now resting on a, what? A catafalque? Sounded a bit grand; lying in state, that sort of thing, but in a crematorium? Well he didn't know. It would have to do, the coffin was resting on it. It was an unnerving feeling, to think, there's someone in there. His wife. His daily companion of two decades. Looking, if he could see her, perhaps much the same as she always looked – perhaps a little paler, but drained of everything, good and bad, that she ever was. Just inert matter finely shaped, and soon to be reduced to ashes. He had in moments of desperation sometimes wished her dead – and now she was. But he hadn't really meant it – had he? That would be really evil and he wasn't that, was he?

The congregation stood as the minister climbed the steps to the pulpit. He fidgeted with the lectern, then, looked down over his glasses at those assembled. The 'Ave Verum' faded disconcertingly – like pop songs always seem to these days, as if their creators had never learned endings, Aidan thought.

'Please be seated,' the minister said.

She had never been a churchgoer – not, at any rate, since the first years of their marriage – yet she had never admitted to the kind of amiable atheism he embraced. It was so many years since they'd been able to have any sort of discussion of deep things anyway, and even then, matters like this were never resolved on a live-and-let-live basis. She could never settle for less than bloody attrition, no matter how trifling the original disagreement. So in the absence of any specific intelligence, he had concluded that on matters of belief, she was hedging her bets and thought it would meet the case if he went for the traditional rites of the Church of England.

The service proceeded. Numbly, he sat, stood or kneeled, according to the minister's instructions, automatically, without sense of meaning, uttering the words on the sheet he held in his hands. A hymn; readings. Then the minister was talking. Talking about her. As far as Aidan was aware, he didn't know her in life, but nevertheless, in death, he was talking about her. Aidan didn't think this outrageous. It was part of the job; what else could he do? Someone, not wishing to burden the bereaved husband with the matter, must have briefed him.

'... and we remember her above all for her great love of the children ...' Aidan felt Bobby wince and she looked up to him.

'Not me Dad,' she whispered loudly, 'she didn't love me though. Did she?' Aidan reached for her hand and squeezed it. Those behind and within earshot rustled their Order of Service sheets and exchanged shocked glances. The minister went on with the bit about suffer the little children ... and then told the congregation about how devotedly the children had loved her in return, how they were grieved by her death, how she was an irreplaceable loss ...

As her soul was eventually commended to God, the curtains closed smoothly in front of the catafalque – the cinema again, Aidan thought – and the 'Ave Verum' recommenced.

There – it was all done. The minister took up his position at the door, and Aidan and his two daughters led the way out. He acknowledging the restrained smiles of sympathy on the way, Dora and Bobby, their eyes fixed on the ground before them, feeling, he supposed, rather different things about their new status as motherless children. Outside the chapel, as they passed the handful of people waiting for the next cremation, he heard the 'Ave Verum' fade abruptly away, to be replaced by the opening of 'All Creatures of Our God and King'.

Outside, the undertaker beckoned. She would, she said, take them to where the flowers were displayed. She led them along a short path to a place beyond a plantation of cotoneaster, juniper and bare crimson, and green dogwood, where there was a kind of brick bunker – the sort of thing, Aidan thought, you might see in a market garden, holding manure. The flowers from the day's cremations, each in separate mounds, lay there on the grass. An elderly man and woman from the previous one lingered, heads askew, this side and that, as they tried to read the inscriptions on the cards attached to the cellophane wrapped bouquets. They left, perhaps not wishing to overlap with someone else's grief, as Aidan and his daughters approached the most recent pile, followed at some distance by the rest

13

of the mourners. Aidan dropped to one knee, turning and twisting the cards, to read the messages of condolence. Who had remembered her then?

Standing just behind him, Bobby said, 'Dad, why are they all wrapped up? Why don't they take them out of the cellophane?'

'I don't know, Bobby. They never do. I don't know why. Let's do it, shall we? Dora, come on.'

All three on their knees, they set to ripping the wrappings off the bouquets and spreading the flowers, till the area became heady with scent. All three crouched there for a while, as though dazed by the fragrance, then standing up, Aidan with an armful of crumpled cellophane, they surveyed the scene in silence.

As he stood there with unfocused eyes, he allowed everything to dissolve into a riotous pattern of colour and shape. Flowers, drained of the meanings put there by convention and dissociated from their function in nature, were now abstract; pure form and colour afloat in his consciousness. For moments, he held still, detached from the place, the time, the occasion. Then a distant roar he had been barely aware of crescendoed overhead, as a chilling breeze gusted hoarsely through the treetops, setting the bare twigs scratching at the sky, bringing him back to reality. Allowing the crumpled cellophane to fall to the ground, he put his arms around his daughters and drew them towards him.

A little guilty at his surrender to sensuality, he tried to look into his conscience, but could see only mud there. A poor exchange. It was all too new, too sudden, too shocking to get it into any kind of perspective. He had been a widower – unglamorous term – for six days. A single parent. He was what, for some time, he had vainly, impossibly, unreasonably wished to be – free. Well, free from her. There were the children, of course – his sole responsibility now. No freedom there but the freedom to deal with them his way. And for Bobby, freedom from persecution. He hoped Bobby would now grow to be a normal happy child and a sane, balanced adult. Shocking to think that he believed she would be better off with her mother dead. It seemed hardly possible that she would grieve. If he believed in such stuff, he would be praying that she was not irremediably damaged

Yes, he was free from her, but worried, perhaps ashamed at the elation he felt in that freedom, for he would not have wished for it at such a cost. Should he feel guilty that he was not overwhelmed by grief? He didn't know. Feelings, like belief, were not determined by the will. They were an unwitting response to the flow of events on the individual, with his or her unique history and genes. He did not feel remorse; he did not feel responsible that they had parted in disarray, but only regret. She had not regained consciousness, so there had been no opportunity to do any repair work on their ravaged relationship, to stitch together a semblance of reconciliation with Bobby. At best it could only have been a semblance, to make things look decent at the end. To be real, it would have required her to understand what she had done to her daughter. It would have required her to change, to repent, to make restitution. But it had not happened. So he might have to lie about it. How could she, in life, in the face of events, have blocked it from her mind? How could she have shared in the palpable distress of her family and denied her own culpability? She may be dead, but there remained a lingering, suppurating wound. His anger was undiminished, and now, because she was no longer there, unassuageable. De mortuis nil nisi bonum. Sod that.

CHAPTER 1

One winter's afternoon, Aidan Hamilton was sitting in the small room in the old part of the college; the room that served him as both study and studio. It had just been confirmed that the college would close in three-year's time. The expected death sentence: redundancy. But, while drinking coffee at his desk, he was absorbed by a matter of much more immediate concern. The fact was, he was intending to commit adultery that evening (he put it to himself as baldly as that), having fallen in love with one of his students. It was all arranged.

He imagined the outrage the strait-laced founders of the college would have felt at such a thing. They'd set it up in 1872 to train teachers, within the Christian (but non-denominational) faith, and this it had done rather well for just over a century. When it became obvious that closure was inevitable, the older members of staff accepted with resignation the prospect of early retirement, but among the younger ones (and forty-five-year-old Aidan considered himself one of these), a kind of subterranean hysteria seemed to take hold; a kind sense of fin de siècle decadence. It may have been something of this that finally nudged him off the path of virtue and into the arms of Louise.

Two things: one, it would be Aidan's first actual act of adultery in twenty years of marriage; and two, Louise was a mature student – no more than twenty years his junior.

The college had to go. Too many teachers, the government had decided. No nonsense about Small is Beautiful; it was the smallest colleges that had to go first. Not economical. And although Swaleborough College had doubled its size in the sixties (then, the same government had decided there weren't enough teachers), it was still relatively small – so, it was goodbye.

Aidan had taught happily there for longer than would have been prudent for a career-minded teacher (for he was not ambitious and knew where he was well off) and the teaching had been wonderful. He had regularly given thanks to the God he didn't believe in for his having been called to such congenial labour. Now though, even without the death sentence, life would not have been all hunky-dory, for in recent years the quality of his marriage had settled into what he feared was an irreversible decline. Now, he had persuaded himself that, notwithstanding his marriage vows, he no longer owed his wife, Cathy, fidelity.

Thus it was; for the last fourteen years (God was it really fourteen?) of his marriage, he had, in his daily life, been surrounded by students; in the first five years, always female, for it was at that time a women's college; later, with an increasing leavening of men. Always though, there was a preponderance of women (or would you call them girls?)

20

– of every degree of desirability and attractiveness, and perhaps, for all he knew, availability. His teaching brought him regularly into close, almost intimate contact with his students; for to stand behind one at an easel, and discuss and analyse the various bits of a nude model from a common viewpoint, required the close proximity of heads. When the student was female and nubile, the frisson he was apt to feel was not wholly aesthetic; consequently he had, over those years, committed conceptual adultery a dozen times a day. Yes, he knew what St Matthew had written, '... every one that looketh on a woman to lust after her hath committed adultery already with her in his heart', but he'd always thought that unfair. For Christ's sake, how could you help it? His lust was built in, hard-wired. He wasn't responsible for the actual lust – just how he responded to it. And to date, his response had been exemplary. That is to say, in the real world, fidelity had prevailed – though whether this was a matter of principle, indoctrination or of unadventurous lassitude, he couldn't be completely certain.

Often he had groaned inwardly at the irony – the agony – of being the owner of an under-fulfilled libido in a life so abundantly full of desirable but prohibited young women. The arrival and eventual omnipresence of the miniskirt exacerbated his torment; for no matter how commonplace the sight of naked thighs became, he never became inured to it. He observed with envy the casual intimacies that took place in the boy–girl relationships that continually developed, flourished and waned among the students, and marvelled at the free display of sexuality and the insouciance with which it was accepted. So were they inured to it? How could anyone be? He wondered that the lecture rooms and corridors were not perpetually strewn with copulating couples. How could they ever be thinking about anything else when everything was always so conspicuously on display? Aidan was painfully aware that his sexual mores were seriously in need of updating.

To make matters worse, for sometime past, his sleep had regularly been embellished by hauntingly vivid dreams, in which a young woman of surpassing beauty and sensuality falls into his arms. Together they wander hand in hand in an Arcadian landscape, suffused with the golden light of the late afternoon sun. Consumed by happiness, they pay little heed to the man in a white toga washing his feet in the spring which cascades into a meandering brook. The noble lady in the flowing peplum bearing a basket of fruit on her head smiles at them from the far bank of the river. Aidan nods graciously, and he and the girl (he can never put a name to her) continue blissfully along the path towards the ancient walled city nestling at the foot of the distant hills. On the way they pass a group of young people, some bathing naked in the stream, others practising archery. Another little group reclines at the feet of a bearded sage, whose words seemed to hold them in thrall.

Presently, the lovers come to a fragrant olive grove, by a grassy knoll and they lie down to rest in a sun-soaked hollow. Aidan is overpowered by feelings of tenderness which, his soul knows, suffuses them both. Their eyes meet (though he can never remember their colour or any other specific details). The diaphanous gown the girl is wearing has slipped from her shoulder, exposing an exquisitely rounded breast. He tenderly caresses the pink nipple, then, with great delicacy, cups the breast in his hand. Soon their lips touch. It is at first the merest, lightest touch of a butterfly's wing. They linger, as though poised on the precipice of some deep canyon. Then suddenly, all passion ignites and they are writhing together uncontrollably, limbs interlocking. He feels her thighs part and reaches down to draw up the loose shift, which is the only garment he is wearing …

This is the point at which he invariably awoke. He would return to consciousness into a desperate feeling of loss – the anguish of withered tenderness; almost the grief of bereavement.

'Oh Christ,' he would moan inwardly. 'Oh shit, oh shit … God, I can't believe it … even in my dreams I can't bloody well be unfaithful.'

He would fling out of bed, dismally aware of his unemployable erection and more than ever conscious of the lack of passion in his marriage. He could not blame Cathy for this; in fact he had generally inclined to blame his own ineptitude, for, thinking back to those uninviting sex manuals he had furtively perused on rickety tables outside second-hand bookshops, in the days before he was wed, they seemed always to be addressed to the man.

These days, Cathy seemed to need him occasionally, usually he was able to oblige. After prolonged effort had produced from her some modest signs of pleasure she would yield herself passively to him for him to take such satisfaction as he might, in fulfilment of her part of the unspoken bargain. But that satisfaction was not great, he had always felt it should be better than this. Were they right, those manuals? Had it to be much careful wooing in search of a suppressed libido; much arduous labour in pursuit of an elusive orgasm; an orgasm seldom, if ever, achieved during penetration; simultaneous orgasm nothing more than an absurd male fantasy. As with most of the dissatisfactions of their married life, it seemed undiscussable; it was not simply that Cathy denied there was anything wrong or even that improvement might be possible; it was just something she could not, would not, talk about. It was as if this ultimate act of intimacy existed only in a clandestine world which, once the moment had passed, evaporated into oblivion. It was much the same when it came to Bobby.

'There's nothing wrong with our relationship,' she would say. 'We get on perfectly well when you're not around. I do my best for her.' Nothing to discuss.

So that afternoon, Aidan, though dizzy with excitement and hardly able to believe what was happening to him, was, in a more down-to-earth sort of way, anxious about the protocol of a first adulterous assignation. It was all arranged and for that very evening. So he had to decide what to bring. Somehow flowers didn't seem quite the right thing. They were too formal – too conventional – too prissy for an illicit liaison. He had thought, then, that some kind of present would be appropriate. But what? Jewellery, perhaps ... but no ... too expensive ... and with connotations of permanence, which at this stage seemed hardly suitable. In the end, it was television that decided for him. That vivid image of a square jawed, polo-necked hero swinging across dizzying street canyons, to leave a box of chocolates on the lady's dressing table. He remembered the lubricious delicacy with which the first chocolate was placed between the open lips and the promise it evoked. He had gone out and bought a half-pound box of Milk Tray.

CHAPTER 2

That evening he entered his study, locking the door behind him very quietly – though silence was hardly important, in view of the noise rising from the studio below. The music had risen again to a howl overlaid by a head-jarring beat. He had never thought he would ever be able or ever want to respond to that kind of noise. It had always been just a ubiquitous aural pollution. He'd endured it in pubs, escaped from it out of shops, suffered the manic thumping of it blasting out of young men's cars at traffic lights, even walked out of restaurants because of it. Hating it; until tonight. Tonight, it had introduced him to sensations he'd not felt before; he'd actually just been dancing to it – uninhibitedly dancing to it; and, slightly muffled, it was going to provide the aural background to this act of, well, not really seduction (for that entails one initially unwilling participant), perhaps more of co-operative passion.

Having just left the melee in the studio below, he felt hot and sweaty. This kind of dancing was sure as hell more energetic than the ballroom dancing he'd done on a Saturday night at the Roxy, in his youth. He felt sticky and madly aroused. Still with him was the sense of the proximity of her body; her palpable nakedness under that tiny dress, the erotic abandonment of her movement, the lingering fragrance of her perfume, as he began his wait. It was ten past ten when he'd left her at the bar with a dry Martini. They'd agreed she would wait about twenty minutes or so, then slip out unobtrusively, come up to his room and tap on the door three times.

The curtains were still open in his small studio-cum-study. Outside, the moon had just risen above the rooftops. It promised frost, casting its cold brilliance through the bare trees and into the tall window, making rhomboids of light on the floor, fragmenting over furniture and walls. But it was warm inside. The big old-fashioned radiator under the window gave an occasional comforting rumble. Aidan did not switch on the light. He did not want to draw attention to his presence there, and anyway he knew where everything was. He looked at his watch, clearly visible in the moonlight.

'God,' he thought, 'twenty minutes.' He'd put the chocolates on his desk. That was one thing. He'd come up just before the party began, wondering what other arrangements he needed to make. He had ensured that the big, deep old-fashioned armchair, his only comfortable piece of furniture, was free from clutter and conveniently placed. Then after looking at the uninviting lino-covered floor, he had brought a large bundle of sculptor's scrim from the stockroom next to his studio and arranged it in a casual heap on the floor, in the corner next to the radiator. He'd moved his easel and the trolley with his paints and brushes into the opposite corner. Next, he'd gone to the cupboard beneath the bookcase and taken from it a bottle of Dry Vermouth, a bottle of gin, a bottle of whisky and some glasses, put them conveniently on the low table beside the easy chair. Now he poured himself a generous measure of whisky and took it over to the window. Trying to calm himself, he sipped his drink as he looked out at the freezing night.

Oh God, oh God, oh God, he thought, this is insane, mad, crazy. And wonderful, wonderful. He took another, this time substantial, swig at the whisky, moving agitatedly round the room, stopping to look at the familiar things; his drawings on the wall, Bessie, the books, his coffee machine. Christ. It was only at the beginning of term that he first met her. And now ... Oh God, that interview. He remembered every detail. It was the only time he ever saw her in a suit. Well, it was an interview, wasn't it? He was always drawn to the image of the beautiful, high-powered executive from a world so remote from his own. If only he'd known

* * *

'Thank you, Miss ... er ... Parslet. It's been very nice to meet you,' Barbara had said, 'We'll let you know as soon as we can.'

Miss Parslet stood up. Gerry hastened to open the door. Miss Parslet manoeuvred her considerable bulk through the opening and with a weak bespectacled smile bade her interviewers goodbye.

'Well,' said Barbara, 'she seemed like a nice girl.' Gerry groaned. 'Perhaps we could …'

Gerry interrupted her. 'Barbara, she had never heard of Rodin, Magritte or Jackson Pollock.'

'Nor yet Poussin,' added Aidan.

'Well I don't know,' Barbara pressed on. 'I think she might shape up, you know …'

'But we're not so hard up for students, that we need to accept candidates, in what, I may remind you is to be our final intake, who "might shape up",' insisted Aidan. 'I couldn't possibly agree to admitting someone whose only experience of creative activity is tatting and thinks it's a good idea to teach kids how to draw matchstick men.'

'And has such a spotty face,' added Gerry, under his breath.

'You were saying, Gerry?' queried Barbara.

'Er … I agree with Aidan,' he said.

'Oh, very well.' She thought for a moment or two. 'Perhaps you're right. Let's get on then.' She stifled a yawn and looked at her watch. 'Is this the last one?'

'Yes. Now this one looks really interesting,' said Aidan. 'I've just skimmed through her papers. She's from London for a start.'

'Well that's interesting enough,' said Gerry. Most of the students were pretty local.

'And,' continued Aidan, 'she's been to Art College, has an N. D. D. in textiles and has spent the last four years in a London design studio.' He passed the application forms to Barbara. She went through them briefly, Gerry looking on.

'Well she looks good on paper.'

'So why does she suddenly decide she wants to come out into the sticks to a small teacher training college? Has she suddenly found her vocation?' asked Gerry.

'Well let's find out, shall we?' said Barbara. 'Will you call her in, Aidan?'

Aidan got up, opened the door, put his head round it. 'Miss DeGrey?' He stopped, then realised she was looking at him with a puzzled frown. 'Er … please come in.'

He waved her in, stumbled slightly as he resumed his seat. She was quite tall and wore an expensive-looking dark grey suit. It was elegantly cut. The lapels curved in diagonals across her breasts and the deep cut collar of her white blouse formed a V-shaped frame to the emphatic cleft between them. A delicate wisp of scarf, of a red that matched her lips was knotted about her throat. Aidan, because he was now sitting behind the table, could not see all of her legs, but the six inches of thigh visible between the top of the table and the bottom of her skirt boded well.

'Please sit down, Miss DeGrey,' said Barbara. Miss DeGrey put a small portfolio on the table. As she settled into the chair, looking down to adjust her skirt and while the Head of Department was shuffling papers, Aidan and Gerry exchanged glances. The latter pursed his lips in a silent whistle. As Miss DeGrey looked down, a wisp of her shoulder-length black hair came adrift and descended across her face. Looking up, she smiled and with one hand restored it to order. Her eyes were large and brown, her complexion pale, her lips full and bright red.

Barbara put down the papers and looked at the last candidate over her half-moon spectacles.

'Well, Miss DeGrey,' she began, 'I'm Barbara Hedley, Head of Department and specialist in textiles; this is Aidan Hamilton, in charge of painting and this Gerald Scott our potter. Henry Portman, our sculptor is off on a field trip, so can't be with us today. And besides our specialisms, we are all, of course, educators.'

Miss DeGrey smiled at each in turn. 'How do you do,' she said.

'Now what I think we're all most curious about,' Barbara said, 'is why you want to give up a job in a prestigious studio in London to come to train to be a teacher here in the north.'

She looked down for a moment, then, looking back at them she said, 'Well, there is no easy answer to that question. I wouldn't like you to think I've suddenly found a vocation to teach – a bit like a nun.'

Not in the least like a nun, thought Aidan.

'But after four years in London, I was somehow getting sick of the noise and the continual rush of things – of always having to be on the go. Oh I realise that's a bit of a cliché …' Aidan smiled in approval at this insight, '… but it really is how I felt at the time … and how I still feel now. And – well – I thought I should perhaps at least try something more socially useful than designing expensive fabrics for rich people.'

'Yes, but why the north of England? There are many excellent colleges in the south; I've examined in a few of them.'

'Oh yes, I know that, but … well you may think this a bit silly, but just about the time I was feeling the need to make some decisions, I was reading this novel. It was the kind I think you would call a suspense thriller, or something. Well it was full of suspense. There was murder and all kinds of mayhem as well as personal unhappiness. The critics sometimes talk about a book being a page-turner. Well this was one. But at the end, when all is resolved, the two main characters go away, seeking escape and the resolution of their personal problems. Well the author takes them to Lindisfarne and evokes such a moving scene of – oh, I don't know – wild tranquillity. Well, I just felt I had to go there.'

'Hm,' said Barbara, dryly, 'very romantic. But you know, Miss DeGrey, though Swaleborough is a northern town, it's really not that close to Lindisfarne. However, if you should come here I think you'd find some respite from the tensions of the big city.'

Gerry then spoke. 'What would you expect to get out of a course like ours, then, Miss DeGrey?'

'Well I would hope to be able ... for one thing, to be able to develop my own creativity. As you know, I have a good background in textiles and art history, but I would like to expand my range and specialise in painting – with perhaps some pottery.' She smiled at Gerry.

'Oh,' he said, 'I'm sure we could arrange that.'

'But of course I know that's only part of it and really the main thing is to end up a good teacher.'

'Yes,' said Aidan, 'that's right.'

'So,' she continued, 'I'd expect to learn something of the theory of education, some psychology – that sort of thing – and perhaps to learn something of, well some other subjects. I'd like to keep up my languages – French and German –' Aidan's eyes lit up; how nice to practice his German with Miss DeGrey '– oh and, of course, get to work with children in school.'

She spoke quietly and self-confidently in what Aidan classified as a posh – though not affected – southern accent, markedly different from the varieties of northern speech most commonly heard in the college. As the interview proceeded, Miss DeGrey responded to the questions she was asked and discussed the topics which were introduced, in her well-bred voice, with a modest competence quite without a trace of the stridency northerners are apt to associate with – well, people like Miss DeGrey.

34

Eventually, Barbara said, 'Well then, Miss DeGrey, can we have a look at some of your work, now?'

They gathered round the open portfolio. Aidan, standing next to the candidate allowed his eyes to dwell briefly upon her enhanced cleavage as she bent over her work, his nostrils picked up an intoxicating hint of fragrance. They sifted carefully through fabric designs, samples of finished materials, studies from nature and a few rather good life drawings from her art school days. This process was punctuated by murmurs of:

'That's interesting …'

'Mmmmm …'

'Oh, this is very well observed …'

'Rather beautiful …'

Presently, 'Well, thank you, Miss DeGrey. That was very interesting.' This was Barbara.

'Aidan, Gerry, anything else you'd like to ask?'

'No, I don't think so,' they said almost simultaneously.

'But,' said Gerry, 'are there any questions you'd like to ask us, Miss DeGrey?'

'Well, I think I've got the hang of the important things, but here's one … I was going to call it unimportant – but really, it is quite important too, if I'm going to spend three years here. It's, well, what sort of social facilities does the college offer?'

'I'll leave you gentlemen to answer that one,' Barbara said, with just a touch of astringency in her voice.

'Ah,' said Gerry, 'haven't you had a prospectus?'

'Oh, er no, I seem to have missed out on that … perhaps because of my late application.'

'Right then, let me rectify that omission.' Gerry opened a drawer in the desk, shuffled around a bit and produced a copy of the glossy new prospectus which had gone to press not long before, as part of a last ditch attempt to escape closure.

Shit, thought Aidan. There was a picture of him, with a student at an easel. His arm was at full stretch, his hand holding a vertical pencil, as he measured something. He was squinting – and, oh the wrinkles. He hated it.

Gerry passed it over the desk to her. She looked down, picked up her handbag and extracted from it a spectacle case. She snapped this open and from it took a pair of small, oval, gold-rimmed glasses, which she placed near the end of her nose.

'Thank you,' she said, smiling again and looking at Gerry over her glasses. 'It looks very interesting.'

She flicked through a few pages, then, 'Ah, I see you're in it Mr Hamilton,' she said.

'Yes,' said Aidan, frowning, 'I'm afraid so.'

'Well,' she said, after politely browsing a moment or two longer, 'I'll peruse it on the train on my way home tonight.'

Gerry said, 'But to answer some of your question now, I can tell you that you'll find all the usual sports facilities on the campus and we're surrounded by wonderful countryside for out-door pursuits.'

'We've got good drama and music facilities, too.' Aidan said.

'Ah,' she said, nodding.

'And of course, we have a college bar, now, which is very popular.'

'And there are some good pubs in the town centre, well patronised by the students.'

'And some staff,' added Barbara, somewhat sourly. Miss DeGrey caught Aidan's eye, he thought he detected a scintilla of a wink.

'Oh well then,' said Miss DeGrey, 'that's a good start.'

She closed the brochure, slipped it into her portfolio and looked up again at her interrogators, waiting.

'Very well then, Miss DeGrey. If that's all, I think we can declare the interview over. It's been very nice to meet you. We'll let you know as soon as we can.'

Miss DeGrey stooped to retrieve her handbag from the floor at the side of the chair, again displaying the beguiling cleft between her breasts and standing up, took her portfolio from the desk. She smiled at them again and said, 'Goodbye then. And thank you.'

Aidan and Gerry arrived simultaneously at the door to see her out. She rewarded them with a dazzling smile. The door closed, they resumed their seats around the table. There was silence for a moment, then Aidan and Gerry both began at once.

'Well I certainly think …'

'Well it seems to me …'

Barbara cut in. 'That girl is a hussy. How on earth do you think a brassy sophisticate like her is going to fit in with our country lads and lasses?'

'Oh come off it Barbara,' protested Aidan. 'That's pure prejudice. It's an outright social judgement. Okay, she's a bit more metropolitan than we're used to, but I certainly wouldn't call her brassy. Just remember, she was doing her interview stuff. I mean, we're here to assess suitability for the teaching profession. We need people with personality and this girl is exceptional. She's intelligent, articulate … she's … she's …'

'Drop-dead gorgeous?' suggested Barbara with a wintry smile.

'Er … well,' said Gerry, 'let's just say that's a bonus. Anyway, I think you're grossly unfair to our local students. They don't all have straw in their hair.'

Aidan said, 'Look Barbara, I don't really believe you would seriously consider rejecting a student like this on grounds of some kind of perceived cultural mismatch And just look at her talent, for Christ's sake.'

'Huh. Talent for what?' asked Barbara, sardonically.

'I think you're outvoted, Barbara. We have to offer her a place. I'm sure the Education Department wouldn't pass her up.'

'Well boys, if that's your considered opinion, on your heads be it.'

And now ... he looked at his watch. He could swear the hands hadn't moved. He crossed to the window and looked up at the moon for a moment, then turned to the desk. He leafed restlessly through the pages of the large volume of Blunt's Critical Catalogue of Poussin paintings which had an almost permanent place there. He stopped at Venus and the Shepherds. Venus lying, gorgeous naked, on what? A pile of sculptor's scrim?

Oh God, Oh God ... His mind wandered to the events immediately following that first meeting a mere eight weeks ago – or was it nine?

He was, he supposed, trying to fit those experiences into a framework of gender behaviour – his – that was years out of date. He had an idea that young people, these days – that is, the kind of people who were his students – if they really fancied each other, might – what would they call it? Make love? Have sex? Fuck? On the first occasion they went out together. In these liberated days, it might even be just a one-off occasion. A one-night stand – he'd heard of this. When he was that age, when his sexual mores were shaped, you were lucky if you came away from a first date with a goodnight kiss; and whatever intermediate experiences were permitted over time, full sex – fucking – was for marriage. Of course, there were inklings of promiscuity, boastings of intimacies, of particular favours secretly granted and enjoyed. But these were not well authenticated, he and his mates, respectable working-class lads that they were, and grammar school educated to boot, dutifully paired up with nice local girls when in their teens, learning what they could about sex in the back rows of cinemas. Then, they married in their early twenties.

Well, it was two months since he and Louise had first met; tonight they planned to consummate their relationship. Consummate. He thought the word sounded rather legalistic. Was it rather, that they were going to surrender to their lust? Did love come into it? He didn't really know. But what he did know was that his concern for his marriage was no longer a safeguard against his infidelity. He went back over the bewildering transition by which Louise DeGrey, student, was about to become Louise DeGrey, what? Mistress? A bit old-fashioned that. Lover? Isn't that more for men? Bit on the side? That's probably more like it. At least if it came out, that's what others would be likely to call her. (As it happened, she would become known among the students as 'Aidan Hamilton's bird'). He was forty-five and married, with two daughters. She was twenty-five and his student. He was going to have to tell lies. Lots of them, he supposed. You could hardly be an adulterer and not. It was a formidable packet of sin he was planning. He was glad he wasn't a Catholic.

* * *

That was the first time he saw her – at the interview. She could have been just another candidate, out of the twenty-five or thirty he had interviewed over the year. But she was the one who stuck most vividly in his memory. She was so exceptional in so many ways; he had really doubted that, having seen Swaleborough, she would in the end accept the place in it they'd offered her. Anyway it was the beginning of the autumn term and there were many things to think about; he tried to put her out of his mind.

The first week of term was always taken up with administration; the new students were put into groups for the various aspects of the course. The Education Department allocated students to tutors according to whether they wanted to teach in secondary, primary or nursery schools. They visited the PE Department, the Audio-Visual Aids Department and the library, and met the tutors of any subsidiary subjects they might be taking. They visited the local education office and listened to a talk by the Chief Education Officer and they paid introductory visits to some of the local schools. They learned something of the routines of college life – meal times, if they lived in, where to go with their grant problems, the location of the bar and all those necessary details upon which an organisation depends for its successful running.

Aidan liked all beginnings of term, but especially this first week of the academic year. Before teaching started, he had time to think about the courses about to begin; to run through his notes for his Art

41

History course, checking his slides, making any additions or deletions. It also meant he could carry on with his own work for a while longer, for he was trying to get enough paintings and drawings together for a one-man show. Now, in middle age, after all his years of endeavour, he was gratified that one of the smaller London galleries was showing an encouraging interest in his work, he was hoping to hear something definite from them soon. So for quite long periods, he was able to shut himself away in his small studio on the first floor, next to the main stockroom, where he was at this very moment awaiting his tryst, painting dedicatedly, accompanied by music. Inevitably, it was the formal intricacy of Bach he needed.

During the past year, he had been working at a series of paintings and drawings, in which he was attempting to distil some kind of formal essence from the Victorian interplay of architecture and nature, at the south end of the town, especially the park which was its main glory. His hero in this endeavour was Nicholas Poussin. On his first encounter as an eighteen-year-old student with the seventeenth-century painter's pictures in the flesh, he had been moved almost to tears, in a way more akin to his response to music – perhaps the final chorus of the St Mathew Passion. He had been overwhelmed by the sense of order, the light, the tranquillity and the sheer majesty of the landscapes; landscapes which seemed to dwarf the human tragedies – The Man Bitten by a Serpent; The Gathering of the Ashes of Phocion – being enacted there. His artistic ambitions were not so grandiose as devotion to Poussin might suggest. It was just that it seemed to him that the Victorian benefactors who had created the park, and their rich houses too, had been organising real trees and real buildings in the real world into harmonious wholes, in the same way Poussin did it in his mind, with his drawings, his models on his studio table and finally on his canvas with paint. It was principally this visual world that excited Aidan. But if, in working out his ideas in paint, he did leave some hint of the small dramas of human events, then that would be okay; for at what human cost, he sometimes wondered, had the wealth that paid for the park been created?

But always, he downed tools for the morning coffee break. Last year, after a long campaign, and a chat with the bursar, Aidan had persuaded the catering manager to agree to provide real coffee, instead of instant. Now, at half past ten every morning, the corridor between the kitchens and the senior common room was fragrant with it, as the trolley was wheeled in. Even in the remote Art Department, as the time approached, Aidan fancied he could smell it and whatever he was doing he allowed himself to be drawn out of the main door, down the steps, across the road, through the yard of the practice school, along the walkways between the old buildings, into the back door of the main block and along the corridor to the senior common room. In transit, he would join up, perhaps, with Barbara and Gerry. Henry, the fourth member of the department, was a man of austere habits and often went for days without coffee or alcohol passing his lips, so was not always present.

The daily assembly around the coffee trolley was both an opportunity for social exchange and the informal transaction of the kind of college business that didn't require a meeting. Aidan himself found it a useful daily occasion to practise his German, with George Hobson, head of the English Department, who spoke it fluently. It was on such a day, after a moderately successful exchange of German phatic trivialities, that George said, 'Anyway Aidan, I wanted to see you on another matter. Better stick to English for this one.'

'Uh oh, that sounds ominous. What have I got that you want this time.'

'Just your genius, dear boy, that's all – just your genius.'

'George, you know you can talk me into anything when you say things like that. Well pour me some coffee then and I'll be even more amenable.'

George up-ended two cups and placed them on saucers.

'Hmm, smells good,' he said as he detached the jug from the coffee machine. 'You know, Aidan, I'll never cease to be grateful to you for getting us real coffee instead of instant. Can't think why we never did it before.'

'Okay, okay, that's enough bullshit. I'm thoroughly softened up now; you can sock it to me straight and hard.'

'Right. Well it's about the next DramSoc effort.'

'Yeah, thought it might be … so …?'

'Well Percy and I had a couple of drinks together during the vac, and we thought a bit of co-operation between Music and English would be a good idea.'

'Don't tell me … Rogers and Hammerstein.'

'Er … no …'

'Kurt Weill, then.'

'Well … no …'

'Go on then. Hit me with it. Opera … Wagner.'

George laughed. 'A bit too ambitious that, mate. No something more modest. Actually, we thought we'd have a go at Oh What a Lovely War. So not quite opera, but we thought that would be well within our resources. What do you think?'

'Oh well, it sounds okay … so long as you don't expect me to stand up there and sing.'

'No, no – well, I expect Percy'll want your excellent tenor in the chorus.' Aidan nodded. 'Anyway, I'll be in overall charge of the production and of course Percy will see to the music. He reckons he's got some real talent in the Music Department this year.'

Another reason Aidan liked this first week was that, in transit between the Art Department and the main building, you would encounter students again; and he hardly admitted it to himself, but as the long summer vacation wore on, and the obligatory family holiday was out of the way, he began to miss them just a bit. There were students he already knew, of course – some very well, some not so well and some just as slightly familiar faces. So there would be familiar greetings,

'Hi, Aidan. Good holiday?'

'Hi, Frank. Yeah, not bad, thanks. You?'

'Yeah, terrific man.'

'Hope you got a bit of work done.'

Others were more cursory and some just an exchange of smiles. Then there were the new faces. Aidan would try to recognise those destined for his own department, some of whom he would have interviewed quite early in the year. There were usually a handful of applicants that stood out in his memory for various reasons – unusually interesting work, unusually interesting background, unusually interesting appearance and unusually interesting personality. Even without the fact of the recentness of her interview, Miss DeGrey would have remained in his mind on account of all the other factors. She would, he thought, be a great asset in the department if she had accepted the place they had offered her, though somehow, he doubted she would. Why on earth would a girl like that want to come to a provincial town like Swaleborough? He dearly loved the place. It fitted round him like an old glove. He loved the Monday market, with the wellied farmers, the tractors, the groaning cattle, the auction of farm machinery and junk. He loved the pubs, the parks, the shops and above all the college, with its easy-going ambience, its delegation of everything of academic importance to the teaching staff in whose expertise it explicitly trusted; its employment of other experts to take care of all non-pedagogic matters. But really, what attraction could it have for a glamorous young sophisticate from the metropolis? He doubted he would see her again.

On the Wednesday of this first week of term, he was walking, at coffee time, along the main corridor towards the common room, chatting with Henry, when, with a clatter of shoes on the old wooden staircase, a group of new students was shepherded down from the library, by David Lynton, the librarian. They stopped at the foot of the stairs, embracing files and bags, organising themselves noisily towards their respective destinations. Aidan saw, with a slight shock, that she was among them. She looked different from when he last saw her. Gone was the high-powered, executive image. Now her long black hair was tied back in a ponytail; she was wearing tight blue jeans, which terminated at her calves and sandals. She wore no make-up – and Aidan thought her just as beautiful without it. The little oval spectacles were balanced near the end of her nose, as she and a tall, good-looking, blond-haired young man Aidan had never seen before, discussed the contents of the sheet of paper she held. Aidan felt a pang of envy at that privilege of proximity. Who was that fortunate young man, enjoying briefly, exclusive rights to her smiles and her attention and, if unattached, to who knew what future prospects?

Henry was airing his latest suggestions for a minor adjustment to the first year timetable.

'And if we divide them up on Wednesdays into four groups, then Barbara can ... Aidan, you're not listening ... What's up?' he asked.

'Yes, yes I am ... sorry. Go on.' But he wasn't concentrating; his eyes didn't leave her until he and Henry had turned the corner towards the common room. She did not see him, for her attention was engaged elsewhere.

He tried to focus on what his colleague was saying, responding with nods and vague gestures of assent and by the time Henry was nobbled, by someone else on other business, he had agreed to something, though he wasn't sure what. He didn't seek out George for his daily stint of German conversation, but poured his coffee and strolled with it over to the tall mullioned window overlooking the lawns and the front entrance with its flanking columns surmounted by stone globes and the street and little park beyond. He stood there, his back to his colleagues, who by now were congealing into pairs, threes and fours, aware of the familiar swell of conversation, gentle laughter and the tinkle of coffee cups. He had had a particularly vivid version of the dream last night. Now its fading echoes had been disturbingly recalled. Well, she had come. Good. He forced himself to turn round and join his colleagues. Monday would see the arrival of the new students in the studio and the beginning of their departmental introductory programme. There'd been details to be discussed. Barbara, Gerry and Big Henry were already at it.

* * *

He thumped the book shut and looked up at the big round station clock that hung above the door – Smith's Sectric, it said, in black letters on the face – ticking loudly with a synthetic, electric tick. He remembered buying it at the Monday auction for eight pounds. It told him he had still fifteen minutes to wait. Why, he asked himself, does time linger so infuriatingly when you want it to fly?

50

CHAPTER 3

Time. He was drawn back into it. His thoughts drifted back to the following Saturday. He wasn't looking forward to it. He had promised to take Cathy and Dora into town to buy shoes for their younger daughter, whose six-year-old feet seemed to have put on a sudden spurt of growth. Cathy, with her by now usual perversity, had wanted Bobby to come too. To go to town as a family, she had said. Ironic, Aidan reflected bitterly, that she seemed on the way to destroying the family whose proprieties she made such a fuss about observing. Aidan remembered the days when his family, brought pride and pleasure to him – when a Saturday trip to buy shoes for the infant Bobby would have been something to share with pleasure, even look forward to. Then, he and Cathy had rubbed along well enough, sharing their delight in their little daughter. He remembered, with bitterness now, how Cathy would wheel Bobby in her pram to the college, how the principal and staff would fuss over her. He remembered strawberry teas on the lawn, with Cathy the proud mother with her admired and adored infant. But what had happened? Bobby was twelve now; no longer an infant.

Bobby had said she didn't want to go to town – and, truth to tell, there was no good reason why she should. She'd said she had promised to go to see the elderly Mrs Cunningham who lived around the corner and to walk Banjo, her Jack Russell terrier. But Cathy did not like her plans to be thwarted and the row which she immediately provoked, left Bobby in tears and Cathy in a self-righteous fury.

'Right,' she said, 'do as you damn well like,' and taking Dora by the hand, stalked out to the car. Though there was a reasonable bus service, Cathy had decided that the additional convenience of the car was on this occasion required and she did not feel up to driving that day. Aidan as usual had acquiesced in her arrangements. He reversed the car on to the drive, got out to close the garage door and stood waiting in suppressed fury, as Cathy saw Dora into the back of the car, before herself taking the front passenger seat.

'It's all right, pet,' she said. 'I'm not cross with you.'

Aidan glared at her, turned away and strode angrily back to the house, to do whatever he could to comfort his elder daughter; Cathy could wait, her own anger doubtless simmering. Aidan found Bobby in her room. As he entered, she turned towards him and subsided into his arms. By now, Aidan knew there was little he could say; the words did not exist which could ameliorate this misery; there was only the reassurance that came from touch. As she became calmer, he offered to walk with her to Mrs Cunningham's, but, wiping a tear from her cheek, straightening up, in a small gesture of defiance, she said no, she would be okay. Aidan kissed her.

'Okay, love,' Aidan said, 'if you're sure.' He returned towards the car, his anger, that once again Cathy had turned what should have been an ordinary family outing into a battleground, barely contained. He entered the car, slamming the door and turned towards Cathy, murder in his eye. But seeing Dora in the back seat, her brow crinkled, her eyes raised beseechingly, he held back his fury; it would have to wait, but this time it wouldn't be passed over; not this time. He took a deep breath, reversed the car on to the road and drove off towards town. He had not looked forward to this expedition, because he knew from experience that it would be fraught with hazard. It had got off to a lousy start. There was only the consolation of the thought that at least this bit of Bobby's day would be congenial; Mrs Cunningham would comfort her and the ebullient Banjo would monopolise the rest of her attention.

They walked the short distance from the car park to the town centre in tense silence, Dora clinging to Aidan's hand. As they were about to enter the shop, a voice called, 'Cathy, hello.' Cathy turned; it was a colleague. Cathy's face thawed; this was a happy family outing. She greeted her friend with a smile. Aidan nodded his greeting; then, sensing that this encounter might last sometime, looked down at Dora and guided her into the shop. After a few minutes browsing along the shelves, they were approached by an assistant, who smiled at Dora and then at Aidan.

'Good morning,' she said, 'now, how can I help?'

Aidan handed Dora over to the assistant's care and turned towards the window, to watch the comings and goings in the street below.

Presently, Dora called, 'Dad, look; aren't these nice. I do like them. Can I have them please, please? They fit really well.'

Aidan said, 'Mmm, yes, they are pretty, but we'll have to wait and see what Mummy says.'

At that moment, Cathy arrived on the scene. She looked at the assistant, then at the shoes.

'These won't do,' she said, 'they're quite unsuitable.'

'But Mum ...' began Dora.

Aidan looked at Cathy. 'She likes them. Would it be too outrageous to let her have something she really likes for once?'

'They are totally unsuitable,' Cathy said, her voice rising, 'and if you can't see that, why don't you just go and let me get on with it?'

Aidan could see the danger signs. Over the years, he'd learned how far Cathy was prepared to go when she was in this kind of mood. He took a deep breath. 'Right,' he said, 'if that's the way you want it.' He turned to go.

'Oh, Dad ...' Dora looked appealingly at him.

'It's all right, love,' he said. 'Look, we'll get you the pretty shoes in time for your party. You need school shoes now. Just do what Mummy says. She knows what you need ... and I'll tell you what – we'll meet at the tea shop later won't we Mummy? ... about half past three and I'll buy you a raspberry sundae.' He smiled at her and gave her hand a squeeze. Without looking at Cathy, he turned and left.

Outside, he took a deep breath while he decided what to do with this unforeseen bonus of time. It did not take long for him to decide: he crossed the road and turned off into a crowded side street heading towards the bookshop. But he did not go straight to the bookshop, for en-route was The Green Dragon, a pub much favoured by his drinking colleagues and students alike. Closing time was three o'clock. That gave him half an hour for a pint – or maybe two and time enough for his visit to the bookshop. As he passed through the pub door, the familiar fug enveloped him and he sloughed off the tension that had built up during the previous hour. He exchanged greetings with the barman, then walked, pint in hand to his favourite corner opposite the door, nodding to one or two other acquaintances on the way. He unfolded the copy of the Guardian he'd picked up earlier and settled down to his first sortie into the crossword.

He did manage the second pint. Time was called at three. Ten minutes to drink up, then he folded the paper, nodded his goodbye to the barman and considerably cheered, set off for the bookshop. George had ordered copies of Oh What a Lovely War, but pending their arrival, Aidan had decided to buy his own copy so he could get the hang of the thing before the preliminary meeting.

Arriving at the bookshop, he pushed his way through the magazine and newspaper section, through the stationery and up the stairs.

After a quick browse through the new publications, he glanced at his watch and headed for the drama section. Squatting on his heels, he was shuffling through the volumes on the lowest shelf, when suddenly he was distracted by a pair of female legs that had appeared just within his field of vision to the right. A soft voice said, 'Hello Mr Hamilton. What are you doing down there?'

He looked up over his shoulder. Black hair, brown eyes, red lips, smile.

'Ah …' He got to his feet. 'Miss er …' He didn't quite know why he affected memory loss.

'DeGrey.'

'Yes of course, Miss DeGrey. We interviewed you only last week, didn't we? Well, what I was doing down here was looking for a copy of Oh What A Lovely War. It's the Drama Society's next production, and the Art Department is always in on the dramatic stuff.'

'Oh yes I know about it. Dr Hobson talked to us about the Drama Society on … Thursday, I think it was, and I put my name down to be auditioned for a part.'

'Ah yes. I remember. You did mention in the interview that you were interested in drama.'

'Yes, so I'm really looking forward to that.' Aidan could not help noticing that the long denim skirt she was wearing was unbuttoned to the thigh, exposing a sliver of shapely leg. 'Will you be taking a part, then, or do you confine yourself to stage design?'

'Oh well, I usually allow myself to be talked into taking a part – so long as it's fairly small. I never feel like spending too much time memorising other people's words.'

'Oh good. It's nice that members of the department will be working together in another area of college life. It should be fun.'

Aidan laughed. 'Well, yes. It's usually that alright.'

'You know, I'm ashamed to admit it,' she said, 'but I don't really know anything about Oh What A Lovely War. Of course, I've heard of it and always felt uneasy at those two words next to each other. But I guess that's what we're meant to feel – kind of playing games with words.'

'Well you've hit some sort of nail on the head there. You see, a work of art sometimes gets its message across most potently by kind of contrasting the sublime with the ridiculous … I mean, take Stanley Spencer's Resurrection; you know it?'

'Er …'

'… Well it's the end of the world – the end of everything and the people emerging from their graves, going up to meet their maker to be judged, are wearing pinnies and gardening clothes …

'Oh I see. You mean …'

'Yes, you see, the play's all done in Pierrot costume, but with just bits of military uniform; a kind of burlesque, lots of jolly songs and fooling about, but really it's a potted history of four pointless years of bloody slaughter of ordinary men dressed as soldiers … and you wouldn't believe the poignancy that contrast generates ... it just ... I saw the first production at Stratford – must be about ten years ago, and I've never quite got over it. It was so ...'

She was watching him, listening, waiting. He suddenly caught her eye, stopped and laughed.

'Oh God, I'm sorry. Poor Miss DeGrey comes out on a Saturday afternoon for a quiet browse round a bookshop and finds herself getting an unsolicited lecture.'

Now she laughed.

'Oh Mr Hamilton, don't apologise ... it was just getting interesting. You've given me something to think about. It was much better than browsing.'

'Oh well then, let's just consider it part of the service – I'll ...' Then suddenly he remembered the time, the tea room. He looked at his watch. 'Oh God, I was supposed to meet my wife and daughter ten minutes ago. I'd better dash. Anyway, new students get together in the studio on Monday, so we'll meet again then.'

'Yes, okay. Look forward to seeing you. Bye.'

'... Bye.' He took his purchase to the desk and paid for it, thinking damn, if I hadn't had the family in tow, I could have introduced her to the delights of the Green Dragon. Oh well ... He'd now been fifteen minutes late and conscious of the fragrance of the pub lingering in his clothes. As he'd elbowed his way with some urgency along the crowded streets towards the tea room, he'd imagined what a pleasant experience that would have been.

But as he neared the tea shop, the pleasant glow created by the encounter was quickly displaced by his recollection of Cathy's earlier gratuitous beastliness to Bobby. He would not, this time let it fade away into history. There would be a reckoning when they got home.

Through the evening meal, the early evening television, Dora's bedtime, Bobby's later departure to her room, Aidan had kept his anger at a damped down smoulder. After spending some time with Bobby and tucking her into bed, he went downstairs, determined that they would talk. It could not be allowed to go on. He could not allow his wife to go on persecuting their daughter in this way, insidiously poisoning her life. What the hell was wrong with her that she could behave like this? He would be calm. He would be reasonable. He would not allow a row to develop.

But as soon as he saw her, he knew he was thwarted, defeated. She wore her suffering like an all-enveloping cloak. He ought to have known. He knew what he was supposed to do, it had happened so often in the course of their married life. What he ought to have done was to walk out; to refuse to play her game. But he didn't. As always, he fell for it hook, line and sinker.

'What's the matter,' he asked, knowing he was scuppered the moment he uttered the words. She'd been an inveterate sufferer all the years he'd known her. Could he really believe that her body was so flawed? So infuriatingly faulty? His own had, so far, served him well. It was nothing flashy, but reliable. It didn't obtrude. It knew its place. It gave him mobility; it received sensations; it contained his thoughts and was a satisfactory temporary base for his soul; all in all very serviceable. So he had over the years found it increasingly difficult to believe in the torments Cathy claimed to live with. The way she went on, her body was like one of those rogue cars, reputedly made on a Friday afternoon, flawed through and through, and an endless source of trouble. She was cursed. Head usually throbbing, joints stiff, back aching, always problems with the bloody plumbing. Her body did obtrude. Ever shouting for attention, upsetting the even tenor of life – and here was the worst of it – not just hers, but because she needed to spread her discomforts around, his too and the children's. At times like this, her suffering hung like a heavy layer of damp cloud over the landscape of their lives.

'I've got a terrible headache.' Aidan looked at her dully, his simmering anger giving way to a kind of despair. She had him, he knew. She looked at him with her suffering eyes.

'Care about me,' she said, 'care, care.'

'I do,' he'd said limply. 'Would you like some aspirin?'

CHAPTER 4

At the recollection, the anger welled up once more inside him and extinguished any last vestige of conscience that may have lurked in his mind for what he was about to do that night; that very night ... soon. He looked up at the clock again. Oh fly, time, fly, like you're supposed to. He went back to the desk and poured more whisky. Christ, then there was that day in the park ...

It was the following Monday afternoon, the new students began their day in the Art Department with the four members of staff who would be teaching them there. Barbara gave them an introductory briefing dealing first with the mundane things like the whereabouts of various materials, payment records and so forth, following up with a little on education philosophy and the place of Art in it, then ending with a bit about the town, its buildings, cultural facilities, the more general environment and the creative use the observant student might make of them. The rest of the morning was taken up with guided tours of the specialist studios. The afternoon was, weather permitting, to be taken up with a kind of walkabout around some of the environmental features described by Barbara in the morning session. This was another of the things she usually put in the hands of her three male colleagues. They did not object because they knew she would be getting together with Mary, the office assistant and general factotum to deal with some of the drearier administrative tasks from which her teaching colleagues were thereby relieved. More positively, it was an enjoyably informal opportunity for getting to know the students they would be teaching, as well as to show off their knowledge of architecture, geology, local history, botany and any other subject that seemed appropriate.

The weather did permit and come two o'clock the party of students and staff having assembled in the main entrance of the department, were almost ready to set off.

'Better have a quick check to make sure we're all here,' said Aidan to Henry. He had already made a note of Miss DeGrey's presence. She was wearing a long, filmy skirt of deep purple and a loose sweatshirt. Today her black hair was hanging free, the slight breeze detached delicate fronds of it which she chased with her hand and it pressed the skirt around the contours of her thighs in a way which reminded him of The Winged Victory of Samothrace. Aidan was enchanted. She stood at the far side of the group, chatting with the tall blonde young man, whom he now knew was to be one of his own students, along with Miss DeGrey and nine others. His name was Mark Andrews.

'Okay, everyone.' It was Henry, head and shoulders above almost everyone else. 'We're heading towards town. We'll have a look at the town hall first, then St Andrew's Church and a few other buildings of architectural interest, then …'

'How about the best pubs?' suggested a bespectacled young man with a wispy beard, amid giggles.

'Yes, those too,' replied Henry, with a grin, 'then we'll head towards the river and the glories of Teasdale Park and back through the fields. You've all got sketchbooks, I hope. Okay, let's go.'

Knotting together in twos and threes, they set off down the entrance steps: then, 'Aidan!' It was Mary, calling from the main door, 'There's a phone call for you.'

'Damn!' said Aidan, stopping in the gateway. 'Who is it?'

'It's a chap, name of Marcus Price … I think. Anyway, he said it was rather important, so I said I'd try to catch you before you set off.'

'Marcus Price?' Aidan said. 'God, that's the Mierevelt Gallery. Could be good news.' He held up his hands with fingers crossed. 'Okay, thanks Mary. Tell him to hang on – I'm coming.'

Hearing this, Gerry had hung back, while the rest of the group meandered off with Henry. He looked at Aidan inquiringly.

'Gerry, this may be the phone call I've been waiting for. It could take a while, so you'd better carry on with Henry, I'll catch up with you somewhere along the route.'

'Right you are, old son. Hope it is good news. Anyway, see you later.'

Aidan turned back and leapt up the steps into the department, calling to Mary to put the call through to his study. He picked up the phone.

'Hello, Aidan Hamilton.'

'Aidan, hello. We haven't spoken before, but I'm Marcus Price from the Mierevelt.'

'Oh, hello.'

'Look, Aidan, I know it's some months since you sent us your slides and I've been meaning to get in touch, but we've been having such a hectic time recently. Melissa ... er that is Melissa Mierevelt, the Director, would normally have got in touch with you herself, but suddenly, she seems to be in demand all over the place. She was about to embark on a year's lecturing and teaching tour in the US and after that a spell in Germany ... There've been so many loose ends to tie up before she departed. She doesn't much like leaving the gallery for so long, but these were long-standing commitments, and, well you know how it is.' Aidan didn't, but he said he did. 'But ... but, she did see your slides before going off and she was extremely impressed. Anyway, when she handed the whole works over to me – I'm the Deputy Director of the gallery – she gave me full authority to follow your submission up and to act at my discretion. Well, I had to come up to Manchester last week and decided to try to make a fleeting visit to the Bowes Museum – Howard Hetherington's an old chum of mine – and have a look at the pictures he bought from you.'

'Well, I can tell you, the slides didn't lie and I was pretty impressed. If there's more where they came from, and more in the creative pipeline, I think we could offer you a one-man show ...' Aidan looked through the window and up at the sky, opened his mouth in a silent yell of triumph, and with his free hand punched the air.

'... despite all the far-out stuff that's going on there's still a huge interest in good painting – for God's sake, you can't hang a happening on your dining room wall or an installation, can you? Anyway, we think you might do rather well.'

'Marcus – what can I say? That's great, that's really great ...'

'Okay, so we'll need to get together in the near future. I mean, I'd like to come up and have a look at the rest of your work, drawings and sketches, whatever, and then we can discuss all the details and business arrangements, that sort of thing.'

'Oh sure. You just let me know when you want to come up and I'll fix it.'

'Right then. You'll probably hear from Helena ... Helena Georgiades – she's kind of number three in the pecking order, so one of us will be in touch. Now, is there anything you'd like to ask at this stage?'

'Oh well, just the matter of the timescale we'd be thinking about.'

'Oh yeah. Well these things don't happen very quickly, you know. I'd say we'd be thinking eighteen months to two years.'

'Yes, fine. I can get some more painting done.'

'Sure. Well bye then Aidan. Speak to you soon.'

'Okay. Bye Marcus.'

Aidan put the phone down and sprawled backwards in his chair, his arms dangling. His eyes rolled up towards the ceiling and he stayed in that position, his mouth agape, for several seconds. Then he sprang from the chair, raised his arms, shaking his clenched fists in triumph and let out a wild whoop.

'Mary! Mary!' he called out through the door, 'I've got it. My London show, I've got it.' Mary raised her head from the stock book she was working on.

'Wow Aidan, that's great, super. When is it to be, then?'

'Well, maybe eighteen months, a couple of years, perhaps ... but isn't it wonderful?'

Mary smiled and shook her head. He'd been talking about it for so long. She had a sympathetic ear and she'd often found, as she busied herself among the stock, her invoices and ledgers, that Aidan had parked himself in her swivelling chair, idly rotating himself to and fro while he held forth about his prospects.

'Well I'm really pleased, Aidan. Hope I'm on your private view list.'

'Mary, you know I wouldn't dream of a launch without you there.' She turned back to her work, as for the second time, Aidan set off down the steps of the main door, this time in a supremely buoyant mood, a smile on his face. He headed briskly out of the gate and towards town. He slowed down as he took the diagonal path across the little park in front of the college. He tried to focus his mind on his teaching responsibilities, upon this afternoon's project; the students;

the walkabout, but his head was full of the prospect, the implications of a London one-man show. For how many years had he been waiting for this? God knew he was no spring chicken; no young tearaway straight out of the RCA or the Slade, bursting to push back the frontiers of art and falling straight into the arms of some avaricious dealer to be thrust upwards into instant fame and wealth. Huh! The chance'd be a fine thing.

No; his training had been conventional. At art school, for four years he had drawn and drawn from the nude model, the antique, still life, landscape and townscape, and he had studied and painted those things he could see. He became an obsessive observer of the world, a habitual analyser of form and space, solid and void, and the way the everyday details of the visible universe interlocked in complex ways, endlessly realigning themselves, adjusting their relationships as he moved among them. He found that at any location he could conjure art out of what was given, for the art was not in the subject but in the response and the poetry; in the metaphor given form in paint.

But as he developed and matured, he became less and less sure of what art was and even what it was for. It was something like sixty years since Kandinsky painted the first pictures without subjects – pictures without reference to the real world. Others had taken that world apart and rearranged it according to whim – or according to theory. Then pictures had gone huge – wall-sized explosions of pure sensation. No pretence now, that you could take it home and hang it on your dining room wall. Aidan was excited by all this, he worked assiduously and learnedly to help his students towards an open receptiveness. One thing they had to understand; these paintings were not about the world – they were their own world and one had to allow oneself to be drawn into it. Now artists were making art with computers and television cameras; they were constituting themselves and their actions as art; they were claiming that to write about the art act was itself art. It seemed that anything that was claimed to be art was now art.

Aidan thought that the horizons of art had receded so far into outer space as to be no longer comprehensible. He could eventually no longer bear to read about art and particularly not the statements by artists about what they thought they were doing, cringing at their cosmic delusions and their vaporous verbosity. Yet he was compelled to go on making art in his own way using traditional materials and techniques – doing it on the modest basis that asked the spectator, have you noticed how this bit of the world sometimes looks? Have you noticed its structures, its harmonies, its dissonances? Have you? Then saying, but what I'm showing you isn't the real world – it's only a metaphor for it, a parallel world, made out of processed earths, plants and chemicals glued together with linseed oil; what we call paint.

Above all, he loved this stuff, the oil paint with which he mainly worked. There was the penetrating smell of distilled turpentine to satisfy the nose, then the oleaginous brilliance of the colours set out in order round the edge of the palette, to be nibbled at by the palette knife and combined into whorls of intermediate tones and shades as he strove with the brush to create on the canvas, equivalents for the relationships he saw in the world. For that was it; that was the essence, equivalence, relationships. The individual brush stroke as meaningless as a single phoneme in language. Saussure said that in language, there are only differences; there are no such things as positive terms. Everything fits into a system and we understand each term in a system only in relation to the other terms it contains. And this was what his contemporary, Cézanne, said – but in paint. Aidan believed him. So the full brush dragged over the canvas in a dry scumble of viridian, however pretty in itself, is without meaning – until, in its context and within its system, it becomes a distant field. It was this duality, in painting as in language – small null components creating meaning through their relationships, which Aidan loved. How like people.

The problem for Aidan was this; he was good at making paintings, but very bad at selling them. Sometimes he envied those who were so convinced of the excellence of their own product, that they could confidently go out into the world and convince potential customers that it was just what they needed. For, he did need to sell his work. It wasn't just that he needed the money – though he wouldn't want to knock that; it was more the fact if someone was prepared to exchange their hard-earned cash for his work, it showed that his endeavours were understood. That was encouraging, and encouragement, though not essential, certainly did help. Then there was the subsidiary problem; namely, that unsold paintings take up space; they need storing. Aidan believed that most things that were stored did not really need to exist at all.

So, he sold work sporadically, usually on a personal basis and exhibited locally. His most auspicious achievement to date had been a one-man show at the Laing Art Gallery at Newcastle. Some paintings sold, but by no means like hot cakes. By far the best outcome of that was a purchase of six paintings by the Bowes Museum – that wonderful French chateau set down so improbably, a stone's-throw from the Pennines, just outside Barnard Castle, for its school loans collection. Howard Hetherington, the curator, was impressed by Aidan's paintings, which, he told him deserved a much wider showing. You've just got to get to London, Aidan, he'd said. Howard set about furthering this idea, by contacting on Aidan's behalf several London galleries he was in touch with, which he thought would be interested in the kind of things that Aidan was doing. So Aidan had circularised them with slides. The results were encouraging; three of them had invited him to take work to London for inspection in the flesh. They had all expressed continuing interest, but it was the Mierevelt Gallery which had followed up and eventually made a concrete offer.

So here at last, at the age of forty-five, the years of steady and persistent endeavour and development, against the grain of fashion, were to be recognised. He was exhilarated at the thought that even in middle age, new and exciting things could happen. He had not reached that plateau after all. And he didn't know the half of it.

As he turned into Botany Road, he saw the group of students filtering in through the park gates at its far end. This entrance took the form of an imposing Ionic portico and he could see Big Henry gesturing as he held forth on its glories, the students, sketchbooks in hand, turning, heads raised, following his gestures. By the time Aidan arrived at the gates, the students had entered the park and spread out, singly and in groups of two and three. Already some were making notes in sketchbooks; others were wandering, looking. Henry and Gerry had found a comfortable bench and Gerry seemed to be saying something with great earnestness, while Henry, nodding, was going through the ritual of lighting his pipe. Then he saw Miss DeGrey. She had not got far. She was alone and standing quite still, looking into the interior of the park. A small movement of the breeze again caused her skirt to stir against her legs; she was a figure in a Poussin landscape. Aidan approached and stood behind her, a little to one side. For a while, she seemed not to notice him. Then she turned.

'Oh, Mr Hamilton!' she said, smiling, 'I thought we had lost you.'

'Miss DeGrey,' said Aidan. 'No, not lost, merely mislaid. Blimey, that sounded a bit Jane Austin, didn't it?' They laughed. 'Listen, when

I first came to Swaleborough Training College, aeons ago, it was all very formal. Students and staff addressed each other as, "Miss A or Miss B" and staff – they were all female, except me, addressed each other by their surnames. In these informal times, however, we've got round to using first names. I'm Aidan.'

'Oh and I'm Louise …' She looked slightly sideways at him. 'Aidan's a nice name … er, isn't there a Saint Aidan?'

'Yes, but he's no relation. Any way, if we're going in for name associations, I'll have to put on a phoney French accent and start singing 'Every leetle breeze seems to …' you know the one.'

'Yes, I do – and I dare you,' she said, laughing.

'Um,' he said, 'you're calling my bluff. No it'll have to be a more suitable occasion. But, to come back to my saintly namesake; do you know where Saint Aidan is?'

'In Paradise, I'd have thought. But I have a feeling you're going to tell me different.'

'I am. You remember in your interview, you said you'd been kind of inspired by a novel you'd read, in which the main characters ended up on Lindisfarne?'

'Oh, yes I do.'

'Well that's where you'll find him – or at any rate a statue of him, right there, in the ruins of the abbey.'

'Really?' she said, raising her eyebrows, 'oh well then, that's another reason for going there. I can see I've got a lot to learn about the north.'

'Hm, let's see. How long have you been here now?' Aidan asked her.

'Oh let's think … erm … this is Monday … I came last Friday week, so that's nine days.'

'And what do you think of it so far?'

'Oh well … I'm quite impressed. The town feels nice – you know – kind of comfortable, I suppose.'

'Oh yes, It's that all right.'

'But not dull and not complacent, I hope.'

'We-e-ell, that I'm not so sure about. But it is an agreeable place to live, that is, if you can do without the excitement of the great metropolis.'

'Oh well, for me that had got to be more hassle than exciting. Just a little slackening of the pace will be more than welcome.'

'Well … okay,' Aidan said, smiling at her, 'as long as you don't think you can slacken it too much. We don't allow skiving here, you know.'

'Oh no … perish the thought.' She dropped her eyes in mock humility. Aidan noticed how long the scalloped black eyelashes were. It had become one of those exquisite encounters with an attractive woman, the tone, a delicate balance between banality and irony, and always with an unrealisable but subtly and mutually understood erotic potential. And this in a student. Well she was a mature student, by the usual definition. Most of the normal age students, especially the women and more especially those from the local area, had difficulty in breaking away from the mores of the school and were, at first uncomfortable with the idea of using their teachers' first names let alone having bantering conversations with them.

'Well, just so long as you understand.' By now, Henry and Gerry were mingling with the students again and the group was drifting further into the park, some across the little stone bridge over the stream, others taking the path which disappeared round a group of tall graceful ash trees. He knew he ought to say, 'Come on. We'd better catch up,' but he wanted this encounter to go on. And it did.

She said, 'You know, Mr Ham ... Aidan, when you came up behind me then, I was transfixed by the view. As soon as I came in through the gates, I thought, "Poussin. This is almost like being in a Poussin."'

He looked at her, taken aback. She went on, 'Look, there's this grove of tall trees on the right. It's a repoussoir – it leads the eye into the depth of the scene. And there's the little river, but it's not just what nature created; it's been altered, adapted. It's been channelled into stone-built ducts, over a weir – and there's the bridge, the path winding away into the middle distance. It's nature and culture combined in a ... in a ... well, a formal and harmonious whole.'

Aidan watched her and listened, enthralled.

'I mean … the way the land raises towards the distance. Oh well, that really ought to be a medieval walled city, but those rows of terraced houses do almost as well …' she caught his eye, smiling again, '… and it would help if a man in a toga would come and wash his feet in the stream down there …'

Aidan laughed, delighted. 'And a tomb inscribed, ET IN ARCADIA EGO?'

'Yes, yes!' She laughed too.

'Miss DeGrey …'

'Louise.'

'Miss DeGrey, somehow your erudition demands the more formal address …'

'Oh, now you're teasing me. I suppose that must have seemed like showing off, but Poussin is one of my two most favourite painters.'

'No, no, I think it's wonderful. D'you realise, nine out of ten students when they come here can't tell a Poussin from a … from a …'

'Kentucky Fried Chicken?' She suggested, eyebrows arched. Aidan laughed again.

'Oh, that's wonderful, wonderful … and your other favourite? I bet I can guess … Cézanne?'

'Yes, well, it wasn't difficult to guess, was it? But do you agree with me about the park?'

'Yes, of course I do. And they're my favourite painters too'

'They are?'

'Louise, I walk through this park every day. For the last ten years I've been trying to do Poussin all over again, but from ...'

'Nature ...?'

'Uh oh ... not quite like Cézanne. A bit more specific. No – I've been trying to do Poussin all over again, but from Swaledale Park.'

'Ah yes,' she said. 'I'd like to see some of the results.'

'You're bound to sooner or later,' he said. 'Meanwhile, we'd better allow this repoussoir to direct us further into the picture and reunite us with the rest of the group before they disappear behind the walled city.'

'Yes, I suppose we should.'

They looked into each other's eyes for a moment, smiling, then set off along the path towards the bridge. Aidan found himself wandering with a young woman of surpassing beauty and sensuality, through an Arcadian landscape suffused with the golden light of the late afternoon sun. Soon they came upon one or two students still at work in their sketchbooks. Behind the grove of ash trees, they caught up with the rest of the group with Henry and Gerry in attendance.

'Better spread myself around a bit,' said Aidan. 'And we must keep in touch over Poussin.'

'Oh yes,' she said, 'we must.' She smiled at him again, then turned away. Aidan watched her as she walked towards a group of her colleagues. As he stood, Gerry came up from behind.

'Hi,' he said. Aidan started and blinking, turned to face Gerry.

'Oh hi, everything okay?'

'Oh sure … You seemed to catch up with the picturesque Miss DeGrey.'

'Hm, yes … and I can tell you she's not just a pretty face. We've just been having a highly allusive exchange on the finer points of classical landscape. She's amazing, she really is.'

'Yes, well don't let her go to your head.' He looked at Aidan meaningfully.

'Gerry, in view of your own – how shall I put it – deviations, you are hardly the one to advise me on such matters,' Aidan replied.

'Um, well … there are serious pitfalls …'

Aidan frowned. 'Gerry, what the fuck are you talking about? She's good looking and she's extremely bright. But she's a student – and for better or for worse – I'm married. Okay? So no lurid fantasising, if you don't mind.' Even then, Aidan was unsure that his indignation was sincere, for truth to tell, he himself had given in a little to delicious fantasy.

'Right, okay, don't blow your stack.' Gerry changed the subject. 'Er … by the way, what about your phone call? Is everything okay?'

The smile returned to Aidan's face. He reached out, gripped Gerry by the shoulders and stared into eyes. 'Gerry, Gerry, listen,' he said, 'I've got it. I've got my show. They really like my work. I don't know exactly when it'll be yet, but it's all …'

'Aidan, man, that's great. That's really terrific.' Gerry punched Aidan playfully on the chest then put an arm round his shoulder. 'I'm proud of you … you're a credit to the department. Hey man this calls for an early celebration.'

'First opportunity, you're on. Meanwhile, maybe we'd better help Henry out with these students.'

CHAPTER 5

As he sipped his whisky, with one eye on that lingering clock, he remembered how the delicious aftertaste of the day's experiences had lingered as he drove home. He didn't know quite which contributed most to his exhilaration – his encounter with Louise or the news that his ambition for a London exhibition was at last going to be fulfilled. He thought he knew which was most important, but well, you can never be totally rational about these things. He was looking forward to telling Cathy, too. But only about the exhibition. She'd generally been pretty sniffy about his failure to power his way up the academic ladder, choosing instead to invest all his surplus energy in his painting. He'd always been adamant that though he might have to rely on his teaching for an income, he would never, as so many of his art school contemporaries seemed to do, resign himself to the single role of teacher or administrator. He went to art school to learn to be an artist and that was what he was, and would always be. Now Cathy would see the justification. He hoped.

He pulled up on the drive and got out of the car still smiling inwardly. As he locked the car door, Dora appeared from the back garden. He could usually depend on a cheerful greeting from her at least, for she generally seemed to find being alive a rewarding experience; but today she looked worried. His euphoria faltered, but he raised a smile for his younger daughter and held out a hand to her. She grasped it in both of hers but did not return his smile. Instead she let out a big sigh.

'They're at it again, Daddy,' she said, with resignation. Now Aidan sighed and shook his head wearily.

'Well what's happened, love?'

'Oh you know ... Bobby dashed home from school ... it was the horse thing. You know, Dad – horses in the Camam ...'

'Camargue.'

'... that we watch. It was the last one ... and Mum wanted her to set the table and started shouting and she switched the telly off. So I came out as well.'

Oh God, here we go again. He wanted to get back into the car and drive hell-for-leather to nowhere. Instead, he looked down at Dora, then dropped into a crouch before her and, cupping her troubled face in his hands, planted a kiss on her nose.

'Okay love. Don't come in just yet. I'll take a look at the situation.'

It would be, he knew, the familiar situation he looked into with depressing regularity and seemed incapable of affecting in the smallest way. A recent development was that Bobby, who had in the past crumbled into defeat under her mother's anger, was now finding her own anger. She was becoming less apt to respond with passive misery and more likely to stand up to her mother. Aidan's advice to her had generally been along the lines of passive resistance, bending with the wind, letting it all wash over her. Aidan himself had, over the years, perfected this strategy as a way of surviving Cathy's regular fits of unreasoned ill-temper, but he supposed it was asking a lot of a child, unversed in the destructive games unhappy adults play.

Dora looked up at him and smiled ruefully. 'Okay Daddy,' she said and turned back towards the garden. Aidan stood for a while, listening to the rhythmic squeak of the swing as Dora got it going again. He took a deep breath, opened the back door, went through the lobby and stepped into the kitchen. Cathy, her face drawn tight with anger was noisily slapping cups and saucers on to the tea trolley. He could hear Bobby sobbing in her room above. His euphoria had evaporated; he was rapidly sinking into deep gloom.

'What the hell's going on,' he asked. He need not have bothered; it was all so familiar. She turned towards him, brushed away a strand of hair with the back of her hand and pushed her spectacles up on to the bridge of her nose – a gesture which, in calmer days he used to find touching.

'She said I was horrible. She said she hated me,' Cathy said, through clenched teeth, clattering a handful of knives and spoons on to the trolley.

'Oh, yeah, and what had you said?'

'Nothing. I just told her to get the tea ready. She got back from school and sat down in front of the telly. I wanted her to lay the tea things on the table but she wouldn't leave that damned box.'

'But she'd dashed home from school to see the last instalment of her television programme – the one she and Dora have been watching for the last six weeks. How about a bit of flexibility?'

'Television isn't the most important thing in life. She has to learn that.'

'And you chose the moment she was watching the last episode of her favourite TV programme to teach her that? She said you were horrible?' Aidan could imagine the scenario. Cathy would indeed tell her to get the tea ready; tell her, possibly with a reluctant, tight-lipped 'please'. But tell, not ask. 'No: 'Will you?' 'Would you mind?' 'Could you?' 'I'd like you to …' No. Just start with the bare bones of the imperative. She would not modulate her voice in any way that might be interpreted as signifying kindness or affection. It would be just cold and neutral at first. And at first the expression too would be cold and neutral. So no, she would not be allowed to watch the last instalment of her programme. It was ordained that the table had to be laid this very instant. At once. Immediately. No possible room for compromise here. A matter of the utmost urgency.

Cathy began her usual litany of self-justification. She'd been shopping; she'd been cleaning; she'd done an enormous wash. She'd not had time to sit down all day, her daughter came home from school and her first thought was for the television. Couldn't be bothered to set the table.

'Well – she's been working all day too. Seems you just couldn't wait to get your claws into her. You could try asking her politely. You don't seem to understand this, Cathy, but the way you ask matters. She does things for me.'

Now her voice took on an edge of malice the face twisted into scorn. 'Look, I've got no time for niceties. If I want it doing, I want it doing now and I say so in plain words. I don't see why I should slave away in this house all day and then put up with abuse in spite of all my efforts. I don't know what sort of husband you are. You're just so damned weak. You give me no support, none at all. No appreciation of all I do for the lot of you. Not a word of praise. Not a scrap of encouragement; just abuse, abuse. I'm treated like a doormat. I'm trodden underfoot, I collect all the dirt. How can you let her say such things to me? God, how I wish I had a husband I could depend on; one who would support me.'

Aidan, standing rigid with fury, aghast at her blatant inversion of the truth, said, 'For God's sake, how the fuck can I control what she says? People – kids – respond according to how you treat them. If you want to be a bloody sergeant major you should join the army. But that sure as hell isn't the way to bring out the best in people – least of all your own daughter. I just don't know what's wrong with you. You used to think she was wonderful – but now you put her down all the time – at every bloody opportunity. You humiliate her at every opportunity. I mean … you can't say her name without loathing in your voice and a sneer on your face. Look, you are reaping what you've sown … we're all reaping what you've sown … God damn it, we're reaping what you're still sowing … and I'll tell you this, too. Bobby isn't going to let herself be brow-beaten forever. And if you don't start looking at the way you deal with her and do something about changing it, there's going to be hell to pay – and it'll be your bloody fault.'

He stalked furiously out of the room and slammed the door behind him, cutting off Cathy's next salvo. He heard the crash of breaking china as he headed through the hall towards the front door. He opened it and went out into the front garden. The late afternoon sun flung long intense shadows across the green over the road, saturating with a fiery orange, the fronts of the houses opposite. The sky was a deep purple, Aidan tried to switch off his mind and surrender himself for a calming moment to the world of sensation. He had yet to deal with Bobby. She would twist his guts too.

He yearned for a cigarette. He'd always said giving up smoking was only viable if you're happy. So why had he decided to do it at this stage in his life? He breathed deeply for a while and tried to relax a little. When he felt his heartbeat had returned to something like normal, he turned back towards the house. The front door opened and Cathy brushed past him.

'I'm going out,' she said grimly. 'You can damn-well get your own meal.'

'Fine,' said Aidan. 'See you sometime.'

'You might.' She flung this at him, with venom.

She got into the car and started the engine. She reversed through the gates and drove noisily off up the avenue. Aidan watched till the car disappeared over the hill. He did not know where she was going, but at that moment he fervently wished she would never come back.

He went back into the house. There was quiet sobbing from the sitting room. Cathy had doubtless let off another raking salvo on her way out. Bobby was curled up on the sofa, a shaking foetus. He knelt down and put an arm round her heaving shoulders; she turned a tear-wet face towards him. She said, her voice quavering, 'Dad, why does she treat me like dirt? Why do you let her? Why is she always showing me how much she loves Dora and how she doesn't love me at all?'

Why do I let her mother treat her like dirt? Why do I let her mother speak to her like that? The recollection of the recent row made his head ache. I'm trying, Bobby. I'm trying.

'Listen Bobby, she does love you really, you know. You know she gets a lot of headaches and things, and that makes her a bit short-tempered. I try to damp things down, but I can't actually make her behave any differently.'

'Dad, you've got to, you've got to … Don't let her spoil my life – cos that's what she's doing, isn't she? Spoiling my life …' The tears came again and she rocked back and forth on the sofa.

'Bobby love, no one's going to spoil your life. I won't let that happen, I promise you. Because, listen, whatever happens, I love you and I'll look after you.'

She turned suddenly towards him.

'But you don't. You don't look after me. You don't know what she's like when you're not here. You're weak. You side with her all the time. You don't care what happens to me.' She broke again into a storm of sobbing.

'Oh God, look love, you know that's just not true. I mean I can't change her nature; you must understand that. It may be a phase she's going through. But what you've got to do is try not to let her upset you. Just try to keep cool. That way you'll survive, like me.'

'I don't want to survive like you. If she treats me like dirt, I'll get her, I will. I'll kill her or perhaps I'd better just kill myself.' There was hysteria in her voice. 'She'd like that, wouldn't she? She'd be pleased then, wouldn't she?'

Aidan was shocked and frightened. He'd not heard his daughter speak with such ferocity before. He reached towards her and enfolded her in his arms. 'Bobby, Bobby, don't say things like that. Just don't say anything like that again.' He wasn't sure the reproof in his voice was real. He knew he felt exhausted and drained of hope or optimism.

He tried to calm her. 'Listen love, she's gone out – I don't know where and I don't know when she'll be back but I'll round Dora up and we'll have something nice to eat – just the three of us.'

They stayed like that for a while then she withdrew, sniffed and rubbed her eyes with the backs of her hands. They were red when she looked at him.

'I hope she'll never come back,' she said, then, after a moment or two, switching disconcertingly to another compartment of her mind. 'Can I have the television on?'

'Yes, okay,' Aidan said. He looked down at her again, and, with one hand, ruffled her hair and smiled at her. Then he went through the kitchen, avoiding the shards on the floor and into the back garden. He paused by the garage to reflect, Aidan Hamilton is weak. It's official. It must be if it comes from two independent sources.

Dora had finished with the swing and was now upside down, her knees crooked over the top rail of the dividing fence, her long fair hair strewn over the sandpit.

'Daddy,' the inverted mouth said. 'Why are Mum and Bobby always quarrelling?'

Aidan crouched wearily and engaged the upside-down eyes.

'Dora, I don't really know,' he said. 'I think it may be something to do with Mum being not too fit and getting anxious, tired and easily upset.'

He was searching his brain for other emollient things to say, when Dora said, 'I got a gold star today.'

He blinked, swayed on his haunches and tried rapidly to refocus his mind.

'Oh er ... a gold star? Did you now. Well that's really great. So tell me, by what distinguished feat of scholarship did you come to gain a gold star?'

She unhooked her legs from the fence and cast them backwards over her head, detached her hands from the rail and somersaulting, landed, kneeling, facing away from him. Christ, is she in one piece?

She turned to face him.

'Daddy, stop using big words. We had to write about the nice things we do with the family. Mrs Jameson was really really pleased with mine.'

Aidan blinked and shook his head. 'And you got a gold star. Splendid. I am extremely pleased ... in fact delighted. I shall increase your pocket money by point nought nought of one per cent with effect from the beginning of next Michaelmas term.'

'Oh Daddy, you're nuts.' She giggled as she got up and dusted her knees. 'D'you think we dare go in now?'

'Yes. Let's go in and look for food, shall we?'

Later, the three of them sat in descending order of size on the sofa before the television watching Belle and Sebastian, eating fish fingers with specially hand-made chips and baked beans, generously lathered with tomato ketchup. Then Aidan, his daughters safely in bed, listened to music and drank whisky. He did not know where Cathy had gone and he did not worry that he did not know. It was peaceful without her. The evening had been congenial, wonderfully stress-free. He and his daughters were together. They had later played a hilarious game of snakes and ladders, then he had read to them. Part of him wished fervently that Cathy would not come back, but any faint guilt engendered by these thoughts was neutralised by the aftertaste of the teatime mayhem. She did, however, return. Aidan, sometime in the night, emerged into semi-consciousness, disturbed by the sound of the car arriving on the drive. Presently he was further disturbed by the arrival of Cathy in the bed. He gave no sign of being awake and she did not attempt to make contact with him. For a while he was kept awake by her agitated breathing, but once again, oblivion had claimed him, drifting him blissfully into his dream. This time he'd seen that the beautiful young woman had black hair and brown eyes. And she had a name.

My God, he was waiting for her now. He looked yet again at the clock noticing as its substantial tick entered into a mad syncopation with the rhythms penetrating from below. Ten minutes ... still ten minutes. What was she doing down there? Was she dancing with someone else? Was she being chatted up and ogled by some randy student who fancied his chances tonight? He topped up his glass again.

God, those next two days …

CHAPTER 6

During those next two days, the essentials of household business, he remembered, had been pursued without the advantage of verbal communication between him and Cathy. But that was nothing unusual. Somehow daughters were got off to school, all attendant transactions conducted and the family was fed, with hardly a word spoken between the parents. They were 'not speaking'. Aidan knew this was absurd and infantile, that he should not participate in such games, but now he was too exhausted to care. He remembered in the earliest days of their relationship how he had disliked going to Cathy's home because she and her brother and sister seemed always to be quarrelling. As he later came to know the siblings better, he realised they were, on the whole, genial and easy-going, and the tension, anger and the sense of unrequited grudge, which so often disfigured the household was largely fomented by Cathy. It was something he had no experience of in his own home life, but quite soon, in the early years of their marriage, he had come to realise that he was going to have to live with tension much of the time, for it surrounded his wife; she emitted it like the force field around an electrical installation. The minutest variation in her mood would find its reflex in a nuance of expression or gesture. It would be transmitted to those – especially her nearest and dearest – within range. He should have been warned. He dared on one occasion during their courtship to mention the matter of the quarrelling which seemed such a regular feature of her family life, Cathy angrily reproached him for deigning to comment on what was none of his business. The atmosphere in her family was stimulating, she had said. Yes, he should indeed have been warned. He had often heard people make a positive case for having a good row, along the lines that 'making-up' afterwards was so wonderful. He had never found this to be the case. He had found that nothing positive had ever emerged from his conflicts with Cathy. To him, they disfigured the history of their marriage like a trail of detonating mines across a battlefield, each one diminishing a little more his hope of survival. She'd seemed always ready to turn the most inconsequential disagreement into a blazing row, into which he would find himself willy-nilly drawn. Far from this being stimulating, it was for him insidiously corrosive. Each reconciliation, so far from being Paradise regained, seemed to leave the fabric of the marriage depleted by a few more fragments. Yet Cathy seemed not to notice. True to her cultural origins, she seemed to take it for granted that once the deal was done at the altar, no further acts of enticement or conciliation were necessary. Marriage break-up and divorce were something one read about, but did not happen to people like us.

So he supposed that on this occasion, according to precedent, over time and in small increments, full communication would be restored. But before long, it would all happen again. Then one day – sooner, rather than later – the cause would not be trivial; it would be about the welfare of their elder daughter and the future of their marriage; and Cathy seemed blind to the peril. It would happen unless he or someone, or something could change Cathy; or their physical circumstances could be changed.

Aidan turned over in his mind the accelerating deterioration of his domestic life since that row. The exploding mines seemed increasingly ferocious in their effect, the path between them ever more nerve-rackingly precarious. Why did she seem so invulnerable to their effects, while he grew increasingly desperate. The possibility of leaving – of taking Bobby away from her – was beginning to look like the only real option; he tried again and again to think through the possible consequences. To break up a home, however flawed it might be, was to destroy an edifice that had been years in the building. And with other people in there, that was serious. How could he make sure that Dora was not deprived of a father? What about the financial implications? The legal? Where could he take Bobby?

Then sometimes, usually when his imagination was liberated by alcohol, Aidan would fantasise. He had never been wholly confident of his attractiveness to women and fear of rebuff had ensured that he'd not been given to making passes at them. Yet, he'd never been short of female company, so concluded that women must on the whole quite like him. It was one of his greatest pleasures in life, if a woman made the right signals in the right situation, to talk to her, and in talking to enjoy the innocently erotic undertones that often seemed to suffuse such conversations between mutually attractive people. This could happen with students, as much as with certain of his colleagues' wives – or for that matter, shop assistants. He had enjoyed such relationships with many attractive students – especially in more recent years when the atmosphere in the college had become much less formal, but he did not know if any of them could have blossomed into anything more, anything illicit, if he had allowed it to. In any case, he had not seriously contemplated betraying his wife. But as his marriage deteriorated and with increasing contact with Louise, he now believed that such a possibility was … well, possible, and this perception allowed him to think what had previously been unthinkable – it was a dangerous and exciting thought.

As the term had progressed, he and Louise had seemed to find themselves together on more and more occasions. Apart from teaching, when Aidan tried to maintain the officially approved distance; there was the Drama Society, with its readings and rehearsals; the Art Society, with its lectures, demonstrations and visits. Events associated with these invariably ended up in the bar or a downtown pub. There were many more unscheduled meetings, of which every advantage was taken. Louise even turned out to be a modestly competent table tennis player to whom it sometimes pleased Aidan to lose gallantly. So he increasingly allowed himself the fantasy of an affair with Louise and his imagination ranged freely through an Arcadian mindscape of sensual pleasures. Yet it was an unsatisfactory fantasy. There was Cathy. An affair entails a double life and he did not relish the thought of a double life. He did not think he could easily live a life of duplicity and deceit. It seemed to come quite naturally to some of his friends – almost second nature; but it wasn't what he wanted. He had never had an affair before. No, he had never been unfaithful; didn't want to be unfaithful. He wanted a proper, exclusive, above-board relationship. So if he was going to fantasise, he may as well go the whole hog and conjure up a life with Louise and without Cathy, even if this did mean putting himself, as he bleakly reflected, in the egregious company of middle-aged men who've disposed of a worn-out wife in favour a younger and more glamorous model. Despicable as it would doubtless seem in the eyes of an outside observer, however, this scenario grew in appeal in Aidan's thoughts and had become some sort of counterbalance to his despair.

* * *

He drifted back into the present. God almighty. It was happening. It was really happening; that fantasy. Not the lot. Not yet. But who could tell? It looked as if he was settling for the double life, the deceit.

Well it would have to do for the present. He looked yet again at the clock. Five more minutes and she would be here; she would be here in his arms ... Louise ... Lulu.

CHAPTER 7

He remembered when she had become Lulu. He recalled trying to adapt Nabokov's phonetics; the tip of the tongue, two taps on the alveolar ridge, the rounded lips ... She had joined the Art Society at the very start. This was run largely by the students. Its members were mostly from the Art Department, including staff, but with a good leavening of others who had a more general interest in art. The department staff acted as advisors and often made the necessary contacts with museums and galleries, when visits or lectures were to be arranged. Within the first few weeks, Louise had stepped in to fill an unexpected vacancy in the post of secretary and with that, took on much of the responsibility of organising the visits – a responsibility which involved not only writing letters and making phone calls, but also liaising with members of the departmental staff.

Thinking back, Aidan remembered it was a Wednesday morning. He'd just set out for the senior common room in search of coffee. Unusually, he was alone, having been held back by some earnest discussion with one of his third-year students, as he saw her heading towards him, something instantaneous and physical happened deep inside him. He wasn't sure that his heart had actually missed a beat, but it was the phrase that came immediately to mind.

'Aidan,' she called, as she approached. 'Can I have few words with you please?' Aidan heave to and smiled.

'Of course; as many as you like.' Even as the words were coming out of his mouth, he was aware of their leery potential, hoping none of it showed.

'We – the Art Society, I mean – we've got a visit planned for Saturday. By popular request. It's to Durham – the Gulbenkian Museum in the morning and on to the Roman Wall after lunch'.

'Sounds good,' Aidan said, 'should be an interesting day.'

'There's a snag, though.'

'Oh?'

'Yes, well … we've okayed the minibus with the bursar, but you see, we haven't got a driver. None of the students has a permit yet, so I wondered if you – well I know it's a lot to ask for a Saturday – but I wondered if you could possibly think of … well would you come and drive us? Could you … please.' She uttered the last word with a wonderfully calculated note of pleading, as she looked at him meltingly with wide-open eyes. Aidan swallowed hard.

'Er … well, don't you want the expert on oriental art for the Gulbenkian? Henry's your man for that, you know – he usually does this trip.'

'Yes, I know and I did ask him, but he said he couldn't get away on Saturdays – his wife needed him – for shopping and things like that.' Aidan raised his eyebrows in amusement.

'Oh really, and what makes you think I don't have responsibilities like that, with a wife who needs me just as much as Henry's needs him?'

'Well … it's just that I've sometimes seen you working in the department on a Saturday, and I just wondered if maybe … Well we're really desperate. If you can't do it, we'll have to call the expedition off … and you know how valuable the visit would be … I mean, for the course. Anyway …' she looked at him slyly, 'we'd all rather have you to drive us.'

'Now you're using feminine wiles …' She smiled demurely and dropped her eyes. It was a good performance. '… and dammit, they're working,' he said ruefully. She looked up at him wide eyed. And the wide eyes engaged his, unwaveringly. 'Okay, I'll do it.'

'Oh Aidan will you? That's great. I knew you'd help us out.'

'Hm, did you, then? Well what time do we depart?'

'Oh, er, Nine o'clock. Is that okay?'

God knows how he was going to square it with Cathy. 'Better make it half-past.'

'Oh, thank you, Aidan.' She smiled. 'That would be wonderful.'

Aidan did not square it with Cathy. He knew in advance it was totally unsquareable and when, with some deviation from the strict truth, he told her that he must unavoidably be absent on college work on the coming Saturday, Cathy found it opportune to recapitulate in the most ferocious and detailed way his inadequacies, his fecklessness, his failure to give any kind of priority to his family responsibilities, and the general wickedness of his exploitative employers. Then she shut down all communication with him for the next two days. She did not even reply to his goodbye as he left the house on the Saturday morning.

Having done so, when he arrived at the department, a number of students had already arrived, chatting cheerfully as they waited for the group to become complete. He greeted them and joined in the chat for a while, noting with a little inner anxiety that she was not yet there. What if she doesn't turn up? Of course she's going to turn up. She's bloody well organising it, isn't she? He looked again around the group, anxiously.

Then, 'Okay,' he said, 'hang about. I'll go and get the bus and pick you up outside the gates in a few minutes.' Ten minutes later, as he drove up the driveway and looked sideways to pull out onto the road, he saw to his relief that Louise had arrived and was checking off names on a clipboard, looking very efficient, he thought. Oh God, and meltingly beautiful.

He pulled the minibus into the kerb, pulled the handbrake on and switched off the engine. As he opened the driver's door to step down, Louise turned towards him.

'Hi Aidan,' she said. 'We're all here except Harry. He's gone over to the kitchens to get the sandwiches. The domestic bursar said if we weren't going to be eating lunch in college, we could have packed lunches.'

'Oh,' said Aidan, 'Am I included? They don't normally feed me in college.'

'Of course you are. They couldn't leave the driver out, could they? We can have a picnic if the weather stays fine – if you know of a suitable place.'

'Oh I'm sure I can come up with something,' he replied. She flashed him a smile and as she turned back to the students, they broke into boisterous cheer for the arrival of Harry carrying before him a large cardboard box: the sandwiches.

The box was duly stowed, then, 'Come on then, Lulu,' someone called, 'you're the conductor … let's get going.'

'Okay, okay. Come on folks, all aboard,' Louise called out. Aidan, thinking to make certain she sat next to him, determined no one else should take the front seat while she was shepherding the tail end, put down his bag of sketching materials on it. He need not have worried. No one made a bid for it, as it was one of three left when Louise stepped aboard and pulled the door shut. Aidan shifted his bag onto the floor and she sat next to him. He never knew whether it was because the students sensed something intangible, something inchoate, between them and deferred to it or whether her official position and her clipboard entitled her, or in fact whether she had threatened to murder anyone who so much as looked at that seat. But as she joined him, he looked at her and smiled, settling into the driver's seat in every expectation of a beautiful day.

As he navigated the minibus through the northern outskirts of Swaleborough, he was infected by the celebratory atmosphere; as Louise turned round in her seat and joined in the chatter, he happily hummed a snatch of Mozart … couldn't remember what … scherzo … Hafner symphony, maybe. Then she turned to face the front and began to pay some detailed attention to the passing landscape.

Aidan said, 'Louise … you seem to have become "Lulu". When did that happen?'

'Oh I don't know really – you know how it is with nicknames. They used to call me Lulu at school – but no one here could know that.'

'Yes, I do know how it is with nicknames, much to my chagrin.'

'Why? Did you have one at school?'

'Afraid so.'

'Well, what was it? Are you going to tell me?'

'Well only if you promise not to tell anyone else.'

'Okay, I swear secrecy.'

'It wasn't so awful, really – just a simple abbreviation; "Ham". I was called that right through my schooldays and didn't get rid of it till I went to university.'

'Hm, not to awful – unless you're Jewish, of course.'

Aidan laughed. 'Of course, there were variations – like Hammy – even Hamster, sometimes.'

'Oh well, they weren't so bad. There's even something endearing about "Hamster".'

'What about Lulu, then?'

'Well you see, that started as an abbreviation – and then someone said it twice, and there I was – Lulu. I rather like it though; it's kind of a naughty, French knickerish sort of name.'

Aidan smiled. 'I see, and am I to use such a naughty, French knickerish sort of name?' he asked. He momentarily took his eyes off the road to give her a sideways glance, which she met with a quick look from under her eyelashes.

'Hm, well only on special occasions, I think.'

'And what would they be?' Aidan asked.

She gave him that look again, and said, 'Oh … I don't know … I expect we could think of some.' Then someone hailed her from the back of the bus; she turned round in her seat and was, for a while, involved in a rowdy exchange of banter with her colleagues. When she turned to the front again, she said, 'D'you know, Aidan, this the first time I've been outside of Swaleborough since I came here.'

'Hm, well I hope that means you've been too busy for frivolities like sightseeing … working hard and all that.'

'Oh well … let's just say I've been finding my feet.' Aidan smiled. She continued, 'And I'll tell you something else – this is absolutely the furthest north I've ever been in my life.'

'Well, what do you think of it so far?'

'It's not what I expected. I thought the north was all satanic mills and smoke, and grime ... sort of Dickensian,' she said, flashing a glance at him and adding as an afterthought, 'apart from Lindisfarne, of course ...'

'Oh yes,' Aidan said, 'I remember now. It was Lindisfarne that attracted you up here in the first place, wasn't it?'

'... but really, it's quite pretty ... rolling countryside, farms, trees. Almost like home.'

'Which is ... I forget.'

'We live in a village – about eight miles outside of Norwich.'

'Oh yes. Well don't get too carried away with what you see now. We'll be running into the pit villages soon. Durham's a bit of a mixture, as you'll see. Have you always lived there?'

'Yes. Well apart from when I lived in London, of course. Daddy bought the place before I was born.'

Aidan slowed the minibus down as the thirty-mile-an-hour sign hove into sight, where the rolling pastoral landscape gave way to a more intimate kind of cultivation; the allotments on the approach to the southernmost of the pit villages, separated from the main road by a scraggy verge, a ditch and a hawthorn hedge, whose many gaps were filled in by sheets of rusting corrugated iron, old doors and decaying enamel shop signs advertising Saxa Salt and Craven-A. Behind, glimpses of pigeon crees topped by brightly painted palings. Then the light was shut out as the road ran through the deep cutting which divided the village, then under the bridge which reunited the two halves.

'Hm, I see. What is your father, then? No, don't tell me. I bet he's a farmer, isn't he?'

She laughed. 'Good Lord no. Why should you think that?'

'Oh I don't know. Suppose I could just see you as the daughter of a gentleman farmer. What does he do then?'

'Well, he's what people sometimes refer to as "something in the city".'

'I see,' Aidan said, 'a bit beyond my experience, that. I've never been quite sure what "something in the city" people do.'

'Well what they do is work long hours and make lots of money.'

'But doing what?' Something deep in Aidan prickled. Something in his socialist, working-class, cultural background stirred and vestigial traces of a deep-seated grievance tried to escape from its dark remote corner in his head. It wanted to shape his talk. 'My Uncle Ben worked long hours, but that was doing socially useful work.'

Louise looked at him with raised eyebrows. Aidan stared concentratedly at the road.

'Are you suggesting stock broking isn't socially useful?' She asked him. Aidan didn't answer the question.

'Very traditional then, your father, is he? Black jacket, striped trousers, bowler hat, tightly rolled umbrella? Commuting everyday to the City of London.'

'Well, yes. I suppose so. They all dress like that. It seems to be a kind of uniform. Mind you, he does wear a sports jacket and flannels at the weekend.'

'Oh ... I bet he rides to hounds too.'

'Hm ... yes, as a matter of fact he does – when he can find time. He's quite keen. As a matter of fact ... so do I, sometimes.'

'And during the week, he spends long hours moving wealth around from one rich bastard to another, but not doing anything to create any? Well my Uncle Ben worked long hours too. He had a kind of uniform – a helmet with a lamp on it, fustian pit-hoggers and big boots with hobnails and steel toecaps. He came home black from head to foot. He earned lots of money too, only it wasn't for him; it went into the overloaded pockets of the bosses. What he did earn for himself was silicosis and an early grave. He was a coal miner, you see.' Louise was showing signs of agitation.

'Look, Aidan, I'm very sorry about your Uncle Ben. But my father and the whole financial thing ... they're just necessary to keep the wheels of industry turning. I mean, what are you, a communist or something? Sounds as though, come the revolution, you'd have my Daddy stuck-up against a wall and shot.'

Aidan shot a sly sideways glance and laughed. 'Well, no ... probably not. I think I'd forgive him almost anything for producing a daughter like you and sending her to Swaleborough to be my student.'

'Aidan! You've been teasing me, stringing me along, haven't you?'

'Just a bit … I don't know … driving through this crummy, exhausted mining area … something got into me. Uncle Ben was pure invention. But there were plenty of real life Uncle Bens around where I was born. As a matter of fact, none of my family worked in the pits; they were all shipbuilders. I'll tell you about them sometime … Anyway, what about your mother? Does she stay at home and look after the house?'

'Oh God, no way. She has a daily woman to see to that. No, she works. She's head mistress of a small but very exclusive and expensive girls' school. She's very bright – an Oxford double first. She's written several important books on Christo-Judaic interaction in Europe in the middle ages.'

'Good Lord. Important books? Important to whom? I suppose you went to that exclusive school, then? I don't remember from your CV.'

'Blimey, no. Mummy's a woman of principle. She sent me to the local comprehensive, thank God.'

Aidan let out a burst of laughter. 'Wow, what a paradox. Well is she a communist or something?'

'I don't really think so. I think you got it about right. Just call her a paradox.'

'And the rest of the family? Tell me pretty maiden, are there any more at home like you?' Almost as he said it, he thought, that must have sounded pretty corny if she doesn't know her Gilbert and Sullivan. But she did. No culture gap there.

'There are a few, kind sir … but no, not really like me. Different sex, you see.'

'Oh, go on, tell me more.'

'Well I have an elder brother, Daniel. He's following Daddy, working his way up in the city. He has a flat in Whitechapel.'

'Oh, yeah …'

'And a younger brother, Damian.'

'And what does he do?'

'Well … I think you'd call him a dropout. He's nineteen and still lives at home. He seems to be waiting for the world to come up with something interesting and remunerative for him … something that doesn't require too much effort.'

'And what do your parents think about that?'

'Well my father's pretty pissed off with him … but Mummy's inclined to be indulgent. I think she still sees him as the baby of the family. In fact, he still lives in the nursery.'

'There's a nursery?'

'Yes … it's in the attic at the back of the house.' She giggled briefly. 'Of course he doesn't sleep in the cot now or play with teddy bears … though come to think of it, I'm not so sure about the teddy bears … anyway, Mummy let him convert it … record player, posters and stuff. Partly to keep him out of Daddy's hair, I think.'

'It's a big house, then … to have a nursery?'

'Biggish. Used to be a rectory, but eventually the church couldn't afford it ...'

'... but your Daddy could ...'

'So they moved the rector into a new house on an estate. Yes, and Daddy bought the rectory, spent quite a bit making it comfortable. It has a couple of acres of land and a paddock. It's nice.'

'It sounds like it.' He shot a sideways glance at her. 'So you're a pretty classy bird, then Louise.'

'Oh Aidan. Don't say things like that. You make me feel embarrassed.' He grinned at her.

'Okay. Sorry. We'll talk about something else. How'd you like a potted history of Chinese ceramics?'

In fact, a potted history of Chinese ceramics was what Aidan delivered to the students to start them off in the museum; and there was no better place he knew of outside of London to do it. Then he sent them off to explore further and follow-up what interested them, consulting him as and when necessary. They agreed a time to reassemble for the journey west towards the Roman Wall and their picnic on the way.

Meanwhile he himself chose to linger a while among the Sung dynasty stoneware and to lose himself in the austere beauty of those ancient pots. He was pretty sure that if he hadn't been a painter, he'd have wanted to be a potter. The mystery, the mystique of it – the ancientness of the technology – the basicness of the materials the primordialness of it. But in the college, this was Gerry's world. Aidan often went down to the pottery when Gerry was firing stoneware. He could understand Gerry's fascination. He'd stand and watch as the firing came roaring and throbbing to its climax; Gerry nursing his big gas kiln through the final stages, manipulating burners and dampers, watching the curl of flame at the spy hole, calculating the amount of carbon in the atmosphere, how many atoms were free to combine with the oxides in the glazes, to give the colours he wanted; to make the irons turn blue or green, the coppers red and just the right fluidity. Gerry acknowledged he wasn't entirely the master of this thing. He didn't quite feel it necessary to propitiate the gods before undertaking a firing, but he did think it best to enjoin the kiln's co-operation in a matey kind of way; he felt he needed to coax it, to cajole it, hope for its collaboration in his plans, hope that what worked last time would work this time. My God, it was like painting with molten rock, Aidan reflected, and that Chun bowl in the display case went through just the same process a thousand years ago. He thought if you want to confer immortality, make it of clay, and burn it to white heat.

Above almost all else here, he coveted that bowl. He wanted nothing so much as to cradle it in his two hands as though to take from it something of the expertise of its forming. It was perhaps the size of a grapefruit; or a breast. With the taut economy of form nature achieves so effortlessly again and again, but which so often eludes the best endeavours of people. The restrained gleam of that fat, rich, lavender glaze with its dissolving calligraphic flash of copper crimson, the perfect symmetry of the form exquisitely upset where the molten glaze had run down at one side, as honey does from a spoon, hardening during cooling to form an elegant drop above the unglazed foot. If he held it in his hand, he wondered, could he fail to derive from the perfect balance of the yin and the yang, a trace of that cosmic harmony it was designed to transmit. Harmony was something he felt he could do with a bit more of just now.

Then wistfully turning away, he set himself to moving around among the students, by now, spread out singly and in little groups around the display cases, drawing or writing notes, or just looking. He did not consciously look for Louise, but he found her anyway, alone, in one of the more remote offshoots from the main gallery. She was captivated by something in one of the cases. Aidan paused for a moment in the doorway, half minded to turn back, for he knew what she had found. But she turned and saw him there.

'Aidan,' she said in a loud gallery whisper, a delighted smile on her face, 'come and look at this.' Feeling a little awkward, Aidan advanced.

'Hm, so you've found it ...'

'But it's beautiful ... it's so ... I don't know ... just beautiful. Tell me about it.'

'Well … er, it's Chinese. It's porcelain … eighteenth century. It's Tao …'

'Oh? What's Tao when it's at home?'

'It's a Chinese … well, philosophy, I suppose you'd call it. It's all to do with harmony and balance. Sort of being in tune with the cosmos … you know.' She'd been looking into his eyes, as he spoke; now her gaze returned to the glass-fronted display case. She was looking into it, completely entranced, her lips slightly parted.

Then, still staring, she whispered, almost ruminatively, 'They're fucking each other like crazy, aren't they? … they're just so …' she stopped in mid-sentence and looked quickly at Aidan. He noticed that she had gone slightly pink. He felt himself blushing, too; he wasn't quite up to this. Certainly, even in the wake of the much spoken of sexual liberation of the previous decade (from which he, locked into marriage, had derived no benefit) you didn't commonly encounter such blatant images of copulation; but if you did … if you did and you happened to be in close proximity to a beautiful young woman, would you expect such a scandalously upfront response from her? Oh God, wasn't he hopelessly out of date? Were they all like this, these days, so uninhibited, when you got down to it?

She went on rather quickly, '… and it's so tiny, isn't it? Must only be about two inches high … and, well …'

God, and they look so happy, don't they? Aidan thought. Just look at the big grin on his face and her smile of satisfaction. The modelling was so exquisitely perfect. He, Lord Yang, is on his back, his knees drawn up to his chest, his legs entwining her waist. She, Lady Yin, straddles him, kneeling. With her left hand, she offers her breast to his open, delighted mouth. From behind, the archetype of the phallus; the shaft, entering her, surmounts the symmetrically disposed balls; the Jade Stalk at the Vermilion Gate; the whole apparatus modelled with minute care. The little sculpture had a white glaze, with something of the quality of ivory, yet with the subtlest hint of blue. The eyes, eyebrows and hair, were delicately black; the lips, including those of her vagina, a vivid red.

Louise went on, stumbling a little, 'It's so … well, beautiful, and unexpected, I just got carried away.' She interrupted her flow and looked again at Aidan, '… Oh Aidan, you're not embarrassed, are you?' she asked.

'Embarrassed? No … no, of course not,' he replied embarrassedly. Then something snapped and they both laughed with a kind of mutual relief.

'Well, it is a bit naughty, though, isn't it?'

'Um … yes … it's pretty shocking to us, I suppose … but in Taoism, this coming together, the Yin and the Yang, feminine and masculine, was supposed to bring about the purest harmony – a kind of connection with the flow of the cosmos. They tried to introduce this balance, this harmony into every aspect of life. But the idea had special potency in … well, er … sexual congress.'

She was looking at him round eyed, her lips slightly parted. 'Yes, yes, go on.'

'Er … well they had what they called the Thirty Heaven and Earth Postures. This one is number eleven, if I remember rightly; it's called, Hovering Butterflies.'

'Wow, what a wonderful idea.' Louise bent forward again and resumed her scrutiny.

Aidan went on, now rather excited at having a conversation with this beautiful young woman about matters so intimate. 'You see, they weren't messed up about sex the way we are, tying it up with all sorts of prohibitions and taboos. Making it a central criterion of morality. Oh God, the amount of frustration and trouble it causes … it just …'

She straightened up and, smiling, not quite engaging his eye. 'Oh is that how you see it, then?'

He consciously avoided her eyes. 'Oh well, I don't know … I heard someone famous say, recently, that consenting sex is really one of the most harmless things that humans do to each other. And basically, he was right. I mean, compared with other favourite human occupations like murder, extortion, torture, pillage, generally making war and things like that that people do to each other, it is harmless – apart from the collateral damage – the nasty diseases you can get, unwanted babies, the jealousy, the rivalry it causes …'

'But the Taoists had got this all sussed out? You know Aidan, I think Taoism's got a lot going for it. Can anyone join?' she asked.

Aidan couldn't suppress a laugh which echoed through the gallery and he clapped his hand to his mouth to kill it, looking round guiltily. Then he looked at her again, her eyes, rounded, met his straight on. He moistened his lips, then took a deep breath, not sure where to go from here. Away from this dangerous territory, he rather thought. So he said, 'Er … okay … look, Louise, we were supposed to studying art, not … er, human relations, so …'

'Hm, just as it was beginning to get interesting … oh well … I suppose. Okay I think I'll settle down and do a little drawing. I've just got to have this in my sketch book.'

Aidan, smiling, nodded. 'See you later then.'

It was a couple of hours before they were all back in the minibus. Aidan drove northwest, through the heart of County Durham and did not stop till they encountered the River Tyne at Broomhaugh. He remembered a quiet spot, a tree-shaded bend in the river, a grassy bank, which would be perfect for their picnic. The morning mists, which, when they had set out, had necessitated headlights, had begun to lift just before they'd entered Durham and now relocated themselves overhead as cloud, seemingly determined that the sun shouldn't get a look in that day. But by the time the bus was halfway across the county, they had conceded and the sun was breaking through. As Aidan turned off the main road and parked the minibus on the worn and rutted verge of a side lane, it had burned away the last vestiges of the cloud layer and was setting about providing some early autumn warmth. This, temperate though it was, seemed to ignite a lurking pocket of high spirits in the students, sending them leaping and whooping ahead through the gate and across the field Aidan had pointed out ahead.

He couldn't help smiling as it reminded him of his early teaching days, taking a class of nine-year-olds on a nature walk. Would they pick flowers and make daisy chains? Aidan followed maintaining a little dignity. Halfway across the field, Louise had hung back. She turned round and beckoned. 'Come on Aidan ... Where do we go from here?'

Aidan pointed and made 'go on' gestures. He called out, 'To that corner, where the trees are. There's a stile. Through that and follow the path down to the left ... the river's just through there ... at the other side of the hedge.' The group followed his indications, but Louise waited.

They strolled across the field together, towards the stile. Louise looked around her, gesturing at it all, said, 'Aidan, do you always picnic in Poussin-ish places?'

Aidan looked at her and laughed. 'Well who wouldn't, if they could find them? But hey, aren't you starting to see the world through Poussin-shaped spectacles?'

'So don't you?'

'Hm ... I suppose I do – where appropriate.' The rest of the students had disappeared through the trees, the sounds suggested that they were making camp beside the river. 'Now for instance, you wouldn't find a stile like this in a Poussin landscape, would you?'

'No, I suppose not. But there are lots of other things about it ...'

It was a swinging-gate stile. Aidan indicated to Louise to go first. The gate was stiff with lack of use and because of some evidently displaced woodwork, the gap particularly narrow. Louise made a play of breathing in.

'Phew, tight squeeze.' She turned, to hold the gate for Aidan. He too breathed ostentatiously in, as he squeezed into the style, he said, 'We call these granny stoppers,' and he feigned being jammed there.

She said, 'And we call them kissing gates.' She bent forward, reaching up on her toes and planted a swift kiss on Aidan's cheek.

He froze and stared at her, speechless for a moment or two. 'Christ, Louise ...'

'Lulu ... special occasion ...'

'... er, Lulu – don't do things like that. Don't even say things like that or I'll ... or I'll ...'

'Or you'll what, Aidan?'

'Or I'll ... or I'll not be responsible for my actions.'

She backed away from the stile, allowing Aidan egress and turned away, giggling. 'That sounds like a challenge,' she said over her shoulder, as she made off at a run towards where her colleagues had disappeared. Confused, Aidan followed, unsure whether to try to reclaim some dignity or to throw in his lot with the spirit of the day and become one of them. Sod the dignity ...

They had found a spot just up from the gravelly edge of the river, where it curved, making a stumpy peninsula, surrounding them with water on three sides. They'd dropped untidily to the ground on patch of dry, springy grass, bordered on one side by a fallen tree trunk. When Louise arrived, with Aidan close behind, they were engaged in sorting out the picnic. Someone had thought to bring along an old table cloth – or perhaps a thoughtful member of the kitchen staff had provided it – and they were spreading out the contents of the box, packets of sandwiches, crisps, apples.

Bill Dixon called out, 'Hey, Aidan, come on. Look, we've got a special seat for you.' He made an elaborate courtly gesture with one arm, indicating the tree trunk. 'You're our teacher, our guru, the master. You can sit on that and we'll sit at your feet, while you dispense words of wisdom ... and Lulu can sit down there ...' He indicated a spot on the grass, next to the tree trunk, '... and be your handmaiden ... or footmaiden – whatever gurus have.' There was an uproar of approving laughter, Aidan sat on the tree trunk and Louise flounced on to the grass at his feet, looking up at him with feigned reverence.

Aidan said, 'Well, thanks for the tribute. No words of wisdom, though. Not part of the job specification. Not qualified, you see. Art. That's what I'm paid to teach. But not now,' he said, reaching down, as Jane Parker handed him a sandwich. 'For the next fifteen minutes, my face is going to be full of egg and cress sandwich. I'm ravenous.'

After the meal, there seemed no great urgency to recommence the journey. Aidan had lowered himself from the tree trunk, which had turned out to be rather uncomfortable and had settled himself with his back against it. Louise was now reclining by his side, the rest of the party sprawled informally round about. Then Jane Parker, always diligent in her pursuit of knowledge, said, 'Aidan, are you going to give us a run-down on the Roman Wall, before we set off again?'

A mixture of groans and noises of qualified approval ... 'yeah, but make it short and not boring.'

'Now would I ever bore you?' Aidan said. 'Okay, twenty-minutes flat, I'm sure you could survive that ...'

'Yeah go on then ...'

For twenty minutes, by the banks of a river, the sage of his dream, held his students in thrall. It was his alter ego.

But ... then ... it was Aidan's brief mention of bath houses and the Romans' management of personal cleansing; water ... cooling water, that delayed things. The sun was now shining in a clear blue sky and its warmth, trapped in the still air by the surrounding trees, was a lingering reminder of the summer, now gracefully transmuting into a balmy autumn. There seemed no pressing hurry and gradually, the questions and discussion subsided and a luxurious indolence took over. Some of the students, from sitting attentively, cross-legged, allowed themselves to melt a little, sprawling more comfortably, soaking the warming sun, sighing and groaning, as they stirred, with the sensual pleasure of it, lulled by the hum of insects in the gorse and long grasses, the soft shriek of martins, skimming the surface of the water. Aidan, now propped comfortably against the tree, caught the mood and half-closed his eyes against the glare of the sun. Louise, still at his side, had also subsided and in readjusting herself, her hand had somehow come to rest lightly touching his. Unwittingly, a thrill ran through Aidan's body. Not otherwise moving, he allowed his eyes to slip sideways. Louise made no attempt to reposition her hand; her eyes were closed, a half smile on her lips. It was like his dream; that beautiful girl – but unlike in the dream, he could not, he knew, surrender to his feelings. Oh God, he thought, it's the dream alright. It keeps coming true. But the reality, like the dream, could not come to fruition.

Nevertheless, with some alarm, he became aware of a developing erection and hastily, he made a small concealing adjustment to the conformation of his legs, being careful not to break the delicate contact that was its cause. He lay there, next to Louise, his eyes half closed and his heart racing. A man, in middle age, aroused, excited, like an adolescent in half-contrived contact with a girl in the back row of the cinema on a first date – wanting more, but not knowing what to do next, in case he should lose what he had already gained, so spending the whole performance holding on to what he'd got. So did Aidan now.

For some time they lay there, bound, whether by accident or design, by that fragile contact. Then there was a scraping of gravel and the snap of a twig as someone moved. A shadow fell across the slit of his eyes and he eased them open, to see Lizzie Allen moving to the water's edge. He watched, as, balancing on one leg, she stooped to remove first one shoe, then the other, dropping them on the gravel before poking her big toe into the water. Then she immersed a whole foot, swishing it round just below the surface, sending up little sparkling showers. Seemingly gratified, she bent down, rolled up her jeans to just below the knees and set off, wading, towards the middle. Whereupon others raised themselves on to elbows, taking notice.

'What's it like, Lizzie. Is it cold?' Jane called to her.

'No ... it's lovely. Come and try it.' Jane sat up, then after a moment's thought, took her shoes off, got to her feet and joined Lizzie, dabbling in the edge of the river. This seemed to signal the end of the siesta; others stood up, blinking, and, shedding shoes, joined them at the water's edge.

It was Harry Pierce, furthest out into mid-stream, who shouted, 'Hey, come over here ... it looks deep enough to swim.' He stood among some half-submerged rocks, facing the opposite bank, looking down into the deeper water, where, halfway through its thousand-year enterprise of creating an ox-bow lake, the current had scoured the bank away on its outside curve. Harry splashed his way back to dry land.

'Anyone fancy a swim, then?' he asked, pulling his shirt over his head. Looking about him for takers, he unzipped his jeans and letting them drop to the ground, stepped out of them.

'Harry,' called Aidan, 'what the hell're you doing? ... You're indecent. You'll get arrested,' he said, laughing, but half alarmed.

'No way ... no cops around here, Aidan – it's too good a chance to miss.' He looked round at his pals, 'come on then, you guys; how about it?' Whereupon, clad only in his underpants, letting out a joyous whoop he splashed out again into the middle of the river, paused for a moment, before flopping forward in a kind of ungainly semi-dive, disappeared in an immense splash. He emerged, turning, spouting water, his hair, like seaweed, sprawling over his eyes, the river up to his chest.

He waved, calling out, 'Hey, come on. It's great ... deep enough to swim here. Look.' He gulped in a breath and plunged head down again, legs kicking, in a clumsy surface dive, disappearing for a second or two before emerging, gasping in air, laughing, splashing water at the two wading girls. Jane twisted sideways, arching backwards and screamed as the cold water cascaded down her back.

'Owww ... stop it, Harry. I'm gonna get you for that. I'm coming after you.' She splashed her way back to the bank, pulled off her tee shirt and dropped her jeans. Then wading into the middle in bra and knickers, launched herself into the deeper pool in an explosive splash, which drenched Harry. Before Aidan had time to consider his responsibilities, a mass undressing was under way.

'Christ … what's going on?'

'Come on, Aidan.' It was Louise, now on her feet, 'You coming in?' He looked up at her in confusion.

'What? … I don't … I … no … NO …'

'Oh come on … come on.' Louise looked at him, and laughing, slipped off her shoes, unzipped and discarded her jeans, dropping them next to Aidan. She turned and skipped towards the water's edge, where she paused to discard her tee shirt. She was not wearing a bra. Jesus Christ! Aidan's jaw sagged and his eyes boggled. She turned slightly and waving to him, waded through the shallows, before launching herself into the deeps. Jane looked at Louise and laughed.

'Hey … topless is it …?' she shouted and reaching behind her, unhooked her bra and flinging it onto the little beach, turned to flop into the water beside Louise.

Louise called to Lizzie, 'Come on Liz … you're overdressed.' She and Jane made a grab at her, going for her bra fastening; they all three toppled over together in a huge splash. In the melee, another bra landed on the little gravely beach. Then they emerged, disentangling themselves, onto the shore, laughing, gasping. They stood for a moment in a group, recovering. The four boys looked on cheering and making lustfully appreciative noises. For a moment, it was

Venus, born from the sea in triplicate: it was The Three Graces, the Judgement of Paris, all rolled into one. It was as though every image of provocative nudity that he had ever seen flashed before Aidan's eyes. The sun lit their wet, naked breasts. Through their knickers, now translucent in their wetness, he could see the dark deltas of their pubic hair. Flabbergasted and enflamed, he could, for a while, do no more than gape, as the three young women wrestled each other back into the deeps and joined in the melee with the young men; his students cavorting nakedly and noisily in the sparkling water. They leapt and flopped, splashed and dived, sending up fountains of droplets, showers of diamonds glinting in the sun, shrieking and bawling, intoxicated. Aidan was intoxicated; intoxicated to the point of dizziness, as Louise detached herself from the confusion of bodies and turned to face him, waist deep, her hair draped, many stranded, down the side of her face and shoulders, the sunlight glistening wetly on her breasts. God almighty, what tits ...

'Aidan ...' She waved to him. 'Come on ... come and join us. It's super.'

'Yeah, come on,' other voices joined in, laughing, encouraging, tempting, scooping handfuls of water in his direction. 'Come on, you're supposed to be looking after us.' More laughter.

Aidan was within a hairsbreadth of abandoning caution and plunging in among them, when a newspaper headline flashed through his mind; STUDENTS IN RIVERSIDE ORGY WITH LECTURER.

For God's sake, he had a Saturnalia on his hands in a small corner of Arcadia; it would not have surprised him if cloven-hooved Pan himself had been lurking in the bushes. He would have given anything to join in, to frolic in the water among those beautiful naked bodies ... but ... he knew it – he was out of date – couldn't do it. Couldn't leap the age gap, the culture gap. Couldn't abandon himself. Couldn't parade himself in his Y-Fronts before his students. Especially with an erection. Defeated by his inhibitions. He swallowed hard and became the guru again.

'No ... you enjoy yourselves my children. I'll look after affairs on dry land and be your life guard.'

Watching them, devouring them, he thought bewilderedly about nudity. He'd seen plenty of it; of course, the privileged nudity of the connubial bed; the mass voyeurism of Hair and Oh Calcutta; countless hours of drawing from the nude model in the life class – these, remote, sanitised nudity. But nudity in the course of professional interaction? In a life that depended so much on clear-cut categories, this was an interstitial experience. No precedent for that. Should he not look? Impossible not to; even clothed, breasts, however provocatively displayed, could not be looked at directly – well not in his book. A paradox; they are wantonly displayed, but may only be looked at, well, sideways or distantly, clandestinely, through dark glasses. For the eyes to lose contact with eyes and slip down a cleavage, is seen as lascivious. God – and he'd been trying to converse sensibly with near-naked nymphs drying themselves in the sun, sprawling there in a kind of augmented Dejeuner sur L'herbe.

So it must be true; the sixties had produced a revolution that he had not noticed – or had at any rate been aware of only in peripheral vision. It had all happened while he was dedicatedly and as it seemed on a day like this, boringly, doing what was expected of him; looking inwards to a family – ingrowing eyeballs – and not noticing the exciting things going in the larger world, or at any rate, the world just outside his, where young people were sticking flowers down the barrels of guns and making love not war, taking their clothes off at rock festivals and on sunny beaches. And now, after missing those ten years of shedding clothes and taboos, he'd unexpectedly gained entry to this wondrous land. Today, this glorious warm, sunlit day in early autumn, his students had shed their clothes and splashed in a limpid pool in the upper reaches of the River Tyne.

It had gone on and on. They didn't want to stop; why would they? It was a foretaste – or a recollection – of Paradise; or Arcadia – what's the difference? And he didn't want them to stop. He could not take his eyes off the spectacle, but he could not join in. They tried to persuade him, but he couldn't; he didn't qualify; he belonged to the wrong generation; he hadn't gone through the apprenticeship; he had a wife, two daughters and a mortgage. So he'd attempted an air of amused detachment, a veneer of urbanity which belied, he hoped, the shock, the wonder, the raging lust – and maybe the love inside him.

128

For these were his students; he was their tutor. Hardly in loco parentis … but nevertheless … So he'd looked on and somehow his lust, the raw longing, in this vision of beautiful, naked young bodies in joyful play, was at least in part assimilated to art. Dazed, his consciousness flowed into the Prelude a l'Apresmidi d'un Faun; The Rite of Spring – even though it was autumn. He was Pan with an erection, on a Greek vase, peering lubriciously between the bushes at nymphs and satyrs at play. An Arcadian dream, if ever he saw one. Oh God, oh God.

He couldn't tear his eyes away and groped blindly behind him for his bag. He fumbled out his sketchbook and a bundle of charcoal wrapped in tissue. Selecting a blank page and a slender stick of charcoal, he began employing the artist's alchemy, transmuting lust into art. His drawing was usually a patient, meticulous analysis of some fragment of the world – but he could shoot from the hip when he had to. Now he drew rapidly; the charcoal cracked and splintered, as feverishly, he pushed it beyond its strength. It was a confusion of flying limbs and breasts; fountains and spouts of water, arcing rainbows; a dynamic chaos of line, form, pattern and colour. With eyes flicking rapidly between the scene and the image, registering micro-second fragments, translating them into line and mass before they should fade. He worked while they played.

Now they were behind schedule. If they wanted to be back before the bar closed (and not to be was inconceivable), something would have to go, so by general assent, the Roman Wall was rescheduled to a later occasion. Now, in a palpable state of exhilaration, they boarded the minibus and Aidan drove it southeast down the A68 – a straight, straight road, draped like a length of grey ribbon over the undulating landscape, disappearing over the summit of the next hill, reappearing, narrower, climbing the one beyond and one beyond that, in ever diminishing, converging lines, towards the distant Cleveland hills, the glory of the setting sun in the driving mirror. With the blissful presence of Louise at his side, his mind was still reeling from the impact of that tableau enacted before his eyes. Oh Poussin, was it not your 'Bacchanal Before a Term of Pan', re-enacted in that secluded curve of the river Tyne? That was a bucolic knees-up, if you like.

It had been a day detached from normality; a day where wild things were happening. He felt that he had somehow come adrift from the real and was bobbing along in some sort of ocean of fantasy, where the normal rules and constraints were temporarily waived.

He seemed, by the unspoken assent of the whole company, to have had exclusive access to the beautiful young woman at his side. It reminded him of another such day, when many years ago and still a first-year art student (yes, but for God's sake – he was nineteen then), chance had brought him together in just such a temporary liaison, with Lissa Dennison. She was one of the goddesses of the fourth year, remote, beautiful and, he believed, inaccessible to the likes of him.

Yet, for a day, by chance, they had been, as though by fate, thrust together – and for that day, incredibly, she was his. He did not know what had become of her, but he had never forgotten that heavenly day. On the morrow, she had returned to the remote heights of Olympus and was soon to disappear out into the cosmos beyond.

And he knew, he knew, then, this was just as improbable, just as ephemeral. Louise was his student and he had a wife and two daughters. He reminded himself of this to prevent euphoria taking over completely, then pushed the memo to the back of his mind, so that he might at any rate for a while, pretend that things were other than they were and enjoy them while he could, drifting happily in this sea of uncertainty. To exist in the world at all depended, he knew, on the understanding of categories and boundaries. Where categories are blurred and boundaries uncertain, danger lies; that's why tribes have rites of passage, why brides are carried over thresholds, why children don't step on lines between pavement slabs. He sure as hell felt himself in danger; and revelled in it.

* * *

But he'd been wrong. It had not been ephemeral. It had seemed like it, during the following days, when contact with Louise had returned to a more distant professionalism. But oh God, what had happened later? That beautiful young woman, with whom he had, this very afternoon, fallen into a passionate embrace, was coming to him ... coming to him in – he looked at the clock again – Christ seven, eight minutes – to give herself to him.

Impatiently, he fumbled open Blunt's Poussin, again. Hah! Another bucolic knees-up – The Adoration of the Golden Calf. Same group of dancers – but back to front. What you can do with a sheet of tracing paper! Oh Nicholas, you cheat! Or just sensible economy? But never mind, they're having a whale of a time, happy, laughing – but watch out; Moses approaches with Taliban intent, fresh from the mountain with his stone tablets. Comeuppance! STUDENTS IN RIVERSIDE ORGY WITH LECTURER.

The rhythms from below resounded through the floorboards. He looked again at the clock. Seven minutes. I swear it's going backwards. Oh come on Lulu, I only said 'about' twenty minutes.

She'd come to the table tennis match, he remembered. He remembered particularly his disappointment, that night ... but also the small triumph ...

CHAPTER 8

Table tennis matches were played on Thursday evenings, sometimes in the college table tennis room in the lofty attic space of the main building, up three flights of stone stairs and one of wood; at other times, on away nights, in a variety of factory canteens, civil service recreation rooms and school gyms. This evening Aidan had made his usual contribution to the domestic necessities. He and Bobby had washed the dishes. On Cathy's teaching days, Aidan cooked. But today it had been one of her free days, so she had prepared the evening meal.

On these days, after the meal, she was absolved from all further kitchen duties, so Aidan had rounded up Bobby and together they had washed the dishes and tidied up the kitchen, while Bobby regaled him with a gloomy account of the day's events in school, followed by a passionate argument in favour of her having her own dog instead of having always to walk other people's. He had listened sympathetically, though being careful to avoid commitment – knowing that Cathy was emphatically not an animal lover – and had then been able to talk Bobby into her piano practice. Later, he started her off on her homework. After that he had helped Dora to get ready for bed and read her a story, leaving her, dressed in her pyjamas and glowing from her bath, arranging her dolls for the night. He hoped that the state of relative peace he had achieved would continue in his absence.

He went into the bedroom and changed into his tracksuit and sweatshirt, and after a brief rummage in the bottom of the wardrobe produced his tennis shoes and sat on the bed to put them on. He looked at his watch. He had a little time in hand. He thought he'd better spend it with Cathy and went downstairs into the living room. She had put down on the floor beside the settee the folder of children's writing she'd been working through and was watching the television. She glanced briefly up as he sat beside her on the settee but then resumed her viewing.

'How's it going?' he asked.

'I've got this pile of marking to do.' She gave a Herculean sigh. 'But I thought I'd take fifteen minutes off to watch the gardening programme. That is if you've no objection.'

'No … Why should I have any objection? It's nothing to do with me.'

'Exactly,' she said, 'it's nothing to do with you … just like the pile of ironing. I've got to do when I've finished this lot's nothing to do with you.'

'Oh well,' he said, 'I don't know why you make such a meal of that. I've no objection to a few wrinkles in a shirt.'

Cathy took a sharp breath and turned her whole body towards Aidan. Too late, he realised she was finding the potential of the conversation of more interest than the television.

'Well of course you wouldn't. You've no standards. I was brought up to do things properly. I wasn't dragged up on a council estate.'

Despite his familiarity with this game, Aidan could not suppress the anger rising up inside him. 'I may have been brought up in a council house but I wasn't brought up to be a snob. And for Christ's sake I don't know what gives you your misbegotten sense of superiority. You think because your family had a house with a mortgage on it that puts you in the upper classes?'

'Well there you are,' she said, 'that chip on your shoulder again. You can never get away from it can you?'

'You ... I ... For God's sake ...' Aidan took several deep breaths and bit his tongue. He looked at his watch, paused, then said, as calmly as he could, 'Well I think I'm going to leave you to enjoy your television programme. I'll see you later.'

'Oh, so now you're going out, are you? Once again you're going out to enjoy yourself, leaving me on my own to do all the work? And where is it tonight then?'

'It is Thursday. I'm sure you can't have forgotten what I do on Thursdays.'

She replied, her voice heavy with sarcasm and an expression to match, 'Oh of course … out playing ping-pong with the little boys. Well don't do yourself an injury.'

It infuriated Aidan when anyone disparaged his favourite game – the only sport he had ever been any good at. And well she knew it.

'And I suppose you'll be going boozing afterwards … well lucky you. Just spare a thought sometime for your wife slaving away at home while you're enjoying yourself.'

Aidan reined in his outrage and attempted a poisonously sweet smile of the kind Cathy so often bestowed on Bobby.

'I'll try to,' he said and left the room, firmly closing the door on Cathy's savage rejoinder. Fuming and angry now with himself, not only for having allowed himself to be once again drawn into an exchange of pointless and destructive recrimination but also having, himself, recourse to one of Cathy's favourite devices, he went to the little cloakroom off the hall, pulled on his leather jacket and zipped it up. Reaching up to the high shelf he picked up his bat in its red plastic case and dropped it down inside his jacket. Then, his spirit pounded, he reeled towards the back door and stumbled out into a cold drizzle. He resisted the urge to slam the door, but instead, shut it firmly and carefully. He tried as firmly to shut his mind on her familiarly angry face.

As he squeezed past the car in the drive he lurched, its wing mirror dug painfully into his ribs. He winced and kicked furiously but ineffectually at a tyre. Then he took a deep breath and made his way unsteadily through the chilling damp of the night, past the last few tarnished roses, their colour distorted in the crude orange glare of the street light. An outstretched tendril of neglected briar caught at his sleeve.

'Bugger it,' he hissed furiously, as he snatched his sleeve away, ranting inwardly at the malice of the inanimate. He strode out fiercely and tried to soothe his mind with the thought that whatever happened, the rest of the evening had got to be an improvement. He might even see Louise.

But his mind would not be soothed; the sour aftertaste of that encounter lingered. He was enraged by the way that Cathy could turn the most innocuous transaction into a bruising conflict. Why does she always seem to think she's being done down? Why the hell does she need to be a martyr? Aidan had never thought himself a candidate for sainthood – even less so now that was entertaining lustful thoughts of Louise – but he was pretty sure he'd always pulled his weight in their relationship. It was not that she didn't get recognition outside of the family – she was a damned good teacher – everyone said so. He'd stopped caring very much that she did it to him, but why did she do it to Bobby? How could she do it to Bobby?

He tried again to put it all out of his mind. Table tennis. Think table tennis. Think Louise. This evening's match was a home one. He was glad of this, for it meant that he didn't need the car; just as well for his anger would have made him a danger on the roads. He hoped it would not affect his table tennis. But he could not leave it. He had wanted and tried to avoid the row, the shouting, the abuse, the noise. He did not want his daughters as involuntary participants in their strife. He had failed, it had happened anyway, but he consoled himself that time had permitted only a single controlled explosion rather than a prolonged pitched battle.

By the time he turned into the college gate, his breath clouding, he was damp, cold and dispirited. A sudden gust of wind set the skeletal trees flanking the drive swaying, emitting a dry, rattling sigh. The front of the old building was lit by a single tall street light rising from the centre of the heart-shaped lawn, around which the drive looped. The light it cast was strangely yellow, in contrast with the orange glare of the lamps in the street. One or two of the pointed windows on the second floor showed cracks of light, but there were no other signs of life.

He walked up the three steps leading to the massive studded door set into the Gothic arch of the main entrance. It was all singularly cheerless and menacing. Turning the wet iron ring handle with a loud echoing clank, Aidan felt for a moment as though he were walking on to the set of some horror film and likely to be confronted by a black-cloaked figure with prominent canine teeth. He pushed one of the doors open, letting himself into the vestibule, which was lit by a single feeble light.

The reception office was in darkness, its sliding glass window locked shut. He went through the double glass doors that opened on to the main corridor. It too was dimly lit and deserted, but now he could hear the faint, muffled sound of music and voices. There was life in the bar. Well that was cheering. Doubtless the team would sample its consolations later. As he headed along the corridor a door opened briefly, releasing a distant explosion of sound. He headed towards it, to the end of the corridor and round the corner into the long conservatory with its floor of inlaid tiles and its exotic plants. Resisting the call of the bar, he turned off into the archway leading to the foot of the staircase and made his way up. Turning at the second landing, he could now hear the subdued sound of play, the soft shuffling of feet, the sound of bat against ball. Who called it 'ping-pong', he wondered. No feeling for onomatopoeia, that's for sure. More like a sort of 'te-pik, te-pok', with variations. He arrived on the top landing and waited until he could hear that the game had ended before slipping silently through the door and taking a seat next to George Hobson to one side of the table. The players were changing ends; it was Gerry against a rather stout but surprisingly agile teacher Aidan had come up against before.

'Gerry should have slaughtered this guy. One all. Hope he finds his form for the decider,' whispered George. And, reprovingly, 'cutting it a bit fine weren't you? You're down to go on next. You okay?'

'Yeah, fine,' replied Aidan untruthfully, as the scorer looked round enjoining silence. A pyramid of bright light flooded the table, green, with its white edges, tautly bisected by the net. From the lofty beams above, behind each end of the table, single lights hung to illuminate the further reaches of the playing area, to which a hard-pressed player might have to retreat, under determined attack. Through the pyramid of light, Aidan could see against the dark of the background, the pale ovals of the faces of the few spectators; supporters – wives and girlfriends of the opponents and a handful of students – interested or with nothing better to do that evening. With a lifting of the spirit, he noted that Louise was among them.

Then play recommenced. Definitely te-pik, te-pok, thought Aidan. Gerry found his form and moving with his short, quick rhythm, methodically and remorselessly returned the little white ball for his increasingly thwarted opponent to hit into the net or off the table. First blood to Swaleborough staff.

Aidan's first opponent was a gangling, bearded, bespectacled young man in a piercingly blue tracksuit. He had, Aidan remembered from previous encounters, a repertoire of beguilingly twisty serves for which he threw the ball high into the air and which required the utmost concentration to deal with. Aidan, as they knocked up, doubted that at that moment, he had much of that.

When play began and all through the first game, he could feel that the accumulated tensions of the evening were infecting him. He could not clear his mind. It was clouded by lingering residues of unresolved problems – problems, after all, of life-affecting importance – compared with which the antics of a little white celluloid ball seemed immeasurably trivial. He felt awkward. His joints seemed not to articulate properly. If he tried aggression, his attacking strokes just seemed like wild swipes, the ball hit the edge of the bat or his thumb and either soared off to the ceiling or ended up in the net.

He looked down at his bat: a sandwich; a plywood frying pan, sort of oval, six inches across the middle; spongy rubber both sides of the blade; one side, black, the other red; a handle of smooth wood comfortably fitted to the hand. With this cheap and simple device, he was to propel an also cheap celluloid ball over a six-inch-high net in such a way that the young man, similarly equipped, facing him at the other end of the table would be unable to return it. To achieve this trifling end he must exclude all else from his consciousness and focus all the power of his mind – a mind the like of which had sent men to the moon and was presently engaged in unravelling the secrets of the cosmos – on this patently meaningless endeavour. What, he had often wondered, would an intergalactic traveller with a penchant for anthropology make of table tennis.

So he tried being cautious – but his defensive strokes were ineffectual pokes offering easy kills to his energetic opponent. He tried to maintain an outward calm, as though he knew something his opponent didn't, but inwardly he was swearing bitterly. Worse, he was aware of his teammates' eyes critically following his every stroke.

He was angry with himself, appalled at his present ineptitude at even this non-crucial activity. No wonder his bloody life was so chaotic. He'd once thought he was quite good at both. Once again the ball crashed across the net and deflected from his bat and dropped to the floor. Sighing, he stooped to pick it up. It had come to rest by Louise's foot. As he rose, she caught his eye and smiled encouragingly. He had a sudden flash of fantasy. He was a medieval knight at a tournament. He extended his lance towards the pavilion and the lady, smilingly meeting his eyes, adorned its tip with her favour. In acknowledgement, he bowed his head. The way things were going though he seemed likely to end up with a morning star embedded in it, if not a lance through the throat. He lost the first game. He was really pissed off.

Five points into the second game, however, he thought he was beginning to focus a little more sharply, he felt that bearing the lady's favour was something of a responsibility, which seemed to help him to concentrate. Then he retrieved a fearsome forehand smash – whose rebound sent the ball up among the rafters – from twelve-feet behind the table, imparting such a powerful backspin to the ball that his opponent returned it into the net. George and Gerry – he saw this through the corner of his eye – nodded their encouragement. He was encouraged and began to feel a new fluidity in his movement; he also began to divine the psychology of his opponent's play.

As his confidence seeped back, he began to see the whole thing as a duel. He dumped the lance and morning star. A rapier was more the sort of thing he needed. His opponent was an enemy to be vanquished. Perhaps he had insulted his lady. Aidan crouched, watching the enemy's eyes through his own, narrowly slitted; registered the tilt of his opponent's bat and the angle of his wrist as he prepared to serve. The spin no longer seemed a problem and with the ball in play, his movement became more and more supple, agile, cat-like. No, he wasn't after all a medieval knight. He was Cyrano de Bergerac, that's who. His bat was a rapier. With it he probed his antagonist tauntingly; he parried with careless disdain, moving with a fluid elegance; he riposted with insouciant grace; his finishing thrusts were the deadly poetry of the assassin. He won that game and the decider that followed it. Well that was the first of his three challenges of the match and with his recovered form, his good luck mascot in the audience, it all augured well.

The match ended in victory, giving them three league points, they felt mightily pleased with themselves as they escorted the opposing team to the bar for consolatory drinks. His eyes signalled an invitation to Louise. She smiled. He and Gerry stayed to switch off and lock up. When they arrived in the bar, he did not immediately see her. She'll come; surely she'll come. She didn't – and how should it matter to him anyway? She was his student. What had happened that day on the banks of the Tyne was a dream; the reality was he was married to Cathy. But he didn't give up hope till the bar closed. He and Gerry were the last to leave. They took cans of beer to the senior common room and Aidan was late home that night; and gloomily, discontentedly drunk.

* * *

He looked at his glass and from that to the whisky. Drunk tonight, too. But by God, not gloomy, not discontented. No, just dying from suspense. Shit, mustn't overdo it though. Too much supposed to make you impotent. The stirring in his trousers told him he'd no cause to worry on that score yet. Now there was an allegory fit for Poussin; The Triumph of Lust over Booze and Impotence.

Time. Why doesn't she just come? Lulu, come on. There'd been a row that night alright and no doubt there'd be one tonight if Cathy were still awake when he got home. Unlikely at the late hour it's going to be though, he thought. Anyway, this time he didn't give a shit.

CHAPTER 9

The fact was he was feeling less and less inclined to fall in with the unwritten rules, which for years had governed such matters. Well, governed him. (Who unwrote them, for God's sake? he asked himself. Not me, that's for sure.) He had been looking back over the long history of their relationship and become increasingly aware of the extent to which in every aspect it was governed by unwritten rules. He supposed that relationships, like language needed agreed rules for them to work. But the essential rules of language, the grammar, were given; they were just there in the infant, waiting to be activated from the outside. On the other hand, the rules governing relationships had to be invented on a pragmatic basis. There might be cultural guidelines, but didn't the practical details have to be hammered out in the light of experience? For years, it hadn't been an issue for him because their marriage had seemed as satisfactory as anyone was entitled to expect, but recently he had come to realise how little of the hammering out he had done. Household practices in respect of times for going to bed and for getting out of bed; times of meals and their composition; the number of nights he could routinely go out, for what legitimate purposes, what time to return had, over time, attained the status of rules – laws, even; laws from which any

145

proposed deviation had to be negotiated – and any deviation not negotiated suffered for.

Well, some rules were related to external things – working hours, shop opening times, holiday periods; these were pretty immutable. But he was more and more conscious that where there was flexibility, where the options were wider, somehow the constraints were almost universally on him, he had acquiesced because for so long there seemed to be no big issue involved. But he could not think of anything that Cathy might want to do that he would want to put constraints on. Short of fucking the milkman. And he wasn't even sure about that. On the contrary, he wanted her to do more things that he would not stand in the way of. For himself, he wanted flexibility. He wanted the right to improvise, to respond to the moment; he wanted adaptive control. God, he asked himself, how many people are there bound into hopeless routines they have never assented to, but nevertheless act on as though they were natural laws?

So now he was in a mind to change matters. These were not natural laws that one had no option but to adapt to; they were rules dreamt up by people – and, as such, were mutable. He intended to mute some. He no longer cared enough about domestic consequences to want to give first priority to appeasement. Cathy's war with her elder daughter was in any case so disruptive of family life that he no longer felt any inclination to submit to Cathy's plan of family conduct; he was prepared to meet the consequences head-on.

Well the consequence of last night's row was a lingering poison that made the morning routines for all of them less than pleasant. It seemed like the uneasy lull after the bombardment stopped over the trenches; a kind of respite, but with no one deceived as to its permanence. However, though nothing was resolved, the atmosphere lightened after Cathy left for school – she was always first to leave, having furthest to travel and a bus to catch. Then he was able to set Bobby on her glum way down the hill to her school and accompany Dora, more cheerfully up the hill to hers. From there, it was no more than a ten-minute walk to college, but the inauspicious start to the day, the unresolved row had left him feeling deeply dispirited.

The weather was no help. It was all November. Cheerless. Rush hour too. The white breath of nudging cars fed the fog; exhaust pipes dripped and headlights burned bright discs into the chill morning. He needed to escape the maddening grumble of traffic and decided to take the path which cut the small park from corner to corner. Once he was through the gate, somehow the traffic noise seemed to fade into the fog. A curlicue of robin song wound through the wet trees, and suddenly, as though he had crossed some invisible threshold of the mind, he felt good. A shower of spiralling tawny leaves gusted about his head. He wanted to run; to run fast and to make wild leaps at the dripping branches overhead. He remembered how they used to do it on the way back from school, after rain. The rowdy gang, slightly mad in their renewed freedom from the day's graft. The trick was to time your leap at the tree so it discharged its stored water on your following friends. For the sake of decorum he decided against doing this and settled for a clumsy chassé between two puddles and an inaccurate side-kick at a pile of damp leaves. He knew that he would sustain this mood of buoyancy among his students and he would be set up for the day.

Emerging from the park, dodging through another line of creeping cars, he crossed the road, trotted through the college gate and leaping up the steps, entered the front door. He went first to the staff study, checked his pigeonhole for post, stuffing a couple of periodicals under his arm, greeted one or two colleagues, looked at the notice board, then set off towards the Art Department via one of the back exits. Crossing the playground of the practice school, he could hear the day getting underway with morning assembly; Give us this day our daily bread, the chorus of young voices intoned, he could almost smell the chalk dust, Forgive us our trespasses ... Aidan wondered what trespasses the little darlings had to forgive, but fervently hoped He would do all those things.

Then, about to exit the yard through the gate leading to the Art Department, he saw coming through the other gate that connected with the halls of residence, the entire force of the maintenance staff, led by Wilf Baxter, the college engineer. They were proceeding with a flat handcart piled high with junk. Aidan had sometimes thought that if he didn't teach at the place, he could think of worse things to be

148

than a member of the college maintenance staff. Under Wilf's jurisdiction were Cyril, the assistant engineer; Charlie the plumber; Bert the joiner; Pete the brickie/labourer; and Albert and Roy the porters, as well as doing a lot of useful work keeping the college functioning, they always seemed to be having a hell of a good time. They were engaged in what Aidan could see was one of those undemanding though necessary occasional tasks, in which their individual skills were put aside and all mucked in, seeming to make a carnival out of it. With them there always seemed to be many occasions for carnival.

Aidan never missed a chance to pass the time of day with this lot. Apart from enjoying a laugh with them, it was prudent to keep in with Wilf because one never knew when one would need his services – and these were on no account to be taken for granted. So he waited; then, 'Morning Wilf. Morning chaps,' he said as they approached.

'Morning Aidan,' the engineer said (he was important; they were on first-name terms).

'Morning Mr Hamilton,' said the others.

'What've you got there, then?' Aidan asked. 'It looks interesting.' Charlie delved around with a brass stair rod he'd picked up off the cart, then waved it aloft bearing what looked like a large pink bat. Pete, who'd been pushing, brought the cart to a halt, they all raggedly saluted the trophy.

Aidan laughed. 'What the hell's that,' he asked – suddenly recognising it as a corset of the kind that used to adorn his mother's washing line of a Monday when he was a child. 'Where did that come from, for God's sake?'

'Right put that down Charlie, before the principal turns up,' said Wilf, as though threatening a child with a bogeyman, then to Aidan, 'Yesterday, the boss said, "It's three years since Miss Featherstone died, and it's about time we cleared the rest of her stuff up and reclaimed that flat." (Miss Featherstone, in the days of the old principal had been college secretary for something like twenty-five years. When the old principal had died in harness, Miss Featherstone had gone into long-overdue retirement. Since her replacement had been a young man with a family and a mortgage, he had no need of the flat, so the governors had voted that Miss Featherstone should have tenancy of it for as long as she needed it)."We've got a new member of staff coming, who wants to be resident," the principal said, "so we're going to need it next term." Anyway I thought we'd better make a start … and Aidan, you wouldn't believe the stuff we found there.'

Aidan looked again at the corset. 'I'm not sure I want to know,' he said.

'Well what're you going to do with this lot then?'

'Oh it's all headed for the skip. We haven't time to mess about with stuff like this.'

'Okay, okay, just hold on a bit,' said Aidan, 'there might be something we could use in the department. Let's have a look ... Hm, nice chamber pot. Might do for fruit if it weren't for the crack. Wait a minute, though.' He noticed that there was a bicycle wheel, just visible under a pile of old clothing and what seemed to be curtains. 'There's a bike under there ... let's have a look.'

'Oh aye, she used to ride her bike, during the war, but when the roads started getting busier afterwards, and she was getting on a bit, I think she got frightened and gave it up ... so it's been in the shed mouldering away ever since.'

Aidan pulled back the bits of curtain, to reveal a very old fashioned and stately lady's bike, covered with dust and grime.

'Well, listen Wilf I'm going to rescue this. It's too good for the skip.'

'You can have it if it's any use to you – bit old fashioned though, isn't it?'

'Yeah, well you know what they call something this old-fashioned don't you, Wilf – an antique – and I'm going to rescue it for posterity – okay?'

'Antique? You're daft, man ... oh well, I suppose ... Right, well bounce it off there Charlie, and let him have it if it'll make him happy ... I don't know – these bloody daft artists ...' Charlie lifted it off the cart along with the perished tyres and let it down on to its rims.

Aidan stood back, head on one side, surveyed it. 'Hm, got potential, that,' he said. 'Don't you think so Wilf?'

'I think it's a load o' junk, but if it'll make you happy, you can have it as far as I'm concerned. Now come on lads – there's work to be done ... let's be having you.' So saying, with a wink at Aidan, he got his procession noisily on the move again, leaving Aidan standing in the middle of the yard with his prize.

'What's this, then Aidan? Going into the scrap business, are you?' Three of his students were passing, laughing.

Aidan looked at them. 'It's an antique,' he said, wheeling it off with as much dignity as he could muster in the direction of the department, accompanied by a rhythmic scraping noise as the deflated tyres rubbed against the forks. He took it in through the back door in the basement and put it in the workshop to deal with later.

The bicycle had slipped out of his mind and it was some days before he remembered that it was there in a corner of the workshop, awaiting his attention. It was a Friday afternoon and as was usual on a Friday afternoon, the department was peopled by a motley population of students working independently, and tutors working independently, consulting each other as and when necessary. Also on Friday afternoons, Dora came to college to the Music Department after school for her violin lesson, usually walking the short distance with the Fletcher girls, both a little older than her and qualifying as a responsible escort. Percy and Zena Fletcher lived in a large semi-detached house conveniently next to the college, Dora would usually end up playing there with Jeannie and Angie until Aidan was ready to take her home.

Aidan had not been much troubled by students questing for knowledge that afternoon and had been fitfully tickling at his latest painting; it was in that slightly indeterminate stage of near completion, in which the real problem was when to stop. Aidan for the umpteenth time was standing back, ruffling his hair with the end of his paintbrush, trying again to make the decision, when suddenly, he remembered the bike and thought how agreeable it would to defer the problem and go down with a bottle of paraffin and a handful of rags to clean it up, then really have a good look at his trophy. Nothing like a spell of displacement activity to refresh the mind, he thought. He gave his brushes a quick swish round in the paraffin bucket, wiped them on a rag and stood them up in the salt glaze jar. He set off for the workshop in the basement.

The bike was covered in years of dust and fluff; oily dust and fluff round the wheel and pedal hubs and steering head. It was a tall galleon of a bike. It must have been almost four feet from the ground to the handlebar grips, via an immensely long, backward sloping steering head. The thought of the fragile Miss Featherstone in control of this noble machine astonished him. Some of the muck had rubbed off the handlebar grips and he could see they were of shiny black celluloid. The saddle, a fraction lower than the handlebars, was of exquisitely sculpted leather poised on three chunky springs – one at the nose and two behind. He imagined it cradling her dignified posterior. The wheels seemed huge, with thick tyres, now depressingly flat and cracked round the circumference. There were the twin low crossbars that ladies' bikes had – the upper one nicely curved, in the old-fashioned way, to offer unimpeded transit to long-skirted legs. The chain was completely enclosed in a neat chain case. It had luggage provision; strapped to the handlebars was a large wicker basket in a sad state of disintegration, and above the rear wheel, a carrier. Aidan stood back and admired the bike's shape and proportions. He could tell it was a Raleigh even without rubbing the dirt off to look for the name, because of the dimples in the ends of the crosspiece at the top of the front fork. Raleighs always had them.

Aidan rolled up his sleeves and set to with the rags and paraffin. An hour later, he sat back on his heels to survey the results. The original black paint was remarkably intact. It was embellished with thin red and gold lines, with the Raleigh badge on the front stem. He noticed around the edges of the rear mudguard, tiny holes two inches apart; these, he remembered would once have cords strung through them to converge on the hub, to protect long skirts from entanglement in the spokes. The back part of the mudguard had been painted white and fitted with a reflector in accordance with wartime regulations.

He wondered if that size of tyre was still available. He wanted the bike to be restored to complete working order now. He wanted to ride it now. He looked at his watch. He reckoned if he went straight away, he had comfortably enough time to slip down town to the bike shop and back before Dora came to seek him out.

Within thirty minutes, he was back with a pair of new tyres and tubes of the right size and a pump with which to inflate them. In another half-hour, they were fitted, he was just completing the inflation of the second tyre when he heard Dora clattering down the stairs, singing Oh where are you going my Anna Marie? She stuck her head round the door.

'Oh, there you are Daddy. I've been looking for you everywhere. Barbara said you might be in the workshop.'

'Hello love. I heard you coming. You were singing. Does that mean you've had a good day?'

'Not bad, Dad,' she said, then, liking the sound of it, said it twice more. She put her arms around Aidan and gave him a hug, then stood back and looked at the bike.

'Gosh, what a funny old bike, Dad. Whose is it?'

'Well, I just rescued it from being thrown on the rubbish skip – so I think I can say it's mine. I fact, I was just about to take it into the car park and give it a road test. You want to come?'

'Are you going to ride it then?'

'Yes, I hope so. Come on.' With Dora tagging along, he wheeled it out of the workshop, along the corridor and out into the department car park.

'Come on then Daddy, let's see you ride it,' Dora said.

'Okay, okay … don't rush me. I've just got to work out how to do this.' He tried swinging his leg over the saddle, but it was too high, threatening, he thought, an acute danger of groin injury. After thinking a moment, he put one foot on the nearer pedal and pushed off with the other. Having gained some wobbly momentum, he slipped his free leg through the gap above the crossbars, found the other pedal and dropped into the saddle.

'Hooray!' shouted Dora, laughing with delight. Aidan did a dignified circuit of the car park, at an altitude which enabled him to see right over the tops of the few parked vehicles. Then he did another, as he tested the brakes and the gears, fiddling with the little quadrant on the crossbar.

'Dad, you look just like Mary Poppins. Mary Poppins! Mary Poppins!' called out Dora, giggling. Aidan laughed, slowing the bike down and by concentratedly reversing the mounting technique arrived at a halt. Feeling extremely pleased, accompanied by his daughter, he wheeled the bike inside, then after a moment's reflection, decided it was much too valuable to be left in the workshop and that it would have to live henceforth in his room. 'Come on Dora,' he said, 'we're going to take it upstairs to my room.' He manoeuvred it with some difficulty up the stairs, with Dora helpfully holding the back wheel, through his studio door, to a temporary resting-place against the radiator. Then they stood back, holding hands to give the bike a last admiring look before going home to tea.

Then Dora said, 'Dad, what's she called?'

'Is it a she? And why should it … she have a name? It … she's only a bike.'

'But she's a really, really special bike and she should have a name.'

'Okay, if you say so. Well you can give her a name, then.'

Dora tucked her lower lip under her teeth and allowed her eyes to roll upwards, thinking. After a moment or two, during which Aidan took down his coat from the hook on the door, picked up a book he needed to take home, she said, 'Bessie.' 'That's her name … Bessie. Hm. Yes. Her name's Bessie, that's what.'

'Okay, if you say so. Bessie she is,' said Aidan

'Wow, just wait till I tell Mum about it.'

'I can't wait,' Aidan had said.

He'd said that with irony. He was waiting now. For Lulu. No irony. Excitement. Tension. Waiting. He looked at Bessie, pinged the bell. He'd made a space for her against the wall opposite the window. Lit by the moonlight, she looked spectral, Aidan thought. He conjured the shade of Miss Featherstone into the saddle. Then he looked at the clock again. Oh no. He checked it against his watch. Oh God. He shut the Poussin book with a thump, turned impatiently to the shelves and picked up his copy of Oh What a Lovely War.

He flicked it open …

CHAPTER 10

He remembered that rehearsal – the one he couldn't go to because of that sodding committee meeting. He hated committees. After two hours, his attention had drifted far from the agenda and he was thinking longingly of beer. Then his thoughts turned to the rehearsal he was missing, picturing George Hobson seated on a back-to-front chair in the centre of the auditorium a little way back from the stage, a sheaf of papers in one hand, unjacketed, in his braces, shirt-sleeves rolled up, tie loosened. Percy Fletcher seated at the Steinway below the front of the stage, turning over sheets of music, restoring them to their proper order while discussing some point of technique or emphasis with one of the cast who was leaning over the open top of the piano. And Louise; would she be there?

But by the time he got back to college, the hall was silent and dark, so he by-passed it and headed straight for the bar. After the prolonged spell of ordered tedium he'd just endured, he rejoiced in the wave of noise and confusion that hit him when he opened the door. Across the animated heads, he saw that the cast was assembled in a group at one end of the bar. Aidan made his way towards them, his briefcase under his arm, through the throng of bodies, exchanging greetings and banter here and there en route. On arriving at the bar, he gratefully accepted the proffered pint from Percy, who'd seen him coming, thrust his face into it and took long, deep draught – on emerging from which, with foam-flecked lips, he let out a sigh of contentment.

George nodded at him, took a long pull at his own pint, then carried on with his inquest, '… so it's pretty rough at the moment, but it's early days yet. One thing you should try to remember is this: all the time you're doing this larky stuff on the stage, there'll be two things happening above and behind you. One, there's a bulletin board carrying news – the progress of the war, casualty figures and stuff like that; two, slides are being projected – pictures of actual events at the front. So there should be this terrific tension between the frivolous-looking stuff on the stage and the appalling reality presented behind you.

'Now, it's all so episodic that at this stage, we can carry on doing it in bits. I'll put up a list of people I'll need at any one time, so keep an eye on the notice board. And listen … by next week I'll expect a bit more progress with learning your parts – we're getting past the reading stage and no one's got a huge amount to learn. That means you especially, Noel. At this rate you'll be coming on "on the night" waving your bloody script around. And Mandy, see if you can get rid of that cold by next week and lose that corncrake voice.' Into the eruption of impolite rejoinders and catcalls he interjected, 'Okay,

okay, that's enough for tonight. Let's concentrate on getting a few pints down now, shall we?'

Then he turned to Louise. 'Ah, Louise, that was good. I can tell you've put in a bit of time at the words.' There were catcalls:

'Yah goody-goody.'

'Teacher's pet.'

'Yerrr! Swot'

Louise laughed and stuck her tongue out, as they chanted their mockery.

Then she turned to Aidan, 'We missed you, Aidan,' she said. He looked at her over the rim of his glass, but it was George who spoke.

'Okay, next week we'll have Aidan here …' he looked at Aidan, '… won't we, Aidan? And we'll see if we can get some more of the props and get on with the ideas for the set.' George turned to Louise, 'And just ignore that lot, they're only jealous.'

Eventually, the cast split up and mingled with those already there. Louise heading to join a group in a corner, flung a quick smile at Aidan. It was crowded and, as usual, the jukebox was pounding out its remorseless rhythms, against which the conversation competed in a rising cacophony. George was at the bar with Percy. Gerry and Henry, who had been working on some preliminary ideas for the lighting, backstage, were nearby. Glasses were empty, now.

'Pints, chaps?' asked George, turning his head. He didn't really need to ask. Henry was out tonight on licence and would want to make maximum use of his liberty. And Gerry – he just was a habitual drinker of pints. George nodded to the student barkeeper, who, seeing the need had been hovering nearby. Anticipating, he had glasses at the ready and in minutes, they were standing on the bar, gloriously full, while he attended to matters at the till. It had been thirsty work.

'I thought you couldn't make it tonight, old son,' Gerry said to Aidan.

'Couldn't make it to the rehearsal, that was all. While you lot have been enjoying yourselves and having fun on the stage, I've been locked up with a bunch of time-wasting half-wits having a committee meeting. The Civic Arts Committee,' he said, glaring pointedly at his two departmental colleagues. 'You remember, lads? They wanted to co-opt someone from the department. It was on the wrong night for Barbara … I mean … she bloody loves committees … so we drew straws.' He paused for another swig of beer. 'I drew the short one, didn't I?'

'Well … just the luck of the draw, mate.'

'Yeah, but I hate sodding committees. Can't stand the buggers. God I'd rather have my balls nailed to a table than go to a committee meeting.'

'Need a bit of stoicism there, Aidan … you know, like your old Poussin. Learn to bear life's burdens without complaint, that's the thing,' said Henry, with an expression of feigned compassion.

162

'Yeah, come on,' said Gerry, 'I bet it was really interesting. Fascinating people too, I should think.' They all laughed.

'Well you think wrong, mate,' said Aidan. 'They're a load of professional committee nuts – you know – the kind of people who get off on spending half an hour trying to decide whether the Culture Coach to London should leave at eight o'clock or a quarter past.' His colleagues laughed sympathetically. 'You know what? We spent an hour and a half discussing the nitty-gritty of flower planting on the municipal roundabouts – and they'll be calling on my special skills as an artist to help them to decide on colour combinations … so that's why I really, really needed this pint.' Aidan knocked back the rest of his drink in one mighty swig. 'And I need another one. Now. Okay?'

'Oh you poor bugger.' Gerry said, summoning the barman, 'Okay, you made me feel guilty. I'll get you a pint.'

With another pint in his hand and the prospect of one or two more before time was called, Aidan was beginning to feel a bit more relaxed. The conversation moved round on to the subject of the play. It was the kind of play that suited him, with plenty of minor – and preferably not too serious – parts. In fact, George was trying to persuade him to take on more than one.

'There'll be very little to learn, really,' said George, 'and if you're good at playing generals, you may as well play two as one … er … so long as they aren't both on at once … which they aren't.'

Aidan considered whether to dispute this arrangement and picking up his pint, turned round to lean with his back against the bar and survey the scene. It was very crowded – groups of drinking, chattering laughing students and one or two staff in addition to his present drinking companions. Then a small group next to him, having decided to finish off the evening elsewhere, drained their glasses and dumped them on the bar. With cheery nods and grins towards their lecturers, they set about forcing their way towards the door, on their way, collecting another two or three groups.

'Oh-oh, looks like a party brewing,' said Gerry.

'More like a nightclub,' George said. 'Where the hell do they get their money from, these students? When I was at college, I couldn't even …' Then across the brief lacuna created by their departure, Aidan, with a barely perceptible flutter somewhere inside him, saw Louise. He'd been hoping she hadn't gone. She was sitting at a table in a corner with Noel Wilson, an English student, whose robust ego, general presentability and love of exhibitionism made him ideal for leading roles in college dramatic productions – notwithstanding his casual attitude towards learning his words.

Then she looked up and Aidan caught her eye. She smiled and waved. He smiled and waved back. The gap healed over and she was obscured from view. But not from Aidan's mind.

The conversation proceeded and eventually arrived via a series of unrecorded mutations to the gloomy subject of the probable closure of the college. It was a likelihood that none of them could yet take wholly seriously. No one entering the field of education at any level within the last twenty years would have thought that redundancy could ever be their lot. Wasn't education what you could never have too much of? Their contemplation of a hypothetical life after Swaleborough was always, at this stage, tempered by the thought that, surely it won't happen; surely they won't let it happen; surely it can't happen. By the time Aidan came to order the third round, optimism had reasserted itself and he himself was at the stage of mild intoxication when the attainment of bliss required nothing more than an attractive woman to converse with and perhaps flirt a little.

So picking up his brimming glass, he said to his colleagues, 'Well, excuse me, chaps … I think I'll just go and spread myself round a bit.'

'Well, if we're boring you,' said Henry, 'don't feel you have to stay with us.'

Aidan smiling, looked round at them and said, 'I've bought my round. Reciprocity maintained. Obligation discharged. See you later chaps.' He slurped half an inch of beer out of his glass for easier portability and carefully nudged his way through tight packed bodies. Via a series of small encounters with other students, he found himself in discussion with Jenny Bell, an earnest second year with urgent things to say about the relationship between the Arts and Crafts Movement and the rise of interest in English folk song in the late nineteenth century.

Jenny was small and blondly vivacious. Appealing, Aidan thought, but her vivacity was, at this moment employed wholly in the service of scholarship. No sexual undertones there; no drifting pheromones; to Jenny, he was clearly beyond the outer periphery of eligibility. He was only her teacher. All very proper; so it should be – but what the off-duty and now slightly drunk Aidan wanted was a smidgen of impropriety.

Pushed about by the comings and goings in the crowded bar, Aidan and Jenny seized two suddenly vacant chairs – which happened to be opposite Louise and Noel who were giggling at something Noel had just said. Louise seemed not to have noticed his arrival and was deeply involved in her conversation with Noel. Her black hair was hanging loose about her shoulders. As she turned from her drink to address him, it lifted a little and swung, in a way that made Aidan think of the swirling skirts of a flamenco dancer. She was wearing little make-up – perhaps a hint of shadow around the eyes, a touch of lipstick. She looked stunning, Aidan thought, trying to keep his mind on what Jenny was saying when Louise stood up, her empty beer glass in her hand, and turned towards the bar. As she rose to her feet, one long thigh escaped from the only partly buttoned calf-length, blue denim dress she was wearing; she made no attempt to retrieve it.

'Damn, I should have got to the bar before that lot came in,' she said to Noel referring to the new wave of arrivals who'd just colonised the bar. 'I'll wait.' With a resigned sigh, she sat down again.

'Louise ...' Aidan's attenuated connection with Arts and Crafts suddenly and decisively snapped. 'Here, have some of mine.' He leaned over the table and decanted half of the contents of his glass into Louise's. She turned towards him, seeming to notice for the first time that he was no longer at the bar.

'Oh Aidan, what a chivalrous gesture – I mean for a man to share his beer.' She picked up her glass and looked over it into Aidan's eyes. 'Thank you,' she said, and Aidan raised his glass to her.

'Cheers,' he said.

Noel got up and moved round the table to sit next to Jenny. His interest in the Arts and Crafts Movement was well known. Louise moved along the bench, and Aidan, trying not to notice the delicious sliver of escaped thigh, moved round to sit beside her.

'You didn't make it to the rehearsal.' Louise said, taking a sip of her beer. Aidan explained to her about the Civic Arts Committee, making her laugh with his lurid description of its members and its arcane proceedings. She, in turn gave him a lurid account the rehearsal, fending off Noel's interventions from across the table, as the imperfections of his performance were gently and, for his benefit, derided. She told Aidan that George was expecting to do some work on the Palm Court scene, next week – the one where they danced together – so she hoped he would be there for that. Aidan, smiling into her eyes, said he would – thinking that wild horses wouldn't keep him away from this one.

Somehow, one thing led to another and when last orders was called, then last drinks, then can we have your glasses now, please? They were still deep in conversation. The music had stopped, the crowd had imperceptibly, little by little, drained away and eventually they were aroused from their self-engrossment by the cool draughts seeping through the open doors and the clatter and slap as the barmen upended chairs upon tables and plied dishcloths and brooms.

'I think they want us to go,' said Louise.

'You could be right,' said Aidan, sighing. 'I hate our blasted licensing laws ... really uncivilised. I'm always just beginning to enjoy myself when they want to throw me out.'

They got up. Aidan retrieved his briefcase, Louise her shoulder bag, and, exchanging goodnights with the bar staff, they made for the door of the now empty and quiet bar. The college seemed deserted, as they walked along the corridor. At the exit, Aidan held open the door for her and said, 'I'd have offered you a lift if I'd got the car, but ...' He paused to turn and pull the door shut with its heavy iron ring. It clanged resoundingly.

'It's okay,' she said, 'I haven't far to go ... I live in Stanforth Crescent – really just around the corner.'

'Oh well then, if I can't give you a lift, at least I can walk you home. Stanforth Crescent is on my way.' They set off down the drive and through the gates. 'I didn't know you lived there. I'm surprised I haven't bumped into you before. I usually walk along it at least twice a day. Are you in digs? What's it like?'

As they strolled without urgency through the autumn night, mild and damp, their breath clouding, a fragment of birdsong drifted from a nearby garden, as a robin, disturbed in its roost and mistaking the drenching orange of a street light for dawn, began its song. They looked at one another and laughed with pleasure.

'Oh, it's fine,' she said. 'I have a comfortable little bedsit with basic cooking facilities and a desk. Mrs Pickles, my landlady, is very motherly. She seems to think of me as some helpless foreigner, you know. She speaks very slowly and always explains difficult words. But really, I'd like a bit more freedom to come and go as I like, so I'm hoping to find a flat before too long.'

Aidan laughed, 'Well, let's face it, you are a foreigner as far as we Yorkshire folks are concerned. You know, I'm still wondering what really brought a foreigner like you to this remote backwater.'

'I did tell you why at the interview. Don't you remember?'

'Yes I remember, but you know, I wasn't altogether convinced. I felt sure there was more.'

'Hm, well maybe … but if there is, I'm not telling. Not now anyway – because this is where I live.' She indicated a wooden gate with peeling paint of a colour Aidan thought might have been green, were it not for the distorting orange light from the nearby street lamp. It opened upon a path through a dishevelled garden, leading to a rickety-looking porch. 'I'd invite you in for some coffee, but I don't think Mrs Pickles would approve – especially as late as this.'

'A nice idea,' said Aidan, 'but as you say, it is getting late and time I returned to the bosom of my family.'

'Thank you for walking me home …' she looked at him, more seriously, this time, '… and thanks especially for sharing your beer,' she said.

Aidan laughed, 'It was nothing,' he said, 'any time. Well, back in the real world tomorrow. See you in the department … goodnight then.'

'Goodnight Aidan,' she said, and smiling briefly into his eyes once more, she turned away and into the gate, as Aidan set off towards home and his problems, which for a while seemed somewhat diminished in the afterglow of this special evening.

* * *

But it was fantasy then. Could he ever realistically have imagined it turning out like this? For him to be waiting here in his room … waiting for her to come to him, for him to fuck her. Jesus Christ. But something had distorted time. It must have got stuck or something. He'd been standing, all this time, or prowling, as far as the bounds of his room would let him. Like a caged animal, that was the image. Somehow standing and prowling eased the passage of time. He felt that if he sat, time would congeal and solidify around him.

He went over to the bookcase, slotted Oh What a Lovely War back into a vacant slot, made an almost random grab into another shelf and came away with his worn copy of Catch 22, the pages swollen and loosened, the spine broken. Some pages fell out, and as he bent and picked them up, he saw the fly leaf, inscribed, 'Christmas, '61. Love from Cathy.' Oh God. He slipped the pages back in place and held the book for some moments against his chest, still, looking into nowhere. Then he took a deep breath and opened it. It came open at the beginning of a chapter. It was headed Dunbar. Aidan thought, Wasn't he the guy who cultivated boredom, so time would drag and he would therefore effectively increase his lifespan? There were other ways, though. Here he was, almost insane with excitement and ill-contained lust – and could time pass any more slowly than this?

CHAPTER 11

He recalled that it was some weeks later that he first actually properly touched her. Touched her. If his visual sense was, of his five senses, the most highly developed – him being a painter – his tactile sense came a close second. He felt that seeing was something that happened in the mind; and the mind was so prone to duplicity, that to be sure, sometimes, tactile verification was needed. This was why he always wanted to touch paintings. It was a way of re-establishing actuality, of retreating from the ambiguity that all painting trades in. Some, like a late Rembrandt so completely embodied the tactile in the visual, that seeing was almost enough. Just as well, for galleries were not fond of touchers: and so with people. But he felt that he could no more legitimately indulge his tactile sense with people – well most people – than with paintings in a gallery. In either case, it could get you arrested.

Among his friends, the male ones especially, but not exclusively, there was a fair amount of comradely touching and this he generally found agreeable – he liked the warmth of it. But with students, it was different. Well, yes there was that glorious day of the Saturnalia, when his hand had twice come into contact with Louise's; pure accident, he had to convince himself, in the sober light of a normal day. But ordinarily, he spent much of his teaching time physically close to students and it was with them that his tactile impulse was most fiercely restrained. One of the most ignominious sexual roles, he believed, was that of groper; it was a role he would not like to be allotted.

But there he was, somewhat downstage to the right, in close propinquity to his student, the glorious Louise DeGrey. She was wearing low-slung jeans and a cropped top terminating at her waist. She was looking at him, smiling, waiting.

'Okay, come on you two. Aidan, put your right hand on her hip.'

Oh God ... but this was orders.

'Louise, put your left hand on Aidan's hip ... aaahhhh ... Right. Okay. Now hold your other hands.' As their hands touched, it was as though a circuit had been closed, allowing a current of pent up longing to surge through his whole body.

'Right, now stretch those arms out a bit ... that's it, a bit further. Yeah, now relax a bit ... come on, it's not a bloody tango you're going to do, it's a waltz ... you know this is how they used to do it. It was considered quite naughty at the time. Come on – a bit closer together.'

They shuffled a little, converging, till Aidan felt her breasts against his chest. Aaahhh ... She looked into his eyes, and, meeting her gaze under half closed eyelids, he smiled uncertainly, and swayed a little.

'Okay. Gerry, Trudy, Bill, Eva, the rest of the dancers, shape up like that ... right. Now look ... okay, relax for a minute. You've got this bunch of British staff officers and generals, bitchy as hell. They're either lording it over their subordinates, bum-crawling their superiors or in some way conspiring, according to their place in the pecking order. The sum total of their achievement at the end of the war will have been to send hundreds of thousands of khaki-clad brickies, tram conductors and grocers to their deaths – to no good purpose whatsoever. Oh and quite a few public school lads. And they've got their mistresses or whatever with them. It's a reception in some palm court or other – unspecified. Now, you'll be backstage right, at first, and when the music gets going, you'll come on dancing, okay? Right, well each couple has a short bit of dialogue to deliver; it has to emerge from the general conversation and hubbub, so I want each couple downstage at the exact moment when their turn comes, so the audience gets every word.'

'Er, George. Problem.' George raised his eyebrows. 'Eva and me … we don't know how to do a waltz.' This was Bill Dixon.

'Blimey, don't you kids know anything these days?' He thought for a moment. 'Right, Trudy, you're the dance specialist. You've got fifteen minutes to bring them up to scratch on the waltz. I'm going for a smoke. Okay, Percy?'

In reply, Percy struck up with The Blue Danube.

During the course of this monologue, Louise had remained in Aidan's arms. There seemed no good reason to undo the arrangement. His right hand cupped the curve of her hip, the thumb unwittingly fallen across the waistband of her jeans, touching her flesh. The extended arms, relaxing, had been withdrawn, and the still clasped hands now reposed between her breasts. His tactile cup overflowed.

'Come on Aidan.' It was Trudy. 'You can be my partner for this demonstration – okay?'

'Okay,' Aidan said obediently, reluctantly putting Louise down. Trudy, propelling Aidan forcefully, demonstrated the basic steps, then, talked the rest of the actors through them. Then Percy came in with The Blue Danube ...

When George returned from his smoking break, he stood for a moment or two, arms akimbo in the centre of the floor, looking up at the stage. Then he clapped his hands noisily.

'Okay folks, take up your positions ... let's try it again. Now you're all competent waltzers, it's got to be good.' Turning to Percy, 'Maestro ... you ready?' Percy nodded and struck up with Morgenblätter.

It was better. As the generals and their ladies drifted off stage to the fading strains of the waltz, Aidan and Louise danced into the wings and turned to watch the next scene. They remained standing close, touching, as if unwilling to relinquish the roles which legitimated such a liberty. In the wings opposite, soldiers began singing a cheerfully bitter parody of a popular song. George had, only that day, taken delivery of the slides which were to form a changing background to the action, showing the horrifying reality behind the burlesque. Norman Madden, the technician had put in some sterling work that day to fix up the necessary technology for their deployment, with George at his side, he was at the projector. Other members of the cast, waiting in the wings, turned towards the screen above and behind the empty stage. As the song began, the screen became lit with the sequence of slides: the scenes of carnage. Night photographs, flares and Very lights illuminating the sky; cloud formations; three British soldiers walking across duckboards in a muddy field; dead Germans in a trench in a peaceful-looking field; a young French soldier on burial duty, laden with crosses; dead French soldiers; a field of white wooden crosses, stretching as far as the eye could see.

'Fucking hell.' Someone, awed, spoke sotto voce behind Aidan. He looked at Louise and turned a little. It was Helen Miller. The petite, quiet, shy Helen Miller; too shy to take a part, but working backstage, her eyes, fixed on the screen; they were brimming with tears. She turned her head to look at Aidan.

'Sorry,' she said, her voice quivering, 'I had no idea ... it's terrible ...'

Aidan smiled at her grimly and nodded.

As the scene closed, there was silence. The cast, wherever they were stood as though frozen. No one seemed able to speak.

Presently, George did.

'Okay folks,' he said, 'I think we'll call it a day after that. It's a bit early, but I think we all need a drink.'

They sat round a table in a corner of the bar, mostly staring thoughtfully into their drinks. The silence in the group was uncanny. Then George looked round and with determined cheerfulness, said, 'come on folks. Let's not sink into terminal morbidity.'

'I'd heard about the Great War,' Noel said, 'but it didn't really mean much before … but that … my granddad was in it, but he never talked about it. He's dead now, so I'll never be able to ask him.'

'And my father,' said Aidan. 'He came back from it, but he was a wreck. Died when I was still at school.'

The mood lightened a little as the evening wore on and the alcohol worked its therapy. The group subdivided and Aidan was successful in manoeuvring himself next to Louise, at a corner table. The general discussion was of the relationships depicted in the play. Then, somehow, in one of those fissions that are wont to occur in groups in conversation, there was just him and her, dealing with some sub-issue.

After a sudden momentary silence, she looked at him directly and said, 'Aidan, may I ask you a serious question?'

He put down his glass and engaged her eyes, sighing. 'Are we going to be serious for the rest of the evening, then? It's that damned play, isn't it?'

She laughed. 'No, this is nothing to do with the play.'

'Well then … I don't know really … it depends on, er … well let's put it this way. Yes, you can ask me a serious question, but whether I'll be able to answer it – or even want to answer it is another matter altogether.'

She pulled a face. 'But Aidan … not be able to? Oh come on … I've come to regard you as the fount of all wisdom, don't you know that?'

'Miss DeGrey, if you think you've anything to gain by flattery … you're probably right. Even if you are lying.' She laughed. 'Okay,' Aidan continued, 'try me.'

'Right … well, erm …' She took a deep breath. 'Well, do you think marriage is a good thing?'

For some reason, his heart sank a little. His lips tightened. 'Why on earth do you want to ask me a question like that?'

'Now you've responded by asking me a question. We could go on forever like that and never get an answer. So come on. Are you going to give me an answer or are you going to chicken out?'

Aidan smiled wanly and shook his head. 'So … you're putting me on the spot, then, are you? Well you know, marriage is like the parson's nose … or do I mean the curate's egg?'

'What on earth do you mean, Aidan?'

'Well you know what the saying is don't you? Good in parts.'

'That's really not very helpful, you know.'

'Then why do expect me to be able to give a sensible answer?'

'You see you're asking questions again. Well I expect you to be able to because you are married, aren't you?'

'Yes, I am. But everyone's experience of marriage is different. I couldn't possibly generalise. I suppose the institution is socially useful as a stabilising factor in society.' Aidan was getting a little irritated at this line of conversation. He wanted to enjoy the frisson afforded by this verbal contact with this beautiful young woman. He did not wish to be reminded of marriage. In particular, he did not wish to be reminded of his own marriage. The rules of this sort of intensely pleasurable sub-sexual encounter, tacit though they were, did not permit references to marriage – especially to one's own.

'Aidan, I'm not talking sociology; I'm talking people.'

'Okay,' he said rather testily, 'tell me why you want to know. Are you about to do it?'

She frowned slightly and looked down, pausing before replying. 'No … no. It's just that I've … well, just avoided it.'

He knew that the relief this reply brought was irrational, but it welled up inside him anyway. 'What, just avoided it? You mean this afternoon? Or was it yesterday?'

'Oh Aidan don't be daft. Of course not.' She smiled at him. 'No, it was just that I saw you with your little girl in college the other day, and watching you together, I somehow got a sense of the feeling there seemed to be between you. I just wondered if I had thrown something good away.'

Aidan was touched. 'Yes, I have a great relationship with both my daughters and that's wonderful. But you know, all the time, you worry about your kids. You know that the worst possible thing you could ever experience would be for some harm to come to them. But that's only part of marriage. The whole thing has a lot of advantages … and a lot of pitfalls.'

'That doesn't sound like an unqualified endorsement.'

'Well I told you it was impossible to generalise.'

'You don't think I made a mistake, then?'

'How could I possibly say – I don't know the first thing about it,' he replied, then, changing the subject, 'look I'm going to the bar. What would you like?'

'Oh, are you buying me a drink?'

'Well of course I am.'

'Then I'll have what you're having – please.'

Aidan gestured to Gerry and Percy, and they gestured back. In some situations spoken language was unnecessary. They used the ultimate restricted code. He returned from the bar with four pints of beer. Passing two to his colleagues, he resumed his place with Louise. She smiled up at him.

'Thanks Aidan. You see, I'm picking up wicked northern habits already – drinking pints of beer.'

'Oh I'm sure that's just the start.' He picked up his glass, and, looking into her eyes over the top of it, said, 'Cheers.'

'Cheers,' she said, doing likewise.

'Right then,' said Aidan. 'What shall we talk about now?'

'I haven't finished about marriage yet. You know that night, right at the beginning of rehearsals – you'd been to a meeting and you walked me home after we got chucked out of the bar?'

'Mm, yes, of course I do.'

'We talked and you wondered why I'd really fled the south and come to Swaleborough.'

'Yes.'

'You didn't think the reasons I gave at the interview were convincing ... you thought there must be more.'

'Yes.'

'Well, you were right ... Oh, I don't know why I'm telling you this ...'

'Because you think your tutor should be your agony uncle as well?'

She laughed. 'Aidan, I don't in the least think of you as an uncle ... Oh I don't know ... I suppose I just got started on this chain of thought; well you know how once you've made an important decision, and it's irrevocable, you go over it again and again, wondering if you really made the right one. I haven't much thought of it since coming to Swaleborough – but seeing you with, er, what's your little girl's name?'

'Dora.'

'Dora ... brought it all back again.'

'Right then, you'd better tell me all about it.'

She looked at him and smiled wryly, 'Well ... I was engaged ... I was engaged to be married ...'

'You were what?' Aidan looked at her wide eyed. For some reason that surprised him.

'Why do you look so astonished? I am of marriageable age – aren't I?'

'Well, yes ... it's just that, I supposed that bright young people didn't do old-fashioned things like that these days. I imagined that your life in London would be so full of excitement, variety, creativity and God knows what else, that ... Oh I don't know ... to get engaged seems so ... so provincial.'

'Well weren't you engaged?'

'Yes, but for God's sake that was in the fifties, in a grubby industrial town, where there was a much higher premium on respectability. If you didn't do things right you might be thought to come from the lower classes.'

'But I thought workers in industrial towns were the lower classes,' she said. Now she was wide eyed.

Aidan was amused. 'Oh don't you believe it. You can get much lower than those lower classes.'

'Well anyway, whatever you may think, people in the south, even in London, the great metropolis, do sometimes agree to marry and seal the arrangement with a ring. For want of a better word, they call it engagement. That's what happened to me.'

'Okay. I stand corrected. What happened, then?'

'His name was Michael. He was ten-years older than me. I met him in my final year at art school. As a matter of fact, he was on the staff there. He taught ceramics.'

'Hm,' said Aidan, slightly frowning. 'It was like that, was it?'

'Well don't look so disapproving. These things happen.'

'Correction. They don't happen – people do them.'

'Oh well, whatever, 'she said. 'Then I got the job in London and we saw each other mostly at weekends, either there or in Norwich. He was in the throes of a messy divorce when we first met, I didn't take things too seriously; and you were a bit right about my life in London at that time. It was new to me and exciting. Lots of the people I met were – or at the time seemed – exciting. I loved working in the design studio and I was making quite a lot of money too. Oh, I'm not boring you, am I? You're not sick of being an agony uncle, are you?'

'No. No, I'm enthralled. For God's sake don't stop now.'

She looked at him anxiously. 'Well if you're sure … well then, eventually Michael's divorce came through and our relationship, sort of intensified. We established some kind of commitment, I suppose. Then, later, he suggested marriage.' She looked into Aidan's eyes and smiled. 'I suppose I could be old-fashioned again and say he proposed to me … and I couldn't think of any really convincing reasons why not …'

Aidan looked at her, bemused, '… and you said, "Yes".'

'Yes.'

'Well if I may say so, the way you tell it, the whole thing seemed to lack much conviction.'

'Yes, I suppose that's true. I still don't know if I was really in love – but Michael was very keen and sort of carried me along with his enthusiasm. Oh and my parents were all in favour – I think they feared for my moral well-being on the streets of London and would be glad to see me settled down with a good man …' She smiled ruefully. 'I suppose I got myself psyched up for it.'

'So how did it all go wrong,' Aidan asked.

She thought for a moment, bringing her interlocked hands to her pursed lips, frowning. 'Last year,' she continued, 'he was offered a visiting lectureship in the States – quite out of the blue. Someone had seen his work in an exhibition in New York was impressed by it and decided they wanted him. Well it was a career move he could hardly turn down. He wanted me to go with him. I suppose I was tempted in some way. But that would have meant giving up my career, my friends and the life I was making for myself, I couldn't do it. So for him, it meant me or his career. In the end, despite his pushing the marriage idea, it was his career that came first. I didn't think I could sustain an engagement to someone on the other side of the Atlantic – so that was the end of us.'

Aidan looked at her sympathetically, while feeling intensely glad that that arrangement had come apart, that she had ended up at Swaleborough and that he was now sitting beside her in the college bar, the privileged recipient of these confidences. 'But now I'm confused,' he said. 'It seems to me that the very things that caused you to reject Michael have anyway happened. I mean, you did give up your career and you did give up your friends – not for somewhere exotic like New York but for homely little Swaleborough, in the north of England. It doesn't make sense.'

'Yes well you see, that wasn't all; there were other complications.' She sighed. 'Shall I go on?'

'Yes, please do.'

'Well I told you I loved my work, and I really did, I believed I had a good future there. The firm liked my designs and, you know, they were getting into production. Aidan, I can't tell you what a thrill it was to see someone at a theatre or in the street wearing a dress made of one of my prints. Then one of my bosses started … well, paying me unwanted attention; nothing much at first, just kind of light flirting, slightly suggestive remarks, compliments on my dress, that sort of thing. I knew that this guy was married, at first it didn't bother me too much, and bearing in mind that he was my boss, I sort of played along with it – up to a point. Then he began dropping hints that my future career might be enhanced if I was nice to him – this was where I began to draw the line. By this time, he was into physical contact – you know, rubbing up against me, concealed groping, that sort of thing, I began to get really pissed off. So I told him, quietly, in a corner one day, in the nicest possible way, that I would prefer it if he would keep his hands to himself. I tried to avoid him as much as I could, but he was very persistent. Well one day, just about the time when the thing with Michael was right on my mind and I was feeling miserable and hurt, I felt his hand on my bum. I just burst into a fury. I totally lost control and I yelled out, "Get your filthy hand off my arse, you dirty bastard."'

Aidan let out a yelp of laughter. 'Oh sorry,' he said. 'I know it was serious, but it's just the picture of the exquisite Miss DeGrey producing a stream of invective she might have learned from a costermonger. What happened then?'

Louise smiled ruefully. 'There was total silence in the studio for a few seconds. The guy went bright red, then, he went into kind of controlled fury. He told me to get my things together and get the fuck out and never come back, he'd make sure my future prospects in the industry would be zero. But anyway I was halfway to the door before he even got to open his mouth.'

'So now you'd lost your man and your job. You must have been pretty unhappy.'

'You could say that.'

'So what then? A new start? Well it wasn't as simple as that. You see there was more.' She looked down at her hands and took a deep breath. Aidan looked at her intently and waited. Then she looked up at him again and said, 'A fortnight before Michael was due to fly to the states, I found I was pregnant.'

Aidan's jaw sagged a little and his eyes rounded. 'Jesus,' he said. 'Well when ... what ha ...'

'I didn't want to tell Michael. I realised that the pangs of parting were not as agonising as they should have been and I realised that it wouldn't have been right to commit myself long term to him ... I suppose I realised then that I wasn't really in love with him. Couldn't see myself as a component of a nuclear family; so I didn't tell him – and he went.'

Aidan sought her hand and squeezed it. It somehow seemed a natural thing to do. He was at once shocked and moved. She flinched a little and looked at him, smiling ruefully, but did not withdraw her hand.

'Louise,' he said, 'that's terrible. But what about the baby?'

'I was still living in the flat in Bayswater that I shared with Tess, a friend and workmate. I had quite a bit of money saved up and I reckoned I could keep myself going with barmaiding, waitressing and that sort of thing till I got myself sorted out again. But when I discovered I was pregnant ... well it just changed everything.'

'But what about your parents? Didn't you think of going back to them?'

'No. Well, I've told you a bit about them. I think Mummy would have been able to cope – but Daddy ...' She gave a little shudder, '... he'd have gone ape. I just felt at the time that I couldn't take that.'

'So?'

'I had an abortion.'

There was a long silence, then, 'Jesus ... I don't know what to say ... I really don't ... Poor Louise ...'

'Aidan, there's nothing to say. It's history now. But now you know why ... when I saw you with your little girl – Dora, it got to me a bit.'

Again they were last to leave the bar. Together they walked back to Stanforth Crescent. As Louise turned to go through the gate, she looked into Aidan's eyes and said, 'Thanks for listening, Aidan. As well as many other things, you're a good agony uncle.' She gave him a quick kiss on the cheek. 'Goodnight.'

She turned quickly, put her key in the lock and opened the door. As she disappeared inside, she blew him a kiss. Aidan stood for a while looking at the closed door, then turned for home.

* * *

Agitatedly, he topped up his glass again, then standing quite still, listened for the opening and shutting of a distant door, the release of a burst of noise, some audible sign that she was on her way. There was only the sound of the clock, an artificial, contrived kind of tick – not the crisp clarity, the metal on metal, of an escapement. Why should an electric clock have a tick at all? he wondered. For the same reason as an electric fire should have artificial logs? Or maybe the passage of time just needed its increments stating audibly, even electrically. Smith's Sectric, it said on the face, just below the twelve. He watched as the gap between the last minute mark and the minute hand widened, as it approached the six. She'd asked him about marriage. She'd asked him about marriage. He didn't want to think about the wreck that was his own.

CHAPTER 12

It was not until the beginning of the last week of term that something happened which had given him a little hope; hope not that the wreck could be salvaged, for that no longer seemed possible or even desirable, but that somehow Bobby could be rescued from the misery of her life with her mother. He'd been in the studio with his first-year students. The studio floor was strewn with drawings and studies, and other work was propped against the walls. Aidan was conducting a crit. He was leading a discussion about the work, eliciting from the students analytical comments about their own and each other's work. Aidan always enjoyed this bit of his teaching and regarded it as one of the most important things he did. He liked to provoke the students, then watch them draw on their critical resources and begin to strike sparks off one another. They were in full flow, when Mary, the department secretary stuck her head around the studio door.

'Aidan,' she called out. 'Sorry to interrupt but there's a phone call for you.'

'Blast! Who is it? I'm a bit busy at the moment ...'

'It's someone from Bobby's school. Says it's important.'

'The school?' Oh, God, what had happened? Looking at his students, he said, 'I need to take this. I'll be back as soon as I can.'

There was a murmur of acknowledgement as he left the room. Aidan turned and followed Mary out of the studio up the steps. Mary said, 'I'll put it through to your study,' and disappeared into the office.

Aidan entered his study and picking up the phone, perched on the edge of the desk. 'Hullo, Aidan Hamilton.'

'Hello Mr Hamilton. This is Fiona McAllister, Caedmon School. You may remember we've met before … parents' evenings and …'

The voice was what Aidan thought of as educated Edinburgh. He tried to put a face to it. 'Yes, of course.'

'I'm sorry to be ringing you at college. I hope it isn't too inconvenient but I thought it best to get in touch as soon as possible, so …'

'What is it? An accident? What's happened?'

'Oh no. Nothing like that. No, it's just that we've been a bit worried about Bobby. For some considerable time now, her work has been deteriorating. She's been getting – oh I don't know – more and more – well, withdrawn, I suppose you could call it. Several of her teachers have said she hardly seems to be there at all in the classroom. She certainly looks a very unhappy child. As you know, I'm her tutor and responsible for her general welfare, so I thought I'd better have a chat with her. Anyway, this morning I asked her, very unobtrusively, to come and see me in my room, at break. Well, to cut a long story short, when I said that we were a bit worried about her and asked her if there was anything she would like to talk about, she burst into tears. It was all rather disturbing, and because of some of the things she said, it seemed necessary to speak to you, at this stage, rather than your wife.'

'Well what did she say? Did she ...?'

'I don't think we can discuss it over the phone, really ... I was wondering if you could come in to see me and Mr Liddell, head of lower school, within the next couple of days.'

'Well, er, yes ... I suppose I could ... Could you hold on. I'll check my timetable.' He put the phone down and stood up to scrutinise the chart taped to the wall over his desk. He picked up the phone again. '... Let's see ... yes ... er, I could probably make it tomorrow afternoon – say half past two?'

'Right, that would be fine ... er, and I don't like having to say this, Mr Hamilton, but it would be inadvisable to involve your wife at this stage.'

'Yes, I think I can probably understand why. Okay then. Thanks, Mrs McAllister. See you then.'

Aidan sat down heavily on the chair, his elbows on the desk, his hands steepled in front of his mouth, his fingers tapping together in a restless rhythm. Presently, he opened the drawer and took out a packet of cigarettes and a lighter. He looked at the packet, flipped the top open and took out a cigarette. It was only three weeks since he had given up, he wasn't sure why he had kept that full packet; perhaps as a kind of emergency resource – like the lifejackets on the channel ferry; reassuringly there, though no one seriously expects ever to have to use them. Or was it some kind of talisman? He turned the cigarette in his fingers for a moment then put it back in the packet, which he then replaced with the lighter in the drawer.

Was it all going to come out? Was the shit about to hit the fan? Anyway, from now on, thought Aidan, it looks as if it's no longer going to be exclusively a family matter, something will surely have to be done.

He got to his feet and crossed the floor to the small cupboard under the bookcase, opened the door and took out a bottle of whisky and a glass. He poured himself a generous measure and took it over to the window. He looked out over the tennis courts, where four students in tracksuits were knocking up and towards the row of stately elm trees beyond. Through the trees, fragments of the exposed backs of the Edwardian terrace which formed the college's northern boundary were visible, the red brick patterned with a mess of windows, drainpipes and fire escapes. As he sipped the whisky, felt it abrade his throat and irradiate his stomach, he allowed his senses to overwhelm him. With unfocused eyes, he soaked up the patterns of light and dark as somehow they fused trans-dimensionally with the irregular pock of struck tennis balls outside and the insistent clack of the old electric station clock on the wall above the study door. His thoughts subsided into a sludge on the floor of his mind and time was suspended.

Presently he was restored to the here and now by a knock on the door.

'Aidan, are you there?'

It was Barbara. Aidan started and turned from the window. 'Ah, Barbara, come in. I was just ...'

'I thought you were down in the studio. There's a couple of things I wanted to confirm with you but Mary said you'd had a phone call from school. Nothing wrong, I hope ...' She eyed the whisky glass '... Hm ... Was it that bad?'

'Just thought a little stiffener would fit the bill ... yes, it was Caedmon.' He looked down and shook his head despondently. 'Worrying ... a bit of a problem with Bobby ...' He stopped short, then began again, his voice rising. 'A bit of a problem? ... like hell. It's a big problem ... it's a ...' He felt his emotion getting out of hand.

Barbara was his oldest friend on the staff. He wondered what she knew, what signals she had picked up. He wanted to let it all out. But she was too kind, too impartial. He knew she got on well with Cathy. It would pain her to hear bad things about her. She wouldn't want to believe them, would want to believe there was another side to it – an explanation which would leave no one culpable. Like wars that could be stopped if only the antagonists would stop behaving like human beings. He did not want that. He knew what was wrong, he lived with it every day and no matter how he tried, he seemed not to be able to stop it. He wanted others to see that, to give him moral support. So, making an effort to calm himself, looking up at Barbara, he forced a smile and said, 'They want me to go in tomorrow to discuss a few things with them. Afternoon, two thirty. I've nothing too pressing, so ...'

'Well, I don't want to interfere, but Aidan, if there's anything ...'

'Yeah ... I know ... well I'll ... Oh shit, listen, I'd better get back downstairs. Can we talk later?' He knocked back the rest of the whisky and, avoiding Barbara's eyes, passed her in the doorway.

'Okay then. It can wait. Bye.'

'See you later.'

After he'd finished his teaching session, he went up to his room and went back to the whisky bottle and glass. He poured himself a double, raised the glass to eye level and studied for a few moments the amber, distorted world he could see through the whisky. He thought, God, I'm drinking a lot of this stuff. He looked again, this time at the whisky, not through it. He swilled it round the glass and inhaled its fragrance. He took a large sip and enjoyed the mysterious pleasure of an incandescent mouth, before allowing it to trickle down his throat like lava down the slope of a volcano. Thank God for it, anyway, he thought, for he had great faith in its restitutive powers.

Emitting something halfway between a groan and a sigh, he subsided into a sprawl across the arms of his easy chair. He had at first been shocked to be approached by the school. Somehow he'd not considered the possibility that his problems could escape from the domestic realm into the outside world. But on reflection, if the school became involved, there would perhaps be help available. He felt some modicum of relief at the prospect of someone sharing his burden. This was his spark of hope.

Tuesday was the day of his appointment. On Tuesdays he had the whole day with his third-year students – a pleasant and easy-going group of ten. It being almost the end of term, they were all well advanced in their projects and didn't need his constant attendance. He would spend the morning helping them individually, as necessary, so to take an hour off in the afternoon would be no problem. Because of the appointment, he'd driven to college that morning and setting off at twenty-five past two to keep it, he had been optimistic. Surely now something would have to happen. Surely, with the school involved, something would get done. Things would improve. Cathy, would by some means, come to see the ill she was doing, would face up to the impending destruction, would agree to seek counselling, be restored to the caring mother she had once been and start loving her elder daughter again.

He pulled the Renault into the Caedmon School car park, locked the door, strode across the playground and up the few steps of the main school entrance. There was a reception office to the right with a sliding glass window. He crossed over to it and pressed a bell push. A stout middle-aged woman with steely-grey hair tied back in a bun turned from a large wallchart she'd been attending to, saw Aidan, smiled at him and came to the window, sliding back the glass panel.

'Hello,' Aidan said, 'my name's Hamilton ... I have an appointment with Mrs McAllister and Mr Liddel.'

'Ah yes, Roberta's father, isn't it? Just a moment, now, where is it? Let me see.' She rummaged among some loose papers, picked up an appointment book and thumbed through it. 'Let me see now ... ah yes. Here we are. Two thirty.' She looked up at Aidan and smiled again. 'Just a moment, Mr Hamilton, I'll give Mrs McAllister a ring.'

Aidan looked round the entrance hall. There were paintings on the opposite wall. With a small pang of pleasure he recognised among them one of his own. It was a small version of one of his park paintings – the Poussin influence rather striking. It had been quite a coup, selling that batch of his work to the Schools Museum Service.

'Good afternoon, Mr Hamilton.' It was that educated Edinburgh voice. 'Yes, I see we have one of yours in this term's selection. It's a beauty.'

He looked round. He had not noticed her arrival. 'Mrs McAllister ... Thank you.' He greeted her, taking the offered hand and shaking it gravely. 'How do you do?' He didn't really remember her. He was surprised that she was so young and pretty, and that she was wearing an elegant trouser suit.

'Bobby's quite proud of you, you know. She tells her friends, "That's one of my Dad's," and they say, "Oh I didn't know your Dad was an artist".'

Aidan laughed. 'Well I think she probably needs all the cred she can get, at the moment, though she'd probably do better if I were a footballer or a rock musician.'

'Yes, she is going through a bit of a bad patch isn't she? But anyway, let's go along to my room and talk about it.' She led him through swing doors out of the lobby and a short way along a corridor. She opened a door on the right, inviting him in. Mr Liddel was waiting by the window.

'Hello Mr Hamilton – we have met, I think.'

'No need for introductions then.' Mrs McAllister said.

'Mr Liddel ... yes, of course ... parents' night ... and the concert. How are you?' He too was younger than Aidan. No baggy sports jacket with leathered elbows here, but smart suit, white shirt, striped tie; carefully cut, but not obsessively ordered dark brown hair, with signs of early greying in one or two streaks. A man on the way up, thought Aidan, whose own ambition had dwindled to zero, once his teaching career had reached a comfortable plateau.

Mrs McAllister positioned herself behind the desk.

'Shall we sit down?' She indicated chairs to the others, while she herself took the expensive-looking swivelling chair behind the desk. She picked a folder from a wire basket and put it in front of herself. Then she placed her elbows on the desk and lowering her eyes, brought her interlocked hands to her lower lip.

After seeming to think for a few moments, she looked up at Aidan and said, 'Mr Hamilton ... er, as I expect you realise, we have something of an ethical problem on our hands.' Aidan looked at her and waited. 'In situations where home and school are involved, we would normally expect to see both parents together. In this case, we didn't think that would be ... er, well ... helpful at this stage, you'll see the reason for that if you agree that we should proceed.' Mr Liddel nodded. They both looked at Aidan, awaiting his response. Aidan, an elbow on the arm of his chair, passed his hand over his forehead in a gesture of dejection. After a moment he looked up.

'Yes. I can see you have an ethical problem and I have one too. But look, for me, the most important thing in all this is what's happening to Bobby. I mean ... for her sake, I think we may have to be – well – not too fussy about the ethical niceties. So ... I think I'd just like you to give it to me straight ... if that's okay.'

'Right then,' Mr Lidell said. Then turning to look at his colleague, 'Do you want to carry on, Fiona?'

'Okay,' she said, 'here we go.' She picked up the folder from the desk and tapped it with the back of her hand. 'I asked for reports from all the teachers who take Bobby. I don't think we need to go into them individually; there's nothing in them indicating bad behaviour or anything like that at all, but without exception, they report a serious decline in performance in the classroom, work in general, attention span and things like that.' She opened the file and leafed through it. 'Doesn't seem able to concentrate.' 'Never smiles now.' 'Contributes nothing in oral work.' 'Always seems desperately unhappy.' She looked up at Aidan. 'You begin to get the picture?'

Aidan nodded wearily. 'Yes ... please go on.'

'You see, it's not just a case of the kind we're only too familiar with, where a pupil just isn't doing the work because of, well, laziness, getting in with the wrong sort of peer group or parental indifference. There seems to be something deeply wrong that's affecting her whole life. Well, as I told you over the phone, Mr Hamilton, when I got her alone and talked to her, she more or less broke down and told me worrying things about her life at home ... and this is where the ethically dodgy bit comes in, because what she said concerned your wife's behaviour towards her.' She stopped and looked intently at Aidan. 'Do you want me to go on?'

'Look, I have to tell you that none of this is a surprise to me, Mrs McAllister, I would like to – I need to know what she has said to you ... and of course this is my ethical dilemma. Any discussion about my wife's relationship with our elder daughter brings up the question of marital loyalty ... but Bobby is, to me at least, more important than any of that. And anyway I'm getting to the state of desperation where I think some outside help is needed, so please carry on with that in mind.'

'Right then.' She went to the folder again and took from it a small notebook. 'I jotted down some of the things she said in her own words as near as I could.' She opened the book and thumbed through a few pages. 'She said more than once, "My Mum doesn't love me." "She must hate me." "I can never do anything right for her, no matter how hard I try." "She's always shouting at me, whatever I do." "She only loves Dora." "It got like this after Dora was born." "She cuddles Dora and looks at me with a smirk on her face." "I want my Dad to take me away but he won't." "I wish I could go to foster parents."' She closed the notebook, put it on the desk and looked up at Aidan. 'Do you want me to elaborate, Mr Hamilton? Or would you like to comment, now?'

Aidan looked down at the floor, tugging at his lower lip, seeming for some moments engrossed in the pattern on the rug. When he looked up, he was close to tears.

'I think,' he said unsteadily, 'you've outlined a tragedy in the making ... and I don't seem to be able to do anything to avoid it. What you get from those things that Bobby said is a pretty accurate picture of how things are. The fact is that when Dora was born – and she's six now – she seemed to absorb all my wife's energies and interest, and Bobby seemed to get somehow excluded. In the years since then, the situation has got steadily worse, so that now, it seems hardly an exaggeration to call it rejection – even persecution.'

Mr Liddel, who had seemed to be compulsively examining his finger nails, looked up.

'And before the second child came along – how was your wife with Bobby then?' he asked.

'When Bobby was born, we both thought it was the most wonderful thing that had ever happened – like I suppose most parents do. Cathy – my wife – adored her. I don't know how you get to stop loving a child – but that is what appears to have happened with Cathy.'

'This must be extremely distressing for you, Mr Hamilton as it clearly is to Bobby,' Mrs McAllister said. 'How are you coping? I mean can you yourself see any kind of solution or strategy? I can see you're in an extremely difficult position and obviously we'd like to help in any way we can.'

'Well, I try – I've tried again and again to talk about it to my wife, but she refuses to admit that there is anything wrong ... well, to be more exact, if there is anything wrong, it's nothing to do with her. As you can imagine, we're having a pretty stormy time of it at the moment – we seem to be in almost permanent conflict. My wife then blames it on Bobby – as though she was some kind of malign influence ... for God's sake, she's a twelve-year-old child. And of course, I'm anxious about the effect on Dora. She's a pretty well-balanced child, but I can see what all of this is doing to her too.'

No one spoke for a few moments. There was the sound of footsteps receding along the corridor. A distant door opened, allowing a burst of laughter to escape, then abruptly, it shut.

'Then what about Bobby?' Mr Liddel asked.

'I suppose I act as a kind of buffer whenever I can. I make sure she knows I love her. I suppose I try to make excuses for her mother. Bobby thinks I ought to take her away from it all – and I often feel like doing exactly that – but of course she doesn't think about my responsibility to Dora, which is just as pressing as my responsibility to her.'

'And presumably it can't do much good to Bobby's relationship with her little sister, who seems to be enjoying her mother's favour all the time to Bobby's disadvantage ... and as you say, it must be extremely bad for Dora, too.'

'Well, you might think Bobby would be wildly jealous of Dora – and sometimes she is ... but much of the time they get on pretty well. Bobby has always thought of Dora as her little sister and even now she still does.'

'The situation does sound a bit desperate, Mr Hamilton,' said Mrs McAllister. 'But let's just try to think of what we can do to help. Of course we'll keep a close watch on Bobby. I've already said she can come and see me any time she wants to talk, although you can be sure that everything that's been said this afternoon will remain confidential, I'll have a discreet word with all her teachers so they'll know to make allowances.'

'Yes, now that's what we can do in school,' Mr Liddel said, 'but we also have the resources of the Schools Psychology Service if that seemed likely to be useful. There is a family counselling service, but from what you've told us, it would seem unlikely that your wife would go along with that.'

'Oh God, no. I've tried to get her to agree to seeking some sort of counselling – together, I mean. Just total refusal. No chance at all, I'm afraid,' said Aidan.

'Nevertheless, perhaps we should be prepared to arrange for the psychologist to have a chat with Bobby if matters don't improve. It could be done here, very informally. Dr Bradshaw is very easy to talk to … you know … non-threatening and it might give Bobby a bit more confidence to know that someone else is, as it were, on her side.'

'Perhaps,' Aidan said, 'but it would compound the problem of the non-involvement of my wife. I think I'd like a bit more time to think it through and really to have another go at getting her to see some sort of reason.'

'Well then,' said Mrs McAllister, 'how would it be if we had another meeting after the holiday?'

Aidan thought this was a good idea and agreed that he would get in touch again at the beginning of the new term. The meeting then ended with the usual courtesies. They thanked Aidan for coming.

Aidan thanked them for their concern and for inviting him. They had resolved to keep in touch. Aidan had gone back to his students, knowing that nothing had changed, yet a little grateful that he'd been able to share a bit of the burden. Somehow the fact of this sharing had seemed to make the fracture in his marriage more official. It had snapped the last restraint holding him to fidelity; he was soon to discard, without a pang of conscience, the habit of a lifetime.

* * *

But dammit now she was late. She was five minutes late. Come on, Lulu, come on. Where was she? Somehow the clock seemed to have speeded up. He thought he'd go mad if she wasn't here in the next thirty seconds.

CHAPTER 13

It was the night of the Art Department's Christmas party. In recent years, this function had, in keeping with the increasing liberalisation of the college regime, which followed the retirement of the saintly Miss Wilberforce, principal of twenty-seven-years standing, acquired a reputation, much exaggerated, for wild goings-on. Students of the department had de facto invitations, which entitled them to bring one guest. There was much competition for those guest places among the rest of the students, as well as a good deal of connived-at gate-crashing. All other members of the college staff, as a matter of courtesy, were invited, too. Few, in practice, came, but those who did, represented a distinct, though not overtly acknowledged, subset of the senior common room. It contained those, male and female, who were most likely to gather in the newly-established senior common room bar, after, and sometimes between lectures and even, according to some students, during lectures too, to drink beer from cans or bottles; those given to sneaking at odd moments up to the big room in the attic to play riotous games of table tennis with the students; those who generally took lunch in any of several pubs in the nearby town centre, noisily discussing politics, sport or – less noisily – sex.

That day, the last day of term, had been spent decorating the big painting studio in preparation for the night's revels. Gerry and Aidan always took charge of this operation. Big Henry, who was a sculptor, had lost interest, since Janet, his wife, who had heard some unsavoury rumours about goings-on at these events, forbade his attendance. Barbara, the head of department and a much-treasured survivor from the old days, though formidable in some ways, was really a model of tolerance and fall-over-backwards anxiety to see and understand the other person's point of view. She'd always given assent to the annual party because she thought she should try to keep up with the times – but not without some misgivings. Accordingly, she was prepared to give her two younger male colleagues a free hand. Well, they knew better than her what sort of thing was necessary. Indeed they did. So, in accordance with recent tradition, Aidan and Gerry had gathered around them a small group of the most able and lively students among whom to spend an agreeable day of light-hearted creativity, punctuated by a leisurely lunch at the Three Tuns. Aidan had, needless to say, issued a personal invitation to Louise. In the event, there had been many small problems necessitating co-operation between them.

'Lulu, be a love, hold this screen while I shove this screw in.'

'Aidan, could you hold on to the end of this streamer and pass it up to me when I get up the ladder?'

'Lulu, we've got to get those screens up from the storeroom. D'you want to give me a hand?'

'Okay. Hang on a minute while I fix this light. Damn. Can you pass me that screwdriver? Thanks.'

She stepped down from the box she was standing on, hooked an escaped frond of black hair behind an ear and rubbed her nose with the back of the grubby hand holding the screwdriver.

'Here, give me that, before you do yourself an injury.' Aidan took the screwdriver from her and laid it on a chair.

Around the studio, students, singly and in pairs, were casually busy, up stepladders or on knees, tapping in nails or slapping on paint, transforming, with cardboard, paper and paint, the functional, everyday apparatus of the studio into some kind of temporary seraglio. The buzz of conversation was punctuated by a shout of instruction or a burst of laughter, here and there, to a background of subdued pounding of pop music from a radio someone had brought in. Aidan took her by an elbow and guided her in the direction of the door.

'Come on then,' he said. 'Down to the store room.'

He led her towards the door, through it and along the glass-roofed corridor, hung with a small collection of seventeenth-century French drawings and etchings, this term's loan from the Victoria and Albert, through another door and down a flight of concrete stairs and into the dimly-lit basement.

209

'Along there,' he said.

At the end of a short corridor was a black painted door, marked 'Store room.'

Aidan fumbled in the pocket of his fisherman's smock and produced a bunch of keys. 'Hold on a minute. Let's get the right one.'

She waited at his elbow while he inserted the key in the lock. His hand shook slightly. He opened the door and gestured for her to enter. Following, he closed the door behind him. The room was weakly lit by a small window high on the opposite wall. Dimly visible were packing cases, stepladders, sacks, tins of paint, bales of sculptor's scrim and hessian and other ill-defined objects. The display screens they had come for were stacked at one side. Aidan did not switch the light on. She turned to face him. She was almost a silhouette against the light from the high window. The fuzz of disordered hair trapped the light and made a halo round her head. Her face was in shadow.

Contre jour, thought Aidan. He realised every wrinkle on his own lived-in face must be mercilessly lit.

This can't really be happening to me.

Then he thought it must be, for now he could see that her eyes, wide open, were fixed upon his face, asking the question, What now, Mr Hamilton?

He noted, not for the first time that morning, that under the skimpy tee shirt she wore above the threadbare jeans, her breasts were unsupported. Then he looked deeply into her eyes and reached for the hands she was holding out for him.

'I find you difficult to resist,' he said.

'Why should you want to?' she whispered.

'I'm married, have two children, I'm your tutor. I'm old enough to be your father. How many more reasons would you like?'

She looked at him slightly sideways under lowered lashes. 'I'm not prejudiced,' she said, placing her arms around his neck, offering him her parted lips. He rested his hands on her hips, rocking her gently, testing; was she real? Lowering his head, he delicately brushed his lips against hers, as though the merest hint of roughness would shatter this fragile dream. For moments they teased one another like this. Aidan felt that exquisite stirring in the loins, which had for so long been only the stuff of dreams. Then with devastating suddenness they imploded, their bodies compacted into a single mass, lips now crushing together, tongues colluding in sinuous dance.

He ran his hands under her shirt up her naked back, to the nape of her neck, feeling her breasts pressed against his chest and down again into the top of her jeans to the beginning of the cleft of her backside. Wildly, she caressed his neck and clawed at his hair. Then, losing balance, they toppled, falling over a sack, onto a bale of hessian and came apart, gasping.

They looked silently at each other, then burst into laughter. Neither, for the moment, was able to find words to express the deed, but both were unwilling to draw apart. Aidan knew a bridge had been crossed – the bridge separating the grey, duty-governed half-world of domestic life in his crumbling yet seemingly immutable marriage, where the best you could do to reassure yourself that you were not yet soul-dead was to enjoy those bantering encounters with ever-so-proper sexual undertones, with the women he met – separating all this from a new world he did not fully understand.

'Louise,' he was serious now. 'I've never done this before ... I mean with a student ... I ...'

She looked at him, wide eyed. 'I didn't mean this to happen,' she said, 'but I sort of couldn't help myself. And it feels wonderful.'

He reached towards her and drew her into his arms once more. 'And I want you. I really do want you.'

'Then I'm yours for the taking,' she said softly.

He drew back, as though he needed some distance, some perspective, to confirm the reality, to dispel the disbelief. He stood looking at her in silence for some moments, his hands again on her hips.

'Oh God, Oh God ... You're beautiful ... beautiful,' he said. Then in a determined attempt catch hold of the practicalities which had brought them there, 'Listen, Lulu, we've got to get those screens up to the studio. Someone's going to miss us soon and that'll look suspicious. Tonight, at the party, will you come up to my room?'

'Yes, yes, yes,' she said. 'Just tell me when.'

'We'll have to be careful, so as not to arouse suspicion. We'll work it out tonight once the party gets going.'

He got to his feet and bent forward to help her to her feet, pulled her again into his arms and pressed his lips against hers. When he withdrew, he said, 'My God, I can't put you down – but I must, I must. Come on, let's shift these screens.'

As they emerged into the studio, manoeuvring the first screen through the swing doors, Gerry looked up from something he was painting on the floor.

'Aidan. About bloody time. We've been waiting for those screens for half an hour.'

By teatime everything seemed as near ready, as near complete, as these things ever can be. The studio had been magically transformed into an ephemeral palace of delights, the floors cleared of tools and rubbish. The students departed. As Louise left, her hand brushed against Aidan's and their eyes briefly met. Gerry took responsibility for locking up and Aidan, pulling on his heavy leather jacket and thick scarf, set off briskly for the town centre. There he visited first a sweet shop, second, his barber.

Then he'd had to go home. He had now to turn about and retrace his steps over the bridge he had so recently crossed. It was a twenty-minute walk, back to that other world and in the course of it he tried to adjust to the contradictions battering away inside his head. The excitement of the afternoon's events, the outrageous reality, the irrevocability of them made him feel dizzy, as he tried to fit them into the fact of his impending arrival at the semi-detached house containing his wife and two daughters. But he could not get Louise out of his head.

Turning the last corner into Oakdene Avenue, he could now see number twenty-five. The sun had gone, leaving a dirty red smudge behind the bare tops of the trees down the hill. It was cold and the sky promised frost. He could see Dora; she was sitting on the low garden wall; she was wearing her brown duffel coat. When she saw him, she climbed up to stand on the wall to wave. He waved back willing her not to fall off. Then she jumped to the ground and raced towards him. His heart ached for her in one of those moments when the awesome responsibility of parenthood struck him with a terrible force. It clashed harshly with the residues of the afternoon's euphoria.

'Daddy, Daddy, Daddy,' she called out as she ran towards him. She hurtled into his outstretched arms and catching her, he swung her three times round, then drew her up so that the cool roundness of her pink cheek fell against his own and he smelt the fresh, little-girl scent of her hair.

'We're having fish fingers for tea and tomato sauce.'

He put her down and they set off hand-in-hand towards home. 'Oh, wow … your favourite. It must be your lucky day.'

'I got a gold star at school today, so Mum said we could have them.'

'Great. What was the star for, then?'

'It was for my story and it was about two little sisters that live in a dark wood with their Mummy and Daddy, and …' They had arrived at the garden gate.

'Hey, tell you what, you can tell me all about it when I give you your bath tonight. Okay?'

'Okay Dad.'

CHAPTER 14

He and Gerry had arrived early to supervise the preparation of the bar and the installation of the disco.

That done, with the trickling in of the first of the revellers and the testing blasts from the electronic equipment, he said, 'Look, Gerry, I'm just nipping up to my room. I've got a couple of things to sort out. I'll get them done while things get going down here.'

'Right you are, old son. I'll see that things get off to a smooth start.'

Aidan went out through the double doors, whose glazing was now obscured by a lurid pattern of coloured tissue and fabric in imitation of stained glass, into a purple penumbra along the corridor whose strip lighting was now subdued by carefully placed coloured materials and up the darkened staircase, to his study. Fumbling slightly with his keys, he let himself in and switched on the anglepoise, low in the corner. In a jittery state of anticipation, he checked the simple arrangements he had already made that afternoon. But there was just one more detail. He felt that there should be some music. There always seemed to be some, with the obligatory subdued lighting, when you saw similar scenes on television. He had a modest stereo system in his room; he found music an important aid to creativity when he was painting. But then as the party down below got going, he realised that was where the music was going to come from, suitable or not. An insistent base throb was beating its way through the fabric of the building. It would provide all the background music there would be.

He had a last look round the room and wondered if she had arrived yet. He could hardly bear the waiting. He hung on a little while, killing time, fidgeting with things on his desk, taking books down from the shelves, skimming through a few pages, replacing them, then walking to and from the window, until, unable to wait any longer, he switched out the light, let himself out on to the dark landing and headed back to the studio.

He was nervous and unsure of what to do when he got there. He hoped Louise would be there. If she wasn't, he would just have to wait, with the air of someone who wasn't waiting. If she was, he would want to dash to her and enfold her in a crushing embrace so that everyone might see what was between them. But he knew that could not be; that no one must know. He entered the darkened corridor just behind a little group of chattering, excited new arrivals. They greeted him noisily.

'Hi, Aidan.'

'Hey, sounds good in there, man.'

'Hope there's plenty of booze in there, Aidan.'

'Hi, Mike, Joe.' He laughed. 'Yeah … more than enough – even for a load of hopheads like you.'

They pushed in through the swing doors, which, open, let out a blast of raw noise. Inside was already a mayhem of flashing lights, din and writhing bodies. Just beyond the door, he encountered Barbara with her back defensively to the wall. She was wearing a long black dress of stunning and expensive simplicity, a discreet string of pearls and the slightest hint of make-up.

'Barbara, you've arrived in good time. You look absolutely stunning.' He had to shout to make himself heard.

'Well you know me, Aidan. I like to get started early so I can get back for cocoa and bed in decent time. And Aidan … I'm too old to have my head turned by your smooth tongue.' She smiled. 'But thank you for the compliment anyway.'

'Oh, come on, I'm allowed to chat my boss up, aren't I? Anyway, I really mean it, so there. Furthermore, I'm going to buy you a drink. What'll you have?'

'Very well, if you insist. D'you think they'll have dry sherry at the bar?'

'Barbara, I'll go through hellfire and water to get you some.' She drew in her lips in a tight smile and rolled her eyes. 'Aidan, you'll come to a bad end someday.'

As he made his way to the bar, around the edge of the dancing, exchanging fragments of banter with the students, his eyes roamed the room in search of Louise. Gerry was at the bar. Aidan knew he would spend a great deal of the evening there. He was chatting to

George Hobson and Trudy Blunkett, a dance specialist, who had only recently joined the PE Department. Aidan greeted them.

'Ho, Aidan,' George shouted. 'What's yours?'

'Nothing at the moment, thanks, George, I'm getting one in for Barbara – she's playing wallflower over by the door.' There was dry sherry; he ordered a glass and he bought a pint of bitter for himself. Making his way back to Barbara, he could see she was now in the centre of a chattering group of her students. He reached through them and handed over her sherry. She smiled her thanks and Aidan, beer in hand, shuffled round the edge of the milling throng, looking, trying not to look like someone looking. For what must have been three-quarters of an hour, he mixed with the revellers exchanging shouted trivia, communicating with gestures, stifling his increasing agitation, trying to seem like a normal person at a party. By the time he had made a full circuit of the room, ending up at the bar, the party had been going for over an hour and still no sign of her. It was beginning to hurt.

'What can I get you, Aidan?' asked one of the students on bar duty.

'Make it another pint, please Mike. Have one yourself.'

'Going pretty well then.'

Aidan didn't think so. 'Yeah, great,' he said. He took a long pull at his beer, put the glass down and for the umpteenth time looked at his watch.

'Hello, Aidan.' She had materialised behind him. Her voice was very close to his ear. He turned, smiled, said with an insouciance he didn't really feel, 'Louise, hello. Have you just got here?' He thought the question sounded innocuous enough.

'Hope I haven't missed anything exciting. Got held up waiting for a phone call. Seems to be going great guns.'

Aidan felt the tension slide away, replaced by a wild upsurge of exultation. 'Right, what would you like to drink?'

'A Dry Martini, please.'

'Barman.' Aidan snapped his fingers at the barman. 'A Dry Martini for the lady.' Mike grinned and tugged an imaginary forelock.

'Very good sir,' he said, doing a Jeeves. The Martini was brought. They picked up their glasses in a silent toast and drank, looking into each other' eyes. The music changed. A crescendo of raw noise. Speaking was hardly possible; they drank again.

Then Louise put down her glass and mouthed, let's dance.

She had looked into his eyes, taken his hand, backed, gently into the melee of gyrating dancers, drawing him after her. He followed awkwardly, wondering if, among all the other considerations, a man of his age wouldn't look pretty stupid trying to do something like this. His eyes flicked anxiously about the room. He noted that Barbara was no longer standing by the door. He knew she must have gone home by now and was glad of that. She was the one person he would least like to have any suspicion about his intentions. But he glimpsed Gerry in the corner near the improvised bar, pulsating under the strobe lights as he capered uninhibitedly with a sinuous blond girl he didn't recognise. She wore tight jeans and a scanty top, and was fully a head taller than him. No one paid Aidan any attention; except Louise.

'Come on,' she shouted against the noise, 'loosen up.'

'This is something else I've never done before,' he shouted.

She laughed. 'Just feel the beat ... and move. Like this.'

She flung her arms up. They were bare. The dress she wore was black, slightly shiny and very small. She closed her eyes dreamily, her lips slightly moist and parted, and her body took up the rhythm of the music, moving with a bewitching eroticism which sent shivers down his spine. Now nothing seemed to matter outside of her and the all-suffusing rhythm of the music. He couldn't now stop his body and he began, awkwardly, to move in response to the beat. He allowed his eyes to fall upon her breasts. They were unsupported, he could see, and moved deliciously with the rhythm of the music. She opened her eyes. He met them, embarrassed.

'Do you like it?' she asked, smiling. He was confused.

'Oh er w-what?' he said, feeling foolish.

'The dress, silly.'

'God, yes,' he said. 'It's exquisite and so are you.'

She took his hand and twirled expertly under his arm. Some of her sinuous rhythm transmitted itself to him. He was beginning to enjoy himself. He allowed his body to respond to the pounding beat. In fact, he seemed unable to prevent it. He had quite suddenly understood what this noise was for. Here he was – a forty-five-year-old married man – in some kind of unspoken and wildly exciting dialogue with a beautiful and sensuous twenty-five-year-old woman.

She laughed at him. 'You're doing great,' she shouted.

'Never thought I could do this.' He shouted back, panting, taking her hand and now twirling her round, achingly aware of her palpable nakedness under the flimsy stuff of that tiny dress.

When the music stopped; they fell together, laughing. She caught hold of his hand and as they moved towards the side of the room, he felt a hefty pat on the back.

'Well done, Aidan. I didn't know you had it in you.' Aidan looked round. It was Mark Andrews – another student from Aidan's group. Aidan raised his eyebrows in a mock haughty look. 'You'd be surprised at what I've got in me, young man. And don't be so bloody impertinent.'

Mark flashed him a wide grin and headed for the bar. Louise squeezed his hand and looked into his eyes. 'And what else do you have inside you, Aidan?' she asked. 'Will I be surprised?'

Aidan tried to read her face. She was smiling and her eyes were large and brown. He looked seriously into them and said, 'You're beautiful.'

She looked down for a moment, then, met his eyes again. 'Am I?' she asked.

'Yes,' he said, 'and I'm an expert on such matters.'

'Thank you, sir,' she said. Then standing on tiptoe, her arms about his neck, she whispered, 'As a matter of fact, you're a bit of alright yourself.' She gently nibbled his ear lobe. Aidan swallowed hard. They elbowed through the press of perspiring bodies towards the bar. Gerry was having an animated and slightly drunken conversation with the blond tall girl, whose name Aidan could not remember.

'I'm just going for a pee,' Louise said.' Will you get me a Martini?

'Right,' said Aidan. 'I'll wait for you here.' He watched her weave her way through clusters of chatting, drinking, laughing students towards the swing doors, exchanging he wondered what sort of banter, what sort of sly innuendoes – and not giving a toss.

He turned and placed his elbows on the bar and two-handed, raised his glass to his lips like a libation cup. He allowed his eyelids to droop as he drifted into a fantasy of erotic anticipation. Then, suddenly, he found Gerry at his side. The blond girl was now intimately entwined with the ginger-haired Noel O'Mally, vampishly trying to part him from a cigarette, Gerry placed an arm around Aidan's shoulder in a comradely gesture of drunken bliss.

'Aidan, old mate … how are you doing?'

'Ah, Gerry,' Aidan began, 'fine, absolutely bloody fine. I … um … I would be grateful if …'

'Don't worry old son,' Gerry interrupted. 'If you want to … er …' He let the sentence wither on his lips as he caught sight of Louise re-emerging through the throng, joining them.

He looked at Aidan, grinning, then at Louise. 'Louise,' he said. 'Louise, you look absolutely ex … exqu … exquisite … and now I'm going to …' Not finishing this sentence either, he turned away towards the blonde girl who was now devoting all her attention to the exacting task of lighting her cigarette.

'Pissed he may be,' said Aidan, devouring Louise with his eyes, 'but he was sure as hell right.'

'Well then,' said Louise, smiling, looking at Aidan through lowered eyelashes. 'Why don't we …' She took Aidan's hand and turning away from the crowd, into the corner where the bar joined the wall placed his hand on her left breast.

Aidan took a deep breath and moaned his muted ecstasy. 'Ahhh … don't expect me to make decisions when you do things like that.' He half closed his eyes and gently nuzzled his face into her hair, savouring the fullness of her breast in his hand, through the silky flimsiness of her dress. Then, at length, raising his head, he looked cautiously around. No one seemed to be paying them any attention. Was this a generational thing, he wondered, to not care, to let everyone do his or her own thing? And no judgements? If it was, Aidan liked it. Well it seemed a good time. Trying not to look conspiratorial, trying to balance his voice against the noise, he said,

'I'll go up to my room now. Give it about twenty or twenty-five minutes, then come up. For God's sake, make sure no one sees you.' She looked up at him, her eyes wide open and smiled. Aidan reluctantly withdrew his hand to fumble for his keys, never for a moment taking his eyes off her.

'Okay,' she said. 'See you in twenty minutes or so.' Aidan looked at his watch as he negotiated his way towards the door. It was ten past ten when he let himself into his room.

As the hands of the clock passed half past ten, then twenty-five to eleven, Aidan began to get agitated. He poured more whisky. By twenty to eleven she still hadn't turned up. His glass was empty. He refilled it. The nature of time had changed. Since half-past; it had picked up speed and was now, incredibly, prolifically gushing away uselessly like water out of a burst main, taking his life with it. She had still not arrived by a quarter to. She was a quarter of an hour late. He was frantic. Where the hell is she? What can have happened? She's taken ill; been carted off to hospital. She's been abducted. She's changed her mind; thought better of the whole thing. Decided it was a stupid and dangerous idea. It was only a game ... I completely misunderstood. He reminded himself that he had said about twenty minutes. Yes, but for Christ's sake, not that about. He opened the drawer with the cigarettes in, took out the packet and the lighter. Flipped open the top, took out a cigarette. No. Can't do that. She hates smoking. He angrily threw cigarettes and lighter into the waste bin. He decided that if she was not here in five minutes, he would have to go down and find her.

Three minutes later, he knocked back the rest of the whisky, slammed the glass down on the desk and let himself out of his room. No stealth, now. Anxious and angry, he stalked downstairs, along the corridor, through the double doors and into the turmoil of a rip-roaring party. Paying little heed to anyone, he made for the bar and claimed the drink he'd left almost untouched nearly three-quarters of an hour ago.

'Looked after it for you, Aidan.'

'Thanks Mike.' He took a long pull then turned round to scan the room. The noise was deafening. The room was full of wildly moving bodies, made unrecognisable by the flashing lights. Then he saw her. She was involved in an abandoned, outrageous pas de deux with Mark Andrews. Aidan stared in disbelief. How could she do this? She seems totally engaged with him. Has she totally forgotten me? Can't get to her till the music stops. It went on ... and on. He drained his beer and ordered another, engaging smilingly in trivial exchanges with various people clustering around the bar, having to suppress the outrage in his mind.

Serves me right, he reproached himself bitterly. Shouldn't be messing about. I'm twenty years out of my depth. I don't know how they behave. Then the music faded out. Dancers began dispersing towards the edge of the floor. They were near the far end of the room.

They seemed to be heading in different directions, but then the music started up again. This time it was slow and dreamy. He saw Mark catch Louise's arm and swing her towards him. They fell together into a clinch and soon the floor was full again – this time with closely embracing couples swaying sensually to the slower rhythm. She rested her head on his shoulder and Aidan saw him stroking her hair. They looked like two lovers. Jealousy ripped through him with a serrated blade. In a fury, he took up his drink again, turning his back on the scene he couldn't bear to see.

Then he felt a bare arm steal about his neck. Electrified, he turned. Disappointed. It was Trudy Blunkett.

'Come on Aidan,' she said. 'You look as though you could do with a good smooch.'

Suddenly he thought, if promiscuity is the thing, then I'll be promiscuous too.

'Trudy! You're damn right. I could.' She led him into the melee and placing her arms around his neck, drew him close to her. He put his arms around her waist, and, touching everywhere, they undulated gently to the music. She was wearing a long, slinky, purple dress, low-cut, slit deeply at the side and Aidan, despite the turmoil inside him, was aroused as she pressed her small, taut breasts against him, he felt the silky material of her dress slide over her thighs. A saxophone wailed a sultry melody over a languid base. The dancers moved in a smoothly intricate pattern as though the room held some viscous liquid that was being slowly stirred. Despite his anguish, Aidan found it powerfully erotic and bending his head, he placed his lips on Trudy's neck.

'Mmmm, that's nice,' she murmured. They moved for a while like that, swaying lazily to the music. Then, when he raised his head, he found himself looking into Louise's eyes, for the swirl of the current had contrived to bring their partners back-to-back. Her eyes were open wide and swivelling to indicate her partner, and she was mouthing a message Aidan couldn't understand. Exasperated and angry, he signalled his non-understanding with his eyes. Even the erotic friction with Trudy could not now assuage his torment. 'Come on, Trudy, I need a drink.'

'A good idea,' she said, and, arms around each other's waists, they manoeuvred through the dancers towards the bar. There they were joined by George, who, Aidan knew, had something of a soft spot for Trudy. He allowed George to take over the conversation, while he tried to make sense of his pain and Louise's treachery. He paid only vague attention to the conversation which was developing around him, for Gerry had now joined the group. There was only one thing he could think about. Then the music stopped and there was only the sound of animated voices and shouts of laughter. He turned away from the bar to face the dance floor and saw Louise coming towards him. As she was approaching, she hunched her shoulders, turned her palms outward and with her head on one side, furrowed her brow with eyes wide open. The gesture seemed to say Sorry, I couldn't help it. Aidan detached himself from the group and moved towards the corner. Louise followed. Before Aidan could speak, she whispered, 'Aidan, I'm sorry ...'

'But what the hell ...'

'No, please listen. I know you must be angry ...'

'You can say that again ...'

'I know, but listen. This is what happened.'

Aidan looked round to see if it was safe to have this conversation here. Everyone seemed to be taking advantage of the break in the music to engage in boisterous shouting, no one was paying them any attention.

'Mark had been watching us and when you went out, he came over to me and he started kidding about. He was saying, 'Where's Aidan gone, then? Has he gone to his room? You're going up there to meet him, aren't you?' and things like that. Of course I denied it, but he wouldn't believe me and he wouldn't go away, and if I'd gone out then, he'd have known ... in fact, he'd probably have followed. When he suggested we dance, I ... well I just didn't have much option.'

'Oh God ... well okay, I can see you were in a fix, you really did the right thing.' Relief swept over him. His concern that the thing between Louise and him might have been noticed was overwhelmed by his joy that it was, after all really happening. He turned and his eyes swept anxiously over the room. 'Where's Mark now, then?'

'He's gone back to Chrissie ...'

'Who?'

'Chrissie Dixon. He's knocking her off.'

'What?'

'You know ... they're an item ...'

'Louise. I know what knocking off means. But where the hell was Chrissie when her fellow was snogging you round the dance floor?'

'Oh she was wrapped closely around Harry Appleby.'

'Gordon Bennett,' groaned Aidan. 'I'm too old for this. I just don't understand the ways of the young.'

She looked into his eyes and laughed. 'Anyway, you lost no time in sampling the pleasures of the lovely and athletic Trudy.'

'It was only to distract myself from you,' he said, squeezing her hand.

'Good. I wouldn't like to think you fancied her too much ... and I promise I'll compensate you for that anguish when we do make it to your room.'

By now the music had started once more. It was slow and sleazy again and soon the floor was once more full of embracing couples. Aidan and Louise joined them. 'Well I'm not leaving you a second time among all these ravening young men. This time I'm going to give you my key and you can go first.'

They had languidly shuffled their way towards the door, Aidan whispered into her ear, 'Okay ... it's time to go.' He disengaged one hand and felt in a trouser pocket. 'Here's my key.'

Looking into his eyes, she found his hand and surreptitiously took the key. She had nowhere to put it, so kept it concealed in her hand.

Aidan murmured, 'When I say so, slip out, as though you were going to the loo. Make sure there's no one around and go up to my room. Don't put the lights on. The curtains are open so there's enough light coming in from outside. Lock the door and amuse yourself for ten minutes or so. I'll come up as soon as it's safe. I'll tap three times on the door and you can let me in.'

'Oh God,' she whispered. 'Isn't this exciting?'

'No slip up this time, my gorgeous Louise or I shall go completely insane.'

'No slip up.'

'Okay. Go now.'

'Wait a mo; here's something for you.' She pressed something soft into his hand and slid unobtrusively out of the door. He watched her go, his gaze lingering on the curve of her hip. He needed a drink and made his way between swaying bodies to the bar. The student doing his stint as barman saw him coming.

'Hi, Aidan. You look like you need a drink. What'll it be?'

'Hi, Tom. I certainly do. I think it's just got to be a pint.' The barman took a glass from the shelf placed it under the barrel and turned on the tap. Aidan opened his hand to see what Louise had given him. He quickly shut it again. It was a tiny pair of black knickers.

Aidan turned to the bar, the better to conceal his burgeoning erection. Clutching the precious garment, he thrust his hand into his trouser pocket and fondled it there. The clear implication of its presence in his pocket was of its absence elsewhere and that thought was driving him crazy. Sipping feverishly at his beer, he paid scant attention to the chatter of the barman and the other revellers surrounding him. As the level of his beer dropped he kept looking nervously at his watch and then at the scene around him, planning his unobtrusive departure.

Then he felt a nudge, behind him.

'Aidan ...' A voice said. It was Gerry, considerably drunk now, bearing an empty glass for refilling. 'You having fun? And where's the lovely Miss DeGrey now, then?' He said this rather loudly, one or two heads turned a little and grinned. Alarm flicked across Aidan's face.

'Gerry, you're pissed. Keep your bloody voice down.'

'Uh, oh,' said Gerry. 'I think there's something going on here ... is there, Aidan?'

'No comment,' Aidan said, 'but what I was trying to say to you before was, if I'm not around at the end, for chucking out and locking up, be a good chap and ... well, you can manage on your own, can't you?'

'Hey, Aidan … you know … enjoying yourself on the dance floor is one thing … but this is looking a bit perilous, isn't it? I hope you know what you're doing.'

'Well I don't really, but I'm doing it anyway – and it's wonderful. I'm slipping out, now. Keep an eye on things.'

'Okay,' said Gerry, shaking his head dubiously, 'as Barbara would say, on your own head be it.'

CHAPTER 15

Aidan, hand in pocket, sidled towards the exit, edging between cavorting revellers, pushed through the double doors and along the corridor. Through the next door, it was darker and the sound of the music, though loud enough, was now more muted. He stopped and looking round to confirm that he was alone, took the knickers out of his pocket, unfolded them, held them draped across the palms of his hands as though he were holding an open prayer book, then pressed his face into them, intoxicated with their scent. He breathed heavily for a moment, then crushing the knickers into his pocket, he waited a while, his heart thumping madly in his chest, set off up the darkened staircase. At the door of his studio, he knocked softly three times. After a pause, he heard the latch click and the door opened. He slipped inside and shut it behind him. Before he could say anything, she was melding with him in a wild embrace, with his hands seeking to map every crevice and prominence of her in one intense moment. Scarcely knowing what he was doing, he pressed her back towards the chair. Then he felt resistance. She broke free, seeming to repulse him.

'No, Aidan. Not like that. I don't want to be ravished. I want you to make love to me slowly, subtly, like an artist … because that's what you are, aren't you?'

He drew back and waited, his heart pounding. She retreated a little, her eyes fixed on his then slowly sank sideways into the depths of the armchair, crossing her legs and exposing the length of her thigh to the curve of the buttock.

'Come on,' she said, 'take some clothes off. Start with your trousers.'

'But ... I can't. I mean, it's too ... I'll just draw the curtains ... I ...'

'No, don't do that. I want to be able to see you. Come on.' She smiled encouragingly. Aidan, embarrassed, yet excited by the idea, said, 'Oh God ... Okay then ... if you think ...' He fumbled with his belt and zip, and reluctantly he let go his trousers; they subsided about his ankles.

'And your underpants,' she commanded. He closed his eyes and with a mixture of anxiety and excitement, he lowered his pants, releasing his erection, seeing the front of his shirt make a tent over it.

'You look lovely,' she said, her eyes appraising him and then slowly lifting, to meet his own. She turned her body to face him, uncrossing her legs and sliding down in the chair, so that the hem of her dress rucked up to her belly. She splayed her thighs.

'Do you like my cunt?' she said.

He stood for a moment, eyes wide, mouth agape. He did not think he had ever heard a woman utter that word. It had been familiar enough currency among the squaddies he'd done his national service with. It had been, he estimated, the second favourite expletive, rendered normally as 'koont' or something like 'kant', depending on the speaker's native region. But she placed the vowel with cut-glass precision between the two and pronounced it 'cunt', with all the languid clarity of a Third Programme announcer.

Aidan reacted with shock and an excitement bordering on insanity. The simple answer he needed seemed inadequate. His knees collapsed and he found himself kneeling between her open thighs, like a knight awaiting the accolade. (He later thought, What an update for the royal ceremony!) For some moments he lingered over the sight before his eyes. Louise watched him and waited. Then he plunged forward and buried his face in her. His tongue found her opening and he devoured her. She crossed her legs behind his back, imprisoning him. She writhed luxuriously.

'Mmmmmmm, aaaaaahhhh ...' she moaned gently, as Aidan plied his tongue. 'You do ... I can tell.' At the same time, she contrived to wriggle the thin straps of her dress off her shoulders so that her breasts fell free. 'Look Aidan.' She twined her fingers into his hair and lifted his head up from her crotch. 'Put your hands on my tits. That's right, mmmmmmm lovely, mmmmmm. Now suck my nipples.' Aidan did her bidding in a glorious haze of sensation in which there was no time, no reality, save the wonderful now. He did not know how long he floated in this blissful haze, for time seemed suspended. Then she said, 'Now Aidan. Now. Now fuck me. Fuck my brains out.' She pushed him slightly away. Aidan, again deliriously shocked by her words, straightened his knees and looked down at himself. With one hand, he lifted his shirt, now the only garment he was wearing. He had a towering erection. 'Oh, Aidan,' she whispered, 'you're beautiful.' She took it in her hand with what seemed almost reverence. Somehow, he had never thought women found penises beautiful. They may sometimes, he had thought, quite like the feel of them inside them, but only in the dark. Whatever. It felt beautiful, beautiful beyond words, the single focus now of his whole sensory being and she was guiding it towards herself. Aidan closed his eyes. Then suddenly, he remembered the condom in the back pocket of his trousers.

'Christ, Louise, wait I've got to pu ...'

'No, Aidan, no, it's OK. It's OK ... I'm on the pill ... Fuck me ... Fuck me now.'

She was wet and Aidan entered her in long slow thrust, with a delicious restraint he was later to marvel at. They came together. It was a simultaneous orgasm.

They did it twice more, afterwards. They hardly noticed when the music downstairs erupted to a final thumping climax, then ceased, the voices gradually died away to the last few 'Goodnight's' and 'See ya's' and there was the distant rattling of keys as Gerry locked up.

Aidan was very late home that night.

The next day she was gone. When, long after the party had died, they decided it was time to go, they found their way down to the main entrance by the moonlight slanting through tall, uncurtained windows. Outside, the moon was high, small and intense, lighting roofs with luminous silver, the bare trees, etched deepest black. A thin crust of hoar-frost scintillated where the moonlight fell. She had put on, over her tiny black dress, a black coat reaching almost to the ground and had flung a long red scarf round her neck. Aidan wore his faithful duffel coat, its toggles done up to his chin. Bound together by crossed arms and held hands, they walked like lovers do, through that brilliant, silent night, to the house in Stanforth Crescent – lingering, despite the cold, willing the walk never to end. But it did. In the darkness of the porch, they had stayed locked long in a wordless embrace, which neither could bear to end. Yet it had to end, presently, Aidan said, 'I'll be in the department tomorrow morning. Will you come and see me?'

'Oh Aidan I won't be able to.'

'But why not? Why can't you?'

'I'm going home, tomorrow. I'm booked on the nine-thirty train.' Aidan was crestfallen.

'Oh damn, I just hadn't thought of you going off straight away. You'll be away the whole of the vacation – the whole four weeks?'

'Oh God, I wish I wasn't going. It's been so wonderful tonight. I just wanted it to go on and on. But my parents will be expecting me.'

'Will anyone else be expecting you?' he asked, looking intently into her eyes, trying to penetrate the dark, to read what was there. She

239

took his hands and drew them to her lips. They felt cool and dry on the back of his hand.

'No,' she said, meeting his eyes, 'no one else. But we could keep in touch, couldn't we?'

Aidan sighed. 'I don't see how, really. I couldn't be getting phone calls or letters at home. A bit difficult to explain away. I'm going to hate this Christmas so much more than usual.'

'God, so am I. I just wish I wasn't going home.'

When finally they had parted, it was with the resolve to wait with as much patience as possible, the New Year and the new term – and whatever their new life would be, for though nothing had been said about the future – how could it at a time when the cataclysmic present was so all consuming? – Aidan at least knew that what had happened that night had changed his life irrevocably.

When the door had closed upon Louise, he had set off briskly through the icy night. It was too cold to saunter, now that he was alone, though he wanted more than anything, at that moment, to luxuriate in his thoughts. He bared his wrist to look at his watch under a street light. It was almost three o'clock. His family would be asleep. Whenever he was later than expected, he could usually be sure that Cathy would be waiting to interrogate him. But not when it got to three o'clock in the morning. He knew she could never stay awake much after midnight. Just as well. He did not think he could lie convincingly about something so momentous and so vividly real. Not now. Not yet. He knew, too, that he could not yet face home at all, even with the family asleep. He had never felt less like sleeping himself and deciding to keep walking for a while, he turned off from his route home, intending to make a wide detour.

As he walked through the silent, glittering, moon-soaked avenues, his mind was surging with half-formed images of some kind of paradise with Louise at its radiant centre. He knew he was in love. He had known from the beginning that he was putting himself at risk of falling in love. He knew that if once he gave in to her attractions in even the smallest way, he would be lost. He had never had a casual affair, either in or out of marriage; he didn't know how. There had been some painful experiences, in consequence, but he realised now that he had not learned much from such failures. He just could not grasp the notion of sex as a trivial or commonplace thing – the outcome of a frivolous and ephemeral union; nothing more than crude gratification, with no meaning beyond the act itself. It was too powerful and too private not to mean more – much more. Yet he could not be sure that Louise felt the same, though he desperately hoped she did. She was on the pill. For how long had she been on the pill? For whom? Had she planned it for him? Or was it a habit carried over from her previous relationship? These were the explanations he favoured. Or was it a prudent precaution against the casual encounter? He did not want these doubts.

Suddenly, he thrust his mind back into the ecstasy he had so recently experienced. In that instant, his exultation returned, and, aided by the considerable quantity of alcohol surging through his veins, made all seem possible. Eventually, there would be a painless way of parting from Cathy, which would ensure a continuing, loving and close relationship with Dora and in which Bobby would be redeemed and restored, away from the baleful influence of her mother. And he would have Louise.

By the time the detour had delivered Aidan to the end of Oakdene Avenue, the moon had sunk low in the sky. His hands thrust deep into his pockets, breath streaming, he hunched into the lowered hood of his duffel coat, shrinking against the cold and tried to prepare himself for home. He clicked open the latch on the garden gate, as he hoisted the hem of his duffel coat to fumble for his keys in his trouser pocket, he performed an involuntary dance as one of his feet lost traction on the hoarfrost. Recovering, he made a mental note to scatter salt on the icy drive in the morning. He let himself into the unlit hallway, took off his coat and hung it on the bentwood hallstand. He knew he could not sleep in the same bed as Cathy, tonight or, the way he felt, perhaps ever again.

So he made his way to the living room and plumped up the cushions of his favourite easy chair. He went to the sideboard, taking from it a half-full bottle of whisky and a glass, which he placed on the low table next to the chair. He plugged headphones into the stereo, selected a cassette – the first volume of Bach's Forty-Eight Preludes and Fugues, and fitted it into the deck. It had been a bad day for booze, but nevertheless he poured out a quadruple whisky anyway and made himself as comfortable as he could in the chair. Today was Saturday and Louise was gone.

CHAPTER 16

Christmas was imminent, though not immediate. The college term was over. For Aidan it had come to a climax of life-changing significance at the department party. But also in the last week there had been what for him were minor events; the more sedate senior common room Christmas party and dinner – best suits, ties; long dresses, jewellery (all members of staff attended this, with spouses too, of course) and the carol service at nearby St Botolph's Church, beautifully sung by the College Choral Society. As far as Aidan was concerned, this would have done nicely for Christmas, but as he knew only too well, it had hardly got off the ground yet; there was much, much more to come – and he hated it. As a matter of fact, all his friends hated it too – or said they did – but they submitted to it anyway. And so did he. But he was annually outraged to find that, immediately after the summer vacation – straight after 'Back to School', the local branch of House of Fraser had removed half of the gardening section in the basement and replaced it with rolls of Christmas wrapping paper and boxes of Christmas tree decorations. For Christ's sake we're only two-thirds of the way through the year, he would fume. For the next three months, had he occasion to visit the store, he would at all costs avoid that department, though, come

245

December, he would find that particular avoidance more and more difficult to maintain and would grumpily conform to the irresistible mores of the consumer society.

But the school term had a further week to run. There would be two more carol services to attend; Dora's and Bobby's. Thankfully, he was not expected to attend Cathy's, but he had already done his annual duty by her in supplying original ideas for decorations for her classroom and helping her with their execution, so they would be admired and envied by her colleagues. Her class would be enthralled and would send her lots of loving Christmas cards. How the hell can she be so adored by other people's kids and be so awful to her own daughter? Apart from those things, life would be much as normal, but without the students. He would spend the days in college, returning home to prepare the evening meal for his working wife and two daughters. During the day, he would get on with his painting, take coffee with his colleagues, play some table tennis, have lunches with them in the pub, and try, for the present, at least, to think about Christmas as little as possible.

There were two things, however, he knew he would be likely to think about a great deal: one was the situation within his family; and the other was Louise. As to the family, since the meeting at the school, this particular problem had seemed to take on a new urgency. Yet Aidan had no new ideas and none of the old ones seemed to offer wholly acceptable solutions. Furthermore, the more he thought about it, the less possible did it seem to tell Cathy that he had been to the school without her and discussed her relationship with her daughter with members of staff there. Her response – and he could imagine it vividly – would be thermonuclear and all reason would be vaporised. Again and again, he returned the problem to the back of his mind and labelled it, 'Action Pending'.

Now however, since Friday, behind the frustrations and worry, behind the darkest anxieties, there was a half-suppressed optimism. It was like the promise of an emergent radiance behind an overcast sky. Again and again he returned to thoughts of Louise. There was at present only one problem. She was not here. How cruel, after that glorious consummation to be so brutally and totally deprived. He wondered if, with the passing of time, he might begin to doubt that it had really happened, to think that it was just another version of the dream – albeit with a much more satisfactory ending. Then he would put his hand in his trouser pocket and close his fingers around the tiny scrap of material there. That treasured memento would stay in situ to assure him that yes, it had happened and he would smile. But if now the only problem was her absence, at sometime, but not yet, he would have to give thought to some of the problems attendant upon her presence. What about teaching? What difference does it make if one of your students happens to be your mistress? Will It Show? Can you be impartial in matters of academic importance? What happens if you get found out? Where and how do you meet, without being seen? How do you cope with lying and deceit? For the present, Aidan, who was deeply in love, allowed reign to his natural optimism. He felt certain his love for Louise could somehow be legitimised, that they would somehow be able to be together, for people to know, for them to be seen proudly together, for the world to recognise and accept their togetherness. The details had yet to be worked out.

It was Wednesday, exactly one week before Christmas day. Aidan had spent a satisfying morning at his easel. His work was going well; he had perforce been able to manage his longing for Louise; to allocate to it a warming background presence which would underlie his daily activities.

Gerry was also in the department, working in the pottery, they met in the senior common room over coffee. It was no surprise that many other colleagues were still about despite term being officially ended. In an establishment where no one laboured under oppressive contracts, time was freely given as need determined. So for another few days, at the appointed times, social life continued. And that day, typically, there was consensus that luncheon would later be taken at the Three Tuns.

After the leisurely coffee break, Aidan returned to his studio and quickly became engrossed in his painting again. His exhibition would have to have a title; for sure, something to do with Arcadia, with its primary resonances of a past, remote and idyllic, where order and harmony transcended human unhappiness. But he also had in mind

248

its wry equivalence in those present-day areas defined as Arcadia by his favourite architecture critic, Ian Nairn. Those were the areas where mill owners and iron masters had built their tree-protected mansions, out of sight of the bleak townscape that housed the workers and the factories that created their wealth. There was irony here, Aidan wondered how you could get irony into landscape painting. Sometimes he saw menace in his work – but irony – well he wasn't so sure. He worked intently for another hour and a half, until hunger began to gnaw at his concentration. He looked up at the round station clock above the door. One o'clock; lunch at the Three Tuns. He knew he would get no more painting done that day. Lunch at the Three Tuns could not possibly end until closing time at three o'clock – which, allowing ten minutes for drinking up, would leave just enough time to collect Dora from school and be back in time to field Bobby and prepare the evening meal in time for Cathy's return. So he had better clear up.

He stood back from the easel to take a last look at his painting. He squinted at it through half-closed eyes, then through one eye, holding a hand out at arm stretch to blank off a problematic area. Then he took the painting off the easel and replaced it upside down. He squinted at it again for a moment, then sighing, he turned away. He picked up a palette knife from the paint encrusted tea trolley that held his gear and carefully scraped the whorls of mixed paint off his palette, wiping the knife on a torn-off sheet of kitchen paper, throwing that into the rubbish bin. Then he dipped a rag into the paraffin bucket at the foot of the easel and with it wiped clean first his palette, then his brushes. After swishing them round in the paraffin, he dried them individually on another rag and returned them to the salt-glaze pot where they were stored.

He took down his duffel coat from behind the door, wriggled himself into it and wound his scarf round his neck. Crossing over again to the easel, he set the painting the right way up, and, his face six inches from its surface, he scratched at one corner with a fingernail, muttering blast. Then after one last look, he went out, locking the door behind him. He clattered down the wooden stairs, through double doors and down the concrete ones to the pottery. Gerry wasn't there. Must have gone on ahead. Damn. Needed to talk to him. Oh well, in the pub.

Gerry was Aidan's oldest colleague on the staff and also his closest friend. Aidan needed to talk to someone about Louise and at present that someone could only be Gerry. He knew that Gerry knew, so it was not to inform Gerry that he needed him; nor did he seek Gerry's advice (though Gerry, he knew, was experienced in unobtrusively combining adultery with marriage and would perhaps have much advice to offer). No, he just wanted Gerry to listen and approve and to be pleased for him while he spilled out his joy and excitement. He wanted to extol the wonder, the glory of Louise, to laud her beauty, her wit, her intelligence; the fact that, with all this, she wanted him.

He wanted to talk about her without ceasing. To tell of how she had already changed his outlook on life; to describe what harmony of mind and, especially, body, they shared and how each understood the smallest nuances of language the other employed; how each laughed at the same kind of absurdities. He wanted Gerry to nod and smile, and understand, but above all, to listen.

He walked through the pottery, feeling the blast of warmth as he passed the open door of the kiln room, leaving the building through the basement exit. He emerged into a penetratingly cold December day, the bare trees motionless, the sky a uniform, unremitting grey. Gloomy. Yet something about the withdrawn, uneventfulness of it unexpectedly struck a positive chord in him, and suddenly, he felt elated. It was as though the neutral background the grey world presented, foregrounded and emphasised the glow of perilous happiness inside of him. Smiling to himself and anyone else in the vicinity, he set off at a brisk walk towards the town centre and the Three Tuns.

Taking the diagonal path through the little park in front of the college, he looked up at the skeletal trees. It seemed strange, but Gerry had some of their spareness. He was a little shorter than Aidan, but more economically built; muscle wrapped tautly around bone; a face tending to triangularity, a flattish top, crinkled with black hair. His table tennis was also economical. He held his bat in the old-fashioned penholder grip (lately given renewed respectability by the world-beating Chinese) and moved as little as possible, returning remorselessly every ball that came his way. Thus did he win against most opposition, including Aidan, who could not resist the baroque flourish – balletic, but except on really good days, unreliable. Ah, what would he do without Gerry? He remembered having reservations when they appointed him. Yes, he had the right experience, immaculate references and was obviously a consummate craftsman and technician: it was just that he seemed, perhaps a little abrasive, perhaps just a little over self-confident; perhaps just a little deficient in humility, with employment in such an august institution in prospect. The daily transactions between Barbara and Aidan were conducted with a cool decorum, rooted, he supposed, in the decorous history of the college. Could a chap like Gerry really fit in with this? Well they recommended him anyway, as the best of the bunch. The Committee offered him the post, he accepted and was duly appointed – and he duly fitted in. That was seven years ago; the beginning of the close friendship Aidan and he had enjoyed ever since.

It seemed at first that their wives would also become close friends. They had important things in common. They were both teachers by training, but were at the time they met, full-time housewives and mothers of young children. In the early days they had exchanged coffee visits of a morning and walked children in the park together in the afternoons. But it soon became clear that there were dissonances between them. By the end of the second term at Swaleborough,

Brenda had organised a Housebound Housewives Group, had joined the local Methodist Church, its choir and its Women's Forum, was in the early stages of forming a Staff Wives Discussion Group and was a leading light in the Parent–Teacher Association of their children's primary school. Cathy, however, had no patience with such dedicated gregariousness. All she needed, she claimed, was her home, her children and her husband. She focused on these, she stated, while Brenda enmeshed herself ever more complexly in the social world about her. So they drifted apart, meeting only on those occasions when social requirements brought them together with other college spouses.

Brenda's love of social life was much to Gerry's liking – as long as it mostly didn't involve him. So long as the supply of babysitters didn't fail – and while there were still students, it wouldn't – he enjoyed considerable freedom to pursue his own interests. These included his own work as an artist (of some reputation in his own specialist field – austerely elegant thrown stoneware, with more than a backward glance at certain wares of the Sung dynasty); drinking with his friends; playing table tennis (for he was captain of the staff team, which played in Swaleborough League Second Division); and a discreet but satisfying extra-marital love life. Aidan had dearly wished that some of Brenda's compulsive busyness would rub off on Cathy and give him a bit more space; not, at that time, for any nefarious reason, for on the whole he was resigned to the limitations set on his life, but just so that he might feel less oppressed by her neediness. However he wished it in vain. He'd suggested to her that Housebound Housewives would give her a good opportunity to meet others in the same situation as herself – tied to home and young children during the day; it would widen her range of interests, get her out and about a bit more.

Her reply was icy. 'Thank you very much, but I have enough interests and enough to do seeing to the needs of this family. I certainly don't want to waste any time on that lot of gossips and busybodies. It's a pity they don't have something better to do with their time.'

Aidan shrugged. What else could he do? It was not until Dora started school that Cathy felt secure enough to do something about her interest, dormant since her college days, in history and antiquities. It was then that she embarked on a WEA archaeology class. Aidan was only too pleased to do whatever babysitting was necessary for the once-a-week evening class and the occasional weekend school. He rather thought that his daughters approved of these arrangements, too.

He arrived at the Three Tuns some way behind his colleagues. When he pushed his way through the swing doors, exchanging the bleakness of December for the aromatic warmth of the Lounge Bar, his colleagues were already performing acclimatisation rituals, variously divesting themselves of coats and scarves, warming extended hands or behinds at the crackling open fire and reaching for menus and discussing drinks to be ordered. Aidan was noisily welcomed into the company. A corner table next to the fire was colonised and the company of six settled in for an afternoon of conviviality. He found himself nursing a pint of bitter between George Porter and Trudy Blunkett.

'Well then, Aidan,' Trudy said, with all the banality of the season, 'are you all geared up for Christmas?'

Aidan, with the cynicism that was de rigueur, replied, 'Trudy, for God's sake don't remind me about it. It's going to be even more awful than usual, this year.'

'Oh that's a shame. Don't you like Christmas? And what's so especially bad about this one? What'll you be doing?'

'What we're doing is, we're spending Christmas in the Lakes …'

'But that sounds great … I wish I were spending Christmas in the lakes …'

'Yes, I know it sounds wonderful – and it has all the trimmings – gorgeous scenery, old cottage nestling by a splashy rill at the foot of a small mountain, crackling log fire, mulled wine. It's straight off the front of a bloody Christmas card – all it needs is a stagecoach. We're staying with Cathy's sister, Isabel, and her husband Roger. Nice people and they make us welcome, do everything so well – Bella's a really good cook. But when you come down to it, it's just the same as everywhere else. You end up bloated on food, but what's worse, bloated on television too. And then the weather's so awful you can't even get out for a walk.'

Trudy laughed, 'God Aidan, I didn't think you were such a curmudgeon, such a Scrooge.'

'Well the worst thing is, you see, enjoying – or enduring – someone else's hospitality, curmudgeonly is just what you can't be. You can't just retire to your room to escape the boredom, read a book, listen to music; you can't even get pissed, except by prescribed increments, courtesy of your hosts; you just have to grit your teeth or clamp them into a rictus grin and be ritually bored ... Of course it's nice for the kids,' he added, sardonically.

He looked sideways at Trudy. She was very attractive. Her specialism, dance, ensured that her muscularity was well distributed – no over-developed forearm, that sort of thing. She wore a tight sweater of festive red, a feature Aidan found particularly pleasing. Her short blond hair curved symmetrically forward under her high cheekbones. Her blue eyes met his sideways glance.

'And how about you?' he asked.

'Oh well,' she said, smiling, 'knowing now how you feel about Christmas, I don't really think I want to talk about it anymore.'

'Oh come on,' he coaxed, 'is there a man on the horizon?'

'That's none of your business.'

By now, the barmaid was bringing plates of food to the table, cutlery wrapped in paper napkins, trays of sauces, salt, vinegar, drinks were shuffled around to make space, ashtrays removed, conversation adjourned.

Then, Trudy, now sawing energetically at her steak said, without looking at him, 'Tell you what, I did enjoy our one and only dance at the party on Friday … or to be more exact, I was enjoying it until I seemed to lose your attention … the glamorous Miss DeGrey, if I recall …' Now she looked at him, queryingly.

He paused in the act of applying butter to half a roll. 'Oh, well … er … sorry if it looked like that. I enjoyed … I enjoyed it too … it was just that there was … er … some unfinished business.'

He put down the knife and took a bite out of the roll, chewed a little and spearing a chip with his fork, added, 'She is one of my students you know.'

'Yes, I know, but … well, hm … I suppose it depends on what you call business.'

Aidan thought the conversation was taking a dangerous tack. It was dawning on him that secrecy was going to be difficult to maintain – especially since what he really wanted to do was to shout from the house tops that he and Louise were lovers. Fortunately at that moment, Andy Miller, Trudy's colleague from the PE Department, leaned over to ask her to pass the tomato sauce and followed up with a compelling bid for her attention. Aidan, relieved, took the opportunity to embark on a discussion, between mouthfuls of battered cod, with George, on some technical aspects of scenery and lighting for the play.

Later, when the plates had been cleared away and the ashtrays restored, a game of dominoes was mooted, whereupon more drinks were ordered, the barmaid produced the dominoes and there was a shuffling of chairs, and a general rearrangement of personnel. Aidan contrived to find himself next to Gerry at the bar. He signalled that he was, for the moment, opting out of the dominoes and Gerry sensing that there were matters to be talked about, did likewise. They took up the classic stance with their pints, side by side, elbows on the bar, a foot each on the brass rail. They looked at each other. The dominoes slithered and clacked on the corner table. Gerry was about to speak but Aidan forestalled him.

'Gerry, if you ask me if I'm all geared up for Christmas, I'm going to push your face in that pint.'

Gerry laughed. 'Okay then, we'll take that as read. You look as though you've got more interesting things to talk about, anyway.'

There was silence for a while. Aidan contemplatively swirled the beer round in his glass.

'Great party,' he said.

'Yeah,' Gerry said, unhelpfully.

'Look, Gerry ... okay we ... Louise and I we did ... you know ...'

Gerry took a long pull at his beer, then turned to face Aidan looking at him crinkly browed. 'Yes, Aidan, I do know. It was pretty bloody obvious. And probably not just to me. I mean, God, discretion's not your strong point, is it?'

'Oh shit, was it that obvious?'

Gerry shook his head in a gesture of benign exasperation

'Aidan, Aidan, Aidan … I just don't know where to begin.'

'Well I hope you're not going to go all righteous on me … I mean with your record of … um … well, shall we say …'

'No, we shan't say. And no, I'm not going to be hypocritical about it, because I admit I can't justify what I do. It's something that happened quite a long time ago, it's happening still and I want it to go on happening. And don't ask me about conscience – we'll just stick to pragmatics. My mistress – if that's what we want to call her – lives out of town. Like me, she has a marriage she wants to preserve, so what we do is what we both want. But we are discreet, careful; we avoid places where we might be recognised. Nobody knows. Nobody gets hurt. But you, Aidan, you're embarking on this thing with one of your students – in a small community like ours. I mean, people are starting to talk. For Christ's sake, what about your family? The way gossip spreads around this place, Cathy'll find out for sure.'

'Yeah, yeah, I can see all that. You think I'm behaving recklessly? Well I bloody well feel reckless. I expect her to find out. God knows what's going to happen between Louise and me. This is just a beginning; Friday night wasn't just a one-off thing. Gerry, I want her and I think she really wants me. I know it's outrageous, crazy, dangerous and all that, but suddenly my life has something in it more than the debilitating destructive grind – that's what my marriage has become.'

'And the kids?'

'The kids? listen, Gerry, you've got a good idea of what's going on, haven't you? Well last week, I got a phone call from the school, asking me to go and see them about Bobby. Me, mark you, not Cathy and me. I went to see them on Tuesday.'

'Well I didn't know that. What happened? They're noticing something at school, are they?'

'Yes. Bobby's teachers … they were all noticing … they could tell something was wrong, her tutor, Mrs McAllister talked to her, got her to spill the beans. So they know, now. Somebody else knows.' He looked into Gerry's eyes. 'So I'm not just making it up.'

'Christ, Aidan, you don't have to convince me.'

'No … I know that, Gerry, but others may not be convinced – those who haven't been as close to it as you. Anyway, we talked … they were really sympathetic … wanted to help. We talked quite a lot but nothing immediate was achieved. We agreed to get Christmas over and meet again at the beginning of term.

'Well, Aidan,' Gerry said, 'that's got to be a good thing, hasn't it? I mean for Christ's sake, you want a bit of help with this, don't you?'

'Well I could use some help, that's for sure. But they're going to want to bring in the schools psychologist, psychiatrist – whatever. I don't really know what I think about that. But just imagine what Cathy would say to it. God, she's the one who needs the bloody shrink, not Bobby. And listen Gerry, she doesn't even know I've been to the school – and without her. Can you imagine what will happen when she finds that out? No, I think I'm going to have to get Bobby out of it somehow and I don't know what will happen then. Somehow I'm going to have to stay close to Dora too. Oh I don't know; it's messy, complicated. Can't see my way through it at present. But anyway that's the situation, so if and when Cathy finds out … well that will probably be the end of our marriage. And you know what? I don't give a shit.'

Gerry took a deep breath. 'Well, old son, all I can do is to wish you the best of luck – and keep on propping the bar up with you.'

CHAPTER 17

Aidan dreaded preparations for special occasions in the family. He supposed that in any family they might be likely to generate some stress – will we get everything ready in time? Have we forgotten anything? Hurry up, it's getting late! But in his family, it was something special. Cathy was always on a particularly short fuse, which the most trifling setback would be likely to ignite. On such occasions – the children's parties, holidays – events whose purpose was generally to increase the sum of family happiness, Cathy invariably managed by her near hysteria to reduce her family to gibbering misery which could poison whole days. Christmas, the season of goodwill to all men; the family time, was particularly hazardous. It would have been bad enough if spent at home and no one else involved. But add in the prospect of transporting it, presents and all, across the bleakness of the Pennines on a winter's afternoon to be guests in someone else's home and you had a situation explosive beyond reason.

Determined to remove as many of the lurking dangers as possible, Aidan had thought ahead. The night before Christmas Eve, which was their appointed travelling day, he had got together with Bobby and Dora and helped them to pack. They had each made a list, which

Aidan had checked with them and double-checked. All items were laid out on their beds and checked again as they were packed away into their bags. Aidan was made to leave the room as his daughters wrapped and packed the presents they had bought with their saved pocket money. All they needed to remember on the morrow would be their toothbrushes.

After he had seen them into bed, Dora first, Bobby later, he co-operated with Cathy, wrapping the presents for their children. It was an occasion even now, in the parlous state of their relationship, for tender reflection; an occasion with a history – and they both managed to smile a little. Then they packed their own necessities for the three-day stay.

On the morning of the next day, Aidan was awake, up, dressed and breakfasted early, before any of his family. He went out into the garden and stood for a while immobile, looking at the sky and the bare trees, holding his breath, for fear of violating the silence. It was a perfect start to the day. From low in the south eastern sky, the winter sun cast its pale brilliance between the long blue shadows of houses and trees; the sky was a flawless blue, arced by a single line of mare's tail cirrus. The air was cold and still. It lifted his spirits. Perhaps after all it wouldn't be too bad. If the weather was like this, he could at any rate look forward to a walk over Binsey or even up Skiddaw.

Fell walking wasn't Cathy's cup of tea, but Roger and perhaps Bella would provide congenial company. Perhaps the kids. If not, solitude would be fine. It would give him a chance to think; to bring into sharp focus the lurking memories; to fantasise a little; to foreground the suppressed excitement and anticipation that was now always there, somewhere just below the level of consciousness. It reminded him of another three weeks, long ago. It was like when, as an eleven year old, with the eleven-plus under his belt, his Uncle Sam had taken him to a local bike factory to buy him his first new bike – not just any bike you could buy off the shelf, but one to be put together according to his own exact specification. It was to be ready in three weeks. Three weeks! It seemed so long. It was three weeks in which that same feeling of warm expectation underlay every detail of his life and was ever there to console him in its vicissitudes.

When his daughters had breakfasted, Aidan ensured that they were well out of the firing line, suggesting to Bobby that she go and see Mrs Cunningham and take Banjo out for his walk, and that Dora should go and play with her friend Klara, up the road and whose Christmas, because her family was Scandinavian, somehow didn't quite synchronise with her own. Cathy's initial response was indignation that they should not be around to 'pull their weight' and help 'to get things done' – more cynically translated by Aidan as 'Bobby should not be around to be shouted at and bullied.' Furthermore, he had had the temerity to send them off without consulting her.

'They did all they needed to last night,' Aidan said, he left her muttering in the kitchen while he went to the garage and backed the car on to the drive, to check the tyres, the oil and the windscreen washers and make sure it was prepared for the journey.

So it was that on the morning of Christmas Eve, having satisfied himself that all was in order with the car, Aidan began the packing of it. It was a task he really quite enjoyed. It was something to do with organising disparate forms into a given amount of space. (Or so Aidan rationalised it to himself, rejecting the idea that he was essentially a tidy, organising person, on the grounds that that did not chime well with his, perhaps rather dated, self-image as an artist.) Also, it helped to justify the recent extravagance of getting rid of the Austin 1100 and going in for something bigger. He could now congratulate himself on acquiring a car with vastly more luggage space. It was pure utility, of course, he would argue. But he really liked his car – a Renault 16 TX. It was French. It was distinctive. It was eccentric. It somehow was the right kind of car for an artist. He had wanted one since they first came out a year or two ago. He loved the long, sloping bonnet. Its lean look. The way the back swept down in a single flattened curve. No boot. The whole of the back was hinged at the top and opened wide to expose the interior, its large luggage space and its big, comfortable seats – the front ones reclining, the back ones folding flat for special loads – good for carrying stuff from the do-it-yourself store.

He loved the oddness of the gear change sticking out of the left-hand side of the steering column; the handbrake you pulled out from under the dash, and twisted to release; the rev counter. Almost above all, he loved the electrically operated windows and sunroof. Such luxury he had never known and could not have afforded new. Fortuitously – for Aidan, at any rate – a house painter he knew had over-extended his finances and needed to realise capital quickly, and Aidan, who happened to be there at the right time, was the beneficiary. He was the owner of a nearly new, blue Renault 16 TX. As he made his preparations, he wished that his other desires might be so felicitously granted. He doubted they would.

Thus reflecting, he opened the tailgate and set about loading the luggage into the yawning back of the car. Cases, bags, some boxes of gaudily wrapped presents. Coats, hats, scarves, boots, waterproofs; everything necessary for a three-week visit lasting three days. He was feeling relieved that so far, largely because of his anticipation, the preparations had gone untypically smoothly. No eruptions of anger, no recriminations. The car packed, the children back home, they had a light lunch, washed up, locked up and embarked. The children in the back, Cathy in the front, all settled comfortably. Aidan lowered himself into his big luxurious seat, enjoying the way the car's soft springing yielded under his weight. After a last look round, he reversed the Renault out of the drive and pointed it at Cumberland.

The pristine morning had by now given way to a milkier light as the sun withdrew behind a delicate veil of thin, high cloud. Looking at it, Aidan feared he might be disappointed in his hope for good weather. As he took the road to Scotch Corner, Bobby and Dora, subdued at first, being only too aware of the delicate balance between tranquillity and mayhem, gradually began to catch some of the excitement of Christmas. Aidan, sighting them briefly in the mirror was happy to see Bobby smiling and animated, chatting and giggling with her younger sister. It gave him hope. He could see peripherally, the profile of the woman who was their mother, his wife, as she sat, silent, looking straight ahead through the windscreen. He wondered what was in her mind, as he nursed his thoughts of Louise.

He swallowed hard and felt a sudden upsurge of guilt as he contemplated the momentous thing he had done. Whatever the state of their relationship now, he had never before concealed anything from Cathy – well anything of any importance – nothing more than the actual number of pints he had despatched on his boys' night out. Really, there had never been anything of importance to conceal. He looked sideways at her again, thinking how innocent she looked; how ordinary. How ordinary they all must look. Just an ordinary family off to spend Christmas with relatives. Aidan felt stirrings of remorse. My God, he was beginning to feel sorry for her, for what he was doing to her. For the betrayal. He became lost in the present. They were all right, weren't they – him and his family? His wife of twenty years here beside him and their two daughters behind? Did she – did they – deserve what he was doing to them? There could be a future, couldn't there?

Yet as he drove, it felt as though the car were full of some explosive mixture, ready to ignite at the touch of a spark – like that suspenseful film where some guys had to drive a lorry load of nitro glycerine across perilous mountain passes. Damn it! They weren't an ordinary family. They were a time bomb and he wondered if they would get to the end of their journey before they blew up.

Yet again he tried to remember why he had married her. He supposed he must have loved her. Perhaps he still did love her. But much of the time he didn't much like her. He didn't like the kind of person she was. He didn't like the way she behaved, her attitudes to so many things. Can you love but not like? Yet again he tried to remember the good in their marriage, for there must have been some – there must have been a good deal of good or it would not have survived all these years. Why was it now so difficult to remember any? Why was so much of the past disvalued by the present?

He knew quite soon after the marriage, that he had wed a supremely bad-tempered woman. Bad-tempered. Not hot-tempered. Not quick-tempered. Hot-tempered and quick- tempered seemed to contain within themselves a degree of mitigation – a bit trigger-happy, but generally okay. But there was nothing good to be said about bad-tempered. It just seemed to signify a miserable presumption of ill will that the deployer sees no reason under any circumstances to withhold or disguise. A pervasive dissatisfaction with so many trifling details of ordinary daily life, threatening explosion at the slightest mishandling; a lurking potential for psychological violence; the ultimate in destructive self-expression. But he had learned to cope with this. It was not that he had knuckled down and allowed himself to become henpecked – well he didn't think so. He was easy-going himself and had learned to bend with the wind; water off a duck's back – that sort of thing. He later came to see that this had probably been a mistake, wished he had long ago taken a firmer control of things and much more clearly defined the unacceptable. He could have done, for as he had later realised, she needed him much more than he needed her, though she herself did not yet know that.

Anyway, once having learned to conceal his thoughts, to avoid controversy and keep his nose clean, he found married life acceptable. In the early years they had enjoyed happy times. They had shared the building of a home. They had saved for furniture and had been able to afford a motorbike and sidecar, which gave them a sort of crude mobility. They'd enjoyed making a garden, weekly trips to the cinema in Horsham, spare, sun-bright winter Saturdays at Brighton and madrigals once a week at the local Evening Institute.

They'd shared a wish for children and a few years into their marriage, judging it time to start breeding, contraception was abandoned and as a consequence of a calculated act of procreation,

Roberta arrived. Pity, such an old-fashioned name, the Sister had said. Aidan thought Roberta was the most marvellous thing that had ever happened in his life. On his first visit to the maternity ward, his eyes drawn first to Cathy, he did not immediately see the baby. Then he noticed the cot at the foot of the bed. It contained a tiny but perfect human being; not red and hairy; not the small chimpanzee he had expected, but a tiny, beautiful human being, miniature in every respect, but perfect and exquisite. Yes, he thought it the most marvellous thing that had ever happened to him. Cathy thought that too, at the time.

They thought two years was the right time to wait; the children would be close enough together to provide mutual companionship. So once again Cathy discarded her cap and they made love with a new sense of freedom and awaited the missed period, the tender nipples, nausea in the morning. But nothing happened. It happened again every month for the next six years. They often thought wryly of their contemporaries John and Kirsty. She had conceived without meaning to; without actually enjoying the pleasure of intercourse. They were just mucking about, as John said. They had to get married for such was the climate of the time.

At first Aidan and Cathy tried vigorously and ingeniously to bring his sperm into happy conjunction with her ovum by all normal processes. To no avail. So it became a matter of intercourse by the temperature chart. When this achieved nothing but turning the whole thing into a chore, they were turned over to a psychiatrist. Again, nothing. Aidan even took to wearing boxer shorts, when Cathy, in one of the magazines she bought in the hope of finding some new ideas, read that tight underpants could cause partial sterility.

Eventually they had given up and resigned themselves to being a one-child family. Cathy had re-established herself in her teaching career. Intercourse, sans cap, sans condom, became an occasional recreational activity. Then it happened. The missed period. Dora was on her way.

At the time the new baby was due, Bobby was admitted to the children's ward with suspected appendicitis. Along several corridors and up several staircases, her sister's birth was attended by certain complications which prolonged the confinement. Visiting was only allowed twice a week on the children's ward so Bobby did not know for some days that the new sister she longed for had arrived. Aidan was as ecstatic about the new baby as he had been about his first, whom, save for the colour of her hair – she was fair – she closely resembled. He thought it profoundly sad that Bobby could not see her sister for she had anticipated her arrival with mounting excitement. He made a drawing of the sleeping child to show her on his next visit; she longed to see and hold the baby.

This had happened at the beginning of the autumn term, the beginning of the academic year, an important and busy time for the college. Aidan was normally good at keeping his domestic life separate from his professional one. Whatever stresses he endured at home he could usually shrug off, as he became engrossed in his work. But at this time, with all his family in hospital he found it impossible to keep the two spheres apart. He found life worrying and exhausting. In retrospect, he saw this period as the time when the tightly laid strands of his life began subtly and inexorably to unravel.

They had turned west at Scotch Corner to take the A66, and the weather seemed to be adapting to Aidan's more sombre mood. The sun had seemed for a while to struggle with the lowering cloud layer, until its disc, becoming gradually more blurred, eventually dissolved into a pallid stain in the thickening grey stratus, before disappearing without trace. By the time they were approaching Bowes, Aidan had to switch on the wipers to deal with a fine rain that was drizzling the windscreen. He turned on the headlights and focused his attention on the road ahead as it snaked towards the horizon – now a dark purple blur, melding the moors and the sky into a threatening continuum.

Bobby and Dora having expended their initial excitement had settled down into quieter mode; Dora had taken out her book and was quickly engrossed, while Bobby was gazing, unseeing, it seemed, out of the right-hand window, lost in thought. The rain had intensified. Aidan was staring intently ahead through the arc of cleared windscreen as the Renault drew nearer to an articulated lorry, whose rear lights flushed with red the spray thrown up by its cluster of wheels. There were not many safe overtaking places on this stretch of the A66. Concentrate. Cathy was peering expectantly through the passenger's window, now slightly opacified by the rain.

'Look, Bobby,' she suddenly said, pointing out of her window 'Dotheboys Hall!' Bobby was just getting into Dickens at school and Cathy, thorough-going teacher that she was, could never resist an educative opportunity.

'Wha … what?' said Bobby, suddenly aroused from her reverie.

'Great Expectations … Dickens … look, over there. That building. It was what Dickens based Dotheboys Hall on.' She tapped impatiently on the window. Bobby swivelled herself round, trying to focus through the streaming window.

'What … where?'

Cathy clicked her tongue impatiently. 'Oh never mind. We're past it now. You're just too slow aren't you – as usual? It's no wonder you aren't getting anywhere.' She turned her back. 'Stupid …' she added, half under her breath.

'I heard that,' shouted Bobby, furious. 'I'm not stupid. I was thinking and I don't care about your stupid Dothingy's Hall.'

'Of course you don't … you don't care about anything, do you?'

Dora had by now brought her feet up on the seat, balanced her book on her crossed legs, grimly focused her attention on it and, in a well-practised strategy, placed her hands over her ears.

Before Bobby could reply, Aidan, his face tense with fury, but his eyes fixed immovably on the road ahead, intervened.

'Bobby! Don't. Not another word.' There was a lay-by. It was almost too late to stop. But Aidan with a swift glance in the mirror, indicated left and braked fiercely. The Renault's nose dipped and the tyres squealed as he flung the car into the lay-by, brought it to a halt and, in an angry gesture, wrenched on the handbrake. The children, tumbled to one side of the car, let out little squeals of fear, Cathy turned towards him in shock and indignation. As she opened her mouth to speak, Aidan put his fist on the horn button, and held it, howling its two notes for fully thirty seconds. When he released it, the only sounds were the faint purr of the idling engine, the wind buffeting the car and the slashing of the rain against the windows.

Then, his eyes still focused ahead, grim-faced, he said to Cathy, slowly and deliberately, 'If you speak to her like that again, I swear I'm going to turn round at the first lay-by and head for home.' Cathy opened her mouth to reply, but before she could put her words together he turned his head and penetrated her with his eyes. He said, in cold fury, 'Look at me. I MEAN IT.'

She thought better of it and tossing a look of contempt at Bobby, tightened her lips, shrugged and turned away from Aidan towards the window. He turned his head towards his cowering daughters, in the back seats, trying, without words, to reassure them. Then he turned to the front again and, switching off the engine, said, 'Now, we will have two minutes of silence in which to reflect on the meaning of Christmas.'

275

Cathy turned to him in outrage, but before she could speak, Aidan enunciated again, this time in an ominous whisper through his clenched teeth, 'I MEAN IT.'

Two minutes later, he started up the engine, waited while a train of cars sped past, tyres swishing and pulled out once more on to the streaming road, his guilt about Louise now gone. In whatever way it happened, his marriage to Cathy was over.

Irethwaite hardly qualified as a village. It was the place where two ancient farms met by a river, their buildings and yards, on either side of a narrow road, formed the nucleus of the settlement. Over the years – perhaps two centuries – a ragtaggle of stone, slate-roofed cottages accrued, like a burgeoning mushroom colony in slow motion. At some stage in the nineteenth century it had acquired a tiny Methodist Chapel, whose wheezy harmonium was still to be heard of a Sunday accompanying the handful of souls who still attended its austere rituals. Perhaps the presence of early Methodism accounted for the absence of a pub – a deficit which would have ruled Irethwaite out as a possible place to live for Aidan – much though he appreciated its other qualities. In a large house, walled and set back from the road amid tall pines, lived a revered music teacher, who, from time to time was host to an eminent string quartet seeking respite from the ardours of their world tours in the tranquillity of this remote place. A little beyond that was a small village shop and post office.

The house where Isobel and Roger lived was a pair of farm buildings, sensitively converted into a comfortable dwelling, with views over Bassenthwaite and Skiddaw. When Roger had been appointed Head of Sculpture in the John Dobson College of Art in Carlisle, he and Bella had spent weeks combing the Northern Lakes area, looking for just the right spot. It had to be quiet; it had to have a splendid view, a garden big enough to provide self-sufficiency in vegetables, it had to have out-buildings enough to satisfy a working sculptor's needs. 'The Shippen' had all of these. Though it was really more than they could afford at the time, they took a chance and committed all their current resources to it; and a good deal of their future expectations. They had never regretted it and it was not too many years before they were wholly absorbed into the village community, full participants in its informal networks of barter and information exchange.

For Roger, the twenty-mile commute to his daily work was small penalty for the advantages they enjoyed. The weather sometimes posed a problem in winter, but seldom more than his Land Rover could cope with. Anyway, the vacations were generous and afforded plenty of time for him to pursue his own creative ends.

Isobel, like her brother and sister had trained for teaching. It had been something of a triumph of working-class prudence and ambition that all three of the Trimble's children should have attended grammar school and been given this nudge up the social scale. For

277

Harry Trimble's income, even as a foreman caulker at the shipyard, was not great. Furthermore, the Trimbles had by sheer financial diligence, been able to break out of the stereotypical working-class/council house dependency and get a mortgage on a modest but well-built semi-detached house at one end of a tree-lined avenue (a circumstance which afforded Cathy much pride).

Isobel, Cathy's younger sister, had chosen to go to a domestic science college. Her first post was in a girls' grammar school where she taught for a number of years. After her marriage to Roger, since no children came along, there was no good reason to give up, so she continued in her career. Following Roger's new appointment, moving into The Shippen, she had been content at first to play the part of country housewife; to tend the vegetable garden, bottle fruit, and skin the rabbits that were not infrequently left on her kitchen doorstep. But eventually she began to miss the more intensive social contacts of the staffroom and took a part-time post in a secondary school in Cockerbeck, commuting the eight miles in her battered Morris Minor.

Had they had children, the pattern of their lives would have been different. But despite their earnest wish, their best endeavours and current best medical practice, their marriage was not blessed – at least with children. They did not see their nieces that often, but when they did, perhaps by way of compensation, they lavished much affection upon them – a feeling happily reciprocated by the children.

When the Renault, streaming wet and mud-bespattered, arrived, the rain had stopped, leaving behind it a mild, clammy stillness trapped beneath the dense blanket of cloud. Skiddaw was nowhere in sight. As the car disgorged its passengers, Aidan, catching Bella's eye as they embraced, could see she immediately realised all was not well. Roger, a shade less observant, bulldozed into the scene, emanating avuncular Christmas jollity, kissed Cathy, crushed his nieces in a communal embrace, shook Aidan's hand while gripping him by the shoulder and scooped them all indoors before returning to help Aidan with the luggage. Next, he dealt with the matter of hot toddy and mulled wine in the glow and warmth of a crackling log fire, next to the Christmas tree winking its coloured lights.

It was Roger's dedicated good humour towards his nieces and his generosity with the alcohol that allowed the day to progress to a relatively tranquil end. Aidan and Cathy spoke little to each other – only when it was unavoidable.

CHAPTER 18

Christmas afternoon and Aidan could feel the day slipping into post-prandial torpor. He was beginning to feel like the prostrate Gulliver, helplessly immobilised by bonds he couldn't see. He thought he must make a break for it before the onset of The Wizard of Oz; away from the litter of orange peel, fractured nutshells and discarded chocolate wrappings, away from the debilitating heat of that rustling fire. He was disappointed that the weather had none of the cold, clear brilliance that could make a Lakeland winter so invigoratingly beautiful, but he knew that the unremitting, damp monochrome he could see in the squares of the window panes had its austere attractions – in small amounts, at any rate.

'Any one fancy a walk?' He asked the question generally. Cathy glanced up momentarily from the book on the archaeology of the Roman Wall that had been his present to her, sighed impatiently at the preposterousness of the suggestion and returned to her book without saying anything. His daughters looked at each other; pulling faces and then at him, pityingly.

'No thanks, Dad,' said Dora shuddering ostentatiously at the very idea, 'we're going to watch the film.' Roger, already nodding off over the bumper holiday crossword, grunted what was probably dissent.

Bella, though, placing the final segment of a satsuma in her mouth and wiping her fingers on her discarded paper hat, looked up from the magazine spread across her knees.

'Mmm,' she said, swallowing and tossing the paper hat on to the fire, 'a good idea. Otherwise I'm going to get hooked on The Wizard of Oz for the seventh time. It's not raining, is it?' Aidan had crossed over to the window and was peering out at the sodden pastures that rose towards the lower slopes of Skiddaw, dissolving upwards into the ragged curtain of cloud.

'No,' he said, 'not quite.'

Bella stood up and stretched. 'Come on,' she said encouragingly, 'anyone else for a walk? It's lovely out there. It'll put roses into your cheeks.'

'We don't want roses,' said Bobby, 'we want to be pasty and warm, don't we, Dora?' She nudged her sister with an elbow and Dora agreed.

Aidan laughed, delighted to see a smile on Bobby's face, delighted at the rapport between his daughters. 'Huh! Lethargic lot. You don't know what you're missing.'

'Oh yes we do,' intoned Bobby and Dora in unison, giggling.

'Oh well, I suppose ...'

Cathy looked up from her book and scowled disapproval.

Once outside, Bella looked round at the landscape then up into the clouds and as they strode off, she said, with the confidence of one who knows her weather, 'It won't rain – we'll be okay, but with this cloud, we'll have to stick with the roads and the lower paths.'

'Anyway,' said Aidan, 'we'll only have a couple of hours before it gets dark.' He looked sideways at Bella and smiled. 'It's nice to see you again,' he said, engaging her eyes affectionately.

The smile she returned was tinged with wistfulness. She turned her head to look at him, her blue eyes crinkling a little at the corners. A tumble of her long blonde hair had escaped from under her hat, swirling on to her red scarf. The years had not diminished her attractiveness. 'Likewise,' she said.

They had a history, she and Aidan. She was two years younger than Cathy, but Aidan had known her longer. When she was fifteen and he seventeen, for perhaps a year, they had, in the inchoate flux of adolescence, enjoyed more than a few tender encounters. He especially remembered winter Saturday nights, after the cinema; the gang, all exuberant; the brisk walk along the promenade. The exhilaration of the biting wind off the sea; the sweeping beam from the lighthouse skimming the curling tops of the waves as they raced in one behind another to crash onto the beach in an explosion of foam; the sizzling retreat of the sea through the shingle before the next onslaught. Then came the – almost arbitrary – pairing up, to race for the shelter, to get there first to claim with your partner the dark corner not reached by the measured probing of the lighthouse beam. Sometimes Aidan was unlucky, but if he could manage it, Bella was the one he sought. And how vividly could he recollect it. Cold cheek against cold cheek. The kisses – lips at first cool and crisp from the Siberian wind – softening into warm, moist pliability; the electric touch of tongues tentatively contacting. Then the groping, exploring, among heavy winter clothing. Such innocently wonderful nights they had been. In the intervening years, he had often reproached himself with the thought that he had chosen – if indeed the choice had ever been his – the wrong sister. He knew that Bella was happy with Roger, but he also knew she still harboured tender thoughts towards him.

As they set out along the road, they chatted cheerfully. They decided to head north towards Binsey, on a round walk of about four miles – as much, Bella reckoned, as they could manage before it started getting dark. Aidan felt she was as glad as he was at having made the effort to break free of the enervating atmosphere of that Christmas afternoon. He felt that she too revelled in the small excitement of their shared memories given renewed life in this reunion – a reunion, perhaps for the best, which would be all too brief. So they talked of the events of the past year; of Bella's work at school, her involvement in the village; of Aidan's forthcoming exhibition; of Roger's latest commission; of the kids.

They presently turned off the road, through a gate and took the path across a field. The stile in the wall they came to had disintegrated into an insecure pile of rocks and rubble. Aidan scrambled over it first, turning to extend a steadying hand to his sister-in-law. She took it and, descending beside him, did not let it go, but looking into his eyes, reached for the other one. Holding both his hands, she squared up to him, holding his gaze, suddenly serious.

'Aidan,' she said, 'something's wrong, isn't it? Well ... tell me to mind my own business if you like ... but the atmosphere is ... um ... uncomfortable, I suppose you could call it, and ...' She drifted off into silence, but Aidan was suddenly hit, as if by a hammer blow to the guts. Within him erupted all the anguish of his repressed turmoil. He was at once unable to speak for fear of disintegrating into tears and clasped Bella to himself in a fierce embrace. She put her arms around him and rocked soothingly.

They stood for silent moments, wrapped in each other's arms, Aidan looking unseeingly over her head into the distance, trying to keep control. He liked to think of himself as a cool, laid-back individual and he believed – or at any rate hoped – that this was how others saw him. He knew that his life was increasingly becoming a dangerous emotional cocktail of anger, anxiety and sexual passion, but he believed he could cope with it all, pending the solution which he was confident must sometime emerge, doing all the things he was supposed to do, without any of it showing. But somehow, Bella had pressed a button that had come perilously close to releasing the full gamut of his feelings. He delayed another moment, determinedly composing himself, then, gently prising himself free, stood with his hands on Bella's hips, looking into her eyes. She smiled at him uncertainly, waiting.

'What's wrong is your bloody sister.' Bella's brow creased a little. She waited for him to continue.

'If I can't change things somehow or change her somehow, she's going to destroy Bobby. You must have noticed the tension between them. It's there all the time. Haven't you seen how Cathy's eye follows Bobby everywhere, as though daring her to put a foot wrong. You can see the malice in her expression every time Bobby comes into her range of vision. She kills her with her expression ... I just don't know ... I just don't know ...'

Bella shook her head. 'Well ... yes. I have been noticing something ... that was why I just had to mention it. I know we don't see you very often, but it has struck me the last few times we've been together that she does seem to pick on Bobby kind of, well, making a lot of fuss about trivialities ... But she was always like that when we were kids. Somehow she was always managing to get someone worked up into a tizzy. We were always having rows at home and it usually started with her ... the way she'd treat people. Oh we get on okay now, of course, but I was really glad when she went away to college. We had a bit of peace in the home then. And you know Aidan, I thought being married to you might change her. But it hasn't, has it? On this visit it's been particularly noticeable. I can see now that it's got you somewhere near the end of your tether.'

She reached with both hands to Aidan's face, drew it towards her and placed a gentle kiss on his cheek.

'Oh God, don't do tender things to me or I shall burst into tears.'

'Poor Aidan … my poor Aidan,' she said softly, taking him by the hand again. 'Look, let's carry on walking. You can keep on talking. I'll listen …'

They set out along the path, but soon abandoned it to its climb, as it disappeared into the mist, upwards towards the summit. Instead, they branched off along a bridle path, running level not far below the cloud, which hung like a layer of soggy blotting paper, seeming to be sucking the landscape up into its underbelly. This was easy going and Bella held on to Aidan's hand as they walked. He told her of the incident on the journey.

'Oh God,' Bella said. 'Sounds just like her. Just the sort of thing she used to do. But, I mean, she used to adore Bobby when she was younger didn't she? How did it happen? When? What went wrong?'

'Well, looking back, I can see how it happened … I mean, I can sort of trace a process, a history, but I'm buggered if I can explain it. You know what Bobby's like. She's not stupid. But she's not confident or outgoing and she tends to be a bit of a dreamer … not too good on practicalities. Most of the friends she manages to make seem to be in some ways oddballs. Maybe that makes her an oddball too – in the eyes of the other kids, at least. Well it didn't seem to matter too much until Dora was born. Then Bobby's inefficiency started to have practical consequences and inefficiency is something Cathy can't stand. You know, Bella, there's this expression, "Doesn't suffer fools gladly." It's generally used approvingly, but I hate it. It's an expression of self-aggrandisement, really and maybe Cathy wouldn't necessarily apply it to herself – but it's the expression that comes to my mind when I see how she behaves towards Bobby. But for Christ's sake, Bobby isn't a fool – and anyway, who isn't foolish sometimes … I mean how could you possibly apply that principle to a child? I've more than once heard her refer to Bobby as "that fool".'

They stopped to negotiate a sagging gate held shut by a chain. It took the two of them to haul the collapsing structure back into place. Aidan continued. Bella squeezed his hand comfortingly as they set off again along the track.

'And as Dora has grown up, it's just got gradually worse … I mean as the differences between them have become more obvious. You can tell; Dora's turning out to be everything Cathy could want her to be – but Bobby's a gross disappointment to her – and sure as hell she's doing nothing to conceal her disappointment.'

'How do you mean?' asked Bella. 'In what way?'

'Oh in all sorts of ways, all sorts of ways,' Aidan replied. 'Look, Cathy was a devoted and enthusiastic guide wasn't she … right up to the time she left to go to college? She got Bobby to join when she was old enough, but Bobby hated it and after lots of rows, she eventually refused to go. Cathy was furious and it's left a lingering sore that keeps getting inflamed. But, on the other hand, you see, Dora's a Brownie and really enjoys it. So Cathy's able to help her – share things with her – and maybe she's reliving some of her past.'

'It's the same with music. Dora's doing well at the violin, does her practice because she enjoys music; in the school orchestra. Cathy can be tearfully proud of her when she plays in the school concert. But Bobby's enthusiasm for the piano soon wore off. Getting her to practice became too much like hard work. Amid bitter recriminations from Cathy, we let her give up. Well, I was a bit pissed off too but I wasn't going to wreck Bobby's life because she wouldn't do her piano practice. But Cathy had been thwarted again and she couldn't let that go. And so it goes on. Cathy's marked Bobby down as a hopeless loser – and she obviously can't love a loser, so she misses no opportunity to rub it in. Well you can imagine what it has done to Bobby's already minimal self-confidence. She is making Bobby's life hell … utter misery – and she absolutely refuses to admit that there's anything wrong.'

He was suddenly silent, as though emotionally exhausted by the effort of recreating the intractable horrors of the situation. There was no sound save the clatter and slither of their boots on the wet stones of the path. Bella was still gripping his hand in a desperate gesture of reassurance. They continued walking in silence. Bella, her brow furrowed, seeming to need time to take it all in, to think what she could possibly say or do that would be helpful.

Then Aidan said, 'Bella, sorry to have laid all this on you.' He looked at her and smiled wryly. 'But you did ask.'

'Aidan,' she said, 'it makes me so angry. When I think of how much we wanted a child and couldn't ... it just seems unbearable that she should be abusing her child ... because that's what it is, isn't it, abuse?'

'It's psychological warfare. Inflicted by a mother on a child,'

The bridle path had now reached a point where it crossed the narrow road curving around the southern slopes of Binsey. It was where they would turn west along that road for half a mile, before taking the path south on the homeward leg. Aidan unhooked the chain on the gate and dragged it open for his sister-in-law, then followed her through. He turned to secure it again, struggling to close the gap between the recalcitrant gate and its post. Bella added her strength to the task and, the chain connected, they paused, leaning on the gate, arms affectionately around each other.

To the southwest, the soft slate ceiling of cloud terminated in a sharp, slightly tilted line above a strip of salmon-pink sky, which touched slopes of Sale Fell with its luminosity and the northern tip of Bassenthwaite with reflected brilliance.

As they walked back towards Irethwaite they talked about the situation, looking at every possible outcome, from the miraculous resolution in which everyone would be satisfied, to the direst disaster. Bella offered every possible help, including refuge for Bobby if that should seem necessary. As they approached The Shippen, potently aware that this tender interlude in their lives was coming to an end, they stopped again and embraced in the gathering dusk.

'Bella,' said Aidan, 'there's something else … I should …' She gazed at him, her eyebrows lifted in enquiry. He hesitated. '… Well, er … no. No, never mind, it's not important.'

She did not press him.

CHAPTER 19

Aidan had never before looked forward to a term's beginning so avidly, for never before had he been so frazzled, stressed and unhappy during a vacation. And never before had he begun a term in excited anticipation of reunion with a new lover – or, for that matter, any lover. Fortunately, from his point of view, school holidays were two weeks shorter than college vacations, so both Cathy, who this term was teaching full-time, and the children were out of his daytime milieu for the week before the students returned. He was, in consequence able to resume work in his studio and reconnect with those of his colleagues, happy to be shot of Christmas, who had also cut short their vacations. It was more than three weeks since he had seen Louise and his recollections had seemed to become increasingly unreal. He did not know if he could trust his memory. It was just the dream again, wasn't it? And yet he still carried with him a token which should have reassured him that something extraordinary had really happened. But it was like some fantastic story he distantly remembered from childhood, where a boy acquired a magic ship, which would carry him through space and time. Other children did not believe this, so he brought back something, Aidan couldn't now remember what, from some remote age, as proof. Still, however, they wouldn't believe him, though the evidence was tangibly there, in his normal life, the boy eventually stopped believing in it himself and when that happened, the magic no longer worked. So, notwithstanding, the tangible evidence, Aidan had to fight against disbelief. How he wished he had, despite the difficulties, tried to make some kind of arrangement to stay in touch with Louise.

As the week progressed, his excitement and agitation mounted and his mood swung between exhilaration and dejection. He tried to think, where would he see her? When? How would she be? Would there be recognition in her eye, in her smile, of the thing that had happened between them in his room that night a month ago? Perhaps she would avoid him until inevitably the timetable brought them together as student and teacher, perhaps there would be nothing more. Perhaps it would be as if it had never happened.

He was forty-five and he was experiencing the emotional turmoil of a teenager. He remembered again the sweet anguish of that hot summer's day towards the end of his first year at art school. He had just been told he had won the Robin Darwin Prize for life drawing. A coach was chuntering on the forecourt, waiting for its cargo of his fellow students. It was the day of the Art Society's summer trip and they were destined for Warkworth Castle. In the cheerful crushing and jostling along the aisle of the bus, he found himself thrust into an empty seat, and as he organised himself into it, another body stumbled, laughing, in beside him. To his surprise, delight and confusion, it turned out to be Lissa Dennison, a third-year student of some renown; a red-headed stunner – the very archetype of Pre-Raphaelite beauty – he'd so often admired from afar, though never before spoken to her. She apologised for landing on him, but did not, as he immediately supposed she would, get up to find a seat with her friends, but stood up to put her large shoulder-bag on the overhead rack and carefully arranging her New Look skirt, made herself comfortable beside him, looked at him and smiled.

'Hello,' she said. 'You're Aidan, aren't you?' How he was flattered that she knew his name – she actually knew his name! They spent the whole of that glorious day together, in happy, tender communion, strolling across the lawns, exploring the ruins, lunching in the pub, later paddling in the sea – a couple, lovers, among their friends. But, Aidan knew, lovers for a day. It was only a dream. It could only be a dream. Travelling back as the day gracefully died, their talk died too and she let her head fall upon his shoulder. He slid his arm about her and she murmured softly as her red hair spilt about his neck. He kissed her forehead and held her hand. Aidan wanted that journey never to end, for it was a foretaste of heaven. But it did. Disembarking from the coach, they embraced tenderly for a while and kissed. Then she thanked him for a lovely day and they parted.

The next day, he saw her distantly, but had not the courage to approach her. It did not seem possible that the dream could continue into the normal world. Nor did she approach him. So he learned to live with his longing and it gradually sank into memory, among his other precious recollections. But in later years, he sometimes wondered ... and regretted his timidity.

But no. This was different. Wasn't it? But my God, suppose she didn't come back? Suppose that after a term at Swaleborough, returning to the south, she'd decided it was all a big mistake? Suppose she met someone over Christmas – at a party, like the department party. Dim lights, smoochy music ... in a clinch with someone ... like she'd been with Mark. God, anything could have happened. Someone, maybe someone she already knew, someone from her own town – from that design studio in London ... rich, young, handsome, sophisticated, street-wise.

Oh God, he didn't stand a chance, did he? Married, middle-aged, frustrated, care-worn. But it had happened; dammit it had. It wasn't just a sudden impulsive act of mutual abandon under the influence of atmosphere and alcohol. It was the outcome of a developing process whose origins went back to that occasion in the park. Their relationship had been founded then. He had experienced its development. He had fostered its development – and so had she. He knew she had. So he tormented himself, even when most of his consciousness was engaged with judgements about colour, tone, line mass, still these thoughts churned endlessly at the periphery of his mind. Mornings and evenings, he distractedly performed the duties of father and husband in a desperately ailing family, striving to sustain some kind of peace.

He did not see her the first day of term. He found as many as possible reasons to move about the college as he sensibly could. To the senior common room for coffee, of course. Quite unnecessary visits to the bursar, to the library, to consult the engineer. His eyes darting, skimming, probing groups of students; rooms, corridors, wherever she might possibly be. Then reluctantly, home, lingeringly past the house where she lodged, the porch where they had prolonged that last embrace and finally said goodbye. But she was nowhere. The second day was the same. She had not come back. He knew it and despaired.

She reinserted herself into Aidan's life in a way which suggested she had uncertainties of her own. Aidan had begun the third day of term in a state of desperate unhappiness. He was fighting the conviction that she had indeed not come back and that his dream was over. He set out for the college on the route that took him past her digs, in the remote hope that he would see her emerge in front of him, that at least he would know that she had returned. But it did not happen. On arriving at the college, he went directly to the Art Department. As he mounted the steps to the door, he could see Gerry and Henry through the basement window in the Sculpture Department. They seemed deeply engrossed in something – he couldn't tell what. No students were timetabled for that morning and he remembered that Barbara would be at a Board of Studies Meeting in Durham. He met one of the cleaners in the entrance hall, a mop and bucket at the end of one arm, a large black plastic bag of rubbish in the other. Having completed her early morning stint in the department, she was off for her tea break.

'Morning Mr Hamilton,' she said cheerily, 'nice day.'

'Morning Mrs Price. A bit cold though,' Aidan responded automatically.

She exited through the front door, humming to herself. Now the department seemed deserted as he headed for his room. On the way, while passing the door of the room that housed the small department library, he heard the slight grating of a chair leg on the wooden floor. Surprised, he pushed the door open and took a step inside.

What he saw first was her legs, shapely, the calf-length blue jeans, crossed neatly under the table. Black slip-on shoes. He could not see her face. Above the table, on which her elbows rested, her hands held the open volume of Christopher Wright's Poussin Paintings: A Catalogue Raisonné, its dark-blue cover with the title in white above a reproduction of The Nurture of Jupiter. It concealed most of her upper half.

Aidan's heart almost stopped. In an instant, his misery evaporated; in an instant, ecstasy. At first he did not move. He could not move. He held his breath. Slowly, ever so slowly, with the barely perceptible motion of the dawning sun rising over the horizon, her eyes appeared over the top of the book – but only her eyes, large and brown. The eyes were smiling at him, though there was uncertainty in them. He waited a moment or two more, savouring the instant. Then, still saying nothing, he slowly walked towards her and reaching into his trouser pocket, found the knickers, and, holding them delicately between finger and thumb, he dropped them down the inside of the book. She snapped the book shut on them, dropped it on the table and pushing the chair back with a horrendous screech thrust herself to her feet and into his waiting arms. Locked together, uncaring that this was a public room, for moments their tongues were too busy for speech and their coming together needed none. At length, parting, they held each other at arm's length, eyes locked, absorbing each other.

'Aidan ...' Louise said. 'Oh Aidan.'

'Louise, Louise, where have you been? I was convinced you hadn't come back.'

'Oh Aidan, there've been times when I've wondered if I should, when I've wondered if it really happened and times when I've told myself it shouldn't have happened. But I had to come back ... I couldn't not come back. For the last two days, I've been having this kind of tussle ... like, how ... where? Wondering if you ...'

He led her to his room, they talked and talked, like reunited lovers would.

Aidan told what might have been his first adulterer's lie, that evening. Yet it wasn't a lie ... just that something important had come up in college ... a meeting.

They met in his studio in the deserted department and made love ravenously on a pile of sculptor's scrim.

CHAPTER 20

The beginning of that spring term marked the time when Aidan's life split perilously in two. He found that much of his energy and ingenuity must now be expended in not so much reconciling the two parts, as ensuring as far as possible that they ran in parallel and never came into contact. He had always believed in the contrastive principle. If the entire world were blue, there would be no colour – not even blue – just monochrome. For there to be blue there had to be the other colours that weren't blue. The seminal truth for the painter. Saussure; no absolute terms – just differences. How could you know tranquillity if you had not experienced stress, happiness if you had never been sad?

His life had for many years been largely without much contrast, seemingly etiolated into a comfortable monochrome. Oh there were minor incursions of colour; variable satisfaction with the painting, with the teaching; table tennis; friends; kids. But as the situation in the home deteriorated, it had seemed to become more a spectrum of half-tone to black. But now that had changed; how it had changed. Now there was contrast. Contrast with a vengeance. Contrast in abundance. Clashing, bewildering, dizzying contrast. The excitement, the delirium of his relationship with Louise he felt as an exhilarating walk along a beautiful but precarious cliff-top path, far above the crashing destructive power of the waves below, knowing that his fate, his survival, depended on his confident sure-footedness. And luck.

Yet his two lives did impinge on one another. There was no way they could not. His most immediate problem was how to steal time from one to service the other. He resolved that whatever happened, he would not short-change the children, though Cathy was a different matter; the gulf between them seemed ever more unbridgeable and now he no longer even wanted it bridged.

Yet infidelity did not come easily to him. He had always believed in honesty, trust ... But he could not, whatever she had done, betray her lightly. He had to believe that the betrayal was a temporary necessity and that somehow, at sometime – preferably soon – truth would be restored, taking account of changed circumstances and all the elements of his life would conveniently rearrange themselves, like a Poussin landscape, into a harmonious whole.

But in his saner moments, he would reflect that he was building, on his relationship with Louise, a hypothetical future of the 'and they lived happily ever after' kind, when the reality was, he supposed, that such illicit relationships were by their very nature ephemeral. He did not know; he had never had one before. In any case, most of his moments were not sane, in this respect anyway, he had no difficulty projecting his present euphoria into an indefinitely glorious future. But to be sensible, he probably ought to avoid thinking of the future at all. He wondered if Louise did. Or was it for her something that had happened, something to be enjoyed while the going was good, after that, what the hell? He wished he could think like that. An affair. Nice, but no big deal. But he couldn't. He just could not. For him it was a bloody big deal. He was looking quite calmly at the break-up of his marriage of twenty years.

The trouble was this. He could face the break with Cathy. He wanted it. He wanted it very much. A divorce. That was the thing. He liked the idea of a divorce – though without really having much idea of what was involved. Even had it not been for Louise, he would have wanted it. To part and take Bobby with him, increasingly seemed the only solution. He was sure that he no longer loved Cathy. He wasn't sure what residual symptoms to look for. He was, he knew, used to her. But another thing he knew was that most of the time he didn't like her. Didn't like her? He hated what she had done – what she was doing to Bobby. There seemed no way out of that. For God's sake, the woman was deranged.

But what really confused the issue was the imponderables; the collateral damage attending a break. The kids; the house; finance; friends; the deep structures. It was not, after all, like falling off a sheer cliff and ending up dead. More like rolling down a steep rocky scarp, arriving at the bottom alive, but with who-knows-what injuries.

What if the break followed from the coming to light of his adultery? From what he had read of adultery, he supposed it mostly did come to light as unexplained alterations in habitual behaviour patterns. He had read – he couldn't remember where – that men cheating on their wives very often became conspicuously more attentive towards them; that their sex lives attained new heights of passion, that waning libidos were unaccountably revivified. Not so for Aidan. He had found in recent years, as his wife's bewildering and destructive rejection of her elder daughter had become more and more established, and its consequences less and less deniable, it had angered and pained him more and more; and his desire for her atrophied. It was not that she was physically undesirable, for in early middle age, her attractiveness was undiminished; he fancied he had from time to time seen her undressed by the lustful eyes of strangers – even colleagues. No, it was the conflict, the anger that reached down to his crotch, deactivating, neutralising his desires – for her, at any rate. He thought again of those who glorified the reconciliation – how it made the row almost worthwhile. He just didn't see it. For Christ's sake, he could not make love to someone he was forever rowing with – and didn't even like.

So their sexual contact had gradually diminished to the occasions, few and far between, when after just the right amount of alcohol, a modicum of affection seeped in from the past. On such an occasion, some of their status as oldest friends seemed to reassert itself over the hostility that was now virtually the norm. Under the circumstances, he did not think he would give himself away through an excess of passion.

But he might through his use of time. He wanted time for Louise. He wanted, he thought, nothing more than to be with her all the time. He wanted time so they could talk; to have brilliant conversations about classical art; to have intimate and tender conversations about their discovery of each other, to savour the details, to linger over the landmarks, to relive those key moments in their short history. Time to gossip about the college, the people in it, what they would think if they knew. Time to learn more about each other. He wanted time for them to go away to where they weren't known, so they could love each other in the open, in the broad light of day without caring who saw them – in fact rejoicing to be seen; to be seen as lovers. He wanted to be with her to make love, wherever and whenever they could. So he needed time; more unaccountable, untraceable time. And time, throughout the years of their marriage, by habit, had always been quite strictly accounted for.

In the first years, fine; they had done things together mainly – falling into a comfortable routine which satisfied them both. Pleasant things to be shared; cinema once a week; the madrigal group; church things (long before Aidan's Damascene disconversion); a Friday night at the pub with Mike, while Cathy and Shirley, at either of their homes, exchanged recipes and gossip, and talked about books.

But moving on, in time and situation, and with the arrival of children, all this had gradually changed; the balance faltered and their needs began to diverge. Aidan's gregariousness, somehow set aside in the early years, began to reassert itself. He increasingly needed the kind of fellowship without responsibility afforded by the pub. But his taste for the pub, he came to realise, was something that Cathy had acquiesced in only so long as she felt the need to please him. Once the relationship was firmly cemented into place, with marriage, mortgage, possessions, children, she seemed to think such concessions no longer necessary.

Aidan now understood that she did not share his taste for people and beer, and was not prepared to be generous in facilitating his. So he became accustomed to a compromise; a boys' night out on Friday, pre-lunch pint or two with the papers on a Sunday – but woe betide him if he kept the Yorkshire puddings waiting. Other outings which were for well-attested college events – drama, table tennis – usually terminating in the bar – were reluctantly conceded. Anything else had to be negotiated on a case by case basis and was seldom yielded with good grace.

It was not that Aidan strove to exclude Cathy from these things. She wanted no part of them and felt affronted that Aidan very much did. Indeed he went to some pains to seek out events they could share, but there were comparatively few; the occasional theatre, the rare visits of the Northern Symphonia. The fact was, she mostly wanted to stay at home in the evening and she wanted her husband to be there with her. But Aidan, in addition to his need to drink beer with his friends, now had an affair to conduct.

CHAPTER 21

'Aidan, you coming?' Gerry had pushed open the studio door and leaned through it, to call to his colleague. Aidan, stooped over a work table, tapping tacks into the back of a frame, turned his head to look over his shoulder. Gerry extruded his wrist from his sleeve and pointed at his watch. It was coffee time. Everything stopped for coffee. Aidan removed a tack from between his lips.

'Just want to finish this. I'll catch up with you later.'

'Oh, okay then.' Gerry withdrew his head and the door swung shut. Aidan heard his footsteps retreat along the corridor and up the stairs.

He continued till the last tack was driven home, then put down the hammer and turned the frame over. He scrutinised his work briefly, then propped it up against the wall. With a last glance over his shoulder, he headed for the door and along the corridor. The department was silent as he mounted the stairs to his room. She was waiting for him there.

Aidan's absence from the senior common room and the coffee trolley that morning was not especially noted, except, perhaps by Gerry, who was more than any one attuned to Aidan's habits. Aidan himself forwent coffee. This was normally unthinkable, but today it seemed a small sacrifice. Later in the day, he walked into town and bought a coffee machine, coffee, biscuits and other related items. He would have his cake and eat it.

His personal entertainment facilities thereby enhanced, his presence at coffee break became gradually more intermittent. The fleeting contact with Louise during these morning breaks, subject to the coast in the department being clear (Louise was enjoined to caution, to reconnoitre inconspicuously before slipping into his room), provided a kind of regularity in their developing relationship, frustrating in its brevity, yet exciting in its hazard. Exciting too were the chance encounters at other times in the college – she perhaps with a group of fellow students, he in perambulatory conference with a colleague – the quick engagement of eyes, the secret knowing, the suppressed lust.

In the studio, she had to be just one of his students, entitled to a fair share of his time, no more. This was business. But beneath the surface was always the secret knowing, the clandestine touch.

Longer encounters were only possible whenever Aidan could arrange unaccountable time in an evening. Any time after a play rehearsal or a table tennis match was not now spent in the bar, but in his room in the deserted Art Department, making love with Louise. He had had duplicate keys made and, after rehearsals, she would slip unobtrusively away from the group making for the bar. After a quickly despatched pint with his friends, Aidan would excuse himself and head for his room. She would be waiting for him with gin and tonics. They would make love and afterwards lie together seemingly suspended in atemporal bliss. Until Aidan, his attention suddenly drawn back to time by the ticking of the big wall clock above the door would become exasperatedly aware that in the bar now they would be calling, 'last drinks'. In ten minutes, 'Time' would be called and ten minutes after that, 'let's 'ave yer glasses please'. He knew his love-making was just as bound by the licensing laws as his drinking would have been.

'Must you go?' Louise would sigh, unwilling to release him from her embrace.

'Yes,' he would say, also sighing, 'I'm afraid I've got to.' Tactfully, or because she knew the reason and didn't want to think about it, she forbore to ask why and for similar reasons he felt he did not need to explain.

So they would make sure they were properly dressed, and taking all precautions to ensure they weren't seen, they would slip out of the building. So long as the nights were dark, he could walk her to her digs, holding her hand or with arms around each other's waists, they could enjoy a poignant parting embrace in the seclusion of the porch of her lodgings.

Aidan did not know if his friends and colleagues commented on his abrupt change of long-established habits. He only knew that making love with Louise was the most wonderful thing in the world. Drinking beer with his friends was fine, but did not in any way compare.

At first, to meet clandestinely in this way offered all the satisfaction that was necessary. The term-long development of their relationship, from the first tremor in the heart, towards the early exchange of signals, hazardous with ambiguity and the risk of misinterpretation, had for Aidan been a time of exciting uncertainty; a time of what if? and if only. It was a time when the plain impossibility of his dream told him this was just a pleasant game. He reminded himself that there had been, in the past, other students with whom his relationship seemed just a little special; where perhaps there was an empathy with the gentle irony that almost unwittingly underlay much of his talk (and offended some of the less aware as sarcasm) or where he had fired a student up with a real energy and enthusiasm that fed back into his teaching, giving a deeply shared interest. When the student was female and attractive, Aidan would not have denied the carnal stirrings he felt. But there were no irregularities there; then, a student was just a student – and he was a married man with two daughters. It was different, however, with Louise; with her there was more than this. Though fraught with every kind of uncertainty, there was something about this relationship that seemed to say, but not all that impossible.

So when the not all that impossible happened, when they had found each other; when there was no more ambiguity, no more uncertainty, no more misinterpretation, with all doubt removed, it seemed like they had scrambled into heaven. To be able to meet in private, sure now of their status as lovers, knowing their immediate purpose, was bliss enough. It was their secret, to be treasured. And for a while it sufficed.

But it was a secret that was bound to find leaks, like water under pressure finds its way past the most insignificant dry joint. It was a secret whose containment would in time become difficult to ensure; a secret in fact, whose keepers would dearly love to liberate it. Aidan, at first powerfully constrained by the fear of consequences he had not fully thought through, gradually became more lax – beset by the dangerous desire to show the world that he, a forty-five year old had captured the affection of a beautiful woman twenty years his junior. Vanity. He realised that Louise hadn't quite so strong a need to share his caution. Discovery, he thought, could do her little real harm and he supposed that among the students there might be some credit in actually having 'pulled' a lecturer.

Thus, from wishing to spend every moment of their secret time wrapped in each other's arms, a need arose for them to try out their relationship in public. It was a need to be together among other people, not to proclaim openly that they were lovers, for secrecy in that respect still seemed to Aidan to be paramount, but rather in associating with their friends, to revel in the secret couple-ness which only they knew of, in the context of the wider world. So they would now join friends and colleagues in the bar for at least part of the time after functions in college, becoming involved with a calculated insouciance, knowing that the later private coming together would be all the more tempestuous for the exercise of public restraint.

Later, these matters were further facilitated by the fact that Louise had, early in the term, managed to find a flat. It was basic; an L-shaped room, with a bed at one end, a kitchen recess and a bathroom. It was on the ground floor of a small block on the eastern, less salubrious, side of town, where they were unlikely to be recognised. This made Aidan feel more comfortable and though it meant he needed to use the car more, it admirably filled their need for a private space.

Following a rehearsal one evening, they were pressed together by an enveloping poultice of hot bodies in the unusually crowded bar, exchanging unobserved caresses of pleasing intimacy. There seemed no immediate prospect of getting a drink.

Louise looked round at the ocean of animated heads, she put her mouth to his ear and against the din, half whisper and half shout, said, 'Aidan, we're never going to get a drink here. Why don't we go out and find somewhere else?'

Aidan raised his eyebrows. 'What?' he asked uneasily, 'Go out? Go where?'

'Oh I don't know … out … out to a pub … somewhere a bit quieter … more intimate.'

Aidan hesitated a moment, looking into her eyes. She smiled at him enticingly.

'Well … I don't know … too dangerous to go to any of the usual ones – not just the two of us by ourselves.'

'Okay, you've got your car, haven't you? Well let's drive out a bit into the country.'

He thought for a moment longer. 'Well … I …' Then decisively, 'right. Brilliant idea … hmm. But we'll have to get out of here without being seen … look my car's in the front car park.' He thought again. 'Hold on … here's the keys.' In the press of people, only heads were visible. Unobserved, he fished the keys out of his trouser pocket and slipped them into her hand. 'You slide out of here. You'll have to go out of the front door – the side doors'll be locked … just make sure there's no one around. Get in the car and make yourself inconspicuous. I'll join you in a few minutes – as soon as it's safe.'

'Okay. Don't be too long.'

As she turned away, his hand traced the curve of her buttock, through the taut denim of her tiny skirt and she briefly looked round at him through half-closed eyes. He watched as she wriggled her body through the packed people and he lusted.

It was a starless night. The light from the lamp topping the slender standard in the centre of the lawn did not reach inside the parked car, at first he didn't see her. Panic. What's happened? Where the hell is she? He was so easily panicked. The unreasonable momentary fear that he'd lost her swamped his consciousness from just below the surface. He was always afraid he'd awake from the dream. He quickly opened the door and, relieved, saw dimly that she was there. She was crouched on the floor in the passenger's foot well, her thighs outrageously exposed, her knees under her chin. He looked hastily round into the night. There was nobody to be seen. Thank God for that. The car rocked as he flopped into the driver's seat and pulled the door shut.

'Louise, I didn't see you for a moment,' he whispered.

'Well you said to lie low ...'

'That wasn't quite what I meant ... but since you're down there, you'd better stay till we get clear.' Aidan started the car and reversed it on to the drive that encircled the lawn in front of the college building. With a shiver of excitement he felt Louise's hand on his thigh. Then as he snicked the gear lever into first and prepared to pull away, he saw one of the main doors ahead of him, lit by the headlights open and the stout figure of the principal emerge. He'd evidently been working late at his desk. The principal pulled the door shut and turning, raised his hand to shade his eyes from the glare.

Aidan screamed inwardly. 'For Christ's sake keep down,' he hissed. He waved at the principal as he abruptly let the clutch in, causing the tyres to let out a momentary screech. The principal still shading his eyes, with his other arm gestured recognition and the wish to communicate.

'Oh Christ!' In a panic, Aidan looked round and grabbing a rug from the back seat, hastily flung it into the seat well over Louise, at the same time bringing the car to an abrupt halt. The principal approached and Aidan was obliged to press the button to open the offside window. He opened it as little as basic communication required. The principal's eyes appeared at the slit. Somewhere below them Aidan could see a segment of uncovered thigh, gleaming palely, in the light of the overhead lamp.

'Ah Aidan, glad to have caught you,' said the principal. Aidan leaned over towards him, hoping to capture the whole of his gaze and divert it from the contents of the foot well, which seemed ever so slightly to adjust its shape.

'Oh ... er, I er ...' fumbled Aidan.

'Yes, I just wanted to say that the bursar and I discussed the possibility of financing the etching press you've been wanting. We think we may be able to manage it out of this year's budget ...'

'Oh great,' said Aidan fixing a smile on his face.

'... so I'd like you to drop in first thing tomorrow to fill me in on a bit of the technical detail. I'd like to put it to the committee in the afternoon.'

'Super,' said Aidan, 'I'll be there ... first thing ... Goodnight then, Harold.'

He wound up the window as the principal stood back and with a wave, let in the clutch, accelerating a little too vigorously round the island lawn in the direction of the main gate. The principal, looking

315

startled, waved back, as Aidan drove through the gates and with indecent speed headed out of town.

'Christ that was close,' he said, gasping in air. 'Didn't bargain for a conference with the principal.'

'Okay, but can I get up now? I'm suffocating under this blanket – and I'm getting cramp.'

'No, for Pete's sake stay down there till I tell you.'

It wasn't till they had left the orange glare of the street lights well behind that Aidan reached down towards her with his left hand, finding a knee and, momentarily, the inside of a thigh.

'Okay, you can come up now,' he said.

She uncoiled herself. 'Oh … that's better,' she said as she straightened up and arranged herself on the seat, smoothing out her clothes. She pulled down the visor and peering into the darkened mirror, made a few adjustments to her face and hair. Then turning towards Aidan she slipped her arm around his shoulder and kissed him on the cheek.

'Oh Aidan, wasn't that exciting?' she said.

'Lulu, we can do without that kind of excitement, okay?'

'Mmm, yes, Aidan,' she said, snuggling up against him.

By now the headlamps were cutting swathes of light through the blackness of the night, as they hummed along the almost deserted road.

'Where're we going, then?'

'Casterby. It's about six miles. Lies in a loop of the river. Roman fort. Seventeenth-century coaching inn – The Crown. It's got beams, little rooms, dim lights, cosy, discreet. That's where we're going.'

It was their first appearance in public and as with so many incidents in his life now he felt a dizzying mixture of elation and terror. True, they were six miles out of Swaleborough, but this was well within the range of Swaleborough citizens on a modest jaunt or maybe out for a celebratory dinner. And Aidan was known by not a few Swaleborough citizens. He wondered if this really was a sensible thing to do – then decided that of course it wasn't; it was reckless, utterly fucking reckless. But by God he was doing it anyway.

He brought the car to a gravelly halt in the car park at the side of the pub. After a quick look round, to see if he recognised any of the cars already there, he led Louise through the side door into the vestibule of the snug. Holding her hand, he restrained her, pausing before opening the inner door. He scanned the room through the glass of the door and the inner screen. Here were people and here was he with his mistress, for them to see. What if there was someone in there who knew him? What would he do? Well it was too late to worry about it now. He'd just have to brazen it out.

As it happened, there was only a handful of customers; one couple in a penumbral corner, sitting silent behind a pint of beer and something sparkly in a stemmed glass. On the other side of the open fire with its simmering logs, four young men stacked up with lager, playing a noisy game of dominoes; and leaning on the bar, silhouetted against the light, each with a foot on the brass rail, guarding pint glasses of something dark and strong-looking, two elderly men in caps, one in wellington boots – evidently not long from the farmyard.

The room was low ceilinged and beamed, the plastered walls the colour of tobacco; some glass cases with stuffed weasels, stoats or something; framed hunting scenes on the walls, a set of antlers, the floor stone paved. Aidan was correct in assuming that the snug would attract mostly locals. But the fact that the barman, exchanging banter with the two men at the bar, was wearing a white jacket and bow tie reminded him that the more sophisticated patrons in the restaurant and lounge bar at the other side of the wall would present something more of a challenge to his anonymity.

Nevertheless, he took a deep breath, opened the door and escorted Louise through it. She flicked her hair back and looked briefly around, before returning her gaze to Aidan, smiling. There was a sudden silence from the domino players. Louise was wearing a blue denim miniskirt below a tight white polo-necked sweater. She had slung her denim jacket loosely over her shoulders. Aidan did not in the least mind that four pairs of eyes devoured her. She was his – but they could look. He looked at them and smiled, wondering what they saw. The boss knocking off his secretary? Nothing legitimate, for sure. Though perhaps father and daughter? With that age gap, possible, but no, it was not a filial smile she gave him and fathers do not – or should not – caress the bottoms of their nubile daughters.

'Good evening,' he said, nodding pleasantly. Louise smiled and the domino players awkwardly readjusted their eyes, muttering a ragged reply. As they turned back to their game, one of them murmured something sotto voce, triggering a subdued snigger from his companions. The barman turned his attention to Aidan and Louise as they reached the bar. 'Good evening, sir, madam. Now then, what can I get you?'

'Two pints of bitter please,' Aidan said – he had converted Louise to serious beer drinking. The two veterans at the bar turned towards them and looked them carefully up and down.

'Aa do then,' said one and the other nodded amiably. 'Chilly aat there, eh?'

'Good evening,' said Aidan and Louise together. 'Yes, there is a bit of a nip in the air,' Aidan said. The man took a long slow draft of stout, looking at them all the while over his glass.

'Tha'll catch tha deeth o' coold, lass, dressed laaik that,' said the other, glancing pointedly at Louise's thighs. Aidan choked on his first gulp of beer and opened his mouth to speak – but Louise laughed.

'No I won't,' she said, 'I'm used to it. You know, I thought you were a hardy lot up here in the north. Can't you stand a bit of cold, then?' The man grinned, turned his head to his friend and winked broadly.

Then turning again to look at Aidan said, 'Well then, tha best look after 'er, yoong man.'

'Oh don't worry,' Aidan said, 'I will.' And drinks in hand, they made their way to the remaining secluded corner.

He knew he was going to be late home that night. In ordinary circumstances, he seemed congenitally incapable of leaving a pub if there was yet unexpired drinking time; the less so when also it was precious time spent with Louise. But The Crown, like many pubs away from the town had, particularly for customers who favoured the snug, an easy-going attitude to the licensing hours. So when eventually Aidan started up the Renault and switched on the lights to head back to town, it was the last car in the car park and he knew that it was already well after the time when he should have been home. As Louise snuggled up against him, he inwardly railed against the constraints he had to contend with, contrasting his binding time limits with Louise's freedom to dispose of her time as she pleased.

As he drove back between the midnight fields, and Louise drowsed, her head on his shoulder, part of his mind was working at a plausible reason for his late return that would placate Cathy, while another, in indignation, rehearsed a scenario in which he met her interrogation with a blank refusal to account for his disposal of his time, or, even less plausibly, in which he baldly stated the truth; I've been to a pub with a beautiful young woman – who also happens to be my mistress. So what?

By the time they reached the ring road, Aidan had worked himself up into an internal fury that he should be so accountable. It could not go on. It was intolerable. He would, he must, do something about it. Soon.

He drew up gently on the small forecourt of the flats. Louise was asleep. He turned and kissed the top of her head, while reaching for her hands.

'Hey, wake up. We're home.'

She opened her eyes and looked up at him drowsily and smiled. He put his arms around her and they kissed.

'I can invite you in for coffee now, Aidan – now that I've got my own place. Won't you come in?'

'Oh God Louise, I can't really.' His resolution had drained away. 'It's so late. I must be getting back.'

She gave a slight shrug and withdrew a little. 'Aidan, I want to spend a night with you. I hate these partings.'

'So do I. I hate them like hell.'

'Then why don't you do something about it?'

'Louise, I am a married man.'

'Oh God, don't remind me … I just need to have you … well, more, I suppose and I … Well, I guess the need to keep it secret all the time, it's just getting to me a bit.'

'Okay, listen, I'll fix something soon, somehow.'

'Will you Aidan … soon?'

'I promise.'

He was very late home that night. Probably she'd be asleep; nevertheless, he was gloomily prepared for a row. As he drove in through the gates, he saw that the house was unlit. Good. As expected, she'd gone to bed. He did not join her immediately, delaying long enough for the thoughtful disposing of two generous measures of whisky. He could not tell, as he was undressing, whether or not she was asleep, he knew that his washing had not erased the lingering fragrance of Louise. Eventually, taking care to cause as little disturbance as possible, he inserted himself between the sheets, ensuring a suitable distance between himself and his wife. She stirred.

'You're late,' she said.

'Yes,' said Aidan, bracing himself to do battle for his independence.

CHAPTER 22

It had been a fairly normal day of teaching. Louise had come to his room at coffee time and had lovingly compensated for the slight dissonance of their last night's parting. He had lunched with colleagues in the Three Tuns before his afternoon studio session. After its official ending, he had pottered around a while, chatting to the students as they tidied up and in ones and twos drifted away. By the time he'd gone to his own studio, picked up a couple of books he was reviewing and collected his coat, he was a bit late, but not unusually so.

As soon as he entered the house, the tension enveloped him. On a good day, the children met him. Dora especially could usually hardly wait to tell him about her day at school. Evidently no children. He found Cathy in the kitchen, an open book before her on the table, an open bottle of wine, half-full glass; no sign of the evening meal. She did not greet him. Oh, but he'd forgotten; they weren't speaking, were they? Not since last night's row. Well then he'd dispense with the formalities too.

'Where are the kids?' He addressed his question to the back of her head. There was no reply. He asked the question again.

'WHERE ARE THE KIDS?' Again there was no answer and after a moment, he took a step towards her and grabbed her fiercely by the shoulder.

'Cathy, will you please ANSWER ME?' he shouted.

'Take your hands off me.' She spun out of the chair to face him, sending the wine bottle crashing to the floor. The explosion of noise seemed to shock both of them to silence and they glared at each other.

'Dora's gone to Klara's for tea.'

'And where's Bobby?'

Silence.

'WHERE IS BOBBY?'

'Haven't the foggiest. She ran off in a temper.'

'What the hell've you been doing now, you …'

'God I can't help it if she's wet and stupid … I'm sick to death of her whinging …'

Aidan raised a hand in fury, restrained himself, stretched his clenched fists down by his side and bellowed, 'BITCH!'

Kicking fragments of broken glass out of the way, he stormed out of the kitchen, slamming the door behind him and out of the house. He made for the lane that ran past the old cemetery and round behind the houses. Dusk was falling and the idea that Bobby was out here somewhere in a state of distress worried him; anxiety immediately displaced the anger which a few moments before had held him helplessly in its grip. He decided first of all to try Mrs Cunningham.

She seemed now to have some kind of role as surrogate mother and it was likely that she'd be first port of call for a distressed Bobby.

'Oh Mr Hamilton … come in … Aye, she came round … right upset she was, so I made her a cup of tea. After that she calmed down a bit and asked if she could take Banjo out. I thought there would be no harm in it. It'd help her get things under control. She'll be all right.'

'Thanks ever so much, Mrs Cunningham. It's a relief to know she came to you. It's good of to look after her like that.'

'No that's all right, Mr Hamilton, she's a lovely girl and it really upsets me to see her so unhappy. Tell you what; you know she can stay with me any time she wants. Since our Joyce left I've a room to spare – and it's all ready, any time.'

His first priority had been to find Bobby; he had urgently needed the assurance that nothing appalling had befallen her, that she had not done anything awful to herself, not put herself in any danger. In the short time since learning that she was missing, his imagination had run the gamut of every disastrous outcome. But at least Mrs Cunningham's information had given him some reassurance for he knew that at any rate she would do nothing wild or irresponsible while she had charge of the dog. So when the question of what to do about Bobby that night was allowed space in his mind and Mrs Cunningham had volunteered an alternative to returning the rescued victim to the burning house, he was relieved and said, 'I'm really grateful for that offer, Mrs Cunningham. I may need to take you up on it.'

'Well I really mean it, I do.'

'That's really very nice of you … but now I think I'd better get out there and see if I can find her. I'll be back later.'

He set off along the avenue and cut through the snicket between the houses, leading to the lane separating their back gardens from the cemetery. He headed towards the allotments. He was making for the disused one with the hut under the apple tree in one corner. He knew it was her favourite refuge and the well of her fantasies. He was soon squeezing his body through the collapsing gate, into a minor scene of neglect and abandonment. He picked his way along the brick path, now partially submerged by the rotting detritus of last year's grasses, brambles and bindweed. As he approached the hut, a dog growled, then broke into a rhapsody of barks and whines and grizzles, as he pushed open the door. She was sitting on an upturned bucket in a dark corner holding the squirming terrier in a desperate embrace. Aidan knelt beside them, put his arms around Bobby, suffered a face licking by Banjo and began his work of damage limitation.

She dissolved into tears and burying her face in his shoulder, sobbed helplessly for sometime, while Aidan uttered consoling noises – and only noises – for he could think now of no consoling words. He knew now that it would be useless, as well as disingenuous to try to make excuses. After this, there could be no excuses for Cathy and he was no longer going to invent any. He reminded himself of the relief he felt on giving up religious belief, relief that he would no longer have to think up excuses for God's bad behaviour. When she was calm enough to speak she said, hesitantly, but with palpable determination, 'Dad … I'm not … I'm not going back.' She looked at him, her pale blue eyes still brimming with tears. He fumbled in a pocket and produced a paper hanky. He gently dabbed her face dry. He did not try to elicit her account of what had happened. The details would add nothing of value to the situation. That it had happened and in consequence he was now in the middle of yet another act of consolation and rescue was, this time, enough.

'What would you like to do,' Aidan asked.

'I don't know, I don't know, but I'm not going back there. I'm not going back where she is. Dad, Dad …' the tears started again. '… She's spoiling my life.' Her voice dropped to a whisper. 'She's spoiling my life.' Aidan felt the prick of tears in his own eyes.

'Okay love, you don't have to go back. Mrs Cunningham says you can stay with her tonight, in her spare room.' She looked up with relief and pleasure in her eyes.

'Oh Dad, did she say that? Wow that'll be great … and I'll be able to feed Banjo and things …'

'Okay then, you can stay with her tonight and it'll give us a bit of time to think what to do next.'

'Oh but Dad, I've got no things – pyjamas and clean clothes for tomorrow – no school things.'

'Well that's no problem. I'll go home and fetch what you'll need.'

He left her with Mrs Cunningham, who said she would see her to school next day and keep her until he could collect her after school. Then feeling suddenly lightened by the unexpected solution to a problem to which an hour ago there had seemed no conceivable answer, he set out on the short distance home. He knew it was a temporary solution and he knew that tomorrow the same problem would have to be faced anew, but having the bleak future starting in twenty-four hours was incomparably better than having it start now. It left time for miracles.

He found the garage door open. No car. He let himself in through the kitchen door. The floor was still scattered with glass fragments. There was a curt note scrawled on a fragment of paper on the kitchen table.

Dora at the Svensens'. See to things yourself.

Aidan grimaced. Then through clenched teeth said, 'Bitch … bitch … bitch. How did she know I was going to be back? How did she know I was going to find Bobby? How did she know I wasn't going to be spending the night at the Police station, the hospital?' He clenched his fists in silent fury.

He looked at his watch; it was ten past eight. Dora would normally have been back by now. Gudrun Svensen would have phoned before letting her embark on the hundred-yard walk home. If she'd got no answer she wouldn't have let her go. He would ring. He reached for the phone. But first ... He put it down again, went to the sideboard, took out his bottle of Laphroaig and poured himself a treble. He held its pale gold to the evening light in the glass door, watching as the facets engraved in the glass sent out slender shafts of fire. He held the first sip in his mouth till it burned then closed his eyes as he savoured its incendiary descent. Then he picked up the phone and dialled.

'Gudrun, hello. It's Aidan.'

'Aidan. I rang at about a quarter to eight, but there was no reply.' Her English was immaculate.

'Sorry Gudrun ... we had a bit of an emergency ...'

'Nothing serious, I hope ...'

'No, not really, it was just ...'

'Well listen, Aidan, they were having such a good time, Klara asked could Dora stay the night? Dora thought it was a great idea ... but I said we'd have to ask you or Cathy first. So what do you think?' At that moment, quite a different thought struck Aidan.

'Oh well, that's okay by me ... fine – if you don't mind.'

'Right, well don't worry about anything. I'll fix her up with nightie and clean knickers for tomorrow and I'll drop her off at school with Klara in the morning. Oh, and here she is to say goodnight.'

'Hi Daddy,' she said. 'Ooh isn't it exciting? I've got Klara's nightie with the giraffes on an' I'm going to have some hot chocolate.'

'Sounds great love. Okay then see you at tea time tomorrow. 'Night, sweetie.'

'Night, Dad.'

He put the phone down and attended to the thought that had struck him. Louise. Bobby was safe. Dora was safe. Just at the moment, he didn't give a bugger about Cathy. What he wanted was to be with Louise. Suddenly he could. As he despatched the whisky with more haste than it deserved, he wondered where she would be. He had to find her. She might be at college, working late or in the bar, or at home. She was not on the phone. Okay, he would start with college.

He looked at his watch again. Half past eight. Oh, but he had to collect Bobby's things and take them to Mrs Cunningham's. Right then he'd better get on with it. He went up to her room, put the necessary items in a small bag and gathered together the school things she'd been using and put them into her satchel. As he was locking the back door he suddenly remembered, Oh Christ, no car. Shit! Shit! Shit!

When at length he arrived at college, via a diversion in the opposite direction to Mrs Cunningham's, he was hot and breathless, and parched. By now he thought his best bet was the bar and as his thirst urgently needed slaking, he headed there directly. It was quite crowded. Must have been some function, he couldn't remember what. He elbowed his way to the bar and unpricipledly pulled rank to get an immediate pint. Bill Dixon, tonight's barman was one of Aidan's students and he unblinkingly colluded. Turning, to prop his back against the bar, he dipped his face into the glass and took a long deep draught, emerging from which, he began a serious survey of the room. Was she here? Was she? Inconclusive.

He finished his pint, ordered another and set out with it in hand to circumnavigate the room, easing his way through the bibulous throng, exchanging in bits of banter with students he knew and probing the dark corners. There was no sign of her. Damn. Was she somewhere else in college? The library? The department? He was trying to decide which to try first, when he was collared by Melvyn Harper, another of his students, who wanted a decision from Aidan about an Art Society visit to the Laing Gallery in Newcastle (where there was a particularly interesting one-man-show of avant garde ceramics). Aidan had promised to arrange it and Mel had bought him another pint in the hope of getting a firm decision on possible dates. Aidan drank his way through the ensuing negotiation while his eyes hopefully roved the room.

No sign of her. Aidan, beginning to feel gloomy and a little desperate, made his way back to the bar. He wanted her so. He needed her.

Then, leaning on the bar and toying with his glass, he asked the barman, with an exaggerated display of nonchalance, 'By the way, Bill, you haven't seen Louise tonight, have you? Couple of things I need to see her about. I just thought maybe ...'

The barman looked at Aidan knowingly, while carefully polishing a glass.

'Oh yeah, she was in earlier on, talking to Pam Wiltshire … they had a couple of drinks at the bar, and, er … yeah then she said something about home, bath and an early night. She must be overworking, Aidan. You need to keep an eye on her.'

Aidan laughed. 'There are limits to a tutor's responsibilities, my son.' He downed the rest of his beer and looking at his watch, said, 'Well, must get going. 'Night, Bill.'

'See ya, Aidan.'

He pushed his way through the bodies to the door, staggering slightly as it gave way to his pressure. He felt just a bit unsteady as he headed for the Art Department and his room. Just as well he didn't have the car, he reflected. He might have been tempted to use it – and that would have been a really bad idea. But he didn't think you could get nicked for being drunk in charge of a bike.

He hadn't attempted to ride it since that Friday when Dora had come and seen it for the first time, newly cleaned and oiled, and ready for the road. That had only been a couple of unsteady circuits of the car park. Oh well … needs must. His Uncle Sam, riding the juvenile Aidan to his allotment on the crossbar of his Hercules used to counter his complaints of discomfort with the observation that a third-class ride was always better than a first-class walk. In this situation, he wouldn't want to dispute that snippet of wisdom.

He let himself into the deserted department and into his room. He switched on the lights and looked at the bike admiringly. Dora had insisted that she (She?) should have a name. What the hell was it? Nellie ... Betty ... something like that ... but no, no; It was Bessie – that was it – Bessie. Yes and a damn good name too. He was feeling slightly giggly as he set about disentangling her from an encroaching pile of books, drawings, canvas stretchers and paint rags. In its growing clutter, his room was beginning to remind him more and more of the set in a production of John Aubrey's Brief Lives he had recently seen at the Civic Theatre. Only the pisspot's missing, he reflected. Then he suddenly thought, shit, no lights ... damn ... I could risk it, I suppose ... but ... No, I've got it. He went to a drawer in his desk and after a moment's rummaging produced a torch. He tested it. It still had life in it. He next found his roll of masking tape in another drawer and used some to strap the torch to the handlebars. That'll take care of the front, he thought. The back'll have to take care of itself.

He carefully manoeuvred Bessie out of his room, propping her against a bookcase while he locked the door. Then along the corridor, down the short flight of steps to negotiate the main door and out into the cold night, through the gates and on to the almost deserted road. He used the high curb to mount and settling his backside into the saddle, he thrust himself into an uncertain take-off. Soon, as he carefully navigated the quiet streets, he started to enjoy himself and thought of the stately figure of Miss Featherstone, sailing along the quiet pre-war streets, like a Norfolk wherry through the waterways of the Broads.

He found himself high up. He could see into gardens protected by high hedges and saw things going on in uncurtained windows behind them; he could see over the roofs of cars. He allowed himself a mild feeling of superiority over them and their drivers, which he had sometimes seen in the eyes of horse riders looking down at him as he had driven past them on country roads.

Now the early spring night chilled his breath and he puffed out white vaporous clouds, pretending to be a steam locomotive. It was exhilarating, he pedalled faster, intoxicated with the speed he made for himself. After negotiating a roundabout, he found himself on the ring road, nervous now at the frightening proximity of unfriendly, speeding cars. Ah, this was why Miss Featherstone had given it up. He didn't blame her; it was dangerous. But what danger could keep him from Louise?

Following the ring road on its circumnavigation of the northern edge of the town centre, he came presently to the turn off for Eastlake. His heart leapt, for it was in Eastlake that Louise had her flat. The road was quiet again and some way ahead, there came into view a bright window casting an elongated oblong of yellow light across the pavement. With it came the fragrance of frying, which reminded him with a sudden shock of the void in his belly. God, he hadn't eaten since lunch time. He needed food and he needed it now.

He drew up at the chippy, carefully adjusting the pedals to stand Bessie against the curb. He climbed two steps into the fluorescent brightness. He was the only customer in the pre-pub exodus lull. The man behind the counter was big and handsome – more like a Mountie than a fish fryer, Aidan thought, picturing him in the red tunic and Boy Scout hat. In an action which flatly belied this image of manhood, he was delicately lowering battered fish into the seething oil, causing sizzling eruptions of noise and smoke. He nodded lugubriously at Aidan, who wondered why fish and chip vendors always seemed to be so unhappy. While awaiting the completion of the operation, Aidan scanned the greasy, puffed-up golden delicacies in the glass fronted display before deciding he could not manage more than a basic packet of chips while riding a bike. The man rubbed his knuckle in circles on a pile of paper bags on the counter, causing them to fan out. He picked the top one, flipped it open and digging a silvery shovel into the pile of chips, filled the bag to overflowing.

'Salt and vinegar?' He asked.

'Please.' Aidan replied. The man shook salt and vinegar into the bag and in another deft movement he parcelled it in newspaper and handed it to Aidan. Outside, Aidan opened out the newspaper and propped the open bag in the basket strapped to the handlebars. Then he set off again, steering unsteadily with one hand, feeding himself chips with the other.

Soon he had to change into bottom gear as he approached the climb up Norton Bank his feet at first whizzing madly around then gradually slowing as he hit the incline. He suspended his meal, needing both hands on the handlebars and maximum effort in his legs for this. Soon his heart was thumping and to keep going he was forced to make wild zigzags over the full width of the road. Then arriving triumphant at the summit, he despatched the last few chips. He picked up the bag by a corner, tipped the remaining crispy bits into his mouth and, one handed, crumpled the bag and its surrounding soggy newspaper into a ball. He spotted a yellow rubbish bin on a lamp post, halfway down the hill on the opposite side of the road.

He changed into top gear and accelerated, pedalling furiously, his hair blowing, his eyes streaming in the rush of cold air. He was filled with exhilaration and laughed aloud as, ignoring approaching headlights, he banked to the right and zoomed across the road, the rubbish bin centred in his sights and dropped the greasy bomb with a satisfying thump into the centre of the target. As he pulled Bessie out of her dive, the approaching car swerved, angrily flashing its lights.

'Get stuffed,' Aidan shouted, as the car flashed past, turning in the saddle and unloading six rapid rounds of .45 from his two-fingered Colt into its retreating boot.

The flat, when he arrived, was in darkness; and he was breathless. He wheeled Bessie across the forecourt and propped her carefully against the wall. He knocked gently at the door; it was a rhythmic code they had decided on for the security of their clandestine meetings in college. Three dots and a dash; V for victory; Beethoven's Fifth. As he knocked, it wasn't the familiar opening he had in mind, but the less fateful rhythm of the scherzo. He closed his eyes and fervently conducted it, waiting for the light to come on.

When it did, he saw, through the patterned glass of the door, the distant blur develop into the minutely facetted form of Louise. He saw her pause and look; he saw her recognise him. Her hands flew to the security bolts and the lock, and he was inside. In the briefest moment that he paused to look, he saw her as he had not seen her before; her hair drawn back, her face scoured and slick with lotion, her lips pale. It was as if a sculptured head, once polychromatic had been scraped down to the naked marble, leaving just the unalloyed beauty of the material to inform the curves and planes. Then she was in his arms; she almost naked, her breasts ill-concealed by a hastily drawn dressing gown; he scarfed, gloved, duffel coated, booted. As he crushed her to himself an imperfect recollection of something read drifted into his mind: Today my lord returned from the wars. He pleasured me twice (or was it thrice, even) in his top boots.

CHAPTER 23

Cycling back towards the town centre and college, head and shoulders above the roofs of cars and the worst of the choking fumes of the morning commuting traffic, Aidan was in a state of mind swinging between joyful delirium in the wake of the night spent with Louise and the grim anticipation of the reckoning to come in his family. The night before last, when they were late back from the pub, she had wanted him to stay. He himself, as frustrated as she was, at the seemingly unavoidable partings, at the pain of them, the unnaturalness of it all, had understood her need to spend nights with him; he wanted it too, almost more than anything. And he had said he would arrange it – without having much idea of how. Then, the very next day, an agonising, debilitating eruption of emotional violence in the family had, with the assistance of a little organisational opportunism, provided the occasion. Truly, thought Aidan, it IS an ill wind that blows nobody any good.

'Aidan,' she had said, gasping for breath, when he'd released her from that first, fierce embrace, 'what … what're you doing here?'

'You wanted me to spend the night with you; I said I would and here I am.'

She laughed with delight and drew him into the room.

'You're wonderful,' she said, 'wonderful. How did you do it? No, don't tell me. I don't want to know; all that matters is that you're here.'

Like Lord Marlborough (he thought it was Lord Marlborough), such was the urgency, he had pleasured his mistress while still partially clad. Then they had drunk wine, languishing on cushions on the floor, listening to Cleo Lane, toasting by a guttering gas fire, before again making love – this time, precariously in Louise's one-person-wide bed. Then, naked, tessellated spoon-wise, her breasts cupped in his hands, they drifted into sleep.

The morning sunlight flooding the room, the chatter of sparrows in the cotoneaster outside the window, the clinking of milk bottles had woken Aidan into his new demi-paradise. Stirring into wakefulness, Louise put out a hand, which fell inconsequentially upon his erection. They were conjoined before she was fully awake and the new day joyfully consecrated.

After breakfast Louise had seen him teeteringly off, seeing him swerve, as he turned, halfway along the road, to wave. He knew she would join him in his room later that morning for coffee.

It was when freewheeling down Norton Bank, flying down the inside of the traffic queue, past the shuffling cars and past the now shuttered fish and chip shop, that his thoughts reluctantly turned to yesterday's events in the family. He felt relieved that there was a whole working day before he need confront them. The children were taken care of, that was the main thing. But what of Cathy? Had she returned home last night? If she had, he wondered, what had she made of the empty house she would have returned to. Sometime, later that day, he supposed, the problems would have to be faced – but later, not now, not yet. He realised he was having recourse more and more often to the cushioning effect of a few hours of grace to defer confrontation of besetting problems. Sufficient unto the day is the evil thereof. Compartmentalisation – that was the thing to help you survive. By the time he had joined the bypass, the euphoria had returned. By the time he had dismounted outside the department and wheeled Bessie into his room, he was already anticipating coffee break.

It was because of lingering over the coffee cups, unable to drag himself away from Louise, that he was a little late for the Academic Board Meeting. It was an important meeting. At the beginning of term, several sub-committees had been established, charged with examining various aspects of the fast-approaching and, seemingly inevitable, closure of the college. They had been given the specific task of suggesting strategies for averting the inevitable; in short, of thinking of imaginative ways of avoiding closure and securing jobs. Today's meeting was for the purpose of hearing and discussing the first fruits of these endeavours, and Aidan having been detained by his mistress, and in consequence, finding it difficult to concentrate on something so trivial as redundancy, was late for it. A little. Entering the staffroom, he closed the door carefully behind him. With an exaggerated display of contrition, he conveyed his apologies to the principal, who looking up from the papers he was shuffling on his desk, nodded his acceptance. Aidan tiptoed across the floor to a vacant armchair in a corner next to the window. Despite trying not to, he caught the baleful eye of Gerry, below a crinkled brow and somewhat above lips pursed in admonition. He smiled blithely at him, before turning to sink into his seat, arranging his papers on top of his sketchbook on his knee.

After the minutes had been read and accepted, the principal invited the chairman of the first sub-committee to introduce his report. It was a quite well worked out set of proposals for a staff buy-out. It reasoned that if the University of Buckingham could function as a private institution of higher education, it was at least arguable that there could be room for a privatised teacher education establishment.

The discussion was well under way, when the door tentatively opened and Mrs Dobson, from the admin office, made her diffident way to the principal's side and whispered something into his ear. He nodded and she left as unobtrusively as she had entered. The principal caught Aidan's eye and gestured. Aidan got up from his seat, suddenly feeling anxious and crossed to the principal. The discussion had for the moment slimmed down to a series of robust exchanges between the chairman of the sub-committee and Eric Blandford from the Maths Department, a long-time Labour Party activist for whom the notion of privatising teacher training was particularly inflammatory.

The principal waved to Aidan to come closer, and said sotto voce, 'Aidan … call from Caedmon School … they'd like a word with you straight away. Take it in my study, I asked Mrs Dobson to put it through.'

'Oh, okay. Thanks, Harold,' Aidan said, trying not to let the alarm show in his face. He'd meant to get back to the school at the beginning of term, he should have got back to them, but he'd just hung on; he had not picked up that phone. What was the point? He'd got no new ideas. Well, he had no new ones, though he'd had another go at some of the old ones. When things had calmed down a bit after Christmas, he resolved to choose an auspicious time – or as auspicious a time as any that was likely to turn up – and carefully approach Cathy again. He would approach her calmly, rationally. It would be a reasonable, even friendly, approach, treating the matter simply as one of mutual concern, the resolution of which would be of clear advantage to both of them and the family as a whole. He would deploy all his resources of tact and patience. No matter what happened, he would remain calm and pleasant. For God's sake, wars had sometimes been avoided by such conciliatory means. Surely a little family problem could not be so intractable. He would suggest seeking outside help – advice, counselling, whatever. Someone wise, impartial, disinterested.

'Oh right then ... and who would that paragon be, might I ask?' Cathy had responded with sarcasm you could cut.

'I dunno ... someone ... the doctor maybe – or even the Marriage Guidance Council, I suppose.'

'Hah! I wouldn't ask that old sot the time of day, if I could help it.'

'Well I've always found him very helpful – even if he does put away the booze a bit.'

'Forget it. FORGET IT!'

'Well okay then ... okay.' Aidan found his voice rising and determinedly restrained it. 'The Marriage Guidance Council. They're trained and they ...' Cathy gave an ironic laugh.

'The Marriage Guidance Council! You must be joking. D'you know who's a Marriage Guidance counsellor? Linda Smith ... Linda Smith. D'you really think I'd discuss anything, anything at all with somebody like her? Our affairs would be all over town inside a week.'

'Oh, for Christ's sake, it's all confidential. It's got to be or the system wouldn't work. Anyway, look, there are others ... if you would just ...'

'Look, let's just get a few things clear. There isn't any problem in this family, apart from a lousy husband who won't support me in the home. And I'll tell you this, there's no way I'm going to have any dirty linen washed in public. There's no way I'm going to let myself be labelled official scapegoat in this family just so you can have the satisfaction of doing me down once again ... so you can get that into your head.' Her voice had not risen. But had taken on a harshness that roused Aidan, despite his good resolution, to fury, and before long they were once more banging away with the same remorseless, destructive circularity. He had blundered yet again, foolhardy, into the minefield.

Thereafter, he'd just tried to prevent things getting any worse. But despite his efforts, they had got worse. Yesterday they had got to crisis point. He knew they had. He had, as an unexpected consequence, enjoyed a few hours of bliss. It's an ill wind ... He had staved off the crunch. He had reckoned he had another six or so hours before it would be upon him. Perhaps at the school they just wanted to arrange that meeting ... but would that justify dragging him out of an important meeting in college ... just to arrange a date?

He hesitated before picking up the phone, taking a deep breath.

'Hello, Aidan Hamilton ...'

'Ah Mr Hamilton.' That educated Edinburgh voice. 'Fiona McAllister here ...'

'Mrs McAllister, I've been meaning to ...'

'Look, Mr Hamilton, sorry to call you again at college, but it's something rather serious about Bobby ...' Terror pierced him deep.

'What is it? Is she okay?' Near panic.

'Yes, she's alright, but she's in a bit of a state. I think you should get here straight away if you can possibly manage it. I don't want to say anything more over the phone.'

'Right, I'll come straight away.'

'Okay, I'll look out for you in the entrance hall. See you soon.'

Heading in a rush back to the staffroom, he remembered. Damn, no car. And no time for cycling this time ... Gerry, he's got his here. He'll lend me it. In the staffroom, the discussion was by now getting quite heated. Aidan crossed to the principal and told him what was happening. The principal expressed his concern and said never mind the meeting, Aidan would have the minutes anyway, to go at once. Aidan thanked him and said he would, but he just had to see Gerry first. Gerry said yes it was okay about the car and gave him the keys. Aidan took them with thanks and left the staffroom. As he went, meaningful looks were exchanged among Gerry, Barbara and Henry.

Fiona McAllister was waiting for him in the school lobby.

'Ah Mr Hamilton, that was quick. Let's go along to my room.' She led him past a counter-current of migrating juniors, then holding the door of her room open for him, followed him inside. She offered him a comfortable chair. After the rush and then the bustle of moving children, suddenly he was in an oasis of tranquillity. He lowered himself into the chair, somewhat reassured by her calm.

'Thank you, Mrs McAllister. Now please fill me in.'

She looked at him steadily, drawing in breath before speaking. 'Right, I'll start with the most serious bit. Bobby, it seems, tried to harm herself ...'

'What? A suicide attempt?' Aidan leaned forward, his hands white-knuckled, clutching the arms of the chair.'

'No, no. I don't think we should put that interpretation on it, Mr Hamilton. No, it's often, said by psychiatrists, that most apparent suicide attempts are nothing more than a cry for help from someone overtaken by desperation; someone no longer able to cope – and I'm sure that's how we need to regard this incident.'

'For God's sake what did she do? Was she in any danger? Is there any serious damage? I need to see her, Mrs McAllister.' Aidan was in shock. 'I need to see her. Where is she now?'

'No, really there's no danger and no major damage. She's along in the medical room with Mrs Meadows, the nurse. She's calmed down a lot and Mrs Meadows is very good in this kind of situation.'

'But what did she do to herself, for God's sake.'

'Well she made a token attempt to cut her arms with some broken glass she'd found – but the damage is only superficial. I don't think she really intended to go for a vein. Anyway, the nurse has dealt with that and she checked the medical records to make sure she was okay for tetanus.'

'Oh God … does she know I'm here: I'd hate her to think that anything could keep me away …'

'Yes, she knows. I told her you were coming straight away. Look, would you like a drink, Mr Hamilton? I do keep some for medicinal purposes – emergencies, you know. I reckon this qualifies, don't you?'

Aidan allowed himself to fall back into the chair. He smiled grimly, 'I think I could be persuaded.'

She stooped to open a cupboard at the side of her desk, produced a half-bottle of brandy and a glass, and slid them across the polished surface of the desk.

'Do help yourself,' she said, and smiling in reply to Aidan's unspoken question, 'not when I'm on duty, thanks.'

He poured himself a stiff one and swilled it round the glass before taking his first sip.

'Ah, that was a really good idea of yours, Mrs McAllister. I think I'm ready for the details, now.'

'Right, well it seems there was some kind of fracas in the playground at break. A group of girls … I don't know whether it was some kind of bullying – or just teasing, but it got out of hand. According to the children I questioned, Bobby suddenly went berserk and struck out at her tormentor – who, incidentally ended up on the ground with a bloody nose – then ran off out of the school gates. It seems that attention then focused on the injured tormentor. No one, none of the children who were witnesses, thought to mention about Bobby to the duty teacher; she had been attending to a minor accident on the playing field. It wasn't till Bobby was missed by the teacher of her next class that one of the children thought to mention what had happened. The teacher immediately informed me and I got hold of Mr Liddell, and we went out in his car to look for her. One of the girls had said she had seen her heading out of school towards the river, so that was the first direction of our search. Well we knew she couldn't have got far and we found her about three-quarters of a mile along the road. You know that parking place, where there's a style, leading to the river path. Well she was sitting against the wall on the other side of the stile, weeping uncontrollably, staring as though hypnotised at her bleeding arms.'

'Jesus!' Aidan let his head fall into his hands.

'Well – we scooped her up and into the car, applied a bit of first aid and brought her back here, where the nurse took over.' There was silence. After a moment or two, Aidan looked up into the distance and took a thoughtful sip at the brandy. Then suddenly he said, 'Look, before I see Bobby, I should ring my wife. If her daughter has made a suicide attempt – even a token one – she should be here. D'you mind it use your phone?'

'No, of course not; help yourself. While you're doing it, I'll go along to the medical room and check up on things there.' She went out closing the door behind her.

He dialled. He tapped his fingers impatiently as the number rang. It seemed to go on ringing forever. Eventually the welfare officer answered.

Aidan said, 'This is Aidan Hamilton. I need to speak to my wife please … Yes I expect she is teaching. Nevertheless, I want to speak to her. It is urgent … Well make whatever arrangements are necessary.

Just fetch her please.' He looked at his watch. He waited. After some minutes, Cathy spoke.

He said, 'I know … I KNOW. Just shut up and listen … I DON'T CARE. LISTEN. I'm at Caedmon School. I was sent for urgently. I had to leave a very important meeting. Shut up, will you. There was trouble in the playground. Bobby ran away from school. They found her heading for the river. She'd injured herself – deliberately … Yes that's right – the sort of thing people do to commit suicide … She's your daughter – remember? I don't care if you're at the fucking queen's garden party, just drop everything and get over here now. I assume you've got the car. Well get into it and drive … JUST DO IT.' He slammed the phone down, tossed back the rest of the brandy and poured himself some more. He walked over to the window with it and stood, looking out over the sun-lit playing field. Having summoned his wife, he really did not know how he would handle things when she arrived. He just knew with absolute conviction that he wanted her somewhere in the front line. He wanted her to have a close-up view of the latest and most serious consequence of her perverted view of parenting.

Presently, there was a quiet tap on the door and Mrs McAllister's head appeared round it enquiringly.

'Yes, I've finished, thanks, Mrs McAllister. Please come in.'

'Bobby's calmer now and really does want to see you. Shall we go along to the medical room?'

'Yes … but look, Mrs McAllister …' He paused to drain the last of the brandy from the glass, '… my wife should be on her way here. Can you intercept her and fill her in. Don't spare the details.'

'Of course Mr Hamilton, you can depend on me.' She ushered him out into the corridor. 'This way. It's just at the other side of the gym.'

Now the corridor was empty and as they passed the closed doors of the classrooms, there were the subdued sounds of children being educated; the coaxing voice of a teacher, the murmuring of children at work, a piano, with children singing, a burst of laughter.

'Afterwards, we'll need to decide what would be the best thing to do next. Clearly some positive action is unavoidable. We'll have to make a full report on what happened and then … well we'll talk it all through later.' She turned her head to look at him inquiringly. 'I take it your wife will now be involved.'

He met her eyes with a sardonic smile. 'Yes, I think she will.'

'I do think the time has come to seek specialist help. If you'll agree, I'll give the school's psychologist a ring and ask her to get over here as soon as she can make it.'

'Yes. I suppose that's the best thing.'

'Right, here we are then. Come back to my room when you're ready, won't you?'

She tapped on the door. A voice said to come in and Mrs McAllister opened the door for him, then left him.

Aidan took a step inside and Bobby threw herself into his arms, wailing, sobbing uncontrollably onto his chest. He enfolded her, stroking her hair, not attempting to say anything – just making soothing noises. He looked up and met the nurse's eye. Should she go, they were saying. Aidan nodded and she slipped unobtrusively out.

'Dad, Dad … help me, help me … save me,' Bobby cried out between sobs.

'Yes … yes. Listen, darling, it'll be all right … it'll be okay … I'll see that it will be, I promise you.' This time, he had decided.

'Dad, I'm sorry … I'm sorry … I'm sorry. I'm really, really sorry what I did.' She looked down at her bandaged arms. 'It just … it just …' She let out another agonised wail. 'Dad, do you forgive me? Do you forgive me?' She looked up at him through brimming eyes; for Aidan, looking down, it was a Christ's eye view of some Spanish baroque, Mary Magdalene, at the foot of the cross; his daughter was asking his forgiveness; she was asking his forgiveness. He thought, shouldn't she be forgiving him? Shouldn't he be asking her forgiveness for allowing this to happen? He had thought he was doing what he could in the circumstances, but it wasn't enough, was it? He should have done more; he was going to have to do more. He was going to have to remove her from the cause of her distress, at whatever cost; the events of that day had changed the possibility of that action into a hard resolution.

'Bobby, Bobby,' he whispered, 'there's nothing for me to forgive …
really there isn't … nothing at all.'

'She'll hate me more than ever, now, won't she Dad, won't she?'
Aidan groaned, his speech immobilised by the impossibility of a
reply. How many times had he bridled at that intemperate word?
How many times had he tried to persuade her that it wasn't true? But
not this time. What other explanation could he expect Bobby to come
to? Yes, he would concede; yes, she seemed to hate her daughter,
within any reasonable meaning of the word. He was not going to lie
about it.

'It doesn't matter about her now,' he said.

'I won't go back, I won't … I won't.' Her voice rose, approaching
hysteria.

'Okay, darling. It's okay …' he said soothingly, 'you won't need to.'
He had no cogent plan by which to keep this promise, but he knew
that by the end of the day he would have to produce one. He led her
over to the window where there were chairs and they sat down
together, he holding her hands. He did not know how long he spent
draining himself, finding inside himself enough comfort, enough
reassurance. It was sometime before he felt able to look at the
bandaged arms, to hold them carefully and look into her eyes,
shaking his head gently. There was nothing really to be said about
that. Nothing in the least useful.

Presently there was a tap at the door and tentatively, Mrs McAllister appeared.

'May we come in,' she asked. She was followed by the nurse.

'Yes, come in … please do,' Aidan said.

'Well then, Bobby,' she said, smiling a calm, maternal smile, 'are you feeling a little better now?' Bobby looked up, making a quivering attempt at a reciprocal smile, said between sniffs, 'Yes … thank you … Mrs McAllister … a bit.'

'Okay, well if you'll stay with Mrs Meadows a while longer – perhaps she'll invite you to a cup of tea – I'll take your Dad along to my room to have a chat. Your Mum's there too …'

'No! NO!' Bobby reacted in panic; grabbed Aidan's hand; crescendo. 'I don't want to see her … I won't see her … I won't …'

Alarmed, Aidan interrupted. 'Don't worry darling, you don't have to – just relax, no one's going to make you do anything you don't want to.'

'No, no, of course not.' Mrs McAllister joined in with her reassurance, exchanging a glance with Aidan, which said, I see what you mean.

Bobby, her face still fearful, looked anxiously from one to the other.

'Now don't worry,' said Aidan. 'You just relax with Mrs Meadows, I'll be back soon.'

With reluctance, she surrendered Aidan's hand, watching them leave the room, her eyes rounded with doubt. Mrs Meadows came up behind and laid a comforting hand on her shoulder.

As they walked back along the corridor, Mrs McAllister brought Aidan up to date with events.

'I gave your wife an outline of what happened, Mr Hamilton; she's waiting in my room. I thought you might perhaps want to see her alone ...'

'Yes, I think that would be best,' Aidan replied.

'Meanwhile, I was able to contact Dr Bradshaw, the psychologist. Luckily she had some time available, so she's able to come this afternoon. Will two-thirty be okay.'

'For me, yes, that would be fine, though I can't speak for my wife.'

'She – Dr Bradshaw, that is – she'll have a preliminary talk with Bobby and with you and Mrs Hamilton. She will probably want to assess whether or not it would be necessary to call in the psychiatrist.'

'The psychiatrist? Oh God, has it come to that? It's my bloody wife who needs the psychiatrist ...' Mrs McAllister looked at him sideways. 'Sorry. Shouldn't say things like that. Unprofessional,' Aidan said.

'Not to worry,' she replied, with a faint smile. She left him at the door to her room.

Cathy was sitting in a chair by the window, her elbow resting on the sill, one hand cupping her chin, the other holding on to her handbag on her lap. She was looking out across the playing field. She seemed captivated by the view. Beyond the fence marking the limits of the field was a hanger of tall sycamores and horse chestnuts rising up a grassy slope, their tops showing the faint haze of green of early spring. Still visible through them were some triangles of red-tiled roofs. They were at the western edge of the area where their own house was, a mere ten-minute walk away. For a while, she didn't stir. How like her, Aidan thought. She must realise the situation was getting beyond her grasp. The affairs of her family were leaking out into the world at large. But she still had power; power to keep him waiting; and she kept him waiting. So closing the door quietly behind him, he stood with his arms folded and waited.

She did not turn to face him. She did not stand up. When she spoke, it was to the view. She said to it, 'I suppose you're going to blame me.'

'No comment,' said Aidan, taking it upon himself to reply. She turned round sharply, to face him and spoke savagely. 'Well you're not going to scapegoat me. It takes two to raise a child.'

'But only one to destroy one,' he replied. 'I thought you might be more concerned with Bobby's condition than with defending your rectitude.'

She dropped her eyes and took a deep breath. 'I got all the details from the teacher. I'd better go and see her, I suppose.'

'A bad idea. Too late for you to start showing concern.' Aidan was bitter. 'Don't you really, really understand? After what you did to her

356

yesterday, as if that wasn't enough to bear … she came into school today and she got picked on by some little yob in knickers. It was a last straw. She lashed out, ran away from it, picked up a piece of jagged glass and tried to slash herself with it. She may not exactly have tried to kill herself – but it could easily have happened that way.' He strove to keep his voice under control. 'And all you're concerned with is evading any responsibility … keeping your character unstained. Well stuff that.'

She stood up and glowered at him. Untypically, she held her tongue. Aidan wondered, after she'd gone, if what he had said had for once hit her as a piece of truth, rather than as a piece of ordnance. Or was it just that this particular field of battle was not of her choosing.

'Well in that case, I'm going back to my children. I have a job to do.'

'Not your children, somebody else's. Never mind your own. But remember, we, I repeat, we have an appointment at two-thirty this afternoon with the schools' psychologist. You should have enough time to make the necessary arrangements.'

'What?' Taken aback, it seemed that that likelihood had not occurred to her. She seemed not yet to be able to adjust herself to the inevitability of outside intervention.

'Well you don't expect everything is going to drop neatly back into place after all this, do you?'

She gave him a ferocious look as she made for the door. 'You … bastard,' she said, turning, before pulling the door shut behind her.

Aidan crossed to the window and watched her emerge from the main door and cross to the car park. He watched coldly as she fumbled with her handbag, seeking the keys. He watched as she let herself into the Renault, seeing it sag a little in response to her weight; saw her put down her handbag, turn slightly to find the seat belt and then plug it in. He saw the end of the silencer vibrate momentarily, emit a small breath of haze as she started the engine. He watched as she reversed out of the car park and drove out of the gates onto the road and disappeared around the corner. He wondered if she would come to the meeting at which the future of their daughter would perhaps be decided.

He stood for a while longer, gazing out of the window at the space where his car had been, trying to induce that space into his mind; to displace his thoughts with an easeful emptiness; somehow hoping to recuperate some of his emotional capital before resuming the day, for he knew not what demands would yet be made on it.

Presently, remembering time, he looked at his watch. It was now after one o'clock. He needed to organise the next two hours. He left the room in search of Mrs McAllister. He did not need to look far. Over the past two hours, he had come to expect her to infallibly be where he needed her – to be the impeccably efficient facilitator. She had been talking to the secretary in the vestibule; she concluded her business and turned to greet him.

'Well then, Mr Hamilton, I don't think there's much more to be done in the next couple of hours and Bobby's waiting for you. She's looking a little more together now.'

'Yes, thank you, Mrs McAllister. I thought it might be a good idea to take her out to lunch – if that's okay with you.'

'Yes, that's fine … a good idea.'

'But first I'd like to get in touch with the college, to bring them up to date. I should be teaching this afternoon, so I'll need to make a few arrangements.'

'Oh sure. Use my phone, meanwhile I'll sort Bobby out and bring her along here to wait for you.'

Aidan rang the principal and put him briefly in the picture, clearing himself for such time off as he might need over the next day or two to sort things out. Then he spoke in a similar vein to Barbara, making provisional arrangements to cover his teaching commitments and then he spoke to Gerry about everything. Gerry said it was okay to hang onto the car for the rest of the day if necessary. All that accomplished, he collected a subdued Bobby from Mrs McAllister, thanking her once more. He strapped his daughter into the car beside him and drove her the mile and a half to The Waggon and Horses, where they had lunch at a rickety table in an untidy garden overlooking the river where a heron stalked the gurgling waters.

CHAPTER 24

Two days ago, Aidan had never heard of an 'adolescent unit'; now it was already part of his familiar vocabulary. She was not 'mentally ill', in any important clinical sense, the psychiatrist had said, but she was depressed. From his conversation with her, he concluded that she was suffering from exogenous depression. As to the prognosis, there was both good news and bad. The good news was this; exogenous depression, unlike endogenous depression, which seems to come unaccountably from within, had a usually traceable external cause and therefore, if the cause could be determined, its removal would generally effect a cure. But the news would be bad either if the cause could not be determined, or if, once determined, it could not be removed.

In the case of Bobby, there seemed little doubt as to the cause – it clearly lay principally within the home – he would not be more specific than that. This being the case, he'd said, there were two choices: the first would be to change the situation in the home and that was a matter for the parents. Failing that, the second would be one way or another to remove Bobby from the situation. Of the two choices, the first, it seemed, had been attempted, at least by one of the parents, but without success, as the present situation attests. And indeed success appeared unlikely, since the problem was quite long term and revolved around what was evidently an intractable personality problem.

The second choice offered two further possibilities. The first and most drastic, though in view of the obvious long-term tensions in the family, not totally outrageous, would be marital separation in which Bobby would live with her father. This, it was to be hoped, would provide a permanent solution. The second would be a temporary place in our adolescent unit. This of course would only ease the situation short term, but it would at any rate offer respite and time for more permanent solutions to be explored.

The Adolescent Unit? Well, more explicitly, the Adolescent Psychiatric Unit. Administratively, a ward of Woodsend Psychiatric Hospital – yes, what used to be called The Lunatic Asylum – but no longer. Yes, it was quite separate from it. In fact, about sixteen miles away. An old large house in extensive gardens in the southern suburbs of Uremouth. At any given time, usually about five residents, possibly up to eight – we don't call them patients – in the eleven to eighteen-age range. No serious cases of mental illness, no psychoses or anything like that; mostly problems with relationships, in the home or school – that sort of thing. Bobby would be a fairly typical case.

What happens there? A bit like an easy-going co-ed boarding school. Very relaxed. Education continues, but without the stress.

There are visiting tutors, a variety of subjects. Visits to places of interest. Opportunities for creativity – art, music, dance. Even pets.

Treatment? Emphasis on psychotherapy – plenty of talk – working it out, cognitive therapy. Help with coping. Looking at alternative solutions, environments. Small, highly motivated specialist staff.

Drugs? Only in case of special need, as a short-term therapy.

How long? As long as it takes. It depends on response. Perhaps six weeks – a year. Usually not longer than that, but that depends on individual circumstances.

Success rate? Difficult to tell. Almost impossible to predict long-term benefits – so much depends on what environment the subject returns to. But it does offer another chance. It's a step short of disaster. It puts things on hold. Gives everyone an opportunity to reconsider, to learn from mistakes.

Cathy had remained silent throughout the interview with the psychiatrist, her head raised in a studied gesture of disdain, which seemed to say, if her daughter were to go to a lunatic asylum, it would be none of her doing. None of her family had ever been sent to a lunatic asylum and she was certainly not going to collude in this endeavour. Aidan, tense and anxious, had asked the questions. It looked like a solution to the immediate problem. Yes, it did seem to afford a breathing space, time to think, to plan, to try to arrange a new future. But Bobby? It was her life they were attempting to arrange.

The psychiatrist had talked to Bobby about it and said that Bobby had not dissented from the idea and fully accepted the assurance that there was no compulsion and no absolute commitment. If it didn't work, if she couldn't stand it, she would be free to leave. But she thought she would find it okay. She would be much freer; there would be no one on her back. She'd have sympathetic, understanding people to talk to. She would have the time, the situation where she could just be herself. She'd make new friends.

Cathy had to go back to her children. She left the decision making to Aidan and Bobby.

It was as the psychiatrist had said. Bobby said she would go. She said anything would be better than going back to that house and her.

'But Dad,' she'd said, tears starting in her eyes, 'Dad, Dad, you'll come and see me won't you, Dad. You won't just leave me, will you? Please don't just leave me, Dad, will you?'

She'd gripped his hand with both of hers as though it was all that prevented her from being swept remorselessly down some raging river to God knew what unthinkable fate. He'd done his best to reassure her.

The whole thing took three days. Meanwhile, Bobby had stayed with Mrs Cunningham. On the day she was to be admitted, Cathy had taken the morning off to see that she had all that was necessary for an indeterminate stay. As Aidan backed out of the drive, Cathy, who had seemed unusually reflective during the preparations, had come to the car window and had said to Bobby 'Bye love. I hope you'll be alright.' Bobby looked up, her eyes widened. She looked down again.

'Bye,' she'd said.

On this third day, as they drove towards Uremouth, the anticyclone which had given them a few days of idyllic spring, had drifted gradually northward and, in its decline, was pulling in rags of grey cloud across the estuary from the North Sea, trailing chill mists behind them in a last unpleasant reprise of winter. Aidan could smell, even inside the car, traces of the acridity which seeped into the air from the huge chemical complex along the banks of the river to the north, with its vast sheds, tanks, silos and towers, and its countless miles of pipes. He could see the pencils of flame from its flare stacks, which rose like tall, slim candles on the horizon. It was not pleasant to be downwind of that lot. He felt that this delicate and doleful task would have benefited from a little sunshine.

Bobby did not seem to want conversation, so now he had time to think of Louise. It would not be true to say that he hadn't had time, in the midst of his turmoil, to think of her. On the contrary she had been in his mind all the time, but often in an etiolated form; a kind of palimpsest of the mind, whose content was diminished by the intensity of the events overlying it. His mind tried to find ways, through its more urgent preoccupations, to allow thoughts of her into the foreground.

He was afraid that if this did not happen, he would lose grip on the reality; the reality would fade to match the diminished thoughts. It was three days since he had seen her. He'd not been able to contact her. Damn why isn't she on the phone? He knew she would have come to his room at coffee time and there would have been no response to her knock. What would she have thought? He could not now bear the thought of a not knowing between them. He wanted certitude and he wanted it for her too.

Even now, after surviving the four-week separation at Christmas and so much shared time since then, he had no confidence that the bond between them would survive three days without renewal through physical presence – it was still all so new, so beyond his experience, so unbelievable. Its quality was still unproven. He was still uncertain of its durability, its depth. He was still unsure of what category of experience it was.

If asked, he would have said he was in love with her. But was she with him? Love had so far not come into their shared vocabulary. Whatever the case, he felt an exclusive commitment. He had no more yearnings for other women; he felt that all the pent-up frustrated desires of the years had now found a focus in her. He no longer dreamed that dream. He hoped, but could not be certain, that she felt the same. He found intolerable the thought that she might go out with someone else in his absence. Then, when he arrived at this unthinkable consummation, he thrust the thought away from him, told himself not to be stupid and reached back into recent history, reconstructed all that had happened, told himself it was real, it was important, it was durable.

He knew Barbara would have put up a notice for the students. It wouldn't be very informative; just that Mr Hamilton was indisposed – or something – and his students should consult other members of the department as necessary. At least, reading the notice, she would probably just think he was ill. But then what kind of ill? And if he was ill, it must have been sudden onset of illness; he was fine when she last saw him the day before. Sudden illnesses are not usually trivial. Not just a heavy cold; a heart attack? A stroke? All the time Aidan's energies were engaged in the agonising, urgent and crucial matter of his daughter's future, he was fighting off ill-defined, but painful worries about Louise.

The road was now less familiar. He needed to concentrate more. Bobby sat by his side in silence; after several abortive attempts at conversation, he'd decided that it was silence that was needed. It was a doleful situation, which would have been eased by a little sunshine, he thought again, as he peered through the twin overlapping arcs of cleared windscreen fighting against the drizzle. But he doubted that all the sunshine of a Riviera summer would have done anything to mitigate the grimness of the road he was driving along towards the centre of the town.

It was a long, broad road, crossed at regular intervals by narrower ones. It had been ordained that the workers would live in a treeless graticule next to the steelworks that employed them. But because steel could now be bought more cheaply from third-world countries, the steelworks had gone and through gaps where the terraces had decayed and houses been demolished, there were areas of black earth and vestiges of industrial detritus among a few battered-looking parked cars. The little shops that had once served the streets were mostly derelict.

Stopping the car at a pedestrian crossing, Aidan noticed a surviving Asian grocer's, a betting shop and a shabby, but still functioning newsagent. Most dispiriting of all, he thought, a boarded-up pub. He turned right thankfully into the road that would take him out to the southern suburbs.

From the map they had given him, he did not have too much trouble finding the Adolescent Unit. Cleveland Crescent was another outpost of decaying Arcadia. No longer the homes of well-to-do manufacturers, who must years ago have taken their loot and built in the country; the houses they had built themselves at the turn of the century now had the brass plates of doctors, dentists and solicitors; some had, lofted over the tops of hedges, on poles, the slicker product of the graphics studio proclaiming an architectural practice or financial services. The tree-lined road was corroded and crumbling in places; the patterns of its many patchings diverted Aidan's artist's mind in the direction of abstraction – but then again, he thought, why bother? Who needs to make abstract art? It's already there; it exists. Just come and look. Bobby said nothing. She had spent the journey defiantly excluding the outside world, her head bowed, as though studying her lap.

Number fifteen was called 'Roseberry'; it said so in letters once deeply incised in the sandstone cappings to the substantial brick gateposts, but now partially filled in by moss. Aidan carefully swung the Renault between them, crunching on to the drive – gravel, giving way at its edges to encroaching grass. It curved between unkempt grass verges, with glossy green banks of aucuba behind, to a square portal with two steps and four Etruscan columns. Within its shelter, to the left of the incongruously modern frameless glass doors, was a painted sign saying, 'Uremouth Health Authority. Woodsend Psychiatric Hospital. Adolescent Unit.' He parked the Renault in a small area indicated for visitors.

For some time, neither seemed inclined to move. Then Aidan turned to look at his daughter. She raised her eyes to his. 'Are you okay, love?'

She attempted a smile. It wasn't quite successful, but he knew what she meant.

'I don't know Dad ... I suppose so ...'

'We can keep in touch on the phone – and I'll come and see you as often as I can.'

'She called me 'love' – did you hear?'

'Yes.'

'It doesn't make any difference, Dad, does it?'

'I don't know, Bobby … I don't know. But whatever happens, I won't let you go back to that situation again.'

'D'you promise?' She looked at him anxiously.

'I promise,' said Aidan, then, after another silent interval, 'come on then, shall we go and investigate?'

Bobby took a deep breath. 'Okay,' she said, releasing her seat belt and getting out of the car.

Aidan got out, collected her case from the back of the car and walked round to where she was looking up impassively at Roseberry. He took her hand and together they mounted the two steps. Aidan held open one of the heavy glass doors, letting it whoosh shut behind them. From somewhere inside, music drifted from a record player – a singer. Something about an American pie or something like that, Aidan thought. He wondered what the hell an American pie was. They were in a spacious entrance hall, polychrome tiled floor, several doors, some open, some forbiddingly shut. There was a dark wood dado; above it, dull green paint up to the elaborate cream painted cornice. At the end, an impressive uncarpeted mahogany staircase spiralled out of sight to the left. To its right, a narrower, penumbral passage led to some distant interior. Kitchens, Aidan supposed.

Somewhere above, a door opened and shut, releasing from some distant room, an animated conversation. Aidan heard the conversation approach, as one hears with increasing trepidation the siren of an approaching fire engine. There was a clattering of feet as the conversers arrived at the top of the staircase and began their noisy descent. Feet first, two nurses appeared, formally, stiffly, traditionally dressed: one in green; the other in blue; both with starched white aprons and caps. At the bottom of the stairs, they concluded their conversation and the one in green disappeared in the direction of the kitchens. The other, apparently noticing Aidan and Bobby for the first time, came towards them.

'Ah ha,' she said, 'I bet you're Mr Hamilton and Bobby.' She had a rather husky contralto voice. Aidan was quite startled. They had said it was very free and easy-going; he did not quite expect to be confronted with every soldier's dream. She had auburn hair and blue eyes, her cheekbones were meticulously carved to yield delicate shadows, fading to the corners of her mouth that was full and pink. She was the nearest thing he had seen to Katherine Hepburn. About his own age, he guessed.

Aidan smiled at her. 'One hundred per cent correct,' he said. Bobby said nothing, scrutinising her feet.

The nurse held out her hand to Aidan, 'I'm Marian Hardcastle,' she said, 'Sister.' Then she offered Bobby her hand. Bobby looked up apprehensively at her father as she held out her hand. 'Come on

Bobby, cheer up. We're not going to eat you. You're really going to like your stay here. Look, I'll tell you what we'll do. I'll just pop into the office for a few minutes – I've got couple of forms to look up – and while I'm doing that, you can say goodbye to your Dad. When I come back, we'll stick him in the office – I just want a quick word with him before he goes – and I'll take you and your bag up to your room. When we've got you settled in, I'll introduce you to Daisy. She's about your age – mad about animals. She's got a parrot.'

'What, here?' asked Bobby, a little interest finding its way through the torpor.

'Oh yes,' said the Sister. 'We don't mind a few pets around if it makes the residents happy. By the way, we're very informal here. We all use first names, so you can call me Marian. Okay?'

Bobby tried her smile again.

'Right then. Back in a few minutes.' With a smile at Aidan, she turned towards a door on the left and disappeared within.

'Dad, you won't forget about me will you? You'll come and see me won't you? Soon, won't you?'

'Of course I won't forget you, darling. How could I forget my favourite thing? And yes I'll come and see you whenever I can – and we can talk on the phone when we want to. You'll be fine, I'm sure.'

When Marian returned, Aidan gave Bobby one last hug. Then Marian took Bobby's hand in one of hers and the case in the other. Halfway up the stairs Bobby turned and gave him a tearful look.

Aidan, a lump in his throat, waved as she disappeared from view, before turning to the room Marion had indicated, to await her return.

It was Dr Wilkinson's room; it said so in gold letters on a narrow plaque on the door. That much Aidan did notice; but not much else. Unusually, the visible world made no claim on him. It was an office of some kind. There were chairs, but he ignored them and found himself standing in the bay window, his field of vision full of unspecified green stuff, his mind full of agony. Then – he did not know how long after – there was another presence in the room. He turned. 'Ah, Sister …'

She smiled at him. 'Marion, please …'

'Marion …' He wasn't yet attuned to the first name culture. It was different with students; there the relationship was a continuing one and had to be easy-going. But here … Was it really old-fashioned to prefer the more formal address in professional relationships. He found the conflicting signals – formal dress, informal address – problematic. Nevertheless, 'Aidan,' he said, reaching for the proffered hand and shaking it.

There was a large desk with a large chair behind it and a smaller one before it. Books in bookcases on the walls; filing cabinets; shelves bearing box files. She smiled again. Pink lips, perfect white teeth. The smile gave extra prominence to the cheekbones, intensifying the shadows beneath them.

'Well, Aidan … do have a seat.' She indicated the chair in front of the desk. Aidan expected she would take the big chair behind it, but instead, she picked up a small chair from the side of the room and placed it at an angle to his so they were not quite facing each other but were quite close. She was holding a clipboard, which as she sat down, she held on her knee. His powers of observation suddenly restored, he noticed pinned above her left breast, a small upside-down fob watch. She crossed her legs, discreetly, though not so discreetly as not to expose a knee whose planes were fashioned with the same sculptural fastidiousness as her cheekbones. Aidan waited.

'Hm … you look as though you've been through the mill,' she said, looking into his eyes.

Aidan smiled grimly. 'You could say that, I suppose.'

'It's never easy to hand over your child into someone else's care. But I think this will be good for Bobby. I think she's going to make friends with Daisy. At the very least, she'll have respite; time to think things through. And you'll have some respite too – which you look as though you could do with – if I'm not being too personal.'

'Do I look such a mess then? Oh well … I suppose it's not surprising. Look, Marion I suppose I should be asking all sorts of intelligent questions about Bobby and what's going to happen to her, and so on and so forth, but really, I'm so exhausted all I'm capable of is sitting here and looking stupid.'

'Perfectly understandable. Right, well look, Dr Wilkinson isn't in this morning. You'll want to see him and he'll want to see you. What I suggest is for you to come back next week. I mean, I think it'll be best for Bobby if she can make a definite break with her recent past and try to get adjusted to her new situation. It'll probably be pretty good for you, too.' Aidan nodded his assent.

'You can ring us and we'll keep you in touch with things. Of course you can visit at any time and Bobby can ring you if she wants to. Really, there are few restrictions here – but I think it would be best if you just left it for a week and let's see how we get on.'

Aidan was thankful for that suggestion. He was thankful to be able to hand over the care of his daughter to someone else – someone he could have confidence in. What he had seen of Roseberry – not much, to be sure – but what little he had seen was sufficiently reassuring for him to feel some measure of emotional renewal as he drove out of the gate and headed back towards Swaleborough.

Time was, when arriving at college shortly after eleven, on a morning when he had no early teaching commitment or perhaps after a nine-thirty school practice supervision at some local school, he would drive into the main gate, park and head immediately to the senior common room for coffee with his colleagues. But today, his first thought was of Louise.

His latent insecurity taunted him; perhaps after three-days incommunicado she would have given him up; met someone else;

come to see the folly of the whole situation and come to her senses. But he had to be there in case she came. So he drove straight to the department and parked his car as conspicuously as he could. The department seemed deserted as he entered through the back door, made his way through the pottery, up the two flights of stairs to his room. Letting himself in, he shut the door behind him, hung up his jacket and set about the coffee-making routine. The machine had just begun to bubble and dispense its fragrance, when the knock came. Beethoven. He cautiously opened the door and she was in his arms. He swung her round, leaning on the door to close it. For moments, they were suspended there, interlocked. Then they parted and stood facing each other, hands on each other's shoulders, looking into each other's eyes as though unable to give credence to their reunion.

'Aidan,' Louise allowed her eyes to wander over his face. Her face showed alarm. 'Aidan, you look wrecked. What's happened? Where've you been? What's been going on?'

He closed his eyes, put his hands behind her head, feeling the softness of her hair flow between his fingers and drew her towards him again, steering her lips towards his, condensing his whole being into the sensations of this singular circular, contact. When eventually and gradually they parted again, Aidan said, and it was the first time he'd spoken, 'Lulu … Lulu … at the moment there's nothing, nothing but that you're here and with me. We're together. The rest can wait.

I'll tell you everything, when … when … when we've had a cup of coffee – if there's time.'

Louise looked at him seriously for a moment, then shaking her head a little, broke into a smile. 'Oh you do like to get the priorities right.'

Aidan used the rest of the day to pick-up his teaching commitments and do some of the things that had been deferred during his absence. He had spoken to the principal and to Barbara, giving them an outline of the events of the last three days. He held nothing back on the matter of Cathy's baleful contribution to those events. He wanted there to be no mistaking what underlay them. Later, he had found time to give Gerry a fuller account over several pints of beer. He speculated with Gerry how domestic life would now shape up in the absence of Bobby from the home. One element removed from a system requires an adjustment of the relationships among the remaining ones. But he knew there was no adjustment that would reconcile him with Cathy – not with the only too palpable gap where Bobby used to be.

378

CHAPTER 25

After it had been settled that Bobby would go to Roseberry, over the course of the next two tense days, during which he kept her at his side almost constantly, an idea started to form in Aidan's mind. It was at first a germ of an idea, at the time overlaid by the urgencies of his real world. It lingered there, like a pale sun struggling through thick haze. It was on the drive back to Swaleborough, with one burden removed (and he felt slightly ashamed to think of Bobby as a burden), however temporarily, from his back, that the haze dispersed; the sun emerged to full brilliance and he was able to attend to the idea in all its splendour. It was the ill-wind principle again. He felt a moment of guilt as he invoked it but this was followed by a surge of elation as he turned the matter over in his mind.

The Easter vacation was only a week away for him and his students; two-weeks away for the schools. Cathy had weeks ago signed up for a five-day archaeology school. It had been necessary for her to enlist Aidan's co-operation for this and for him to agree to look after the children. In view of the strains in their relationship and in the persistent climate of hostility, it doubtless pained her to have to ask Aidan a favour, but she had no option, so she did. Aidan could not remember the details. More probably she didn't ask at all, but just told him. 'I'm going … and you'll have to look after the children.'

Well, Aidan was not minded to play hard-to-get over this. He found the prospect of getting Cathy out of the house for a week very appealing. Anything that would divert her energies away from their destructive deployment in the family and focus them on something more remote was fine by him, something he would do everything possible to encourage. So he agreed. It didn't seem a chore to spend five days with his daughters. In fact, he thought he might be able to do some useful restoration work with them. He thought too that he would find various occasions to see Louise – remembering Christmas and now having her own flat, she had pretty well decided not to go home at Easter.

But then the Svensens had firmed up their invitation to Dora to accompany Klara and them on a short visit to their native Sweden. Dora was agog with excitement … and that week would overlap the five days of Cathy's absence. It would have left just him and Bobby. Now Bobby was at Roseberry; that was the ill wind. It left just him; just him. And Louise. He told Cathy that since he no longer had responsibilities at home, he might very well go away for a few days on a sketching trip. So if he were not about when she returned, she would know why. There were no grounds on which she could object to this, though Aidan supposed that if she had found any, she would have used them.

So when Aidan arranged to meet Louise that evening it was with some sense of suppressed excitement. She had said she would be working late in the studio on her current project and Aidan said he would come to meet her there, though he couldn't be sure of at what time. As the day wore on though, his relief that Bobby was being taken care of started giving way to anxiety. Supposing she knew straight away that she couldn't stand it at Roseberry. What if there should be an incident like that at the school? There were so many 'what ifs', that he became beset by the expectation that the phone would ring and it would be the Sister – Marion – requesting him to come and collect Bobby at once. Or worse, that it would be Bobby herself in a state of abject, incoherent panic, trying through her tears … to tell him something and wanting him to save her. Come now, come now… please, please, Dad, come now, now, now. He just hoped with all his heart that everything would be all right.

Failing an SOS from Bobby, there should, he thought, be no problems with his arrangements for the evening. He no longer felt obliged to negotiate his absences from home or to explain them. He no longer felt he owed this to Cathy. Henceforth, he had resolved, he would come and go as he pleased – and acknowledge her entitlement to the same rights. This would be subject, of course, to the fulfilment of his obligations towards the running of the house and particularly his responsibilities towards Dora.

Here he would be particularly vigilant. Cathy's relationship with Dora tended towards the doting. It was as if Dora was the recipient of not only her due in maternal love, but of Bobby's entitlement too. There were the makings of another kind of destruction to be visited upon her; she could turn out to be a monster of smugness, self-satisfaction and selfishness. He was sure that this outcome was contrary to her nature, but he was going to be there just to make sure.

On his return home, he had given Cathy an account of the morning of Roseberry and Bobby's installation there. She listened in silence. He wondered what her thoughts really were.

She said, 'I hope she'll be all right.' That was all she had said, when Dora's whirlwind arrival from the Svensens' made further exchange along those lines impossible; Dora's happy chatter about her coming visit to Sweden filled what would otherwise have been a gloomy void of silence. She had spent much of her time with the Svensens during the last three confused days. Aidan had kept wondering what Dora was making of the events which were torturing him. Probably not much, he thought. He was glad that she, having the average six-year-old's capacity to invest all her being in the here-and-now, seemed for the moment to be able to fill her life with that glorious anticipation of a treat to come. These were the conditions under which the evening meal was taken. Then Aidan, helped by the chattering Dora, cleared up while Cathy retired to the sitting room to prepare the morrow's school work.

It was not until later, when he was sitting on the edge of Dora's bed, watching her wriggle into her pyjamas that the subject of Bobby came up. She had been regaling Aidan with a breathless account of the day's triumphs and vicissitudes. Then, clad for sleep, she jumped on to the bed by his side and putting her arms around his neck and pulling herself up to put her cheek next to his, she asked, 'Daddy, where's Bobby gone? Is she coming back?'

Aidan had anticipated this and other questions, but though he'd thought about them off and on since Bobby's admission to Roseberry was first mooted, he'd come up with no answers that satisfied him. Children ask difficult questions and parents spend so much time devising the kind of plausible lie that saves them embarrassment, at least temporarily, on the grounds that they're too young, they wouldn't understand.

But Dora was a witness to what had been happening. Time and again she had been on the sidelines of the emotional violence which was common currency in her family. How was a six-year-old mind to process that? How was a forty-five year old, for that matter? Aidan consoled himself that it was at any rate somewhat easier to answer than 'Where has Granny gone?', and he had no option but to offer a simplified version of the truth. The difficulty was, Dora had a fairly normal relationship with her mother and he did not want to jeopardise that. Just as importantly, he resolved that no fragment of blame would attach to Bobby.

He said, 'Well ... she's gone away ... for a while. But she'll be coming back ... yes, she'll be coming back.'

'Where's she gone, though?' Dora persisted.

'To a place called Roseberry. It's a bit like a boarding school ... you know, where the pupils actually live in the school.'

'But why has she gone there?'

'Oh dear, Dora ... now why do you think she's gone there?' Dora looked down and thought for a bit. Then she turned her head sideways and looked up into his eyes.

'Is it because of Mum?' She asked tentatively. 'Why doesn't Mum like her?'

'Yes, that's why, Dora. But I can't answer your other question.'

'Why not Daddy?'

'Because I don't know the answer myself, love. I only wish I did.'

She sighed, thought for a bit and seemed satisfied for the present. Then suddenly, she leapt off the bed. 'I'll feed the gerbil now,' she said. Aidan watched her with an overwhelming sense of tenderness, as she crossed to the cage that stood on the chest of drawers by the window. After that, he supervised teeth cleaning and watched while Dora, still chattering went through the ritual of kissing goodnight each of her collection of dolls.

When she eventually tumbled into bed, taking pains to ensure the comfort of Betsy, her favourite rag doll, who always slept with her,

Aidan sat on the bed, lowering his head at the invitation of her outstretched arms and they hugged.

Then, 'What did Betsy say, Daddy?' she asked.

He went through the next ritual – the imaginary conversation with the rag doll, calmed his daughter's ensuing fit of giggling, fended off a sequence of further procrastinations and after a final embrace, switched off the light, with a final, 'Goodnight my love.' He knew as he went downstairs that his goodnight to his wife would be less congenial.

He reflected that there had been no emergency phone call from Roseberry or from Bobby. He did not think now that there would be, but if there were, Cathy would have to deal with it.

He let himself into the department by the main door, casually checking the rooms on the way to the studio, greeting the one or two students who were still working in the library. He found her at the far end of the studio, sitting on a high stool at a bench, bent over a microscope next to a drawing board. She was wearing a white coat and would have looked much like a medical student, had the white coat not been smeared and spotted with paint. Aidan opened and closed the door quietly and stood just inside it in silence for a while, looking at her at the other end of the room.

Usually, she wore variations on the theme of scruffy jeans and sweater or shirt, in the studio. This evening she must have been wearing a miniskirt, or, my God, he thought, lasciviously, maybe nothing, under her white coat, for a length of elegant thigh had escaped the opening at the front. The sight of that cool, naked thigh … aahh … a hotline to his genitals … would he ever become inured to it? How could he – ever?

Her hair hung loose and formed a curtain around the microscope. Not functional, he thought, but … beautiful. She was working on some ideas he had suggested to her about proportion in classical landscape – the golden section, the Fibonacci series – that sort of thing. She'd asked him, was it to be found lower down in the order of things – like in cell structure? He'd said he didn't know and suggested she find out. Her hair parted over the microscope as she turned to the drawing board and drew something with great concentration, perhaps a line, perhaps two. As she turned again to the microscope, she raised her hand to draw back her hair.

'Hi,' Aidan said softly. His voice whispered the length of the studio. Her hair streamed over the microscope as she raised her head and slowly swivelled round on the stool. She looked at him, smiling.

'Hi,' she said. He waited a moment longer before he slowly approached her. Their coming together seemed to alternate between the sudden, ravening, instantaneous implosion, like this morning; and the teasing, taunting, breath-holding deferment of the moment, like now; for silent aeons, it seemed, delaying the first delicate touch in a kind of slow motion ballet. But what power there was in this minimal touch – his hand light on the back of hers, their lips poised a hairsbreadth apart; their eyes locked together. It was a public place and the touch of their lips was momentary and gossamer-light.

Still in slow motion, they drew apart. Then, taking a deep breath, she showed him her work, talked about it. He looked, made some suggestions. They discussed them. Another pause.

'You have things to tell me, Aidan,' she said, looking again into his eyes.

Then, voices in the corridor. Crescendo. The doors flung open admitting two students in hilarious conversation. Their noise cut off sharp as they saw that the room was not empty. Aidan's hand brushed her knee in one of those audacious public gestures, flirting with discovery, as he turned to greet the newcomers.

'Hi Aidan ... hi Lulu,' they called.

Louise waved. Aidan said, 'Evening chaps. Planning on a little overtime tonight, are you?'

'Aidan, you must be joking,' then looking at his companion, 'tell him Paul.'

'Um ... well, nothing very virtuous, Aidan. S'matter of fact, we're going to the bar to get smashed. It's all on account of the stress you put us under in this department. I left my fags down here this afternoon ...'

'Yeah, and you can't get smashed without fags,' added his companion.

Aidan laughed. 'I never saw a less stressed-looking lot than you. It's just an excuse for youthful excess, if you ask me – as if an excuse was needed.'

Paul retrieved his cigarettes from the place on one of the side benches where he'd left them that afternoon and the two of them – the other was Garry – headed for the door, where they turned.

'See you guys in the bar, then,' said Paul.

'See ya later,' said Garry as they pushed through the door. There was suddenly silence. They looked at each other in this silence, smiling. Then, 'Hm,' said Aidan, his brow crinkled, 'I rather think they've got suspicions about us.'

'I rather think they have,' Louise replied. 'Does it worry you, Aidan?'

'Perhaps it should … but it doesn't. To tell you the truth, I like it. I would love everyone to know … but … ah well … just, just … but …' He allowed his speech to fritter away into vagueness. There was no conclusive end to this line of thought. Not at this time. Not yet.

Louise, smiling wistfully, began collecting together her gear. She placed the microscope in its box, her pencils in her bag and picked up the drawing board. Standing by the stool, she looked at Aidan and said, 'Right then. Shall we go?'

'Right,' Aidan said, 'but perhaps not to the bar – at least, not yet.'

They left the studio, heading for his room, turning off lights on the way, drawing a veil of darkness and silence behind them. There they made love – the kind of love you make after three days of separation and uncertainty, when the uncertainty has been resolved.

Then he drove her back to her flat. He'd not said anything yet, about the reason for his absence and though she had mentioned it, she had not persisted. Aidan felt that to speak of the events of the last few days at any length, now, would be to resurrect the agony of it all and he could not bear that.

Not only that, though, it would involve disclosures about the state of his family life. This was something that so far, had the status of a no-go area between them. Apart from Louise's one observation about his relationship with Dora, to date, they had conducted their affair – if that was how it was to be designated – as though his wife and family didn't exist; as though he were a free man – albeit with some unspecified obstacle in his life which acted as an irritating, though temporary impediment to the absolute freedom of their association. He supposed that Louise had erected some sort of mental barrier against the unwelcome reality too, and that, in the intensity of their mutual attraction and lust it was, for the present, enough.

Aidan felt too that the present was so overwhelmingly beautiful that the future, though he had recurring hopeful dreams about it, could for the moment be left to take care of itself. But when there were problems – over the stealing of time, for instance, he knew there was an irritant here and he knew that at sometime, something would have to be resolved. He foresaw two possible outcomes. One, either tensions would develop which would in the end destroy their relationship; or two he would realise his dream and be able to leave Cathy and throw in his lot with Louise. The former outcome he could not countenance. But he did not want to set up expectations of the latter in Louise until he had worked out more of the details and was sure she wanted the same. He wasn't, despite everything, certain about that. Love had never been mentioned, nor commitment. It had all been, so far, just a total intoxication with the present.

Over coffee in Louise's flat, that night, Aidan had told her that there had been trouble regarding his elder daughter which had taken several days to resolve. She had looked up at him over her coffee cup and nodded silently, seeming to accept Aidan's reticence, seeming only too ready to enjoy with gratitude the blessing of the here and now.

After the second cup of coffee, Louise said wistfully, 'I don't suppose you're going to cap this lovely day by staying the night, are you, Aidan?'

Aidan was silent a moment, looking down into his coffee cup as he swirled the last dregs around. 'No ... but ...' He hesitated teasingly, almost smiling.

'But what, Aidan?' she asked, expectancy in her eyes.

'Hm ... well ...'

'Come on. Come on ... But what?'

'Well you're not going home over Easter ... are you?'

She narrowed her eyes and looked at him penetratingly. 'Not if you make it worth my while.'

'Right, well ... you remember what it was that first brought you to the north?'

She thought for a moment. 'Well, I, er ...'

'Or rather what you said at the interview brought you to the north ...'

'Oh yes ... Lindisfarne, you mean? Well, what about it?'

'I would like to take you there.'

'What?' she almost yelled. 'Say that again please.'

'I said, would you like to accompany me on a few days in Northumberland, to take in the Roman Wall, the Northumbrian coast – and Lindisfarne?'

'Aidan, are you serious? I mean really really serious?'

'Never more serious, my beautiful Lulu.'

'Oh, Aidan, you're wonderful. I can think of nothing more marvellous. How could you arrange it? What could ...? No never mind about that – I don't care how you did it. It's just a wonderful, wonderful idea.' She took hold of his hands in both of hers and looked at him through eyes round and bright with delight, before flinging her arms around his neck in a rapturous embrace. It reminded him of Dora's response, when he had told her, yes, she could go to Sweden with the Svensens.

CHAPTER 26

Aidan collected Louise from her flat on a beautiful spring day. They drove out of Swaleborough to pick up the A68 at West Auckland, to retrace the route they had taken on the return from the Saturnalia, through County Durham to the northwest, to cross the River Tyne at Corbridge. There they booked into an old hotel. It was the first time Aidan had ever done this. Should they be 'Mr and Mrs Smith?' Wasn't this the archetype for illicit liaisons?

It proved not to be a problem. They spent two nights there, using the day between them to visit the Roman Wall. Louise was captivated by the wildness, the remoteness of the landscape; the landscape of horizontals – not Poussin; you couldn't do Poussin without verticals. They reminisced about that day in early autumn, when they hadn't made it to the Roman Wall, when their hands had first touched.

Then on the third day, they set off early, again picking up the A68, north across the wilds of Northumberland to Otterburn, thence through Rothbury to Alnwick, then up the A1 to Beal, before turning east towards Lindisfarne – the Holy Island. Access to Holy Island is via a causeway, only useable at low tide so they'd had to time their arrival according to the tide tables. Most visitors confine their stay to the interval between the tides, but Aidan planned that they would allow themselves to be marooned, to seek solitude.

They headed first for the village, parked the car and drank coffee. They wandered round the harbour, watching a fishing boat unload its catch. They watched the gulls swooping and squabbling over the cast-off bits, before drifting towards the priory to find the sculpture of St Aidan. Then they wandered back through the village, bought fresh crab sandwiches at the open door of a fisherman's cottage and returning to the harbour, ate them while sitting on the harbour wall, rejoicing in the glory of the sea and the sky, and the air.

They'd left the car in the car park at the end of the village and in the early afternoon, they headed back the way they'd come – back towards the causeway. A sparse procession of cars overtook them as they walked along the broad sandy margin of the road; it was too early in the year for the main flow of tourists. Those who had ventured over from the mainland during the morning slack tide were all heading back now, seeking to beat the incoming sea before it cut them off from the mainland, severing them from the realm of supermarkets, motorways and filling stations. They had 'done' Lindisfarne, now they were on their way back to the real world with their souvenirs and their photos.

Aidan and Louise, though, having decided to allow themselves to be marooned – to foreswear the blessings of the outside world for all of four hours – felt an inordinate sense of superiority over those fleeing back to the mainland with their ephemeral impressions. They wanted to be sure they were properly marooned. They wanted to watch the unstoppable advance of the sea, sealing their isolation.

'Of course,' Aidan said, 'we're still going to be sharing the island with the villagers – but they live here all the time, so that's different.' Louise agreed, laughing, as he directed them away from the road, which here swung round to skirt the very edge of the incoming sea, which now swirled and slapped about the rocks embedded in the rippled sand of the shore, just below its edge, causing clumps of dormant seaweed to stir into life and foraging sanderlings to flee before the wavelets, on their little clockwork legs.

Aidan and Louise, hand in hand, followed a grassy path into the dunes. Quite soon, it unravelled into a network of narrow sandy runnels between waist-high clumps of marram grass, sometimes leading to precariously unstable ridges, sometimes opening out into sheltered shallow basins. Leading the way laboriously upward, Aidan wondered whether it would be better to make love in the seclusion of a sandy hollow, with the risk of being suddenly stumbled upon by a solitary rambler; or on a ridge, somewhat exposed to a bird watcher with binoculars, but with a commanding view of the surrounding landscape and early warning of intruders. That judgement could, however, be left till later; what they now sought was a convenient belvedere from which to observe the incoming tide and verify their marooning.

The highest point in the immediate vicinity was a flattened summit, its tonsure of marram grass enclosing a circular pate of fine, pale gold sand, warmed by the afternoon sun; there they sank luxuriously down to watch and await their stranding. They looked across the glistening sands of the sound to the mainland, where Aidan pointed out the distant mound of Cheviot, quite hazy and blue on the western horizon.

They reclined, he leaning backwards, supported on his elbows, she with her head on his shoulder, rivulets of her hair falling on to his chest inside the open neck of his shirt. They watched as the sea crept in. Soon it had all but covered the shallow sands and the redshanks, oystercatchers and sandpipers which had been feeding in the last redoubt had taken off in little groups and dispersed, piping, to places now more congenial, up the coast. Only the straight line of the causeway was now above the water and though it was well after the advised safe crossing time a few cars were still venturing over.

'I suppose they must be locals,' Aidan said. 'They don't take any notice of official times – they know just how much time they've got and sod the safety margins.'

'Well what's that tower thing in the middle?' asked Louise.

'Oh that. That's a refuge – just in case anyone gets it wrong. It wouldn't be the first time a car's stalled and got swept off into the sea.'

'Look, one more crazy driver,' Aidan said, pointing to a Land Rover approaching fast. 'Must be one of those people who never gets anywhere on time.'

'Well I hope he makes it,' said Louise, shading her eyes from the glare of the sun as she followed its progress. The car reached the beginning of the causeway, which by now was completely awash, and hitting the sea with an explosion of spray, set off across it at high speed, its engine howling, throwing up twin plumes of water like a speedboat. They watched it till it reached the safety of dry land. Aidan almost expected it to stop there and shake itself like a dog, but without slowing down, it climbed the shallow hill on the other side and disappeared towards Beal.

Now they were marooned. They lay there soaking up the warming sun, watching the inexorable rise of the sea, till the causeway was no longer visible and the sea formed an unbroken, glittering expanse between them and the rest of England. Now it was the turn of the terns to feed; they came in a shrieking group, skimming the surface, then swooping upwards, to turn and dive ferociously into the shoals of little fish just below the surface, before throwing themselves once more into the sky, gracefully wheeling.

Louise watched them for a while, then rolled lazily on to her stomach and, looking sideways at Aidan, cradled her head in her arms.

'Aidan ... this is so beautiful. I could just ... just languish here forever. Why didn't I know about it before?' Aidan looked at her and carefully brushed sand off her bottom. The calf-length skirt she was wearing was of very light cotton – one of her own designs she'd told him. She wriggled a little and smiled, in response to his touch. Aidan, distracted for a moment, half closed his eyes to savour the sensation.

'... Er ... because we keep it a secret. For connoisseurs only – just in case some millionaire from the south might want to come and build hotels and lidos on it.'

'Oh Aidan,' she said, laughing, 'that's not fair – we southerners aren't all money-grabbing philistines.'

'No ... you're an exception,' he said, turning on his side to face her, then drawing her towards him. He looked into her eyes, with one hand touched her cheek, parted the curtain of hair that had fallen over it and delicately brushed her ear with his lips. She murmured appreciatively. Then quite suddenly, he leapt to his feet in a flurry of sand, staggering a little as he adjusted his balance to the yielding ground. He reached down and hauled her after him to her feet.

'There's more,' he said, briskly, 'much more. Look ...' Taking her hand, he led her through a narrow gap in the marram grass to the brow of the dune and turned her to face the sun and the southwards sweep of the coast. They shaded their eyes against the glare.

'Wow, I can see three castles,' Louise said. 'What are they?'

'Well the nearest one, a bit pointy, a bit like a volcano, that's Lindisfarne. We're attached to it. We can go and see it later, if you like.'

'And the next one, in the middle distance? That one looks absolutely massive. What's that one?'

'That's Bamburgh. It is massive. Built not long after Durham Cathedral was started.'

'And the one in the distance?'

'That's Dunstanburgh. Just a ruin now, but magnificent. Right on the edge of the cliff – a dizzy drop into the sea, a hundred feet below.'

'Gosh, so many castles.'

'Oh that's not nearly all of them. There's another over there, you can't see from here.' He pointed to the southwest. 'That's Alnwick and another beyond Dunstanburgh – that's Warkworth. Northumberland's full of them. We can see those on the way back if we want to.' She turned to look at him.

'Well why are there so many castles in Northumberland?'

'It's to keep out millionaires from the south, who might want to come up here and build hotels and lidos,' said Aidan, looking sideways at her. For a moment, she looked at his serious face through narrowed eyes, then without warning, gave him a hefty push, which sent him, stumbling helplessly down the hill with absurd giant footsteps as his feet tried to progress through the deep, fine sand at the same rate as his teetering body. He let out a yell. Louise immediately launched herself after him down the hill with the same crazy half jumps and caught up with him as his feet gave up and he totally lost control, tobogganing headlong for several feet down the dune. Louise's flight came to the same disastrous end and they came to rest in a jumble of limbs, half buried in the sand.

Louise's blouse had come untucked, and her skirt was rucked up. Aidan shook himself free of the sand and grabbed her about the waist. Giggling, she struggled to free herself and in the ensuing melee he deftly removed her knickers – against only token resistance. He struggled upright and made to run off with them, but Louise dived at his legs and brought him down again into the sand. For a moment they struggled together, helpless with laughter. Then she fell back into the sand, gasping while he held up the knickers in triumph, like a pennant captured in some deadly skirmish.

'Oh Aidan,' she said, through the laughter, pulling down her skirt. 'I love you, I love you, I love you … I …' she hesitated, the laughter subsided. She was suddenly serious. '… Oh dear, I don't know if I meant to say that … I … I …' Her sentence drifted into silence. They had never before spoken of love. He turned on his side, resting on one elbow, hardly breathing now, looking at her, waiting, as a sudden breath of warm breeze stirred some straying fronds of her hair. Her eyes were wide open, seemingly captivated by the sky. Her mouth was arrested in the articulation of that last syllable, as though she were shocked by the unauthorised escape of words she did not even know were there inside her. The tip of her tongue ran round her lips, moistening them. A smear of fine sand streaked her left cheek.

'Do you, Louise?' he said, 'Do you love me?'

She slowly turned her head towards him and reached for his hand. She looked seriously into his eyes. 'I didn't mean to fall in love. When I came to Swaleborough … I mean … away from all that mess and upset … I didn't want to have to go through all that again … I thought being in love was a bad deal. I think I just wanted to forget about it all and try to start a new phase in my life, and just … well, see what would happen …'

Aidan took her hand in both of his and lowered his head till his lips brushed her fingertips. 'And this has happened. I'm glad,' he said to her fingertips.

'And now I've said it … so it must be true, mustn't it?' Her smile had a tinge of wistfulness. 'That makes it serious, doesn't it?'

'I think it was serious for me right from the beginning,' Aidan said. 'Nothing quite like it has happened to me before. I couldn't bear to think it was something … well, just transitory. I've just kept hoping you would feel the same. And if you really mean what you said …' He looked up again and into her eyes. '… then you do.'

'Oh Aidan …' she said, '… Aidan,' looking, with eyes that were slightly bewildered, into his eyes. Suddenly, the playfulness was gone, the carefree irresponsibility, the sense that only the now mattered; the living hopefully and excitedly from this now to the next one.

Suddenly, these feelings had a context. If this meant that they were not ephemeral, there must be a future and that future contained other people; especially, it contained a family. They fell into an embrace; and it was an embrace with a frisson of fear, but also a new element, an enhancement; a deepening, perhaps something to do with a new sense of emotional security, emotional commitment. For minutes, they lay there in the sand, clamped fiercely together, neither speaking. Then Louise relaxed and withdrew a little.

After a pause, she said, 'Aidan ... I'd like you to tell me about your wife and your family. All this time I've tried to avoid thinking about them. I suppose ... well as long as I didn't think about them, I didn't need to feel guilty but now ... now ... if we really love each other ... I need to know. I'd better start facing the facts.'

Aidan bit his lip. He too had, without at this time really wanting to, been thinking about his family.

She continued, 'I want you. I really want you ... so I need to know what the competition is like ...' she paused for a while '... but not now.' She sought out his lips and touched them with her own, holding the fragile contact in a prolonged, suspended kiss. 'What I want to do now is make love.'

She gently pushed Aidan on to his back. He smiled and looked up at her through half-closed eyes. She sat up and looking down at him unzipped his trousers. He was ready and she released his erection into freedom, the air and the sunshine, then hitching up her skirt, she twisted round to straddle him, guiding him into her. Then she allowed her skirt to fall about them, concealing their conjunction. They made love in the sand, to the whisper of the warm breeze in the marram grass and the distant cry of gulls. And they were not disturbed.

Presently, when the fires had died down and the world had gradually come back into focus, and again they noticed the cry of the gulls and the warm caress of the breeze, they had ever so slowly disconnected and become two again.

Louise said, 'Aidan, let's go to the sea now, to the beach. Can we do that?' She got to her feet, straightened out her clothes and smiled down at him.

'Er ... well ...' Aidan began.

'Er well what.'

'You can't go wandering around Holy Island with your present underwear deficit,' he replied, picking up her knickers from the sand; he had allowed them to fall there when he had earlier needed both his hands free. He waved them round and handed them up to her.

She took them, giggling like a child who has just whispered a naughty word, shook them and inspected them. 'I can't wear these ... they're full of sand. I don't want to get sand in my ...'

Aidan leapt to his feet, laughing and snatched them back, thrusting them into his trouser pocket. 'Okay then. I'll take care of them. St

Aidan wouldn't like it, but it's okay by me. You shall roam Holy Island knickerless.'

They spent the afternoon exploring the dunes and the northern shore of the island, finding their way past the still submerged causeway, on their way back to the village. They had two more nights before them and had decided that if they could find somewhere to stay, they would spend this one on the island.

They did. They found accommodation in a comely fisherman's cottage, with a view over the harbour and a large brass bedstead.

Later that evening, they had, as a matter of course, headed for the pub. Before long, they were at that prime stage of alcoholic bliss where sibilants were not yet a challenge and talk flowed uninhibitedly. It was about themselves – reliving the short history of their relationship. For now they knew they were in love. There were so many reminiscences – even from so short a period of time. Nothing, nothing in the world was more interesting than themselves. They massaged their history and delighted in it. So now when she asked him about his wife, the question no longer seemed such an outrage against their present happiness. That seemed impregnable. No, what she was asking seemed merely a filling in of background.

'Tell me about when you first met her,' Louise suggested. 'I mean, how long have you known her?'

Aidan looked down into his beer, reflectively swished it round in the glass. Then looking up at her again, he smiled ruefully. 'We were at school together. Must have been about fourteen when I first spoke to her.'

'Ohhh, so you were childhood sweethearts,' She said, nodding knowingly.

Aidan looked pained. 'God, I hate that expression. But in any case it wasn't like that. It was only in the sixth form – and then in the … er … context of the gang – when … you know … sort of tentative relationships seemed to develop. Kind of unofficial pairings. She wasn't the only one in the running. You know how it is at that age – things are pretty fluid. Then, anyway at eighteen, I was whisked away by HM Government to serve my country for two years in the RAF.'

'Oh Aidan, how glamorous. Were you a pilot?' Louise asked, wide eyed.

Aidan laughed. 'Like hell I was. I wasn't nearly belligerent enough for that and what I did wasn't in the least glamorous. As a matter of fact, I spent my two years as an instrument mechanic. Most of the time it was extremely boring.'

'Oh how disappointing. I could just see you flying a Spitfire or something, looking really handsome in your uniform.'

'Well no such luck. Now if I'd been born a year or two earlier, it might have been different. But I did actually work on Spitfires. Spent my time mending the instruments on wartime Spitfires the airforce kept in storage – just in case. When I was recalled to arms for a fortnight's reserve training two years later, they'd all been chopped up and burnt.'

'What! Well then the whole thing was a waste of time then. You could have been doing something much more valuable for those two years.'

'Oh I don't know … it wasn't altogether a waste of time. I did get something out of it I suppose.'

'Well, like what?'

'Er … well, I learned to solder.'

Louise choked in the act of taking a swig of beer and burst into laughter. 'What? Was that all? All that taxpayers' money over two years, just to teach you to solder?'

Aidan looked down modestly. 'Oh … I suppose there were a few other things.'

'Well what else, then?'

'I was able to explore one of the most remote and beautiful areas of Scotland. I had a bike and a good friend. Someday I'll take you there. And then there was …'

'Yes. Go on.'

'Well … I lost my virginity.' Louise laughed again.

'Wow, I bet that was the best bit. Go on, tell me about it.'

'Mm …' Aidan had a dreamy smile on his face. 'Sometime, perhaps … well, she was a WAAF named Rosie and it happened, oddly enough one hot summer's day on a remote sand dune on the edge of the Moray Firth.'

'Ah, so today wasn't the first time on a sand dune,' she said, with a piqued expression.

'No – but it was certainly the best to date,' he said teasingly. She tightened her lips, glowered and gave him a playfully fierce punch on the shoulder.

'That's enough of that. I'm getting jealous.'

'Well it was a quarter of a century ago.'

'Yes well, it's retro-active jealousy and I've got it. So you'd better carry on with your autobiography before I hit you with my handbag.'

'Right well after that, four years at art school, then another year doing a post-grad diploma. So there was plenty of scope there for adventures. But Cathy was always there, waiting in the wings ... I don't know ... there seemed to be a kind of inevitability about it.'

'So you got married.'

'So we got married. We all got married. Everyone I knew got married. It was in the air. It was the thing to do. I got my first job – art master in a brand new secondary modern school. And we lived in a brand new semi, rented to us by a generous new-town corporation. In the alien south, what's more.'

'Oh, in the maligned south, was it? And were you in love with her?'

He sighed and looked thoughtful for a few moments. 'Well people usually are in love when they get married ... so I suppose I must have been. But it's a long time ago and things that have happened since have sort of clouded the picture quite a lot. You know when people talk about "the mists of time" ... well it's a pretty good metaphor, really. Time is misty.' He paused, looking thoughtfully into his empty glass as small archipelagos of foam slid down its interior. Then he said, 'Look, we're out of beer. I'll go to the bar.'

He pushed his chair back and stood up. The chair legs grated on the bare wooden floor. He could feel her looking at him as he turned his back on her and made his way to the bar. He wondered what kind of figure he cut. Christ, he was forty-five. He consciously stiffened up his shoulders and drew in his belly. Remembering that ghastly picture of him in the prospectus, he was careful to hold his head up and thrust out his chin a little so offering the best possible view, before turning to the bar and presenting his profile to Louise's scrutiny.

He paid the barman for two bottles of Newcastle Brown, each slightly frothing at the mouth and exchanged convivialities with a pair of elderly, grizzled, gansied locals, on the way back to the table. Louise's eyes followed him back to his place. She was waiting for more revelations. Adjusting himself into his chair again, Aidan reached for her hand, over the table, and, assisted by the Newcastle Brown, he continued, filling in some of the history of his life with Cathy, the birth of their daughters and their present problems. When he seemed to have come to an end, she squeezed the hand she was holding and looking into his eyes asked him, 'Do you still love her, then?'

He held her gaze for some moments before replying. 'I said I love you.'

'Yes, I know you've told me that. But do you still love Cathy too. You see, I don't know if you can love two people at once.'

'Depends on how you define love, doesn't it?'

'Well how do you define it Aidan?'

Still holding her hand, Aidan scrunched up his eyes again and thought. It was a question he had in recent times wrestled with regularly. There had been a time when he could fob himself off with the meretricious thought that love was a bit like art; almost impossible to define, but you recognised it when you saw it. But now, for him, that no longer worked for art, for not only could he not define art, but a lot of the time, he couldn't damn well recognise it either. 'Art is whatever is used as art.' He couldn't remember who said that, but its exquisite circularity seemed to him to make the best of a bad job. He had come to realise that it didn't work for love now, either.

From general observation, he had developed a cosmic image of love which seemed to work for a lot of cases. In some distant galaxy, a star goes nova; it explodes cataclysmically, giving up the whole of its energy in the space of a few days then shrinking, lightless, to a lump of dead matter of incredible density – a black dwarf – for the rest of eternity. A lot of the mature marriages he saw looked to him like lumps of dead matter. He supposed the thing to aim at was a nice, amiable steady state kind of star – like our own sun, reliably radiating light and warmth into the foreseeable future; the odd solar flare, of course, but nothing disastrous. Yet, his own previous experience fitted neither case really. It had certainly not started with a nova in the first place, nor quite shrunk into a black dwarf subsequently – too many energetic flare-ups for that analogy to hold.

He knew he was experiencing the nova with Louise, though, and what an exhilarating burst of light and energy it was! Could he reshape physics and keep the celestial furnace going forever? He felt at that moment as though he could … but realistically, he needed a fallback cosmology to characterise what was to come. Could he hope for a gradual transition to that amiable steady state – to a reliable, familiar, totally satisfying warmth? He needed to know what love was made of. He'd said he loved her, he felt, deeply and believed that he did; it was like nothing he'd experienced before. He just felt he wanted to be with her the whole time, to blend his life with hers. When he was not with her, his mind was filled with her absence.

As far as Cathy was concerned however, for years now, her absence had been no cause for unhappiness – latterly more often a cause of relief. So if that was the crucial test, perhaps he didn't love her. Yet there was more than that, wasn't there? There was a shared history. There was responsibility for another person's happiness and welfare.

But was it love when you became, over time, bound by custom and usage, and a sense of responsibility? Or was it ... well, something else?

He cast about for precedents. Close to him, there were Gerry and Brenda – a steady state couple if ever he saw one. They seemed to like each other for a start; to share jokes, hold hands, administer their household and deal with their children democratically and amiably. No quarrels about money. No jealously monitoring the other's time away. Room to be individuals as well as lovers. Ah yes, but Gerry had access to a bit on the side, didn't he? My God, the thought struck him, does Brenda too? Is that what it takes?

And what about Alan Bradshaw? Arrived at Swaleborough a year or two after Gerry, to be number two in the English Department. A little older than Aidan, he moved into a tiny, but extremely engaging cottage, one up, one down, which he soon filled up with his books, hi-fi and pictures. Alan was good-looking in the shaggy mode. Long, undisciplined hair; black, with matching beard lightly streaked with grey. Battered leather jacket, jeans ... (except when visiting schools!). At that time, in pursuit of a PhD, engaged on a rather demanding analysis of the oeuvre of some obscure early eighteenth-century poet, using a markedly structuralist approach.

He was soon assimilated into the 'younger set'. Useful table tennis player – though never made it on to the team. Dramatic Society. Could knock back a pint with the best and never let an opportunity to do so go by. No woman in his life; he seemed to belong to that saintly minority untouched by lust, and, his colleagues thought, destined for permanent bachelorhood.

His friends all had difficulty with the concept of a woman-free existence; of course they understood about homosexuality, but clearly, Alan was not that. Indeed, over a pint or two, he would hold forth with the best of them on the necessary attributes of the right woman. She must be young, beautiful, intelligent and she must 'know who she was' (he said he'd had trouble in the past with people who didn't – though he was unspecific on this matter).

Although an attractive guy – both to look at and to pass the time of day with, he seemed to have little more than a theoretical interest in attracting women. His friends were inclined to believe that the unrealistic standards he professed were a cover-up for a feeble libido. They rather suspected that he was a virgin. They, to a man, self-professed experts in these matters, were not reticent about giving him advice on pulling – but nothing seemed to work. They concluded that his nerdish absorption in his academic work was reasonably effective as a substitute for sex.

Then quite unexpectedly, his ship came home. He'd been supervising students on the spring teaching practice in one of the local comprehensive schools. Back in college, in the senior common room, around the coffee trolley, he began mentioning to his friends things about the German assistant he kept meeting there. Over the four weeks of the teaching practice, the details accrued. She happened to be working on a PhD too. Subject? Early eighteenth-century English poetry. And wow, did she fit the specification! She was beautiful. She was funny. She was sexy. She knew who she was. And, extraordinarily, she shared Alan's other enthusiasms – for walking, ornithology, football, cooking and baroque music.

They arranged to go for a walk together. Alan would show her some of the upper Teesdale manifestations of the Whin Sill. It was a success. So they decided to do it again. He would take her this time to the remote tarn he knew, where, in the spring – for spring it was – you could hear the burbling of curlews, watch lapwings performing their connubial aerobatics and hear the snipe drumming for their mates.

Alan had not thought he and Gretchen were doing more than enjoying a shared interest in a secular sort of way. He could not credit that such a gorgeous, witty (people were wrong about the German sense of humour, he asserted) and intelligent young woman would want anything more than that from boring old him. Well … perhaps it was something to do with nature's naked display of fecundity in that lonely reach of upper Teesdale, but that day, to his intense surprise and immense gratification, she deflowered him behind a small clump of dwarf juniper.

Nova? SUPERNOVA. Alan was transformed, radiating light and energy. He gave his friends to understand that he and Gretchen were now an incandescent item and how wonderful it all was. For a fortnight he went through his days wearing an idiot grin. At the end of the fortnight, the grin was somewhat compromised by an element of bewilderment.

'She's moved in,' he told his friends, over coffee that morning. He'd often gloated over his, as he saw it, family-oppressed colleagues, extolling the incomparable advantages of living alone and free. He would never, ever want to share his living space, he would assert. 'And d'you know, I'm not sure I agreed to it,' he said, showing some signs of confusion. A week later, a new face looking for coffee in the senior common room. It was a while before recognition dawned; it was the voice more than anything. It was Alan, minus beard, hair noticeably shorter.

'She loves me to bits,' he'd felt bound to explain, 'she just doesn't care for facial hair.' A week later, she'd bought him a present: an electric razor.

'She likes me to shave twice a day; can't abide stubble,' Alan had said. His hair was now very markedly shorter and with the novel feature of a neat side parting. 'She's good with the scissors ... keeps my hair in order,' he said with a slightly sheepish grin. In another week, the leather jacket and jeans were replaced by a navy-blue blazer and grey flannels.

'Well ...' Alan took a deep breath. 'She's a vegetarian. Having me in carnivorous clothes went very much against her principles. Yes I know jeans are vegetarian, well they just didn't go with the new

414

jacket. She kind of likes the English image ... you know ... but the sex is terrific, absolutely terrific – like a ferret on heat all the time.'

One thing Alan had been concerned about was his smoking. He'd been meaning to give up ever since the doctors found out it was bad for you, but he'd just never got round to it. The next thing that happened was that he gave up the fags. Cold turkey. Just like that. Instead he took to chewing gum; the perpetual, frenetic mastication of spearmint-perfumed gutta-percha. His friends wondered what it would take to get him off the chewing gum.

There was now a conspicuous falling off in Alan's involvement in the social life of the bar. Understandable, to some extent in one suddenly exposed to the pleasures of the flesh in unrestricted quantities. But his now occasional appearances were attended by a certain shiftiness, a kind of unease; a guilt, perhaps. An offer of even a second pint was now met with the hand hovering over the empty glass.

'Oh ... er, no thanks,' He would say. Then glancing at his watch, 'I think maybe I'd better ... er ...'

He eventually explained that Gretchen was pretty appalled by his drinking habits, which he'd always thought were pretty okay. But she was right. The doctors were saying that anyone drinking more than a pint and a half a day was seriously jeopardising their health. She seemed to believe he was on the verge of alcoholism. And because she loved him so much, she couldn't bear to see him drink himself to an early grave. He had to break with the pub culture – that culture of self-destruction. He knew she was right. She had the medical evidence. So no, he wouldn't have another half. No, he knew she would never know if he did, but she'd put him on his honour. She had to be able to trust him.

It was later discovered that she was extremely concerned about his dependence on other stimulants too. He would really have to do something about the tea and coffee. Oh and she knew a very good homeopath, who would help him with his addictions and generally set him on the path to a good healthy lifestyle. And we must look very seriously into what kind of past life he'd led, what sort of childhood, to set him on this ruinous road. Undoubtedly some counselling would help. And then, he'd really have to do more walking, cycling, healthy things they could do together. He could do his unwinding in herbal baths, rather than in the pub. Perhaps some yoga too – wholesome things like that. Oh and they would look into detoxification – the latest thing she'd read about – and colonic irrigation, too. He really needed to get rid of all those accumulated poisons.

After six months she had, apparently successfully, reshaped Alan to fit the blueprint in her head. He was unrecognisable as the man she had fallen in love with. But she loved this new man so much that she wanted them to spend every moment of their non-working time together. If he was out she must know where he was and when he would be back. Every time they met, even in the house, she needed them to exchange caresses; she needed to be told again and again how much he loved her. Their language by now had disintegrated into a kind of lovey-dovey pidgin – not only in private, but even, to Alan's embarrassment, among friends. So insistent were her demands upon his attention that he found it almost impossible to find enough time to himself to read a book or do a crossword. He could not even allow himself the simple luxury of a protracted stay in the lavatory in case she should be waiting outside the door with an enema syringe.

Yes, there were minor problems, Alan eventually admitted, but she really, really believed in these things and it was all because she loved him so much. It was just a matter of a bit of give and take. That's what relationships were all about.

The nervous breakdown kept Alan away from college for a whole term, the first six weeks being spent in a psychiatric ward. During that time, Gretchen had to return to München-Gladbach because of illness in the family. She had thoughtfully removed all her possessions from the house during Alan's internment and did not return to Swaleborough. Aidan and other friends set about reincorporating Alan into the depraved world of the sane.

Aidan had to reinvent his cosmology to cover this case; perhaps a celestial encounter between two stars. They enter into a binary relationship, revolving round a central axis. But one proves more massive than the other and gradually strips away its weaker companion's atmosphere, leaving it shrivelled and shrunken to spin forlornly off into the outer reaches of the universe.

'Aidan,' Louise said, looking determinedly at him at him and gripping his hand so tightly that her nails were digging into his flesh, 'tell me. I need to know. I need to know what I'm up against.' Aidan detached his gaze from the picture rail and met hers.

'Listen, Louise, I can't really define love, but I sure as hell recognise it. I recognise it in what I feel for you.' He fell back on that one after all.

'And Cathy?'

'What I feel for Cathy is … well, responsibility. It's the kind of feeling that arises out of knowing that you're capable of actions which could drastically affect someone else's life.' Louise sat silent, still gripping his hand, waiting for him to continue. 'The history we share … well it creates a … sort of bond and that's difficult to deny. You know … not something you can ignore.' Silence again. Then Aidan took a deep breath. 'But I don't any longer love her in the way most people understand the word.'

Louise sighed. She relaxed the grip on his hand, smiled a little.

'I'll just have to be satisfied with that, then, I suppose.'

For a while they sipped their beer, without saying anything. It seemed a time for silence. Then Aidan smiled ruminatively into his glass.

'What're you grinning at then?' Louise asked.

'Oh, I was just thinking about when you first came to college. That day when we went on the walkabout, maybe that was when I first fell in love with you.'

'Did you, Aidan?'

'Well ... in retrospect ... of course I didn't say that to myself then. I mean, you were a student ... I was a married man. It was a fantasy, that's what it was ... and I booted it out of my mind. But it kept coming back again.' Louise smiled at him.

He went on, 'You were so beautiful. And you talked about Poussin, classical landscape, the park. I was completely bowled over.' A shadow of anxiety passed across Louise's face. She looked down. The tip of her tongue emerged and rested on her upper lip. She sighed then looked up again as though undecided about something she wanted to say. Aidan caught the anxiety.

'What is it, lovely?'

She looked thoughtful. 'It's a kind of confession ... I ...'

Immediately, Aidan stiffened. Anxiety. Insecurity lurked. What could she have to confess?

'You know all that stuff about Poussin? Well ... that day I came for the interview ... I don't know really know to put this ...' She glanced up at him sideways as though checking his response ... 'Well I arrived in the morning, but during the journey, I'd kept looking out of the window, asking myself what the hell I thought I was doing. Several times I thought I must be crazy doing this. I kept thinking, I'm going to get off at the next station and catch the next train back. Then suddenly, the next station was Swaleborough. And I got off. But I didn't go back. I thought, well now I'm here, I may as well see what it's like. So I walked into town, thinking to have a look round, but still not sure that I was going to the interview. But anyway I wanted a cup of coffee first. Well I found that espresso bar in Coach House Lane so I went in, got my coffee and sat down. Then two girls came and sat at the same table. They saw my Swaleborough stuff and we got talking. It just happened that they were students from the college – and in the Art Department to boot. So when they realised I was being interviewed there that afternoon, they offered to take me up to the college and give me an unofficial guided tour. Well I jumped at the chance. They gave me a lot of useful insights I wouldn't have got officially. That decided me to go to the interview.' Aidan was looking puzzled, wondering where this was going. Louise had paused.

'Well, go on,' he said.

'Er … for instance … they gave me a rundown on some of the lecturers – particularly those in the department.'

'Oh really,' said Aidan, tightening his lips. 'What did they say about me, then?'

Louise smiled. 'I can't really tell you … oh well …' She hesitated, embarrassed. 'Well they said you were quite dishy – for a man of your age.'

Aidan looked severe and said, 'humph.'

'They also told me that you were mad about classical art ... and Poussin especially. Then when I met you in the interview ... well I thought you were dishy too ...' She paused again.

'Go on then. I can't really see where all this is getting to.'

'Well when I got home, the first thing I did next day was ... Oh Aidan you're going to hate me for this. You see, I didn't know a damn thing about Poussin really. I got out Anthony Blunt ... anything I could find about Poussin. I went to the National Gallery.' She hunched up her shoulders and looked appealingly up at him. 'I swotted it all up – don't you see?' She clenched her teeth, screwed up her eyes, put her hands over her ears and ducked her head down, like a soldier in the trenches, hearing the scream of the transient shell, waiting for the bang, hoping it wouldn't be too close.

Aidan sat up stock still, his eyes wide open, his mouth agape. He remained like that for several seconds. Then he began to laugh. Louise opened her eyes cautiously. He looked up at her and shook his head.

'Lulu ...' he said, through the laughter, '... my God ... I just don't know what to say ... Listen, you deceitful ...' he sought for a suitable word '... baggage. I was completely taken in. Just shows how gullible I am – and how easy to deceive. How can I ever trust you now, eh?'

Louise smiled anxiously. 'Well I didn't mean to deceive, Aidan ... really. It just sort of seemed like a good idea, if you were going to be my tutor, to know something of what you were on about ... but if you forgive me, I promise not to do it again.'

He looked at her tenderly; did she do all this because she fancied him? 'Oh Aidan,' she said meekly. 'You do still love me, don't you? I know it seems deceitful ... but I won't ever be deceitful again.'

Aidan reached across the table, took both of her hands in his and drew them to his lips, looking into her eyes. 'Very well then,' he said. 'We'll say no more about it.' He shook his head and the laughter came back. 'And I still love you ... very, very much.'

They left the pub in time to be present at the day's elegant demise, from the grassy mound on the landward side of the island, beyond the village. Fractured bands of dark purple stratus striped the sky to the west, against the crimson afterglow. Across the water, on the mainland, a few sparse lights pricked the on-coming night and echoed in the waters of the sound. To the south, beyond the silhouetted cone of the castle, the beam of the Longstone light swept the sea from its tower on the Outer Farne, reminding Aidan of his first encounters with Bella, so many years ago. He put an arm around Louise's shoulders, feeling her hair blow gently against his cheek as she nestled her head into him.

The brass bedstead squeaked appallingly. They made mute love on tiptoe that night. In the morning, generously breakfasted, they set off for the causeway to make an early crossing. The weather had changed in the night and beyond the harbour, the sea roared its fury. Inland, the ebbing tide was still lapping the edge of the causeway and the wind, gusting fiercely, funnelled between island and mainland, flayed the tops off the wavelets, spattering the car with salty spray. The sky was unremitting grey, with rags of darker, lower cloud racing towards the land scourging it with fierce bursts of rain which rattled against the car like machine gun fire.

Aidan was exhilarated by the energy, the turbulence of it, for he loved the sea in all its moods and wanted Louise to share his love. She caught his excitement and they revelled in their restricted, intimate existence in this mobile enclave of security, safe from the battering of a hostile world.

They stopped at Bamburgh. In waterproofs and boots, battered by the wind, they stood for a while looking up the wet-glinting face of the basalt cliff, to the massive bulk of the castle above. Aidan explained to Louise about the Great Whin Sill – that layer of molten rock which, from some cataclysmic eruption, millions of years ago, had oozed below the surface crust of the northern landscape, breaking out in places to give it some of its most characteristic shapes; surfacing along the upper reaches of the Tyne, so the Romans could build their wall along it, creating the massive step in the upper Tees for its waters to plunge over at High Force and emerging on the Northumbrian shores to provide impregnable foundations for the castles of Lindisfarne, Dunstanburgh and Bamburgh – and with enough left over to make the Farne Islands.

Later, high up, crouching in the lea of the castle's ramparts, Louise, wet faced and shouting against the wind, said to Aidan, 'Now I know why you love Poussin so much, classical landscape and all that.'

'Oh go on – enlighten me,' Aidan shouted back.

'Well, just look at this ...' she stood up, and, braced against the wind, gestured round her with a sweep of her arm and downwards at the crashing waves. 'Storm-lashed coast, grim castles, implacable nature. You were brought up among all this wildness. It's romantic ... it's Romanticism gone mad. It's in your blood. It's been twisting your guts all these years. And you're trying to find tranquillity ... that's what it is – that's what you're looking for in Poussin.' Laughing, Aidan pulled her towards him and kissed her wet face.

'Lulu,' he said, 'you could be right. Thanks for the insight.'

Later, they dried out and had lunch at the Lord Crewe Arms. It was while sipping their coffee, reflectively, their feet still slightly steaming before the simmering open fire that Louise suddenly said, 'Oh God, Aidan ... it's our last night, tonight ... and then back to normality. How quickly it's gone.'

Aidan sighed. 'It hasn't gone, Lulu,' he said, reproof in his voice. 'There's still almost two days – just a bit less than half – left. Lots of nice things will happen in that time. And they'll go on happening when we get back – though I know it won't be as perfect as now.'

Then having fended off that small intrusion from the future, he explained to her, as they proceeded on the leisurely drive south, his

424

'we'll cross that bridge when we come to it' strategy. He told her of how, in order to survive, he'd worked at it and brought it to perfection in his early teaching days in an inner city school. At first, he'd found that the pleasure of the anticipated weekend respite from the rigours of the classroom battleground lasted only as long as the partial anaesthesia induced by the Friday night binge. Come Saturday morning together with the hangover, he was beset by the dread thought that Monday was only a day and a half away, and those hours which he should be enjoying would be increasingly tainted by the inexorable approach of the new week. It had tended to happen with holidays too. He explained how, realising how much of the time he was supposed to be enjoying he was not enjoying, because he was anticipating its end, he had worked hard at the strategy of compartmentalising parcels of time, refusing to permit the baleful contents of one to leak into another.

Louise looked at him with a rueful smile and placed her hand on his thigh, '… well you're right I suppose. Okay, I'll give it a try. You can start by telling me how we're going to spend the rest of the day.'

By the time they arrived at the little fishing village, where they would spend their last night, the layer of heavy cloud, lying in ever-diminishing rolls to the horizon was showing signs of wear and tear. Far out over the sea, a seam had split and a broad fan of pale yellow sunbeams splayed downwards onto the surface, laying a brilliant slash of light along the tops of the waves. But the breeze was still sharp and as they parked the car, they could see that beyond the protected waters of the little harbour, the fury of the sea was undiminished. They could hear the thunderclaps as wave after wave smashed against the rocks beyond the harbour walls, sending up drenching clouds of spray. They sat for a while in the car; just looking.

'It's magnificent,' Louise said, 'simply magnificent.'

Presently, they got out and put on their anoraks, they skirted the little pebbly beach where the protected waters of the harbour gently lapped the land and stood on the stone pier, arms wrapped round each other, braced against the steady pressure of the wind. Suddenly, Aidan, exhilarated, felt overwhelming optimism. It would all work out.

'Look,' he said pointing to the north, 'there's Dunstanburgh.' Standing against the sky on the horizon of its promontory, the keep stuck up like a badly decayed molar in a fragment of ancient jawbone. Holding hands, they set out towards it and as they passed the last few cottages on the edge of the village, the turf which edged the rocky shore was sprayed with sunlight from a new breach in the cloud layer, now showing long streaks of blue between its folds as it dissolved before the stiff on-shore breeze. In a fantasy of crashing waves and wheeling gulls, they walked, ran and danced their way the two miles to the castle. Only once did Aidan distantly wonder if this was an appropriate way for a middle-aged man to behave. Only if he were drunk, he thought. Well this one is. This one is. It isn't booze, but he's sure as hell drunk.

They entered through the great arched gateway, under the portcullis, paid their money to the custodian in his little cabin. They explored, clamouring among the ruins, then undertook the permitted climb up the worn spiral slabs of the keep's staircase and stood, looking out of the topmost window, hassled by the wind. Looking down, Aidan felt a sudden convulsion somewhere above his diaphragm as he sensed the height. There was no danger but in a moment of panic, he grabbed Louise round the waist and held on tight. She looked round smiling. Her hair disassembled, framing her face with writhing fronds.

'It's okay – I'm not going to fall,' she said.

'Ha, so you say. But I'm not taking any chances. No way.'

He swung her round and drew her to him, enveloping her in an embrace, against the rough stone of the wall.

When they parted, she said, 'You see, Aidan, I am taking your advice. I'm happy … now. And whatever happens to us in the future, I'll always remember the loveliness of these few days. I can just imagine one day telling my grandchildren about it in the years to come.'

'Your grandchildren?' Aidan was taken aback.

'Oh well … you see, I had a grandmother I was very close to. In my teens she used to tell me about things that happened to her when she was young.'

'Oh I see. And who do you have in mind for grandfather?' Oh God, children. He hadn't really thought of that. Christ, imagine starting again at square one with a squalling infant! Imagine being a father again …

She looked down. 'Well I know who I'd like it to be … but the future is so uncertain, isn't it?' She smiled ruefully. 'I should have had more sense than to fall in love with a married man.' Aidan turned again towards the sea, for a while seeming quite lost in it. Okay, if she was going to have children, so be it. He'd have to grit his teeth. They would have to be his. Have to be. He was about to speak …

'No don't say anything. I've got to remember, we're enjoying the present … keeping the future at bay … well, trying.'

He turned back towards her and took her face in both his hands and kissed her softly on the lips. 'Okay,' he said. 'Let's get on with the present.' Then he took her by the hand and preceded her down the steps. They followed the remains of the southern fortified wall round to the seaward side of the castle to where it turned and followed the cliff edge, above a hundred foot drop to the wave-lashed rocks below. They stood on tiptoe to terrify themselves with the peril of it.

'It's the Whin Sill again,' Aidan said. 'If you lean over and tap it with a stick, they'll hear it on the Roman Wall at Cuddy's Crag.'

Giggling, Louise reached forward as if to do it and Aidan grabbed her by the scruff of her coat. 'Oh no you don't,' he said, laughing and in the security of each other's arms and in the lea of a very stout wall they enjoyed the mayhem of the thrashing sea below. It could not harm them.

'Look,' said Aidan, 'it doesn't bother them.' He gestured, as a pair of fulmars in close formation ripped past them almost within arm's reach, surfing the cliff top wind on board-stiff wings, then banking with nonchalant grace, slicing down to skim the breaking wave tops. 'Look at that. If there is reincarnation, I'd like to come back as one of those.' She did not reply immediately, then turning away from the sea, to face Aidan, so that the wind carried strands of her hair across her face, she went back to the future.

'Aidan, if my grandchildren were your grandchildren ... well ... it would mean ...' She paused and the tip of her tongue moistened her lips. '... would you leave Cathy? Would you ever leave her ... for me?'

'Ah the future's leaking back again. You see, Lulu, it isn't just as simple as that. I've told you about my family and the problem between Cathy and Bobby. It goes back a long way. Even before we became involved – you and I, I was coming to the conclusion that the only thing I could do was to leave Cathy and take Bobby away. It seemed the only thing, for Bobby's sake. Well, and for my own sanity.' Now he turned and looked at her intently. 'You see ... it would be me – and Bobby too.' She looked thoughtful. He continued,

'And I have another daughter I care about just as much. She's always going to be an important part of my life too, no matter what happens.'

'Yes, I know. I'd worked that one out. But if you did leave Cathy, we – you and I – we could get a flat or something. We could rent it and Bobby could live with us. You could see Dora as much as you liked … I think I could learn to love them too … if …' She didn't finish the sentence.

Aidan looked at her and kissed her lightly on the cheek. 'Ah, Lulu, how easy you make it sound. But how do you know you could take on a potentially stroppy teenager you haven't even met – a known trouble maker at that?' He smiled wryly.

'Aidan, I've lived with a stroppy teenager. Remember, I've got a younger brother. I've had plenty of experience there.'

Aidan laughed, shaking his head. 'And you think that qualifies you?' Then he became serious. 'Well, Lulu, look, that's more or less what I've been thinking. It wouldn't be easy, but if you're willing to take on the role of stepmother …'

'Oh yes, yes …' She threw herself into his arms and they clung together, her hair stranded across his face. Presently, they drew apart.

'Listen, shall we have another go at the present?' Aidan said.

She nodded. 'Okay, we'll really do it this time.' But now, the future contained at least a glimmer of hope.

Hand in hand, they wandered back, making for the jetty, which earlier in the afternoon had seemed so hazardous, with the wind so wild. It had calmed and it was now safe to walk to its end. They stood there to watch a sleek blue and white fishing coble, its droning engine spluttering as the sea now and again swamped its exhaust. It was loaded with crab pots and they watched it leave the harbour, bucking as it first met the swell, then slicing through the waves with its elegant high prow.

Aidan told Louise how the traditional design was in direct line of descent from the Viking longships that raided these shores more than a millennium before. A man in a flat cap and tan smock stood at the tiller, holding his verticality against the movement of the boat, like a bird does on a swaying branch. He seemed to have set a course for the horizon, while his companion, in a bright-yellow waterproof, busied himself preparing the crab pots in the centre of the boat. They watched it out into the open sea, as it rode the swell, sometimes disappearing completely in the troughs.

Then Louise looked round and ostentatiously sniffed, frowning slightly like one trying to identify a wine at a blind tasting. 'Aidan, what's that wonderful smell?' He closed his eyes and also sniffed – ecstatically.

'Mmm … kippers. Wonderful. Smoking oak chips and split herrings. Beats Chanel No. Five any day.'

'Wouldn't like to dab it behind my ears – but it does smell good.'

'Let's go and see if we can buy some. We can have them for supper when we get back to your flat tomorrow.'

They followed their noses around the harbour to a kind of courtyard. They saw them, hanging in rows in a miasma of fragrant smoke from smouldering oak. They were lucky, they were told. Just come at the right time. There were kippers ready – the best you'll find anywhere, they were told. Aidan and Louise had no difficulty in believing this and they made their way to the pub by the harbour, where they were to spend their last night, clutching their gourmet parcel.

When they set off next day towards the south, it was fine again and they had all the time in the world for a leisurely meander, continuing their castle crawl. They zigged inland to Alnwick and visited its castle, drank coffee, then zagged coastwards again to Alnmouth and lunch, after which they zigged inland to Warkworth – another castle – before zagging coastwards again to the old fishing and coaling port of Amble. As they stood looking over the harbour, now containing many more yachts and pleasure cruisers than fishing boats, Aidan directed Louise's gaze to the south. 'Look ... see those four tall chimneys over there?'

'Hm, you could hardly miss them. They don't do much for the landscape, do they?'

'Well, I don't want to get into an argument about aesthetics. You've got to realise Northumberland isn't all picturesque. You see, we're getting into the industrial southeast. Mining, shipbuilding and coal exporting – well, that's how it was at one time. Not much of it left now. Still, I think they're pretty dramatic. Just think of what Poussin would have done with them …'

'Poussin! You're joking …'

'Not at all. Look … that decisive group of verticals … the intervals, the golden section. Think of them as trees … or slim Ionic columns. Or from closer, a repoussoir. Can't you see it?'

Louise snorted her derision. 'Hah, you've got Poussin-shaped eyes.'

Aidan laughed. 'Anyway, at the foot of them lies the town where I was born, where I went to school, where I lived with my family until I went to college.'

'Oh Aidan, could we … do you think we could go and have a look? I'd love to see the places you knew when you were a little boy.'

'Louise, it's not a beautiful place. It never was beautiful. But it used to be sort of interesting – the way working towns, with their specialisms can be. And I loved it like that. But when the shipyard closed and then one by one the mines – those chimneys, they belong to the huge power station they built on top of the last profitable pit – and the shipping trade shrivelled away with it … well turning out Bri Nylon on a trading estate seemed a poor substitute. Brawny miners going to the technical college to retrain as pastry cooks. Pathetic.'

'Well that's all very sad – but there must be some of it left. There must surely still be places left that you knew.' She put her arm around his shoulder and nuzzled him persuasively. 'I just want to know all about you. Please, can we?' He looked at her and laughed a little.

'Right then, if that's what you want. Nostalgia, here we come.'

They spent their last afternoon in the haunts of Aidan's history. Then when they knew they could stall the future no longer, they reluctantly set off on the journey back to Swaleborough; the idyll was drawing to a close.

The journey back was functional. Purely a matter of 'A' to 'B'. From a perfect 'A', to a deeply problematic 'B'. Louise looked among the handful of cassettes in the glove compartment for music to fit the mood. She chose one and slipped it into the player: Cleo Lane and John Williams. 'Feelings.' Oh God, Aidan thought, music to commit suicide to. He took a swift sideways look at Louise, smiling wanly. She had settled back into the seat and closed her eyes. How he wished he could get into that mind.

How was she now going to feel about reverting to the clandestine role of mistress to the married man who was her tutor? For God's sake, how was he going to fit himself back into the role of dissembling adulterer, tortured parent and tutor to his mistress? For the last four days, he had lived with the conviction, that somehow, it could all be made to come right, but as the reality drew nearer and the problems loomed larger, he began to wonder if it was all total delusion. Yet he could not allow himself to accept that.

He looked again at Louise. It was now dark and the light from oncoming traffic intermittently lit her profile. He took a hand from the steering wheel and put it on her thigh. Without opening her eyes, with a ghost of a smile on her lips, she placed her hand over his and squeezed gently.

Before the cassette had ended, they were back. Aidan drove the Renault on to the forecourt of the flats, pulled on the handbrake, and, reaching for the volume control faded the music. It always seemed to him discourteous, just to switch off and he could never do it. Then he switched off the engine and they sat in silence for a while. Presently, He reached again for her hand and she opened her eyes, and turned towards him.

'Is it really over then, Aidan?'

'For the present, I'm afraid so,' Aidan said quietly.

'It's been lovely. I've tried not to let the future spoil the present. But now the future has arrived … and I don't like it.' She looked into his eyes. 'I suppose you'll be going back to your wife now.' There was an edge to her voice which Aidan found disturbing.

He put an arm around her shoulder and drew her towards him. There was the merest suggestion of resistance. 'Louise, I want you. I want to share my life with you. I intend to make that happen. But you'll have to be patient. It can't happen in an instant.'

'Are you going to tell her … about … us?'

He paused, looking down, 'Yes.'

'When?'

He was a little irritated. 'As soon as I can … I said you'd have to be patient?'

'Right, I'll try, then … but it's not going to be easy. It's not going to be easy going to bed alone tonight.'

'Well look, you won't have to. Not if you invite me in.'

'Oh … well …' She released the tension and relaxed into his arms. '… in that case, I invite you in … for kippers and bed.'

The future had been postponed for a little longer.

CHAPTER 27

Cathy would have got home that same night. Next day, Aidan was in no hurry to return to her, yet he thought that to delay the parting from Louise any longer would be merely to prolong the agony, to risk the re-emergence of the tension which had just begun to surface last night, to risk marring the memory of Northumberland. After breakfast, having arranged with her that they would meet the next day in the department, he said goodbye, left her in the flat and drove himself not home but to the college, to the reassuring comfort of his studio.

After letting himself in, he shut the door behind him and leaned back on it for some moments, his eyes closed, hardly breathing. Out of term time, it seemed to Aidan that this was one of the quietest places on earth. He thought that silence was the most precious of states. It was not just an absence of noise, which there was far too much of everywhere, but rather it was a positive thing with rejuvenating, curative properties.

He had for a long time believed that the malaise of society had its roots in the gross amount of noise everyone was obliged to absorb, just from the fact of living in the last quarter of the twentieth century. He was convinced that people's brains were being remorselessly

437

scrambled, as they unprotestingly soaked it all up. So for a while, he stood, quite still, savouring the silence, reassimilating the familiarity of his room. Then he crossed to the window and looked out over the tennis courts, to the line of trees beyond and the backs of the houses beyond them. His mind shifted kaleidoscopically from the ecstasy of the recent few days, to the murkiness of the future, then to the immediate present; to the question of what to do now – that is, in the next ten minutes.

He knew. What he would do was to make a cup of coffee and then have another think. Yes, that was the thing to do. Having thus decided, he went over to the coffee machine, detached the jug from it, let himself out through the door into the printing studio next door and filled the jug at the sink there. Returning, he topped up the reservoir, got his tin of coffee from the cupboard, found a filter paper to line the filter cone and spooned coffee into it. He operated the switch and the red light came on.

There was absolutely nothing more he could do for the next seven minutes or so, until the coffee machine completed its cycle. Again time was suspended. He went back to the window and stared out of it again – now, his mind a blank. Eventually, the sound of the gurgling and the slow release of fragrance brought him back to awareness.

He waited till the gurgling stopped then went to the machine, rummaged for his mug in the cupboard, poured coffee into it, looked for the little plastic pots of pseudo milk he knew were in there somewhere, found one and struggling with its opening apparatus, let out an obscene curse as a gloop of white stuff spurted out over his desk. Furiously, he shook the rest of it into his coffee, flinging the empty pot in the general direction of the waste bin in the corner of the room and missing it by a generous margin. He cursed again, then after looking in vain for the teaspoon, took a palette knife from his painting trolley, stirred his coffee with it and took the coffee over to the window.

It was hot, strong, comforting. He need do nothing now until he'd finished his coffee. Holding the mug in both hands, he sipped and savoured it. After that – well, the thought came to him that he could postpone the future a little further; he could look for some of his colleagues, of whom there would surely be a good number in the college; someone to play table tennis with, to have lunch in the pub with. Perhaps he could find Gerry. He would surely be around somewhere, he could tell Gerry about the glories of Northumberland and Louise. Gerry was the only one with whom he could relive this experience, with whom he could consolidate it and confirm its reality.

But gradually, the realisation sank in that he could not really indulge himself like this. He knew there was something urgent, that he could not really postpone. Bobby. Despite his resolve to award himself total release from his family – not even to think about them for the duration of his trip with Louise – he had phoned Roseberry from Holy Island. He had hoped not to have to speak to Bobby, not to

439

have to become involved in the tensions of it all again. Not yet; not in the middle of this snatched, fleeting fragment of paradise. Time enough when he got back to Swaleborough.

No, it was just to enquire about the patient. Was that what she was? A patient? Just to speak to the Sister – what was her name – Marion, that was it. Yes, Marion, just to make sure Bobby was okay.

So nervously, he had phoned from Holy Island. He had asked to speak to the Sister. Marion had come to the phone; she had reassured him that his daughter was doing well. She'd settled in and struck up an immediate friendship with Daisy and he was not to worry. She was asking about him though, he should really come to see her soon – just to reassure her. He could come at any time, but he should ring first to make sure they weren't out on a visit. Aidan had thanked her and said to give Bobby all his love and to tell her he would come and see her as soon as he got back from his trip. Aidan now reminded himself that 'as soon as he got back from his trip' was now and accordingly, after refilling his mug, he picked up his phone, got put onto an outside line and rang. Yes, it was fine to visit today. They would tell Bobby to expect him.

He knew he could put it off no longer. He had to go home. He resisted the temptation to return to college but headed glumly for Oakdene Avenue.

It was all so familiar; the roundabout, the garden centre, the right turn at the junction, the trees, the semis with their gardens and verges. Another right turn and he slowed down, to turn off the road, over the short ramp interrupting the grass verge. Crossing the pavement, he registered the familiar slight bump as first the front, then the rear wheels surmounted the irregularity where the flags of the pavement gave way to the concrete of the drive, the loose one giving its familiar double 'clack'. He noted yet again the deep-blue paint peeling from around the hinges of the gate and the incipient signs of rot. He reproached himself routinely for not yet having done anything about it. An outreaching branch of buddleia – he'd been meaning to prune it – brushed against the side of the car as he, with familiar precision, located it, leaving sufficient space in front for the up-and-over garage door to operate and at the side to allow convenient egress, before engaging the handbrake and switching off the engine.

He slumped back into the big black leather seat, unmotivated to leave it. He remembered that buddleia as a healthy nine-inch juvenile, when, years ago, he'd set about its planting with a trowel in one hand and an instruction book in the other. Now its trunk, if that was what it was called, was as thick as his wrist. He remembered its high summer populations of butterflies – red admiral, peacock, tortoiseshell and the pleasure with which he watched their capricious busyness.

Familiar – yet he'd never felt much affection for the house. It wasn't what he wanted and never could be. Not at all the sort of house you'd think an artist would live in. It was what they could just about afford in those early days in Swaleborough – nothing like where Aidan really felt he belonged; perhaps in an austere, white, cuboid composition of Bauhaus pedigree, over a tumbling cataract in the manner of Frank Lloyd Wright, with furniture by Mies Van der Rohe, Le Corbusier and Marcel Brauer, and a lofty studio on the top floor with a deep, angled north light. Or possibly a generously converted fisherman's cottage on some remote shore, ingeniously and sculpturally furnished with salvaged driftwood and rich with natural materials.

Instead, he'd so far had to make do with a rather small three-bedroom semi-detached on an estate of local-builder-vernacular houses on the western edge of the town, among the teachers, bank clerks and draughtsmen, the furniture mostly affordable post-Festival of Britain and junk shop second hand. It was lower middle-class conventional; and conventional was not what Aidan had meant to be. He'd had unconventional thoughts, sometimes unconventional intentions, but willy-nilly he had ended up in a state of total and utter conventionality quite dissonant with his image of himself.

Of course he was aware of contradictions; his notions of unconventionality were at odds with the implied purity of Bauhaus living. He was an artist and weren't artists supposed to be unconventionally living on the margins of orthodox society? He had never meant it to be like this. In his student days, he had read avidly of the turn of the century wild antics of the artists of Montmartre, of

Picasso, Modigliani, Braques, of the Lapin Agil, the Moulin Rouge. They set the conceptual framework, yet that framework, essentially metropolitan, was at odds with both the Bauhaus purity and the remote marine idyll. But what did it matter? It was his own native culture which had shaped his life. Small town, working class.

Silly bugger, he chided himself, thinking of his pretensions. Luck and circumstances had brought him a social step up. Education. A degree. A teaching job, a far cry from the Bohemia of Modigliani and Picasso – but sure as hell a cut above the pits. Then even better, a lecturer in a teacher training college, a wife with whom he was now out of love, two children and a mortgage on a semi-detached house in the local-builder-vernacular style ... He did not know if she was in.

He was not moved by the prospect of giving it up. It had never been what he wanted; doing without it would be no problem at all. All he would want from it would be his guitar, his books, his hi-fi and records, oh, and if it could be negotiated, the Ernest Race Heron chair. All the rest she could have. There would be no trouble, no messing about with lawyers or that sort of thing. He wouldn't quibble. It was the only wealth they had really – they'd somehow never managed to accumulate any more, but she could have it. It was a price he would willingly pay for an amicable agreement to part.

How she would look at it, he wondered. They no longer slept together – either in the literal or in the euphemistic sense. They had not done so since well before he and Louise had consummated their relationship. That event had set the seal upon it. But she had no reason to ask herself why their sexual relationship had suddenly ceased, because it had been a long and drawn out process – a withering on the vine. So there was nothing to indicate that it had stopped. Merely that the intervals were getting longer. But he wanted her to know that it had stopped, because wasn't consummation a vital criterion of a functioning marriage? Didn't undivorceable Catholics get annulments on grounds of a lack of it? Couldn't their marriage thereby be accounted over? Defunct? Dead?

For God's sake, what was she getting out of it? They were standing on opposite sides of a huge spiritual and psychological rift. There seemed no possibility of agreement over Bobby. She refused to see what she was doing and he could not understand how she could not. He could not understand what went on inside her head. He could find no way into it, no way to change it. So he just had to change the situation. God, he just had to get Bobby out of it before she was totally destroyed. And himself too. Well, since he seemed unable to achieve happiness in and for his family, shouldn't he make a grab for his own, while it was available, secure that and then do whatever repair work he could in the wake of his decision? He thought so. He had decided so.

What was she getting out of it? he asked himself again. Well he thought he understood something of it. With a husband and children, she was comprehensibly located in the social structure. Secure. Her status affirmed by the all-embracing orthodoxy she'd been brought up in; parents, the extended network of uncles, aunts and cousins. Never any shenanigans there. Divorce? Adultery? Not for people like us.

He remembered the huge power she attributed to their ritual act of union. That wedding day – anticipated and planned for so long in advance, so toweringly symbolic for her, in the act and in the recollection. A modest registry office job would have suited him fine. But no. It had to be church and all the trimmings – well, as many as her parents and her own savings could rise to – and all the folklore and superstition. For Christ's sake, she had him wearing a morning suit! Pretentious. No one in his family had ever worn a morning suit. Hers either, for that matter, he suspected.

Then later, the anniversaries; the meticulous, moment by moment reliving of the occasion. At this moment a year/five years/eleven years ago, I was walking down the aisle/you were putting the ring on my finger/we were signing the register. The photographs, which Aidan was increasingly embarrassed by, as the years wore on, taken out of the box, lingeringly sighed over; a selection placed on sideboard and mantelpiece, to be changed around daily for a week, before being reverently repacked and returned to storage. It seemed to have been and by a large margin, the most important, the most momentous event in her life. It was in the truest sense a rite of passage, by which she was mystically and ritually severed from one status in society and life and post-liminally, reincorporated into another. She held the new status to be inviolable, unconditionally permanent and, seemingly, strangely independent of the state of the relationship it depended upon.

Slumped still in the seat, Aidan allowed his thoughts to stray momentarily. They returned to Louise. He groaned. How the hell was he going to sort this lot out? He wanted to turn around now and go back to her. He felt a sudden wave of despair and his mind seemed to turn to mush, his eyes became unfocused and he slipped into a kind of meditative limbo. He sat quite still for several more minutes before he found the will to lever himself out of his seat and out of the car.

The back door was not locked. She was back. He entered the kitchen; the remains of a breakfast and probably a supper. Plates, cups, a wine glass, a crumbling wedge of cheese, gnawed toast and an open packet of Special K formed an impromptu still life on the table. In the corner, the washing machine thought its imbecile way through its programme, chuntering, sloshing, humming.

Well then, she was home. He looked into the dining room. Not there. Then the hall. On the floor, an open suitcase, spilling clothes on to the floor. Several shoes scattered about.

He stood for a moment at the foot of the stairs, looking, like a detective newly arrived at the scene of the crime. Looking, just looking. Moving nothing. Yes, he thought, she is certainly home. Definitely. He spoke out aloud, 'Why that's remarkable Holmes,' he said in his Doctor Watson voice, smiling as he always did at his own parody. Then slowly his face became serious. He closed his eyes and took a deep breath. 'Oh God,' he said, 'Oh God, oh God.'

There were letters on the telephone table, some open. One folded sheet – a bill of some sort – lay on the floor. He picked the letters up and shuffled through them, without really seeing them, then put them back on the table; this was no time to be dealing with letters. He leaned against the newel post and closed his eyes again. Then with sudden resolution, he straightened and called out.

'Hello!' No reply, so again, louder, 'Cathy.' Again no reply.

So … the garden then. Detaching himself from the newel post, he headed for the sitting room. The curtains were drawn back, the French window open. The sunlight gushed in, assaulting his eyes with its brilliance. Squinting, he crossed to the window. At first he didn't see her. Then her head and shoulders appeared from behind a flowering currant. Straw hat, sunglasses. He watched as she disappeared again behind the shrub, emerging after a while with an armful of weeds, taking the few steps to the compost heap in the corner of the garden and dropping them there. Then she picked up a pair of secateurs from the low wall along the edge of the vegetable plot and stood looking around for something to apply them to.

He stepped over the threshold on to the small terrace. She had not yet seen him and he had no strategy for the moment of reunion, no idea of what he would say. He did remember, though, that there had seldom been conflict in the garden. It seemed to act as a kind of tranquilliser for Cathy. As he watched her, she repositioned her glasses on her nose and he was briefly moved. It was something about the innocence of the gesture. He found this, that there were occasions – often the unthinking performance of a familiar mannerism, which would send him into a sudden agony of tenderness and anguish, embracing in one fleeting wave of emotion both the individual and the rest of struggling humanity in an awesome portent of tragedy. This was what he felt for an instant, he was left with an aftermath of compassion and in its wake, guilt.

He watched as she snipped here and there at bits of dead stuff or severed a withered flower. It seemed that it was only in the garden that Cathy found real peace. She could not be in contention with the plants. Why, then, could she not be more like that in the rest of her life? Cynically, he had often supposed that it was something to do with the fact that plants can't answer back; they can't have conflicting opinions, so her relation with them was non-problematical, harmonious. Plants were simple. They either thrived or they died. So he had found that over the years, and most noticeably in recent times, their most tranquil moments together had been spent working in the garden.

He could not blame her for how she was, could he? He could not blame her that her life seemed to be plagued by the minor exigencies that should normally pass almost unnoticed. It was the genes and the upbringing. He should be sympathetic that they had combined to provide her with a turbulent, abrasive personality always scratching at the minor irritations of life, inflaming them further, spreading their misery all around. Oh well, thank God, for the garden, the tranquillising garden.

It was hers, really, her realm. In it she was the undisputed authority. Perhaps that was why she was generally content in it. And he was happy that it was so. She was the mastermind. She knew the plants. Horticultural science at school. A distinction. He had always contributed labour, a few ideas about materials, aesthetics. But it was she who caressed the plants into thriving magnificence, she who knew their names, their preferences, their idiosyncrasies, their weaknesses, their afflictions; she who decided which would live and when necessary, which would die, which would rot on the compost heap to provide life for another generation.

Then she turned and, suddenly, she saw him.

'Aidan,' she said, startled 'you're back … I didn't see you there.'

'Hi,' Aidan said, 'when did you get back? Did you have a good time?'

She stepped carefully over a flower bed on to the brick path and came towards him, dropping the secateurs into her jacket pocket and peeling off her gloves on the way. He walked slowly over the lawn to meet her. She looked briefly into his eyes and, with a slight smile, offered her cheek to be kissed. 'Some tea, do you think?'

Aidan also smiled. 'Good idea,' he said. She turned towards the house and Aidan followed her through the French window.

'I'll do it,' she said, going into the kitchen. He eased himself into an armchair. He did not know how to interpret this congenial, almost tender greeting and it made him uneasy. He heard the gushing of the cold tap in the kitchen, as she filled the kettle, culminating in a loud clunk as she turned the tap off. He heard the sound of the plug groping for the kettle's socket, a cupboard door open and shut, teacups clink, her soft movements around the room, the rattle of the biscuit tin. Every sound registered with familiar clarity; each one of their possessions resonated in its distinctive way. The kettle's crescendo abruptly stopped by the click of its cut-out switch, the rattle of the teapot's lid, the descending chromatic cascade of boiling water into the pot. Milk from the fridge, the soft thump of its closing door.

Aidan felt oppressed by the tyranny of the familiar. That was it. Possessions. They had gravity, mass. You accumulated them and they became heavy with meaning, association. And they accumulated a fearsome centripetal power. Perhaps they were, as much as anything else, what held people together. Like a galaxy. All those fragments of matter holding together under the force of their own gravity. How could you escape from that undefeatable force? Suddenly, Aidan felt helplessly and hopelessly in its grip, as he remembered Louise and their plans to live together.

She came in carrying a tray and put it on the coffee table. While the tea was brewing, they exchanged brief accounts of their respective activities. As much as Aidan told Cathy was true – but it was not the whole truth and it was certainly not the most momentous part of the truth. Somewhat thrown by the unexpectedly congenial reunion, he had decided on a brief postponement of the whole truth. How could he drop such a devastating bombshell into such a pacific scenario – when she was being so nice to him?

Cathy set cup upon saucer, dispensed milk, then poured the tea. She opened the biscuit tin and offered it to Aidan. He selected a chocolate digestive. She took one for herself, put the lid on the tin and replaced it on the tray. She sipped reflectively at her tea for a few moments, then put down the cup and saucer, and toyed with the biscuit, staring out at the garden. She nibbled a bit then put down the crescent of biscuit, seeming, for the moment, preoccupied. Then, 'Aidan,' she said, 'I rang the hospital or whatever it is … Roseberry.'

'Oh,' said Aidan, guardedly, 'and …?'

'I rang twice … I asked to speak to Bobby.' Aidan's face was impassive. 'At first they stalled me. Then … then they told me … the Sister told me that she … that Bobby didn't want to speak to me; and she advised me not to insist. She said it wasn't the right time … perhaps later on, she said.'

'Oh?'

'I was very hurt … I've been concerned, worried about her.' She turned her head to look at him. He returned her gaze, giving nothing away, suppressing the wave of outrage that rose inside him. My God … concerned, worried – now! Now that her daughter is in a mental hospital – because, let's face it, that's what Roseberry is, whatever bloody euphemism you might want to wrap it up in – now she's concerned, worried.

Breaking the silence, Cathy asked, 'Well?'

Aidan looked sideways at her. 'Well what?'

She sighed impatiently, 'Well what do you think? What'll I do … I mean, well, you know …'

'What do I think? Well what I think is that you're a bit late with your concern and your worry. After all this time, watching the situation deteriorate, refusing to admit that there was any sort of problem, refusing my offer to go and seek help, doing bugger-all until the crisis hit you in the face – and now that she's in the bloody lunatic asylum – now you're concerned and worried. And you're asking me for advice on what to do … I just can't believe it … I just can't … I …' Aidan's voice was taking on the bitter timbre of conflict.

'Aidan, for Christ's sake stop it. Don't turn this into a row. Don't you understand? …' She paused. Aidan looked at her, conscious of his clenched jaw, of the ferocious downturn of his mouth. As his mind prepared the next phase of the attack, something in Cathy's eyes, something he'd not seen before, not exactly fear or anxiety even

– just something undermining their usual sense of self-justification, caused him to hold back.

Cathy took a deep breath. 'Look … okay, so I didn't see it coming …'

Aidan slumped back, his eyes shut, clutching his hair in furious disbelief. How many times had he warned her of disaster to come? How many times had she angrily dismissed his warnings?

'Aidan, listen to me … I may have been a bit over strict with her sometimes. But I've always done my best for her.'

'I just can't believe this … over strict? Is that what you call it? So you're not accepting any real responsibility for what's happened? You've just been a bit "over strict", have you? Cathy, you've come damn near to destroying her. You've driven her into a fucking lunatic asylum … that's how strict you've been.'

With a sharp intake of breath, she stood up. She walked across to the window and stood there, visibly tense, looking out into the garden. Aidan shook his head in angry exasperation. He picked up the teacup, drained its contents at a gulp and set it down noisily on the saucer. Cathy stood, immobile, for some time; Aidan sat back in the chair, legs outstretched, crossed at the ankles, arms folded, head slumped forward, chin on chest, eyes closed, mouth drawn tight. Silent. After a while, she turned to face him, the flooding sunlight behind thrusting her form into semi-darkness, but lighting a bright halo round her hair and glancing on her shoulder. Aidan looked up. He could see little of her expression against the light.

'Aidan,' she said, in a soft voice, a voice so rare that he might not have recognised it as hers had she not been visible there before him, '... I'm trying to be ... conciliatory, can't you see? I've had some time to think and I would like us to ... to try to get things together again ... to sort of ... well make a new start.'

'Oh, are you? What about Bobby? They're wanting to know what we have in mind when she's discharged and that has to be soon. So what am I supposed to tell them, eh?'

'Well, as far as I'm concerned, she can come back. I'm prepared to give it another go.'

'You're prepared to give it another go? Oh well, that makes it all right, then, does it? Well I think what's more important is, is she prepared to give it another go?'

'What do you mean? What else could she do?'

'Well here's one thing. I could leave you and find other accommodation for me and Bobby. And that's what I intend, if anything goes wrong again. So get that into your head.'

'You're not going to ...' But Aidan was on his way out, not sure he could contain his fury.

'Aidan, Aidan don't walk out like that ... Aidan ...' But by then, he was out of the garden gate and soon out of earshot. There, he had said it.

CHAPTER 28

It seemed a lot of hard work, a lot of sweat over many weeks for just four performances, but it had to be fitted into the year's pattern of college events. It had to be located in the summer term to allow two terms for rehearsals and to allow opportunity for the new students to take part. It also had to be at the beginning of the term, because exams were at the end. As to the shortness of the run, the cast consoled themselves with the thought that there were a few expensive West End and Broadway productions that were closed down after as few performances.

As work on the production proceeded, members of the cast were assembled in threes and fours; small fragments of the play were isolated and tried out with the script, then adjusted and repeated. Passages were memorised and the script tentatively dispensed with. The roughnesses were ironed out, word perfection striven for, scenes and bits of scenes practised again and again, and honed towards a final finish.

The actors, some of whom began the term as strangers to each other, underwent a transformation too; a process of growing together and into their parts, even taking on in real life something of the characters they represented and often the relationships between them. Then as, week by week, the fragments were assembled into larger chunks and the larger chunks eventually into the whole, the cast, backstage workers and production team, the whole of the company underwent a gradual but deeply felt melding into an entity – a distinctive group – a subset of the college population, with a unique internal life, replete with its own vocabulary of esoteric references, its own folklore, its own catch phrases, all tightly bonded. For a time, temporarily, they would constitute a community within a community.

No hierarchical distinctions intruded from the larger world of the college. No staff, no students, no us, no them: it was all us. The distinctive us, the unique us. Everyone seemed moved by the events they were enacting; the savage insanity of the war their grandparents remembered. They somehow felt themselves heirs to events most of their contemporaries knew nothing of. They seemed particularly affected by the counterpoint of tragedy and buffoonery the play offered and especially the unbearable poignancy of the songs. Fragments of these were to be heard during the day in different parts of the college, softly whistled or gently hummed by students working at easels or hunched over microscopes or maps ... There's a long, long trail a-winding ... They wouldn't believe me ... Keep the home fires burning ...

In this highly charged atmosphere, new liaisons grew, one or two souls outside the group, with partners on the inside, felt the bonds inexorably weakening and looked in with helpless jealousy as their partners drifted away, feeling that now, there was an essential ingredient missing, knowing they could not supply it.

In all of this, Aidan and Louise played their stage intimacies for real. Now no need for acting in the dance scene; when Aidan snuggled his hand between Louise's breasts, as they waltzed into the wings and when he looked into her eyes, he knew it was for real. And so, he supposed, did the rest of the company. At other times, waiting backstage together, they held hands or put their arms around each other's waists. Or, in passing, their hands would touch and their eyes meet. In the half light or caught a glancing blow by a sweeping spot beam, their intimacies were visible to whoever was in the vicinity. His students, his fellow actors, his colleagues, saw and smiled. They knew and Aidan was pleased they knew. They were part of the intimacy of the group, in which everything that happened had its own internal legitimacy. To Aidan, it no longer seemed to matter that his secret would thereby be released into the world outside.

The dress rehearsal went off vigorously, but with many imperfections. It was a busy night for the prompter and yielded many inspired but dangerous improvisations; many cues missed, many not delivered. But the imperfections were compensated for with a self-confident aplomb. It was just the spirit George wanted. He would

457

take vitality over accuracy any day. At the end, the curtain came down, the closing music died away and the actors slumped down among the footlights, erupting into a cacophony of chatter and laughter, and self-congratulation. George slumped ostentatiously onto his reversed chair, folded his arms over the back of it, rested his chin on is arms and stared at the floor. Percy slammed down the piano lid, placed his elbows on it and his chin between his cupped hands. He looked at George. George raised his head and looking at his actors revelling on the stage, shook it slowly from side to side. Then suddenly, he stood up, sending the chair clattering onto its back on the floor. There was sudden silence. He placed his hands on his hips.

He said in a loud voice, 'It was crap ... absolute, utter crap.' After a moment's shocked silence, bedlam. Uproar of outrage. Catcalls, protests, shaking fists; a shower of military caps arced and skimmed towards him. He cowered, with raised protecting arms and staggered drunkenly.

'Okay, okay, okay,' he shouted above the melee and as it died down, 'Okay, okay, okay. Only joking.' More catcalls, dying away. 'As a matter of fact, it wasn't bad ... quite good, really ...' mocking cheers from the cast. 'BUT ...' Groans. George produced his clipboard and commenced a scene-by-scene post-mortem, sparing no one's feelings, ending, 'Remember, your mates are going to be out there – maybe your mums and dads ...' whistles and sardonic laughter ... 'They'll

have paid good money to see you doing stupid things on that stage …
Just make sure you give good value. Okay who's for the bar?'

The first real performance was, by custom, the big night for the
students. From the players' point of view, this was a good thing, since
it meant that on this first night, they were not, in the main, on display
to the theatre-going public of Swaleborough. This meant that any
remaining imperfections were witnessed mainly by their pals and
fellow students – normally a forgiving lot, if always ready to toss a
little banter towards the stage and provide, whether wanted or not, a
certain level of audience participation. And this particular first night
was very much along those lines.

It was then usual that each performance would improve on the last,
to achieve perfection on the final night, after which the whole
company would celebrate with a backstage party. It was also
customary that the college staff, the college governors, domestic staff
and staff spouses would come on the last night. The principal would,
after the applause and curtain calls, come on to the stage and make a
short congratulatory speech. After this, the audience would tactfully
fade away and leave the players to their revels. And thus it was in the
case of Oh What a Lovely War.

It was a really good party. It was well supplied with beer and the
domestic bursar had been particularly co-operative on the matter of
laying on sandwiches and other delights. The sound system and lights
had been swiftly adapted from the needs of the play to the needs of

the party. The sense of relief that it was all over was tempered by a deep sense of regret that it was all over; regret that the community which had been so central to all of the participants for much of the year, was at the end of its natural life. But the party got off to a resounding start, for it was the sense of achievement and liberation which now predominated. The music was loud; and after the initial assault on the bar and the quenching of thirsts, everyone surrendered to its powerful beat and the dancing got under way. Aidan was no longer inhibited by his sense of his age. No longer caring, knowing that he was part of a community that understood, he gyrated uninhibitedly with his mistress, giving himself completely up to this glorious, but ephemeral pandemonium.

As the first explosion of energy moderated, the music changed, modulating to a more languid mood. The couples closed up and embraced to smooch together in the dimmed lights. Liaisons tentatively embarked upon over the preceding weeks were tenderly reinforced, connections made and severances confirmed.

Presently another sound began to impinge on that of the disco. It was the sound of the piano. Percy was sitting at it surrounded by a small knot of people. Then out of his extravagant music hall flourishes there began to emerge the theme song of the play – Oh, Oh, Oh What a Lovely War… Some voices joined in – a few at first, then, as someone faded the dance music, others, in ones and twos drifted towards the piano, till the whole company was joined in a last rendering of the music, now infused with a sweet and melancholic nostalgia. They went through all the songs and then started again – unwilling to draw a line under this exquisite moment. Then Percy looked at his watch.

'Okay folks,' he said, 'that's it. Time I was heading for the sack.' Groans, protests, turning to reluctant goodnights – but they didn't want to stop. Bill Dixon produced his guitar and took over the accompaniment. Now, They Wouldn't Believe Me had the real words, the words about love, rather than the bitter soldiers' parody. Love was what they all felt at that singular moment; love for each other, love for themselves, love for suffering humanity.

And so the party lingeringly died in a miasma of exquisite sentimentality. Couples and individuals drifted wistfully away like the players in the Farewell Symphony, as fatigue overtook them, leaving, finally just Bill and Eva, Aidan and Louise. Then as the last chord died, they got up, turned out the lights and left.

Aidan needed to be in place next morning for Dora's early awaking, so he left Louise's flat in the small hours, to return home. Now deeply tired and thinking only of the luxury of bed, he left the car on the drive and let himself in through the front door. With a foot on the first stair, he noticed light under the sitting room door. Quietly he went to investigate. He eased the door open. Shit. Cathy was there, a book on her lap. Wide awake.

'Oh.' Aidan was taken aback. 'I didn't expect you to be up this late. It must be an un-put-down-able book.'

'It is,' she said.

'Oh, well … what did you think of the performance?'

She raised her eyes from the book and looked at him coolly. 'Fine. Are you screwing her?' she asked him.

CHAPTER 29

During the months Bobby was at Roseberry, Aidan had visited her regularly. There were surprisingly few restrictions there – definitely child (or should it be patient?) centred and after an informal chat with the doctor or the Sister, during which Bobby's progress would be discussed – sometimes, but not always, with her present – he would take her out and they would drive to the beach or into the hills, to have lunch or tea, in either a garish café on the prom or a twee and cosy tea room in some picture-postcard village.

It was, for Aidan, in some strange way, a period of calm. For the moment, life seemed to progress in a predictable, ordered way. To be sure, it was a bizarre kind of order, but the important thing was, the parameters, if not the motivations, seemed to be comprehensible – to be understood and accepted by those concerned. Bobby was in residence at Roseberry and evidently a great deal happier there than she had been in recent years at home. To have the constant anxiety attending her life at home, replaced by the assurance that she was well and someone else's responsibility elsewhere, gave Aidan welcome respite.

As for his relationship with Cathy, that had him bewildered, but uncomplaining. When she had asked that question, he'd known in an instant that this indeed was the moment of truth – or of falsehood. It was a moment he'd been nudging before him into the future, like a dung beetle taking home its next meal – though with considerably less relish. It was the moment Louise was becoming increasingly impatient for; the moment, the appropriate moment, the right moment that he assured her he was waiting for and would seize upon when it arrived; the moment when he would tell Cathy. He knew in that instant that it had arrived. He had not chosen the moment; he had walked, without warning, right into it. At first he did not meet Cathy's eyes. His first instinct was self-preservation. Lie, lie.

He fumbled for words, 'What … what the hell are you talking about?'

'Oh come on. You weren't so much like a middle-aged general and his whore as a couple of infatuated juveniles … those admiring cow eyes. That wasn't acting … was it?'

As she spoke, he'd felt blood flushing into his face. Good God, When had he last blushed? He knew he could manage minor untruths without betraying himself, but with this one, he felt the polygraph inside him had already announced the blatant barefaced lie this would have to be? No, he just wasn't up to it. He didn't want to be up to it. She waited.

Eventually, he looked down and met her eyes. 'You could have put it more delicately … but … yes.'

He had anticipated this scenario more times than he could remember. He had rehearsed its possible variants in his mind ad nauseam. He had accumulated an arsenal of verbal ordnance, defensive, self-justificatory, attacking. He expected her to go nuclear. He had not anticipated meeting calm reasonableness.

'Are you in love with her?' she'd asked, her eyes fixed upon him.

Knocked sideways by the question, he was unable to produce an immediate answer; he looked down, breathing hard. Then raising his eyes to her, he'd nodded. Cautiously, he'd said, 'Yes ... I am'. Then more definitely, 'I am in love with her.'

He'd expected bitter derision. But no; she'd looked away from him, seeming for a while to be enthralled by the soft roar of the gas fire and the slight flickering in its incandescent bars. Then she'd nibbled thoughtfully at a finger nail for a moment before turning to him again.

Cathy was a virtuoso of the facial expression. He couldn't count the times when he had found Bobby in bitter tears. 'Oh God,' he would ask, 'What's she said to you now?'

The sobbing reply would come, 'It wasn't what she said ... it was the way she looked at me.' He would know exactly what she meant. Cathy could quell a class of rowdy eleven-year-old children at fifty yards without uttering a word. More destructively, she could, silently, reduce Bobby to helpless grief and anger. She needed nothing more than an almost imperceptible modulation of the corners of the mouth, a minute adjustment of the eyes, to release a silent, scorching barrage of contempt. It would do its malign work and it would leave no trace. A word can be repeated; it can be reported, recorded. Evidence. Proof. But a facial expression is ephemeral; it disappears leaving nothing. Then it is no evidence, merely hearsay. It is related to the wiles of the master torturer, schooled in the techniques of causing maximum pain, while leaving no broken bones, wheals or scars for the victim to show in court.

But now, on this occasion, this instance of real crisis, with its potential to crucially affect their future lives, Cathy's face was without expression. Blank. Neutral. Conspicuously devoid of content. 'Don't for one moment think I'll give you a divorce,' she'd said.

When he'd told Louise that he had told Cathy about her, about them, that he loved her, Louise had flung herself into his arms in a paroxysm of delight. She seemed to see it as a Rubicon crossed, a committed step towards … what? At all events, Aidan felt that a small, but recurrent irritant that was beginning to tinge their relationship had been removed and larger questions banished to the temporal horizon. So their relationship had strengthened, within and in spite of the continuing constraints.

Aidan continued, then, in what appeared to the outside observer a working marriage. Inside it, he did most of the things he had always done – even to some extent forestalling any possibility of guilt by overcompensating. He made his habitual contribution to the running

466

of the household; he took his wife shopping, did his share of the household chores, spent even more time than ever with his younger daughter and continued visiting his elder one.

There was now little constraint on his comings and goings. Now that it was accepted – in whatever way – by his wife, that he had a mistress, the imposition of such constraints would be impossible and in any case pointless. Cathy seemed to regard these comings and goings with casual indifference. Aidan was sometimes uneasy at this unprecedented impassivity, wondering if, behind the mask, some plot was fermenting, to ensure his downfall; if there was something he hadn't thought of with which she could wreak destruction on him and Louise, and find some enduring compensation for all her own frustration. But then he would determinedly readjust his mindset. Seeing that it was all over between them, he reasoned, she was only too glad to have external appearances maintained.

For the rest of the summer term, the uneasy status quo continued. Louise, initially delighted that Cathy now knew about her and Aidan, and satisfied with that for a while, eventually asked the question, 'Where do we go from here and when?' It was the question which came up more and more frequently as the term wore on. They agreed on the answer to the first part: first, Aidan had to move out; to leave Cathy physically. He had to find separate accommodation.

He had to do this in the first place, to provide for Bobby on her discharge from Roseberry. So the motivation for the move need not, as far as Cathy was concerned, involve Louise. Then, despite Cathy's promise of non-co-operation in this matter, divorce. But this was less urgent. So they were united on what must be done, but Aidan was evasive as to the when. He himself felt he needed to build up his inner resources before facing what he anticipated would be emotional Armageddon.

As to the time; well it wasn't a deadline – though Louise was quite forceful in her advocacy of it – but the autumn term would be the time. Aidan was able to keep it to that degree of flexibility.

CHAPTER 30

The summer vacation had come and gone. Aidan had done his duty – only, he told himself – for the sake of Dora and co-operated in a holiday. They had accepted a long-standing invitation from Derek and Shirley Holbrook, friends from the early years of their marriage, to stay with them in their house on the edge of the New Forest. Aidan normally hated staying with friends, no matter how dear, because he hated being smothered with kindness and hated the constraints and obligations such kindness imposed. But in this case, being obliged to holiday with an alienated wife, he reckoned that the presence of old friends would be a useful safety valve for both him and Cathy. They could each renew the old intimacy and bend the ears of their friends with their woes. Dora would love renewing her friendship with the Holbrooks' two boys, Robert and David – both a little older than her.

With Louise, it was quid pro quo. She arranged to go home to her parents over this period, but this time, she and Aidan made arrangements for contact both by phone and via a PO Box number, by letter. On their return to Swaleborough, they resumed their intimate life. Aidan worked assiduously at his painting and Louise worked at his side. When they weren't working, they made love.

The students were back, the term was just under way. Aidan had been to a meeting in Durham. It had been a particularly futile and irritating meeting. He was annoyed, for a start, that it was scheduled for an evening; but due to circumstances in two of the other colleges in the Institute and to the fact that time was running out for setting examination papers, and a deadline approaching at great speed, there had been no other option. He might have consoled himself with the thought that he could drop in on Louise on the way back, but when he had mentioned this to her, she had demurred.

It was the birthday of one of her friends, she'd said, and they were having a get-together at the Green Dragon and going on to a nightclub afterwards. Aidan was crestfallen. He hated the idea of her socialising in this way without him; it had set little worms of jealousy wriggling in his stomach. He could not get out of his mind the picture of her smooching round a darkened dance floor to moody music in the arms of some young Adonis; of her looking up at him and finding him sexily irresistible, suddenly coming to her senses and realising how foolish she'd been to get herself involved with a middle-aged man. A married middle-aged man.

He thought of her deciding there and then to break it off. He thought of his own misery if that should happen; or, almost as unsupportable, he imagined Adonis taking her home after the party, still under the spell of the music: the intimacy; the invitation for coffee; inhibitions loosened by alcohol; the inevitable; the falling together; the unstoppable outcome of the intimacies already enjoyed – the one-night stand. Then next day, the recriminations (he never doubted that he would know). His pain; his rage. How could he ever forgive? How could he ever forget? It would be the end. But hold on – she loved him, didn't she ... he had to trust her, hadn't he? Yet why should that be part of the thing anyway? He had precious little moral claim to her loyalty. What was there about the situation which entitled him even to talk of trust? She was free, free. And he was married. Oh God, oh God, he couldn't stand it.

He wanted to ask her who was going to this party, he wanted to be reassured. Did he know them? Were they students? Were they from this college? But he knew he must not do this. I would be undignified, ignoble, uncool. Louise would get the message that he didn't trust her. Oh God ... jealousy. Did this have to be the downside of being in love? He remembered the corrosive pain of it vividly, from his youth. Middle-aged people should surely not feel like this. Maybe middle-aged people shouldn't be doing things like this. What was the saying? If you can't stand the heat, stay out of the kitchen. How he hated it. Jealousy.

It had simmered in his mind all through the meeting. The last item on the agenda had gone on and on. He hated meetings, but had no choice over the matter when it came to appointments to committees; he had to do his share. But what made it so frustrating was that not everyone shared his loathing. If they did, meetings wouldn't last so

471

bloody long. But in fact, a good number of his colleagues seemed to thrive on them – seemed most wholly alive when tussling with agenda, motions, paragraphs and subsections. This final item had got bogged down on a pedantic quibble over the wording of a single sentence. It had been dismantled, analysed and reconstructed several times, until, half an hour later, half an hour, it was decided that the original version was perhaps, after all, the best.

Aidan was quietly gibbering as he passed through the main door of the building and made for the car park. There was now an insistent drizzle falling, as the light faded. Peering intently through the windscreen, he drove around Palace Green, under the looming mass of the castle and into the narrow streets of the old city, his head beginning to throb. By the time he had threaded his way through the suburbs and negotiated the final roundabout before the A1, he was host to a major headache.

The traffic was unusually heavy for that time of day. Why is it that everyone seems to want to get their car on the road when the weather's atrocious? Why do they seem to drive so much faster when it's black night and the windscreen's half obscured by drizzle, and the water thrown up by the lorry in front? And on this bloody road, with its two opposing carriageways with the intermittent shared overtaking lane in the centre. God, it's hazardous enough at the best of times – but on a night like this ... concentrate ... concentrate ...

His head was full of searing pain and torturing images of Louise, as he thrust it forward towards the windscreen, trying to maximise his vision. The road curved away in front of him, its black wetness reflecting the white lights of cars coming towards him in groups of five or eight, or thirteen, throwing their dazzle through the windscreen. The red lights of the traffic in front curving in diminishing pairs into the distance. Oh God, what's this? He suddenly realised he was closing up rapidly on the red lights in front and lifted his foot off the accelerator, to let the car fall back. There was a slight rise in the road and he could now see that it was a heavily loaded builder's pickup encumbered with a tied-on ladder, a cement mixer and God knows what else. Through all the noise, the rain, the splash of water flung up off the road, the windscreen wipers, he could hear the howl of the pickup's engine, labouring in third gear.

He glanced down at the speedometer. Hell, hardly managing thirty. He could see that a gap had opened up in front of the pickup as the line of traffic ahead pulled away into the distance. He dropped down into third gear ready if the chance came to overtake. No chance yet. An unbroken stream of traffic, headlights glaring were coming towards him. Some in the overtaking lane ... it was hard to tell what was happening. He trundled along in third gear, hammers in his head, eyes straining behind the roaring, crawling pickup. Christ that's all I needed. Bastard! Suddenly the mirror was full of blinding light as the car which a moment ago had been two distant points of light arrived in close proximity to his tailpipe. His eyes strained ahead. A gaggle of cars approaching. Then the two lanes became three again … maybe a chance to overtake.

An oncoming car in the central lane. It's got past, in front of the queue now. It's clear … here's my chance. Aidan glanced in the mirror, floored the accelerator and pulled out into the central lane. He was halfway past the pickup when he saw a pair of headlights detach itself from the oncoming queue. Christ, he's pulling out. What the fuck does he think he's doing? No, no he can't make it. He's got nowhere to go. Collision course. A desperate glance in the mirror. The car behind. The glare of its lights. He's closed up; can't drop back. Fucking lunatic.

Coming towards him four headlights; two of them in his lane. God, oh God he's going to kill me. Quick. second gear. Floor the accelerator. Pray. He felt the second choke come in; the push in the back, the rev counter in the red, the engine howling. The front wing of the pickup in the corner of his eye. NOW. Swerve. The pickup braked as Aidan spun the wheel. Left then right as the oncoming headlights, flashing furiously, horn blaring, swept past him with barely inches to spare. The note of the horn swooped into its Doppler diminuendo as the car passed and died away into the distance as its driver continued his insane progress to God knows where.

Sweating and shaking from the terror of it, Aidan put some distance between himself and the pickup, saw a lay-by ahead, signalled left and pulled into it. He unplugged his seat belt and slumped back in the seat, his eyes closed. Then he sensed lights behind him and heard the boggling of a diesel engine die into silence. A door banged and then the driver of the pickup was peering in at the window. Oh God now what? Aidan lowered the window and looked painfully up at him.

'You alright mate? I saw that. Right fucking maniac he was.'

'Yeah, just a bit shaken, that's all.'

'He could've had us all killed. Bloody dangerous road this, and some fucking dangerous people on it. Anyway ... if you're okay, then I'll get going. Take it easy mate.'

'Yeah, I will. Thanks for stopping. See you.' The driver waved as the pickup pulled past Aidan's car and out into the traffic stream. Presently, Aidan clicked the seat belt into its socket and wearily, warily resumed his journey.

By the time he arrived back at Swaleborough, he was a wreck. He needed aspirin and rest. He needed them now. He decided to stop at the college. There was aspirin in his room. He parked outside the department and let himself in, and into his room. He went straight to the desk drawer, found his bottle of aspirin, unscrewed the top and shook three of the tablets into the palm of his hand. Moaning, he looked round for his glass.

'Oh bugger ...' It was nowhere to be seen, so letting himself out into the textile studio, he staggered to the sink. He tipped the tablets into his mouth and turning on the tap, followed them with a slosh of water scooped up in his cupped hand. He jerked back his head in a convulsive swallow, just catching a tinge of acrid bitterness as the tablets went down. Then using both hands, he scooped up more water and doused his face and forehead, before fumbling his way back into his room, to slump painfully into the armchair.

After half an hour of fitful dozing, the pounding in his head had settled down to a steady dull ache. He looked at his watch. A quarter to eleven. Past closing time. He thought of Louise, imagining her all animated in a tipsy group of giggling friends, heading for the Blue Lagoon. What would happen next? He groaned and dragged himself miserably out of the chair, put on his coat; let himself out of his room, out of the building, into his car. He wanted only bed and oblivion. Tomorrow, a new day. Tomorrow it would be over; relegated to history. Yes. If nothing happened. For Christ' sake stop it. Nothing's going to happen; she loves me, she loves me. Yes … yes … yes, but what if?

He had hoped to go straight to bed. He had neither the will nor the energy to put the car away, so he left it on the drive, locked it and let himself into the front door. The automatic pilot of habitual action took over and he bolted the front door, went into the kitchen to check the back one. Then he took a glass from a shelf, went over to the sink and filled the glass with water, to have it by his bed with his bottle of aspirin; he might need it in the night. He was strongly tempted to go to the drinks cupboard for a soothing glass of Laphroaig to hasten oblivion, but the continuing dull ache in his skull told him that would be a bad idea; so having hung up his coat on the hallstand, he set off unsteadily up the stairs towards the consoling privacy of his bed in the spare room. But there was a sliver of light showing under the bedroom door. Oh God, no. He winced and his forehead creased …

'Aidan …' the voice came; how many ways were there to say 'Aidan'? Well Cathy knew them all; knew all the intonation patterns, the variations in timbre and Aidan knew what message each carried. The combination he was hearing now had not been much used lately. It lacked harshness, hostility, a sharp edge. He could not quite characterise it, except he knew it could not be met with defiance or aggression. Nor could it be ignored. He waited, swaying slightly. Oh, shit … what the fuck now? He put his hands to his forehead and massaged it gently with all ten fingers.

'Aidan … please ...' Pleading.

He crossed to the bedroom door and fumbled it open. Chiaroscuro. A Rembrandt; a Joseph Wright. The cone of light from the bedhead reading lamp spilt brilliance over her head, giving her a golden halo of disturbed hair and making pools of dark shadow under her eyebrows, nose and chin, leaving the rest of the room in enveloping twilight deepening to impenetrable black under the furniture. She was lying on her back, the striped quilt drawn up almost to her shoulders. They were bathed in light, too, their contours, like lines on a map, evoked by the thin black straps of her night dress. She did not turn her head to look at him. Aidan waited. She said nothing.

'Well what?' he asked. He did not trouble to conceal his impatience. He'd had a hell of an evening, bored stupid in a meeting while being tormented with jealousy; a nerve-racking drive back, incorporating a skirmish with death; a merciless headache. And that was just tonight. Add to that the long-term bitterness lodged deep in his soul. So what the fuck did she want now, when all he wanted was solitude and sleep?

She took a deep breath and released it through her mouth. 'Will you stay with me tonight?'

'What?' Aidan reacted with astonishment. They had not shared the same bed for some months. Things had changed. She knew they had changed. He would be being unfaithful – not to his wife; with his wife.

'Look, I know you don't want …' Not finishing the sentence, she drew in a sharp breath. '… but not for that. It's just … well, I need to have someone close, tonight.'

Aidan groaned. 'Why the hell … look, I've just had a lousy …'
'Please …'

Something in her plea stopped him. He bit his lip in agitation. She had turned her head towards him, to look at him with upturned eyes. Aidan, irritated, perplexed, gave a sigh of resignation. 'Okay. I'll … just go and clean my teeth.'

From the bathroom, he went to the spare room, which was now de facto his room. For most of their married life they had slept naked, until the attrition of their sexual activity had somehow made this seem indecent and night clothes had crept back into use. Aidan, once confirmed in possession of his solitary bed, had resumed nakedness for he liked the coolness of sheets on his body. But tonight's situation called for pyjamas, so rummaging in the back of a drawer, he found a pair of crumpled blue ones. As he pulled on the trousers, he remembered from when he had last worn them, that the elastic in the waist was shot. Why the hell don't they make them with cords like they used to?

Holding them up with a handful of waistband, he searched one-handed through the drawers and in the bottom of the wardrobe, looking for a stray safety pin. None was to be found. Shit! He stood for a few moments, clutching his pyjama trousers with one hand and massaging his pounding head with the other. Then with an under-breath curse, he hooked his slippers from under the bed with one foot and one at a time, insinuated his feet half into them, crushing the backs with his heels. He switched out the light and shuffled across the landing.

She had now switched off the reading lamp and the bedroom was penumbrally lit by the orange of the street light outside, diffused through the drawn curtains. He could see that she was lying, curled foetally, facing the door and him. He could see that her eyes were open. He navigated himself round the foot of the bed stepping over a small pile of her shed clothes, to the opposite side, still clutching the waistband of his pyjama trousers. Then as carefully as he was able, so as not to expose any of Cathy, he peeled back the quilt and sheet, and inserted himself into the bed, carefully replacing the covers. There, for some time, he lay rigid on his back, to attention, ensuring that no part of him came into contact with any part of her.

It was sometime before he was able to allow his body to relax, to surrender to the seductive yieldingness of the mattress, to enjoy the blessed horizontality of it. He put his headache to bed, but his mind lingered ... Why am I here? Why does she want me in her bed? I feel embarrassed. Why did I agree? He repeated the questions to himself as he began to lose his grip of consciousness. Why does she want ...? Why does she ...?

He was jerked back into wakefulness as Cathy suddenly turned onto her back, causing something deep inside the mattress to twang. Then there was stillness. And in a few moments Aidan had resumed his blissful slide into unconsciousness. But again something stopped him. Now Cathy was lying rigid. She somehow radiated rigidity. Though he was separated from her by a decent gap, he was acutely aware of her wakefulness and it infected him. Oh God! Why doesn't she go to sleep? Why doesn't she let me go to sleep? In his impatience and irritation, he took a deep breath and uttered an involuntary snort. Cathy was breathing audibly, but not the regular heavy breathing of sleep; it was breathing that was tense; breathing through a mouth that was open. It was breathing that was punctuated by small clicks as somewhere above her epiglottis, a small bubble of saliva formed and burst; the lips, closed for a swallow, parted audibly as the moist seal broke.

Oh God, Aidan thought, how does she do it? How, by doing nothing very much, does she disseminate tension enough to drive anyone mad? How can she so effortlessly invade other people's tranquillity and destroy it? He lay there, now wide awake, staring furiously at the patterns of light and shadow on the ceiling. He heard a car approaching. As it drew abreast of the house, the glare from its headlights swept across the ceiling, temporarily swamping in their whiter light the resident patterns he'd been listlessly studying. He heard the engine note modulate as an unknown hand changed down a gear for the hill and the bend. The sound tapered away into silence. Cathy breathed, radiating wakefulness.

'Christ!' Aidan suddenly and violently sat up. 'Cathy, for Christ's sake why don't you go to sleep?' The shock seemed to release something in Cathy, something that had been trying to come out. She moaned softly and her moan dissolved into a soft sobbing.

'What the hell's the matter?' He asked her. But he thought he knew. This was it, wasn't it? He was engulfed a sudden wave of apprehension. He'd known quite soon after he had taken up with Louise that he couldn't for long deceive Cathy; that she would have to know. And that it would become more and more important to Louise that she should know. He had postponed that piece of the reckoning, cowardly in the face of sheer difficulty of confronting Cathy. When it had happened, it had been thrust upon him by Cathy. He had not chosen the time; it had been brought about by Cathy's own perception She'd seen what was going on and had forced the truth out. She had responded to that truth in a way that he neither expected nor understood. But it had made things better, so he gratefully accepted the situation. He was both having his cake and eating it. He did not need to lie, now that she knew and there had been no trauma. And Louise was reassured of his commitment. Other bridges would be crossed as and when.

Since then there had been this period of eerie stability, but it was a fragile stability and it was necessarily temporary, for sooner or later, there had to be a resolution; a resolution leading to a permanent change. He did not know on what basis Cathy was prepared to be visibly cuckolded. But he felt he was sitting on a time bomb and he would either have to take his fate in his hands and defuse it or put on his flak-jacket and wait for it to blow up. Now it looked as though the crunch time had again been chosen by Cathy. She had come to the end of her tether. This was to be the end of the ... what? The phoney war? That uneasy period of armed non-belligerence, when he was free to come and go as he pleased, without hindrance? He never thought it could last. How could she possibly put up with it? Its reasonableness was quite beyond reason. There had to be a showdown. It could be horrible. Surely the reasonableness couldn't continue. But he had to be firm. Okay then, so this was it. He braced himself for it.

The bed now shook gently to her sobs. Then, more kindly – he could never stand up for long against her tears – he said, 'Cathy, come on … what is it? What's the matter?' The sobs went on, as she tried to control herself. She breathed in sharply through her mouth, then sniffed. She was silent for a while. There was only her breathing, more normal, now. Aidan reached out a hand under the sheet and found one of hers and squeezed it encouragingly. Maybe it wasn't going to be a row. She was upset, naturally. But she was resigned. She was going to be reasonable. Well of course he would be reasonable too. After all, they could still be friends – all those years couldn't just go for nothing. He would be fair. He would see her all right.

'I … I think I've got a lump.'

Aidan, having now convinced himself that a major and painful act of reorganisation of their lives was about to be initiated; that this was the crunch he'd been expecting for weeks; this agonising act of rationalisation which would give concrete form to their de facto separation and which would bring closer that longed for union with Louise, was sandbagged by the shear bathos of it.

'A lump.' He repeated the word. A lump of what, for fuck's sake? The collocations: a lump of coal; a lump of rock; a lump in the mattress. He scrolled the meanings through his mind, looking for a context.

Cathy supplied it. She sobbed again, 'A lump … a lump in my breast …'

Aidan said nothing immediately. His first inward reaction was, Oh God, here we go again. Why is she always seeking attention? Why does she want to be the sufferer now? How does that fit with the pitiless despot she wants to be with Bobby?

'I noticed during my period. Things can happen then. I thought it would go away after, but it hasn't and I …' Her voice faded away. Aidan, still sitting upright in bed shook out his thoughts, trying to put together suitable words, words that would make the problem go away. They were slow in coming.

Then Cathy, in a sudden explosion of energy, which shook the bed, flung herself bolt upright. 'Aidan. For god's sake say something. Do I have to spell it out to you? I've got a lump … a lump. Don't you see? It might be cancer.'

Aidan was struggling. 'Oh … I … Oh God. D'you really think it's …'

'I don't know, I don't know … I don't know …' her last 'don't know' reduced to a miserable squeak, segued into another sob. Fear, panic.

'But it may be harmless. I think that most of them are … aren't they?'

'Oh for God's sake ... Aidan, listen ... I want you to feel my breast ... see if you can tell. I may be imagining it or something.'

Aidan flinched. Feeling breasts was something to do with making love, with sex. He adored them, was fascinated by them. Always had been a boob man. Not that he was immune to the attractions of a taut, mobile arse or a shapely pair of legs. But essentially he was a devotee – a worshipper almost – of the bosom. Oh God ... but here, now?

Cathy had splendid breasts: generous, but avoiding pendulosity. They were nicely rounded and well separated on her deep ribcage; and firm. She could not have held a pencil in her sub-mammary folds. Her nipples were pink and pleasingly responsive. Or at least they were in the heyday of their marriage, when they did get it together. In those days, on those good days, her breasts had given him much pleasure. Her too, he'd hoped. But now ... Oh God ... now ...

'Well ... okay, if you want me to ... er, just tell me what to do.'

He'd let himself fall back against the pillow. Cathy tugged at the cord, switching on the light. Aidan lay, his eyes screwed up against the sudden shock of light, dazzled by the floating reds and greens of the aurora inside his eyelids. When he opened them, she was sitting upright. He could see the swell of her breast under the black flimsiness of her nightie and despite himself, felt a stirring in his loins. He groaned inwardly at his susceptibility and tried to disconnect his eyes from his genitals.

Cathy looked at him. She seemed embarrassed. Christ, embarrassed. Embarrassed after all these years. All those years of sleeping together and mutual revelation. He thought about that – mutual revelation, when each knew what the other was like on the outside. But inside – God, another matter altogether. She took a deep breath and slipped the straps of her nightie off her shoulders and it slid down over the roundness of her breasts to fall about her waist. A small shock penetrated to Aidan's testicles and he flinched.

'Okay,' he said, 'tell me what to do.' Without looking at him, she took his hand and placed it on her left breast. Oh God. His mind quite without his consent, momentarily flashed back again to that night when a girl took his hand in hers and placed it on her naked breast. Fifteen. The Lyric cinema. He remembered her name now: Doris Wilmot. Not exactly notorious, but said to be generous with her favours. Couldn't remember the details of how they'd met. He'd hardly ever even spoken to her before, but somehow in the middle of the week, they'd found themselves together in the cinema queue. He could even remember the film: Cover Girl. Betty Grable. The girl with the torch saw them as a couple and Aidan saw no reason to object when she showed them to the back row. Nor evidently did Doris. Emboldened by the offered Smarties, Aidan, inch by inch sneaked his arm around her. Then she, perhaps impatient at his timidity, grabbed his other hand and sliding it under her blouse, clamped it emphatically on her left breast. Aidan, already fired up by this unexpected erotic encounter and in charge of a healthy erection, swallowed hard and stared fixedly at the screen. She didn't look at him or say anything. Aidan, in a sweat of lust, did not know what to do next. So he did nothing, fearing to do anything which would jeopardise this heavenly, heaven-sent sensation.

They parted after the show. He didn't know what to do; how to extend the experience, how to arrange for a repeat performance. He was just paralysed by shyness and embarrassment. So they parted; she to catch her bus; he nursing the erection which felt as though it might be permanent. Nothing intimate ever again occurred between them.

And now ...

'There. Can you feel it?' The pleasure of her breasts had always been immediate; the sense of their weight, mobility, warmth, smoothness. Instantly electrifying his libido; sending direct and urgent signals to his genitals. But this wasn't supposed to be like that.

'Move around a bit.' Now, for the first time tentatively searching, his fingers encountered a subtle world of submerged structure he did not know how to interpret. What the hell should be there? Is that rib or muscle, or gristle. How should it be? What are breasts made of? What's inside them?

'Can you feel anything?'

'I don't know ... I really don't know.'

'There ... just there.' She redirected his hand, and pressed his fingers deeper.

'Cathy, I don't know. There may be something, but I just don't know. I don't know whether there's anything really. It's hard to tell … I mean, I'm not sure how it's supposed feel … in this way. Look, you'd better go and see the doctor. I'll make you an appointment tomorrow.'

She was sitting up rigidly, biting her lip. He tried to comfort her. 'Listen, it's probably nothing. Probably nothing at all. But better be on the safe side and see the doctor.' He soothed her as best he could. He knew what he was saying was trite – but what else was there to say but words of hope. Quite soon, sleep crept back over him and he left Cathy to her anguish.

It wasn't nothing. It was a malignant tumour.

CHAPTER 31

Next day, as soon as the surgery was open, Aidan rang to make an appointment with the doctor. It was for two thirty. Then they went through the motions of breakfast together, though little was eaten. Cathy was silent, tense, subdued. Aidan was solicitous, anticipating, doing everything possible to remove from her path anything that might cause the slightest inconvenience or generate the slightest friction.

On emerging from sleep, he usually experienced the return of consciousness as a procession of half-formed thoughts jostling with each other on the way to full awareness. He would experience inchoate intimations of events scheduled for the day, pleasures and pitfalls. His senses would gradually come into focus and incorporate his first impressions of the weather; and all would, as full consciousness developed, amalgamate into his anticipation of the day. Despite the vicissitudes of his life, more often than not, his optimism prevailed and he looked upon the coming day with pleasurable anticipation. But this day, his emergence into consciousness had been perplexing and overlaid by an ominous black shadow. Where was he, for fuck's sake? Where? Where? Oh Christ! He was in Cathy's bed. What was he doing there? Had he been pissed?

Surely not that pissed. His mind clawed at the fragments of recollection, and suddenly the bits came together, and he remembered. Oh God, oh God, oh God ... His cry went up and he knew it was not just for Cathy, but also for himself, as, suddenly, a whole range of likely consequences and ramifications hit him. He groaned inwardly and waited a while, staring at the ceiling.

When he had got his faculties into rough working order, he slipped out of the bed, leaving Cathy apparently still asleep. Not knowing what else to do and needing time to think, he went to the bathroom, showered and then to his room to dress. He returned to the bedroom. She was awake and in her dressing gown.

He did not know what to say. So he said, 'Hi.'

And she said, 'Hi.'

'I, er ... I'll ring the doctor's ... get you the earliest appointment.'

'Okay. Thanks.' Then she'd gone to the bathroom.

'Two thirty,' he told her, when they'd assembled at the breakfast table.

'Right. Thanks. That means I can go to school this morning.'

'Oh, d'you think that's a good idea?'

'The best. I'll take my mind off it.'

'Okay. If that's what you want. D'you want the car? Or I could give you a lift if you like.'

'No thanks. I'll do what I usually do. I'll get the bus. I'll have lunch at school then get the bus back. But Aidan, I'd like you to come with me to see the doctor. Will you, please?'

'Oh …' Aidan thought for a moment. He had not expected this. But he knew he could not refuse. '… right if that's what you want. I'll see you at the surgery at half two.'

No, he hadn't expected that. Nevertheless, he was in some way relieved. He remembered the agony last night and marvelled at her tense stoicism this morning. Her intention to act normally, as long as it was possible to do so, meant that so could he. So having given her a brief encouraging hug, he watched her leave, carrying as usual, her capacious shopping bag full of her school things; he returned to the kitchen and set about organising Dora's departure.

He did not need to set off to walk to college for another half an hour yet. Punctuality was not essential on studio days like this. He knew that when he got there, he'd find more or less the right number of students, starting work on their individual projects or standing around, discussing their work – maybe even just gossiping. One of the nice things about his working situation was that days were fuzzy at both ends. The only important thing was that the work got done and there were no bosses to prescribe how or, within reason, when. He knew he was the expert in his own domain and that was that.

More coffee. He took the jar of beans off the shelf and shook some into the grinder, pressing the button that set it off with a yowl. He reached for the coffee pot, unscrewing the top half. He swilled out the bottom bit then filled it up to the safety valve with water. Then he tipped the finely ground coffee into the top bit, screwed both halves together and set the pot on the smallest ring on the cooker hob. He didn't think he was obsessional, but he found the small rituals of daily life important; they were small way-stations en route through the day; they divided it up into manageable chunks. This one should have seen him embark, as was usual, in high hopes – if not spirits. But it didn't. He waited, immobile for the coffee to start bubbling, then turned out the gas. He took the coffee pot to the table, collecting a mug and the milk jug on the way.

He sat down, poured coffee, added milk and with his elbows on the table, holding the mug two handed, he tilted his head forward, to inhale the steam and allow his thoughts to assert themselves. Now he had a little space to himself, his mind leapfrogged backwards to the evening before – before his wife had laid her discovery on him; the evening came back and engulfed his mind in another wave of despairing jealousy. God … that bloody party. Who did she end up with? Did somebody take her home? How could they not end up in bed? Both half pissed and randy after an evening of frotting to erotic music in subdued lights. No. No. She wouldn't. She couldn't. She loves me. We're going to be together … aren't we? Aren't we? But what if? Oh God, stop it. Stop it.

Okay, sod waiting. He had to see her. He'd thought he'd play it cool; be ever so casual. However much he was pained that she should go to a party without him – should even want to go to a party without him – he wouldn't show it. He had to see her, but he couldn't let her see his anguish. He just couldn't go up to her and confront her with his suspicion. She'd have to come to him. It was up to her ... wasn't it? No. To hell with that. He wanted to know. He wanted to know now. He'd be able to tell. He knew he would. She was in his class this morning. He looked at his watch, knocked back the coffee, put the mug in the sink with a clatter, went to the hallstand, grabbed his coat, let himself out of the back door, pulling it shut with a crash; set off down the drive and up the road at a feverishly brisk pace.

As he walked, he tried to restore some rationality to his thoughts. Come on, Aidan, you're a middle-aged man, behaving – in your head anyway – like an adolescent. What're you doing? You're rehearsing in your mind a silly psychological game – the kind juveniles play. Just fucking well grow up. Be honest, upfront.

By the time he arrived in the studio, he was calmer. As the door swung shut behind him, some of his students looked up and there was a murmur of unco-ordinated greeting. He saw Louise in the far corner where she usually preferred to work. She turned and flashed him a smile. Aidan gave an unobtrusive wave. He usually avoided going to her first, though it was his instinct to grab her into his arms and ravish her on the spot. She turned back to her work.

Aidan, though now knowing every detail of her body, never failed to be excited at first sight of her. She was sitting at an angle to the bench, on a high stool, bent over her drawing board. She was in working gear. Her jeans were faded and patched, sandals shabby and worn. The familiar knitted beige top she wore ended a little above her navel, so in her forward stoop, exposed a crescent of flesh above the waist band. Her black hair was tied back with a scrap of red material. She wore no make-up. Christ, she's beautiful ... and ... My God she lets me fuck her. The question ... did she let someone else, last night? Tried to sidle into his mind, but he determinedly suppressed it before it had time to completely form.

He stood for a few moments looking round at his students then said, 'Okay, who needs me?' He always began this way. It was a well-worn formula, but useful. He knew that when he first came into the studio, the students would expect it. It was his catchphrase and he had often noticed a student motionless, waiting for it, to roll his eyes and mouth it silently, in synchronisation. Three students needed him and it was not until he had helped them with their problems, that he allowed himself to approach Louise. She had before her a double elephant drawing board covered with a tautly stretched layer of Whatman watercolour paper. It already bore a complex of inter-related black lines of varying thickness. By the side and on another, but smaller board were the dissected pieces of a reproduction of Poussin's The Gathering of the Ashes of Phocion, an open copy of Le

Corbusier's Le Modulor and a number of strips of wood of differing lengths. She was wearing the small oval glasses, she looked up and over them as he arrived at her side.

She smiled. 'Hi, Aidan,' she said.

'Ah, Louise,' Aidan said, thinking of last night. She can't have done. She couldn't have done and everything so normal. I'd be able to tell ... wouldn't I? 'How's the search for perfect harmony progressing?'

'We-e-ell, er I'm still working at it. Look, I made these.' She indicated the wooden strips.

'What ...?'

'Thirteen, twenty-one, thirty-four, fifty-five, ninety-one ...' Aidan picked up the sticks and examined them.

'Ah, the Fibonacci series.' He thought of Cathy. Oh God, What chance of perfect harmony now? Louise bent forward over the drawing board as he arranged the sticks on it. She did not look at him as her breast brushed the back of his hand. He sometimes found it difficult to focus on the teaching. They had developed, for use in public, other, non-vocal, languages. They had learned to kiss with their eyes, to speak with their bodies, their hands secretly, briefly finding the intimate places, their thighs, in delicate frottage. 'Well ... a good idea ...' This couldn't have happened – what's happening now – if that had happened last night ... could it? 'The higher up the scale, the closer to the golden section ... so what are you going to do next?'

'Shall we talk about it after coffee? I'm gagging for some and it's about time.'

The concentration in the group was on the point of breaking up. There was the clatter of a displaced stool, the swish of brushes in the paraffin bucket, outbreak of fragments of conversation.

'Coffee time, Aidan,' someone called.

'Okay folks,' Aidan replied, then to Louise, 'probably a good idea …' An exchange of glances, 'See you later.' Aidan made for the door.

Five minutes later, she was secure in his arms and they were locked together in a raging kiss. When they came up for breath, they stood for a while facing each other, panting, needing oxygen. Then she said, 'How was your meeting last night?'

'Horrendous.' After a pause, looking at her intently, 'I'd rather have been at your party … but then, I wasn't invited … was I?'

'Well you really wouldn't have fitted in Aidan.'

'No. Too old, I suppose.' He could not keep an intrusive tinge of bitterness out of his voice.

She smiled at him and gently patted him on the cheek. 'Aidan! It was a hen party,' she said.

'What?' A wave of relief swept over him, dispelling the black cloud that had fuddled his mind for the last twenty-four hours. The relief was quickly followed by an onset of shame that he had allowed the poison of suspicion to seep into his mind, that he had thereby insulted Louise. He had allowed her to be fickle, promiscuous, even;

had not credited her with the love she said she felt for him, had not believed in it. He saw that she was trying to read his face and he let it collapse into laughter, as eventually the relief prevailed over the guilt. As the laughter died away, he looked down, sighed and shook his head.

Louise, looking slightly bemused, said, 'What was all that about then?'

'Oh, I er ... oh nothing ...' She made a swift grab with both her hands and caught him under the armpits. Taken by surprise, he gave a yelp.

'Come on, tell me or I'll tickle you to death.'

Aidan, wriggling and about to yield to hysterics, but trying to sweep her arms away, cried out, 'Okay, okay, I'll tell you.' He paused for a while. He took a deep breath, 'Well, it's silly really. I wondered why you were going to that party by yourself. I wondered why you hadn't asked me to go with you and there was this awful meeting. I didn't have even the consolation of being able to see you afterwards. And because you were going to a bloody party.'

'But Aidan, it was a hen party.'

'Well I didn't know. You didn't tell me ... and I started imagining things. I got angry and jealous. I know it was stupid ... but I just couldn't help it. I kept remembering the Christmas party, when you didn't turn up in my room. I had to go and look for you – and found you in someone else's arms.'

'Aidan, you know why that was. I hope you're not going to hold that against me forever.'

Aidan smiled at her ruefully. 'No, of course not. I suppose it just shows how insecure I am. I'm not used to having a beautiful young woman as a lover. I sometimes find it difficult to believe.'

'But Aidan, you must believe it. I love you. I do love you. And I wouldn't have wanted to go to a proper party without you. Even if I did find myself in that situation … well, remember, I'm not about to fall into bed with any Tom, Dick or Harry … I would never do anything to put our relationship at risk.' She snuggled into his arms and let her head fall on his shoulder.

'I love you,' Aidan said. But he said nothing of the other problem which haunted him, only that he had something on at half past two that afternoon and might not be back afterwards.

CHAPTER 32

Half past two. A short wait, skimming through out-of-date Tattlers; then the doctor. A woman, young, smiling,

'Come this way please,' and looking at Aidan, 'you coming too, Mr Hamilton? Good,' as Aidan nodded.

'Okay Mrs Hamilton, can you take your top off and your bra?' She leafed through a file, stopping in a couple of places to give closer attention. 'Yeah, thanks. Can you come over here a wee bit? That's it.' Palpating. 'Mmm … There's something there. Can't always tell with these things … could be just a cyst.' Palpating. 'Better have it looked at. I'll get you an appointment at the hospital. It'll be quick. Can't hang around with something like this … just in case. Try not to worry.'

But worry she did. The hospital appointment came within a week. Aidan took time off to drive her there. X-ray. Biopsy. Several days waiting in anguish. Phone call from the surgery.

'You'd better come in for a chat.' The doctor's face was serious. 'The news is not so good, I'm afraid.' There was no way to soften it. 'The biopsy results indicate that it's malignant.'

Aidan put his hand on Cathy's arm. She sat in frozen shock.

'But there is some good news, though. We can get an almost immediate operation. We caught it early so there's every chance of a complete cure.'

'But I come out of it minus a breast.' Tears were running down Cathy's face.

'I'm afraid so. But the main thing is to get you well again … and they do marvels these days with prosthetics.'

He took her home. Once inside the door, she turned to Aidan and collapsed in tears. He put his arms around her and she wept inconsolably onto his shoulder as he tried to think of what he could possibly say to help her. It seemed that some situations were impermeable to words; the words just did not exist. In such a situation, there was nothing for it but to submit oneself to the utter bleakness of it and get on with the suffering – and try to find room for hope. Aidan, realising that the comforting arm was the best he could offer, did enough hoping for two.

The grief gradually subsided and they went into the living room where Cathy lowered herself into the cane chair by the French window, turning herself towards the garden, in silence. After a while, Aidan suggested some whisky. Cathy did not normally like the stuff, but this time agreed; it was a special occasion. He fetched the bottle of Laphroaig from the sideboard and two of the best crystal glasses – two of the four survivors of the set someone had given them as a wedding present. He'd thought them pretty useless at the time, before he had discovered the glory of a good malt whisky, but later in his marriage, he'd changed his mind about that; he found them increasingly useful, as he came to appreciate the restorative and consolatory properties of the fiery liquid. Then he marvelled at the givers' foresight. He poured a good measure into each glass and they sipped in silence, looking out over the garden.

Then, seemingly reinforced, she said to the garden, 'I'll go into school tomorrow. I want to carry on. No point in hanging around just thinking about it. Best to keep busy.' Aidan agreed. It meant that life could be fairly normal for him for the time being and he felt some relief for that.

The letter came four days later. The designated day for the operation was a week ahead. Cathy continued, in the meanwhile, to teach her children and associate with her colleagues. At home, her spirits rose and fell unpredictably, Aidan did his best to administer comfort – in a situation in which comfort was hard to find. Sometimes, in those few days, Cathy wondered aloud if death was preferable to life thus mutilated. Aidan gently scolded her for such negative thoughts, while wondering on his own behalf, if death was preferable to a life mutilated in the way his now, inevitably, it seemed, would be. Physical mutilation; emotional mutilation. His hopeful journey towards an eventual life with Louise was now blocked by an impassable gate labelled CANCER. Leaving Cathy was now a moral impossibility. When not being nice to Cathy, he was inwardly screaming his fury at a fate which had played him such a diabolical trick. His imagination now began to reinterpret his life as gruesome game of snakes and ladders, and he was now at the bottom of the tail of the biggest snake on the board.

He had not, at first, said anything to Louise; he really didn't know how to handle it. But she soon seemed to sense that something was amiss. For one thing, constraints seemed to have been re-imposed on their meetings. Aidan felt unable, now to come and go with the same freedom as before; he felt that the emotional situation was so fragile that he could not leave Cathy alone too much. Okay, she knew about his relationship with Louise, but he'd never managed to work out the basis on which she seemed to tolerate it. So he was nowhere near to understanding how things stood now. He wanted to say, 'Look, I know you've got cancer – and that's terrible, but it doesn't make any difference to Louise and me. I still love her and want to go to her.' But he knew he couldn't. Not at this moment. And it could be a long moment. What was Cathy doing with that knowledge? Was she suppressing it? She can't have forgotten. Maybe it just seemed now less important than trying to stay alive, under the threat of the most feared of diseases.

Then there was Dora; they were unsure of how much to tell her and when. And, of course, Bobby. He did not attempt to discuss Bobby with her. Cathy did not mention her – she seemed to have forgotten she existed at all. So this was something for him to decide.

But Dora was the immediate concern; being present through it all, it was clear that she seemed to sense something amiss. Aidan could see difficult times ahead and wanted to be around for her as much as possible. So he had to make excuses to Louise for his altered behaviour, for being not so available. It seemed that they were back to an earlier phase – snatching at moments where and when they could – and she, not understanding, clearly seeing it as a surrender of territory recently gained, did not take readily to it. Then there was Aidan's behaviour – abstracted for much of the time, but punctuated by episodes of despairing passion, when he would take her in his arms and they would cling together, like a couple in the last seconds of ecstasy before approaching death. In his blackest moments, this was what it felt like to him. Then, in his room at coffee time, after one such embrace, she pushed away from him, took his hands in hers and fixed him with her eyes.

'Aidan, what's the matter? There's something wrong – isn't there?' He looked away, frowning and took a deep breath. While he tried to assemble the words, she went on, 'Look, you've been behaving strangely, these last few days. I'm getting worried. Are you going off me or something?' He reached out and pulled her back, close to him, wrapping her fiercely in his arms, nuzzling his face into her hair.

'Lulu, how could you think such a thing? I love you … I adore you … I want you forever.' She gently freed herself from his embrace, so she could engage his eyes again. He looked down and moistened his lips, 'Well, something's come up these last few days ...'

'Something that affects us?'

'No ... well, it can't affect how I feel about you ...'

'Well then ...?'

He thought for a moment. '... But it could affect how we see each other ... for a while.'

'Aidan ...' she was getting exasperated, 'For God's sake tell me. What is it?'

'It's Cathy ...'

'She knows about us. She does – you told her, didn't you?'

'Yes. Yes, of course she does. You know I told her after the play.'

'Well then what is it ... what about her?'

'She's ... she's got cancer.' there was a long pause; she stared at him round eyed.

'I ... I don't know what to say ... God, that's awful ... terrible. Oh Aidan, I'm sorry ... really sorry.'

'Yeah, it is terrible. Breast cancer. So sudden ... a real blow. I'm just trying to get my head round the implications. Trying to keep in focus that it's worse for Cathy ... I mean ... she's the one with ... she's got the cancer.'

'So this is why you've not been so available this last week?'

'Yes.' He hesitated, 'Lulu, I hope you understand. It doesn't make any difference to us – it can't – I won't let it. It's just that for the time

504

being, well I've just got to be around for her more. She needs help, support. She's got to have an operation – soon – within a fortnight, I should think. I'm going to have to do everything – transport, visits, looking after Dora – as well as visiting Bobby.'

'But we'll still be able to meet, won't we? I mean, we just can't not meet, can we?'

'Christ Lulu, of course we will. We can still meet here every day and I'll be able to manage some evenings. It's just that it's going to be a bit difficult for a while. I … I just can't see the way clear at the present moment.' He took her into his arms again and held her. For a while, she didn't speak; she just held still, her chin resting on his shoulder, her eyes looking away into some unfathomable distance. Aidan held her tightly, entrapped in his arms, as though the fierceness of the entrapment was a guarantee that all would be well. When he released her, she walked slowly over to the window and stood, silent, for a while, looking into the distance.

Then she said, 'If I want you … if I want you, I'll just have to stick with it, won't I? I've no option … have I? Because I do want you – very much.'

CHAPTER 33

He'd not yet told Bobby about her mother's illness. In fact since Bobby's admission to Roseberry, they had never, either of them, mentioned her. Bobby had never asked and he, seeing no good reason why she would want any tidings of her mother, had never attempted to impart any. But it was different, now; she really should know.

The next day, he had an appointment with Dr Wilkinson, at Roseberry. At the time he'd arranged it, he'd afterwards spoken to Bobby on the phone and arranged to take her out for the afternoon. The evening before, he had rung Gudrun Svensen and arranged for her to collect Dora from school. She'd again offered an overnight stay and Aidan accepted with relief the gift of a few more hours of freedom.

The Sister rapped briskly on the door. The voice from inside said, 'Come.' She smiled at Aidan and with a hand on his arm, opened the door and led him in.

'Mr Hamilton to see you, Wilkie.'

'Good morning Mr Hamilton,' the doctor said, looking briefly up from his desk. Aidan had been relieved that the intimacy of first names and diminutives had not extended to his relationship with the consultant. The practice, in use from the first day with the Sister – she had introduced herself as Marion, emphasising the prevalent informality – had led to an increasingly flirtatious relationship which, though appealing to Aidan's vanity, seemed not always to give appropriate weight to the reason for his being there at all – namely the plight of his daughter. He had no great wish to be flirtatious with the consultant.

'How are you?' and without waiting for an answer, 'do have a seat.' He indicated the chair facing the desk, opposite him. 'Can you just give me a few seconds while I sort this lot out?' He flipped briskly through a sheaf of papers on his desk, scribbling a note on the occasional one with a ballpoint. Again looking up briefly, 'Marion, could you fetch the file please?'

Then after dealing with the last sheet, he put down the pen, picked up the pile of papers, shuffled them into orderliness and slipped them into a folder. Looking up at Aidan, this time giving his full attention, asked again, 'Sorry about that. Bloody paperwork. How are you, Mr Hamilton?'

'Fine, thank you,' Aidan gave that reply more because it was the only answer the rules permitted than because of its truth.

'Oh good … Marion …' He spoke without looking up at her, holding out his hand and she placed the file in it. He put it on the desk in front of him. 'Let's see … when did we last see you?' he opened the file and thumbed through the pages. 'A fortnight ago … y-e-e-s. Well we were talking then about discharge, weren't we?' He looked up from the file. 'Marion ...' Marion, now half sitting, her legs elegantly crossed, on the edge of the desk, smiled at Aidan.

'Yes ... well she's made great progress here. She was so withdrawn and apathetic at first. But I think we won her confidence quite soon.'

'Yes ...' the doctor agreed, 'and she very quickly palled up with Daisy, didn't she? That was really good for both of them.'

'Well they certainly formed a formidable alliance ... the life and soul of the establishment. We've had a lot of laughs with them – and they've been so creative – art, music, drama – the lot.'

'When I spoke to Bobby on Tuesday,' the doctor resumed, 'she told me she didn't want to go home. She wanted to stay here and become a psychiatric nurse. I rather think she's a great admirer of Marion.' He seemed amused and looked up at the sister and smiled.

The sister, also smiling, looked down at her hands, clasped on her lap then said, 'Well, in a few years ... who knows?'

'But,' continued the doctor, 'dealing with the present reality, I think we've done everything we can – all that we set out to do and we've really got to be thinking of discharging her. So really, Mr Hamilton, what I wanted to ask you today was how have your negotiations at home gone? How do you see Bobby's future, now?' Both doctor and sister looked at him in expectation.

Aidan, looking down, almost imperceptibly shook his head and shuddered. 'Look, Doctor Wilkinson,' he slowly raised his eyes and looked at both of them. 'There was a time, round about Easter, when

Cathy, my wife, indicated that she was interested in some sort of reconciliation; she suggested that we might all make a new start. Well, in the light of history, I didn't think that idea stood much of a chance from the outset. Then, for various reasons, the possibility became … well, no longer even a possibility. So I'd come to the conclusion that the only thing I could do was to leave my wife, to find a flat where Bobby and I could set up on our own but where I could stay in close touch with Dora. In fact, I had one or two possibilities lined up.' He looked down again and fiddled with the gold ring on the third finger of his left hand, while they waited. Then he took a deep breath. As though about to dive into a swimming pool.

'But you see, things have changed, since we last discussed Bobby's discharge. The fact is, my wife … she's just been diagnosed as having cancer – cancer of the breast.' There was a long silence.

'Ah …' Dr Wilkinson nodded thoughtfully, 'I see. I'm sorry to hear that.'

'Presumably Bobby doesn't know. I mean, if she did, we would certainly know she knew,' Dr Wilkinson said.

'No. No she doesn't. I'll have to tell her, of course. It's going to affect all our lives, so it would be difficult to conceal – even if that were desirable.'

'Yes, I agree,' the doctor said. 'Knowing her so well as we do now, I think we can confidently predict she can handle it. It might have been more traumatic for her if she had a loving relationship with her mother – but, things being as they are …' He let the sentence go unfinished and turned with a quizzical look to the sister. She signalled her assent with a smile and a nod.

They agreed that, in the circumstances, it would be undesirable to discharge Bobby, just yet, so they would keep her on until the situation was somehow resolved.

'Anyway,' the doctor said, 'I expect you'll be wanting to take her out now. I know she was looking forward to your visit.'

'Yes, she always does,' the sister said.

Aidan took his leave and went up the broad staircase to find Bobby in her room. Not knowing what kind of response to expect, he decided, for better or for worse, he would tell her that day. The door was labelled in a bold, bright scrawl, illuminated with prancing horses and fish, BOBBIE'S PLACE. He rapped the door with his knuckles.

'Hello-o,' he called.

'Dad,' she replied, 'come on in.'

He found her cross-legged on the floor, surrounded by sheets of paper, dozens of cut shapes and all the ancillary requirements for making a collage. She stood up in a shower of cut paper and flung herself into his arms.

Then he asked her where she would like to go. She went over to the open window and inspected the day.

'Oh it's a seaside kind of day, Dad. That's what I want ... the sea, the sea. There'll be a lovely breeze. Maybe we'll be able to fly the kite. Can we do that, Dad can we ... please?'

That was fine by Aidan. 'Yes, of course we can ... just the day for it. I've still got it in the boot from last time. We can go to Sandsend and we can have tea at one of those caffs on the seafront.'

'Yeah, that one where they do those gorgeous jammy doughnuts ...'

He drove around the northern edge of the Clevelands, meandering at a leisurely pace down the coast road, dropping down the steep twisted descent into Sandsend. He parked the car in the village car park and they stepped out into a warm, gentle stirring of the air. Walking round to the back of the car, Aidan opened it up and got out the kite, in its long oilskin bag.

'Is there going to be enough wind, Dad, do you think?' Bobby asked. Aidan looked up at the sheltering trees. It was calm down here, but up there, the tops swayed languidly, as the wind played in the leaves, flipping them over in waves to show lighter undersides to the sun.

'I think there'll be plenty when we get out of the shelter of these trees and down onto the beach.'

They left the car park, walking over a little bridge and crossing the seafront road, dropped down immediately onto the beach. The tide was far out and there were miles of sand. They headed first towards the sea, across the band of fine dry sand, the colour of bleached bones, its miniature dunes sparsely peppered with half a day's sweet papers and ice cream wrappers. On reaching the line of darker, rippled sand, firmed and corrugated by the now distant sea, the breeze suddenly hit them. It was still warm – unusually, from the south – but carrying with it the tang of the sea. There they turned north, up the coast and away from the holidaymakers with their shouting children, barking dogs, beach balls, Frisbees, deck chairs and wind shelters. They seemed, as ever, reluctant to stray far from the reassuring presence of the shops, stalls, tea rooms, their cars and each other. Aidan was always thankful for the gregariousness of holidaymakers and the considerate way in which they left large areas of emptiness for those who had a taste for that sort of thing.

They stopped and made base in the lea of a substantial chunk of fissured, sea-washed tree trunk, stranded by the tide at the end of some mysterious voyage from God knows where. Bobby held the bag as Aidan extracted from it the folded kite, with its bright red sail and aluminium struts. It fluttered in his hands as the wind caught it, like a huge and brilliant butterfly struggling out of its pupa case.

'Okay, Bobby, hold it down while I get the struts in,' Aidan said kneeling down on the compacted sand. Together they assembled the kite, resisting its struggles to go with the wind.

'Oh no you don't,' said Bobby, 'not yet …' as her father clipped the control lines onto the twin bridles. Then to Aidan, 'Bags me first go, Dad.'

513

'Oh well ... I suppose so. Here, take the handles. Don't forget, red one in the right hand, green in the left ... they mustn't get swapped or ...'

'Da-a-ad ...' Bobby interrupted, 'don't try to teach your grandmother to suck eggs.' Aidan laughed. He knew she was an expert with the stunt kite – an ace, in fact.

Gripping the kite firmly from behind, he stood up, staggering a little as the breeze snatched at it, snapping the fabric into a taut aerofoil.

'Okay, off you go.'

Bobby, letting the lines run through her hands, unwinding off the dangling handles, walked briskly backwards upwind, while Aidan backed downwind, wrestling with the bucking kite, which seemed to be making a decisive bid for liberty. It reminded him of trying to restrain a cat, to get it into the carrier for a visit to the vet. When the lines were fully extended, they both stopped, now sixty yards apart. Bobby pulled the lines taut and Aidan held the madly struggling kite aloft. Bobby lifted her hands together to show she was ready and Aidan let go.

The kite roared vertically upwards and thirty feet of tubular tail uncoiled with a crack, becoming supple and serpentine as it inflated with air. Bobby threw the kite into a triple loop to the right, its tail following in a graceful spiral, followed immediately by three loops to the left. Then for a few moments, she held it still, poised high, almost above her head, a translucent, red diamond against a sky of the most intense blue, the yellow tail swaying vertically below, the wind whistling in the lines. Aidan, watching, saw it begin to tilt to the right, gradually accelerating, till it was hurtling down towards the ground, its tail describing a perfect arc behind it. Then a split second before disaster, Bobby pulled it out, to send it screaming, horizontally to the left at head level, its tail now straight as a bar behind it. Just in time, Aidan ducked and it whooshed a few inches above his head before rocketing up, to hang, almost stalled across the wind as though deciding what to do next. But Aidan didn't wait. In a fit of exhilarated laughter, he ran towards Bobby, knowing that the closer to her he was, the safer he'd be.

'God, you trying to kill me, daughter?' Aidan asked.

'No Dad – just giving you a fright,' she said happily.

Aidan stood by her side, squinting into the sky, following with his eyes the graceful ballet of loops, spirals, rocketing climbs, perilous dives and fast ground-hopping horizontal runs, the long yellow tail tracing the serpentine geometry, the wind howling in the strings. She seemed wholly absorbed in the pleasure, the excitement of the here and now. Aidan didn't know why he thought this would be a good time to tell her.

'Bobby,' he said, taking his eyes off the kite and looking at his daughter, her face in profile, tilted up towards the sky, 'I've got something to tell you.'

515

'Oh, what?' she asked, not for a moment taking her eyes off the kite. It really needed complete concentration.

'It's about Mum.' Bobby snorted impatiently, allowing her eyes to flick momentarily sideways, giving Aidan a minimal glance, then sending the kite hurtling into a vertical climb, to hover almost directly overhead. There she held it, making it sway languorously from side to side.

'What about her, then?'

'Well … she's ill.'

'Huh, isn't she always ill – or pretending to be?'

'This is a bit different …' He bit his lip, then, 'She's got cancer,' he said.

'What?' She turned suddenly towards Aidan, losing her grip of one of the handles and the kite gave a lurch and went into an ungainly, fluttering decent like a pheasant winged by an inexpert shot. Aidan grabbed at the other handle and helped the kite to a crippled landing just where the little waves were breaking at the water's edge. Bobby stood still, facing him, her eyes round with alarm.

'Is she going to die … is she?'

'No … no … of course she's not going to die. She …'

'But people do die with cancer. They do, don't they, don't they?' There was panic in her voice. She does care, then, despite everything, Aidan thought. He saw that there were tears welling in her eyes.

'Well some do – but it can be cured if it's caught early. Lots of people do get cured …'

Bobby burst into tears. 'Dad … Dad …' she wailed, 'it's my fault … it's my fault …' the words faded into a desperate moan. Aidan, alarmed, uncomprehending, took her into his arms and soothingly stroked her hair.

'Hey, hey, don't be daft. What on earth do you mean? Of course it's not your fault. These things are nobody's fault. They just happen … How on earth could it be your fault darling?' She let out another despairing moan.

'… cause I … cause I … when she was being horrible to me … when she was being horrible … I prayed to God to help me … and … and sometimes I asked him … I said to him, I hope she dies …'

'Hey, hold on a bit … Bobby, God doesn't work like that. You were angry and you had a lot to be angry about. God would understand. He doesn't go round making people die just because someone asks him to. What's happened to Mum's not something that God's done – and it's certainly nothing to do with you.'

'But he does, he does make people die … we learned about it in Sunday School, when he had all the first-born killed in Egypt and helped the Israelites with their wars and things.'

'Listen Bobby … no, it's not like that …' How he hated having to make excuses for God's bad behaviour.

'… and he made Abraham kill Isaac.'

'But he didn't – he sent an angel to stop him …'

'… but it doesn't matter. It was a terrible thing to do to tell him to kill his own son. And if he can do things like that … he can kill Mum. But I didn't mean it … I didn't really mean it … it was … she was just so horrible to me, all for nothing … and I was angry with her …' She buried her face in his chest and sobbed, gasping in breath, the whole of her body shaking.

Aidan held her tight and looked despairingly into the sky.

'Listen,' he whispered, 'those stories are from the Old Testament – way before Jesus was born. Most people don't take them literally now … more like sort of myths, you know … and the God Jesus talked about is much kinder and really understands peoples' problems, and forgives them when they do bad things.' He hated the pious twaddle he was putting out, but realised that this was not the time to put the record straight. What else could he do? She looked up at him with wet eyes.

'Ohhh … Dad. Will it be all right then, do you think … I mean with God. He won't punish me in hell, will he … for saying that?' She asked him, snivelling into his shoulder. 'I didn't really want her to die … I didn't.'

It took Aidan sometime to calm her down, to convince her that she had in no way incited the Almighty to visit misfortune on her mother. He wanted to say, but forbore to do so, that the Almighty needed no prompting when it came to dishing out misfortune.

They decided that kite flying was at an end for that day and by the time they'd got through the necessary chore of winding in the lines, dismantling the kite and packing it in its bag, Bobby's slightly wrinkled brow suggested a mood of quiet reflection.

In the tea room, waiting for doughnuts and tea, Bobby, completely calm now, asked Aidan for more information about her mother's illness and her prospects.

Aidan, his own mind in turmoil as he considered every possibility, answered her questions as best he could and she listened without emotion to his answers.

CHAPTER 34

Cathy had recovered quickly from the operation. The consultant said they were pretty confident that they had got it all and it had not been necessary to remove the lymph gland. To be on the safe side they would want to follow-up with a course of radiation treatment as they did with all cases like this. In such cases, the survival rate was very good, very good indeed. So with a bit of luck, she could look forward to a good quality of life for years to come. No, of course they couldn't give any guarantees or put a figure on it, but the five-year survival rate for this operation was excellent and many went on for ten or even fifteen …

She was in hospital for ten days. The first visit Aidan made did not seem to count. Not long from the operating theatre, she was tubed and somnolent, her eyes fluttered once or twice, but nothing seemed to register. The next, she opened her eyes and gave him a wan smile. She looked pale, drained of all energy, uninterested in the world outside. He held her hand. On the next visit, he brought flowers, grapes, orange squash. The one after that, he brought her books, one of the new Walkman cassette players and some tapes, some knitting she had started in a short-lived outbreak of interest a year ago. The day after, he took Dora for a dose of maternal reassurance. Then by the next day, she began to recover her strength and her interest in life.

Her colleagues began visiting. They brought flowers too, and grapes, chocolates and Lucozade. They all said how brave she was; how well she was standing up to this terrible ordeal. They talked of school. They much admired her fortitude and determination in the face of adversity. Later, they brought get well cards, hand-made especially for her by the children in her class. The children all said how much they missed her and hoped she would be back soon, and sent her lots of kisses.

He didn't take Dora again until the recovery was well under way and Cathy began to lose her post-operative haggardness to regain her normal appearance. When he visited alone, the Svensens were very good about looking after Dora, inviting her around to play with Klara. If the children had got so deeply involved, they were more than willing for Dora to stay overnight. When that happened, Aidan, thanking them profusely, lost no time in seeking out Louise. The nights spent with her in this way were precious and enabled him to attempt to soothe away some of the stresses his newly restricted life was placing on their relationship. He took every advantage of these occasions, fearing that when Cathy came home to convalesce, they would be few and far between.

He was right. She'd gone from strength to strength and was discharged after ten days. Her return home made the situation with

Louise much more difficult, for Aidan was in sole charge of her convalescence – apart from the district nurse who visited regularly to change her dressings. In addition to his normal responsibilities towards Dora and Bobby, and his teaching, he had to see to all Cathy's needs and to keep life clear of any possible impediments to a calm and peaceful recovery. This left little more, than snatched moments to be spent with Louise. She had said she would be patient – or at any rate try to be patient. Aidan had said to her that things would change as Cathy regained her strength. Then, he would not need to be in such constant attendance and they'd be able to see each other more.

Then soon, Cathy would have to go into the cancer hospital for a three-week course of radiotherapy. Then they might be able to meet a bit more. Yes, he would have full-time charge of Dora and would still be visiting Bobby, but there would be time; there'd be babysitters and friends Dora could stay with. So Louise had to be content with these hopes. Yet Aidan knew she was far from content and he felt a distressing unease about their future.

To some extent, what Aidan had forecast did happen. During the three weeks, Aidan drove the thirty miles to the hospital twice a week to visit Cathy and replenish her supplies of underwear and whatever else she needed. He visited Bobby once a week and did all that was necessary for Dora. So in the gaps, when Dora could be looked after, Aidan and Louise were able to see more of each other. But it was difficult to recover the carefree passion of the days before cancer descended upon their lives, for that was stoked by hopes for a future – a future about whose possible shape they still regularly hypothesised, but in which, whatever optimistic gloss Aidan tried to put upon the situation, Louise seemed no longer to have much faith. Yet when the circumstances were right, when Aidan had managed to negotiate a free night and when just the right amount of wine or whisky, or beer had been consumed, they would make love wildly or tenderly, and remind themselves of what they were in danger of losing.

It was when Cathy started work again, first of all, half days, then quite quickly full-time, that things started going really wrong. Cathy was not, of course, cured; 'cured' was a word used with great caution in the field of cancer. For the next year, she would have three-monthly visits to the consultant and only if there was no recurrence after five years would she be given some sort of qualified clearance.

But, nevertheless, there was a deceptive appearance of normality. She now looked glowingly healthy; she'd lost some weight, which made her look younger and they were right about the prosthesis. Her harrowing experience and the applause she'd enjoyed for her fortitude, had given her a new lease of life. Everyone who met her said how well she looked, how cheerful, how optimistic. But that wasn't how she appeared to him; what he got was the furrowed brow, the suffering silently born; intimations of mortality.

He was inescapably oppressed by her suffering and inescapably trapped by it, almost blamed for it; God, almost blaming himself for it – and when he was drunk, which, these days was often, he hated her for getting cancer, as if she would do anything to frustrate his escape, even though their relationship now rested on ties of mutual resentment. When he returned to sobriety, he was ashamed of that hatred. He reminded himself that she was the one who'd got the cancer. She'd got the dirty end of the stick. This was why he seemed helpless and unable to act.

Time and again, he tried to explain this to Louise, to get her to understand why it was taking so much time for him to get round to it, to confront Cathy with his decision. He explained that she was still under surveillance – three-monthly checks. When she was through that phase, with her future reasonably assured, he would then be able to …

'But for God's sake, Aidan that's going to take a year, a whole year.' Louise had said. Aidan could see that her understanding was wearing thin; there was a limit to how far her patience would stretch. And at the time of Bobby's return home, it became clear that that limit was drawing near.

Aidan's angst was intensified by the now looming problem of Bobby and her future. It was not a problem that seemed to tax Cathy, though. She never asked about Bobby. Returning from his visits, he would tell her he'd been and he would attempt to interest her in what

525

they'd done and what progress Bobby was making. But she never replied other than in the most abstracted way and she never asked questions. It was as if he were trying to interest her in the boring life of some distant maiden aunt she'd never met, rather than their elder daughter and her future. But, like it or not, Aidan decided, she had to be confronted, for time was getting short.

It was only two days before, when he'd gone to Roseberry to an appointment with Dr Wilkinson, prior to taking Bobby out for the afternoon, that Dr Wilkinson had said he would really have to discharge Bobby within the next week. The place she'd been occupying was urgently needed for another patient and now he was looking for confirmation that Aidan had made appropriate arrangements. Aidan had no option but to confirm. He had no confidence that the arrangements he'd made were appropriate, but they were the best he could do. It seemed at the time they were all he could do. There seemed to be – there was – no alternative to Bobby returning home; he had not, at any rate, been able to think of one. Somehow, the fact of Cathy's cancer had inflicted on him a kind of paralysis which restricted his action in every direction. He could not walk out on her while she was still recovering from her cancer.

Bobby's sojourn in Roseberry had removed one source of pressure for a while and his predisposition to push the future ahead of him as long as possible had prevailed. So the truth was that when the plan to move out with Bobby had had to be shelved, he'd got no more ideas and had not really made any attempt to do anything about it. Now the future had caught up with him; it had arrived. As he was driving to Roseberry, he wondered if there was a flaw in his time-management philosophy. Perhaps it should be, 'Never do today what you can put off till tomorrow – and watch out for the consequences.' He just had to hope that Cathy's own crisis had given her a little more compassion, a little more insight and that he might be able to have more control over events.

He had taken Bobby out after his meeting with Dr Wilkinson. They'd gone to the seaside, walked along the beach, dabbled in rock pools, finished up with tea and jammy doughnuts. On the way back, they'd pulled into the cliff top lay-by, a place where they often stopped to enjoy the view along the coast. This was where, as gently as possible, he told her that she was to be discharged next week and he wanted her to come home. When she heard this, she was silent for a moment, her eyes rounded in horror and then she burst into tears.

'No, no,' she wailed, 'I won't go back there … Dad you promised … you promised when that thing happened at school. It was her fault, because she made my life miserable at home. I remember how angry you were with her and you said, you promised you wouldn't let it happen again. You were going to take me away, weren't you … you promised. Dad, don't make me go back to her … please, please.' She looked beseechingly at him with her wet eyes.

'Yes, I know I did, love. But everything changed when she got cancer. It's a terrible disease and while she was going through that, I had to be around – I had to stick by her.'

'But she's had her operation. She's better, now, isn't she? She's back at work, isn't she?'

'Yes, but she's got to go through a lot of things before they can say she's better. After a while, we'll be able to think about it. Perhaps look for a flat – you and me.' She looked at him through tear-filled eyes and he was shamed to think of how often he had seen her in this state, how often distress had filled her life and how little he seemed to have been able to change it.

'Dad, you just can't face up to her, can you? That's the trouble, isn't it? You can't face the aggro, can you? But she doesn't mind it, does she? She loves it, doesn't she?' She started to wail again. Aidan winced at her words. He put his arm around her and smoothed her hair.

'Bobby, don't say things like that. Can't you see the position I'm in? I mean, I just can't pack up and go … not just like that … not at this moment.'

Eventually, he managed to calm her down. He promised her things would be different, though he had little confidence that they would be. He promised to redecorate her room; to fit it out like bedsit, with her own television, so she could spend more time there and that he would look after her. He reminded her of how nice it would be to see Mrs Cunningham again and take Banjo on his walks. For good measure, he held out a distant possibility, when the time was right, that she might have a dog of her own.

Then she said, 'If she's horrible to me, I won't stay. I'll run away … I will.'

'Okay, okay, okay,' Aidan said.

He drove back in a grim mood. He'd survived one emotional volcano, but not unscathed. He had an idea he was heading almost immediately for another, which was rumbling away and on the point of eruption. For though Cathy had come through her experience into some sort of renewal, he had no evidence that it had in any way changed her attitude to Bobby. But he had to put it to the test. Now. Well, after stopping off at the department to look at his painting, to remind himself of how good it was; something positive and after he'd soothed his nerves with a couple of stiff shots of whisky.

So, after they'd eaten and Dora had gone up to her room, he said to Cathy, 'Cathy, look, we need to talk. We need to talk about Bobby.' They were in the kitchen, after the evening meal. She'd been about to leave and he stood between her and the door.

'Well?'

'Is that all you can say?'

'Look, I've got marking to do and preparation …'

'Cathy, this is important. We need to talk about the future of our daughter.' Not a promising start.

'Listen, I've just had a major operation. I'm recovering from cancer. I don't need all this.' Not promising.

'Yes, I had noticed.' He tried to prevent anger creeping into his voice. 'But this has got to be faced. When you came back from your archaeology course, you said you wanted to make a new start …'

'That was before I knew you were knocking off that … that bimbo. You expect me to …' Her voice rose in anger.

Aidan faltered. So she hadn't forgotten. It was the first time she had directly referred to Louise and he didn't like the word she'd chosen – but he could hardly expect respect, could he? But that was a matter for later. So ignoring it, he pressed on. 'We have to talk about Bobby. Bobby, don't you understand? She's had an extension while you were ill, but now they want to discharge her. They are going to discharge her – next week.'

'Well?'

Aidan took a deep breath. He must stay calm.

'She will be coming here, home. It is her home, remember. I was hoping we could just talk about it a bit to make sure that she'll not be returning to the same situation as before.'

'Well then you'll have to make sure she behaves herself, won't you?'

Aidan was outraged. Okay, so it was open warfare. Back to the trenches. Business as usual. 'It's you who've got to change, and if you don't … I will leave you and take Bobby to live with me.' There, he had said it.

She said, 'And you would just leave me with my cancer, would you? Just what I'd have expected from you. Well we wouldn't have had that situation if you'd stood up for me, your wife. But you couldn't stand up to your own daughter. You let her wrap you round her little finger. That's your trouble – can't face up to hard decisions. Weak. Weak, that's what you are.' She pushed Aidan aside, picked up her school bag from the hall and went into the dining room, slamming the door resoundingly.

Furious, Aidan slammed his fist down on the table, causing plates and cutlery to rattle. He stood clutching, white-knuckled the edge of the table for some moments then stormed out into the garden. Why shouldn't he slam a door, too? He went down the path and headed down the hill to the pub. It was the early evening lull. Just as well; he did not feel sociable – yet. He took his pint to the farthest corner and flopped onto the worn, plush covered seat. Leaving the house in anger, he'd not thought to bring the paper. So no solace from the crossword, no respite from reality. Except … he drained his pint and went to the bar and ordered another. It seemed his character was deeply flawed. His wife and his daughter too, both said so.

At first, things had been peaceful. There had been some signs of an attempt at goodwill between mother and daughter; but quite soon small areas of friction began to appear. It was the usual things, trifling, inconsequential; nothing, however trifling or inconsequential escaped Cathy. However, this was a different Bobby. This Bobby had learned a thing or two during her sojourn at Roseberry. This Bobby was not going to be intimidated by bullying. By the time Bobby had been home for a week, Aidan was feeling most of the time like a referee in the ring, holding in tenuous restraint two bloodthirsty thugs who above all wanted to tear each other apart.

That made problems with Louise. He found it difficult to get out in the evening. He was afraid of what might happen if the referee left the ring, so their time together was snatched and limited. It was unsatisfactory and unsatisfying, Aidan had to keep trying to convince himself and especially Louise, that it was a temporary state of affairs, that they would fight their way through it and happiness would, in the end, be theirs.

Then there was an evening when he was free. Dora was sleeping over with Klara; Cathy was going to a meeting at school; and Bobby was going dog-sitting for Mrs Cunningham. So Aidan and Louise had arranged to meet in the college bar, at eight o'clock, to have a few drinks before drifting over to the seclusion of Aidan's room.

But Louise did not turn up at eight o'clock. In fact, it was ten o'clock before she arrived in the bar. Aidan had tried every way and everywhere he thought he might locate her. Without success. Eventually he sat in the darkest corner of the bar, in the blackest of moods, resisting every opportunity for cordiality; and with one eye on the door, he determinedly set about getting drunk.

The bar clock was reading just after ten o'clock when she came in. She was not alone. She was laughing and in animated conversation with Mark Andrews. They were closely followed through the door by Harry Pierce and Lizzie Allen. They all made their way to the bar – a noisy bunch of students, enjoying themselves. Aidan watched, stunned, ripped apart by jealousy, as Harry ordered drinks and induced a yelp of laughter in the barman, as he involved him in their conversation.

He watched in agony, as Mark said something to Louise; there was another eruption of laughter, as Louise grabbed him by the ears and baring her teeth in his face, gently shook his head. He watched as the laughter subsided and Louise picked up the pint of beer Harry had put before her and dipped her face into it. As she drank, she turned and over the heads of other drinkers, over the curve of the glass, her eyes met Aidan's. Slowly, she lowered the glass. Her face was flushed and the laughter in it died. She looked at Aidan for a moment, turned briefly to say something to the others then began to make her way across the crowded floor. Her companions, noticing Aidan for the first time, waved to him cheerily. He nodded. Louise slid into the chair next to him, placing her glass on the table and her hand on his. It was a lump of rock.

'Aidan ...'

'Hello Louise,' his eyebrows were raised, his greeting was cold. 'Well, you've arrived.'

'Aidan ... I'm sorry ... I, er ...'

'Louise, you're pissed; you're fucking pissed, aren't you. Where the hell have you been? Eight o'clock. Remember?' His voice was tight with anger and jealousy. 'I've been sitting here, waiting, since eight o'clock ...'

'Okay, okay,' Her voice was slightly slurred, 'I meant to be here, I really did, but we were working late in the studio and, well we just thought we'd go down to the Green Dragon for an early evening drink. I was going to be back for eight ... but then we had another ...'

'By which time you'd forgotten all about me ...'

'No, Aidan ... well one thing just led to another, we had a couple of games of pool and the next time I looked at my watch – well you know how it is – it was a quarter to ten. I didn't know if you'd still be here ... we came back. I am a bit pissed,' she finished lamely.

'I just can't believe this; you'd ... you'd actually stand me up – on the one night I could get away ...'

She interrupted him, 'Oh, look, Aidan, I'm sorry, but I don't think you've much right to complain – you seem to have had no compunction about standing me up recently.'

'Look, I always let you know somehow or other if I can't make it. You know it's more difficult for me to get away at the moment.'

'But you always expect me to be available when you can fit me in, don't you?' Now there was anger in her voice. It frightened Aidan; he was not used to her anger. She went on, 'Well I just wasn't tonight.

Aidan, it's time you made your mind up, whether or not you really want me. It seems to me you don't want me enough, if you can't find the guts to tell Cathy you're leaving her. You just seem to find it easier to put me off than to confront her. Maybe that's a flaw in your character. But anyway, it's getting me down, Aidan. I'm getting sick of playing second fiddle.'

Lulu too, Aidan thought. They all think I'm weak. He saw tears welled up in her eyes. This was something he'd not seen before and these were tears of anger, tears of frustration. To conceal them, she took up her glass and sipped at her beer. The rock melted; Aidan reached for her hand and took it in both of his. The anger, the anger of both of them subsided. Louise sniffed and a shadow of a smile appeared. Aidan clutched her hand to his lips.

He locked the door of his room behind them and wrapped her in his arms, kissing her savagely. Then they pulled apart and eyes locked, they undressed each other with a feverish urgency, till they stood naked, face to face.

'I love you.'

'I love you.'

'I love you.'

'I love you.' They said to each other. Louise subsided backwards into the worn softness of the chair, drawing Aidan after her, for him to kneel between her parted thighs. There were, tonight, no preliminaries; he entered her and they lost themselves in ecstasy.

Aidan's torments swilled away, like wet leaves hosed from a garden path. For a short eternity, his whole being was compressed, with the density of a neutron star at that place of their union. Arcadia.

The next day was Friday. The first part of Aidan's morning was taken up by a Curriculum Committee Meeting. As soon as it finished, he evaded the post-meeting inquests and headed straight for his room. She was not there. Oh well ... held up by something or other, he told himself. It was when he went to set up the coffee machine he noticed the envelope that had been slipped under the door and partly concealed by heap of paint rags. He stooped to pick it up. It was not addressed, but it bore a message; Ich liebe dich. Aidan tore it open. Inside was a postcard. Poussin; The Burial of Phocion.

The message:

Aidan,

Last night ended wonderfully. It could always by like that. But as usual, you had to go back to your wife. I'm finding it now almost impossible to cope with.

I decided to go home for the weekend to get away from the situation for a few days to think things through. I hope you'll do that, too.

All my love,

Lulu.

Aidan flopped into the chair where last night they had made ecstatic love, his legs stretched out in an ungainly splay, his arms dangling over the arms of the chair, the postcard still held in one hand, his head tilted back against the cushions, his eyes wearily shut. They had always managed to meet at some point over the weekend. It was what made the weekends tolerable for him. He closed his eyes in despair. Oh shit, oh shit. This one would be bleak.

He did not know then how bleak.

She did not come to his room at coffee time on Monday. He looked for her, while pretending not to look and discreetly, he asked around if anyone had seen her. No one had.

'She wasn't in Education, this morning,' Lizzie had said. 'She was going home for the weekend. I don't think she's back yet.' A cloud of gloom and anxiety settled over Aidan as he ploughed his way through the day. Where is she? Where the hell is she? He asked himself again and again. The next day, he couldn't wait to get to college. The two periods before coffee time seemed to last for aeons. Surely she'll be there, there'll be an explanation. She wasn't. There wasn't. He didn't bother with coffee. He went straight for the whisky bottle and treated himself in quick succession to two generous slugs.

After coffee break, there was the weekly meeting of the college Academic Board. He could hardly face the prospect of being pinned down for an hour and a half, trying to attend to matters which, in his present frame of mind, were to him surpassingly trivial. There was only Louise's not-here-ness that mattered. He needed to be wandering the college, looking for her. With a few cursory nods to colleagues, he made his way to a seat in the corner of the room and pretended to interest himself in the agenda and attached papers.

Aidan detached his brain from the events around him, managing to make the right noises at the appropriate times. Once or twice, Gerry's eye, the eyebrow quizzically raised, caught his, but his window on the world was, at that moment, impenetrably opaque. Then, nearing the end of the meeting, the chairman got to the item before Any Other Business. It was Individual Students. One or two names were mentioned, of students with minor academic or medical problems.

Then, 'Louise DeGrey ...'

Aidan started. Full awareness returned like a sudden electrical charge. The principal went on, looking up from his notes, 'She rang me last night. She'd gone home at the weekend. Illness in the family, apparently. She's asked permission to be away for a few days. So, concerned tutors please take note. She's one of yours, I believe, Aidan.' He looked at Aidan over his glasses.

'Er ... ah, yes,' Aidan said. 'Yes, she is.'

The few days extended into a week. Aidan lived through it, mechanically doing the things he had to do, as best he could through the alcoholic haze with which he determinedly buffered himself from reality. By the time of the next week's Academic Board, she had still not returned. Nor had she got in touch with him. He learned why, when her name came up again under Individual Students. Louise DeGrey was item eight on the agenda.

Aidan listened aghast, as the principal outlined the situation; in view of continuing problems at home – bit of vagueness here – something to do with parental illness – she had requested to intercalate a year; a whole year. Aidan was devastated. She wants to be away for a year. A year, a whole year … He couldn't believe it. He caught the sideways glance from Gerry, but had no option but to keep his feelings concealed. As Louise's main course tutor, his views were the first to be invited.

'What do you think, Aidan? Any reason not to accede to her request?'

Yes! Yes! Every reason. I love her. I want her. I want her back here now. I want to stroke her hair; I want to thrust my hands down her knickers; I want to kiss her breasts; I want to fuck her in the old chair in my room. I want … I want …

'No … I suppose not … can't think of any … apart from the fact that this college is closing the year after next.'

'Yes, well with the Institute's consent, she'll need to do her final year at one of the other colleges. It shouldn't be a problem.' Aidan wanted to get out of his chair, cross the floor in three mighty strides and crash his fist down on the principal's table and shout at the top of his voice, Oh no, it shouldn't be a problem. It IS a problem! It's a fucking great problem.

So it was agreed.

The working day ended. He knew he had to go home. Like an automaton, he followed the familiar route without noticing any of the familiar things by which he measured his normality, his mind numbed by both the shock of the loss of Louise and the considerable amount of alcohol he'd steadily dribbled into himself throughout the day. As he rounded the corner into Oakdene Avenue he became aware of the two little girls sitting on a garden wall, halfway down the hill. He made an effort to sharpen his focus; it was Dora and Klara, on the Svensens' wall. They were playing. How nice, he thought. Playing. His mind was suddenly swept by a longing for that innocence of the world, in which there could be play. Dora saw him and got to her feet and waved. Klara joined her and waved too, though in a shyer, more restrained way. Aidan tried to take command of his faculties and when Dora ran up to greet him, he managed the usual ritual; his arms around her, under her own, to swing her round in a couple of twirls before setting her down again. But he staggered a little and Dora looked up at him, wide eyed.

'You okay, Daddy?' she asked him, anxiously.

'Oh fine … Just a little bit tired, that's all.' He turned to Klara. 'Hi, Klara,' he said.

'Hello, Mr Hamilton,' Klara replied.

'Dad,' Dora pulled him away by one arm and cupped one hand round her mouth, 'I want to whisper something.'

'Oh okay,' he said, allowing himself to be drawn away from Klara and bending down towards Dora, cupping an ear in a reciprocal gesture towards her cupped hand. 'What do you want to whisper?'

She crinkled up her brow. 'Dad, it's happened again.'

Aidan's heart sank to even remoter depths. 'What's happened again, darling?'

'There's been another row. I think Bobby's gone away.'

Aidan groaned. 'Right, thanks for the warning, love. I'd better go and see what's what, then hadn't I? Well look, you stay and play with Klara, for the time being … okay?' He straightened up, closed his eyes for a moment or two, swaying a little. Just then, Gudrun emerged from the back garden with a trug over one arm and a trowel in her hand. She smiled.

'Hullo Aidan. How are you?' Then, after a pause, 'Are you alright?'

Aidan tried to smile at her. He said, 'Not really. There seems to be some trouble at home. I guess I'm just steeling myself up to go and investigate.'

'Oh dear,' said Gudrun, 'well look, Aidan, if it would help, you could leave Dora here for the time being – you know, till you've got it sorted. She can stay the night if need be.'

'Gudrun that would be really helpful – not the first time you've come to the rescue. Bless you.' Then turning again to Dora, 'Is that okay love?'

'Ooh yes, Dad,' she said.

'I'll ring,' Aidan said, as he set off, this time in a hurry, once more down the hill.

He went in at the back door, arriving in the kitchen at the same instant as Cathy arrived there from the sitting room. Aidan dishevelled, panting, his mouth slightly agape, a bead of saliva in one corner; Cathy, silent, showing no emotion, they stood in mute confrontation for some moments. Aidan wiped the corner of his mouth on the back of one hand. Focusing his eyes on hers, as best he could, he said, 'Well?' He hoped that commonplace monosyllable, used a hundred times a day on every English speaker's lips would somehow carry the crushing burden of all the unspeakable meanings that were trying to burst out of his head.

Cathy said, 'You're drunk.'

'You've done it again, haven't you? Where is she?' It had all happened before. Against his hope, it was so predictable. Déjà vu! Déjà vu? More a recurring nightmare, the more horrifying for its familiarity.

'Don't you accuse me? You don't know anything about it.'

'Is there anything new to know? Where's she gone?'

'I don't know ... I expect she's gone to that woman with the dog ... Look, I shouldn't have to put up with this sort of thing. I'm just recovering from cancer and ...'

Aidan's voice had been quietly, drunkenly venomous. Now something snapped within. Now he bawled at her, 'SHUT UP. FOR

542

CHRIST'S SAKE, SHUT UP.' He lowered his voice again and said, 'I'm sick of hearing about your fucking cancer. Does it give you a license to abuse your daughter, to do anything your distorted mind fucking well tells you to?'

He turned away from her and went into the dining room, slamming the door after him.

He stood still for a moment, staring dully out of the window, breathing heavily. Then he turned, picked up one of the dining chairs and with the blood-curdling cry of an infantryman plunging a bayonet into an enemy's guts, raised it above his head and smashed it into the floor. It fragmented. Then he did it again and once more, till all he was left with was a fragment of leg in one hand. Cathy flung the door open and stared, wide eyed at Aidan, then at the wreckage.

'Aidan, for God's sake ...' she began.

'Fuck off!' Aidan said, advancing towards her, still holding the chair leg. She gave a little scream and backed off. Aidan slammed the door shut and collapsed into the easy chair. Vaguely, he heard the back door open and shut and the sound of the car starting and driving away.

He looked at his watch; it wasn't late; no need to start worrying ... yet. But anyway he'd go round to Mrs Cunningham's; it was very likely she'd be there and what a relief that would be.

But she was not. Mrs Cunningham concerned, said she'd look out for her and if there was anything else she could do ... Aidan thanked

543

her and headed for home, checking out the derelict allotment hut on the way. Now he needed the telephone.

As soon as he got back, he checked the few possible numbers he could, without success. There was nothing he could do now but call the police. He did. They took down necessary details and said they would alert all cars, and send someone as soon as possible. Aidan put the phone down. He stood for a while, desolate, his eyes closed, then, moaning softly to himself, he stumbled towards the stereo in the corner. From the LP rack, he took out the last disc of Tristan and Isolde, and after several attempts, managed to fit it on to the turntable. He located the track he wanted and tripped the lever to lower the pickup arm on to it. He turned up the volume and was slumped in his chair before the stylus hit the groove and the music began. It was The Liebestod. As the music enveloped him in its voluptuous tragedy, he allowed himself to weep.

He was awakened by a persistent tapping, tapping. It took some moments for him to work out where he was and to remember what had happened. Christ, oh Christ … His mouth was dry and tasted foul; his head was aching. He traced the tapping to the vicinity of the window and using his elbows to lever himself up from the deep recess of the chair, painfully, he screwed his neck around. A face. Eyes peering in beneath interlaced hands. Christ; Gerry. What's he doing here? Aidan forced himself out of the chair and kicking aside the debris, made his way out of the room to the front door. He opened the door. Gerry was standing on the step. He looked Aidan up and down, alarm in his face.

'Aidan, for Christ's sake, are you okay?'

Aidan laughed a weary laugh just on the edge of hysteria.

'No, Gerry … It's no use me pretending, I'm definitely not okay … but it's nice of you to ask. Do come in,' he said, making a dramatic sweep of the arm. He guided Gerry into the sitting room and sagging once more into the easy chair, waved him into the sofa. 'To what do I owe the … well you know … and all that shit?'

'Aidan, what the hell's been going on? Cathy turned up at our place, a bit hysterical. Said you were smashing the place up. Said you'd gone berserk.' Aidan smiled faintly. Gerry indicated the wreckage on the floor. 'Is this all?' Eyebrows raised, he looked at Aidan.

'Yeah. Not too terrible, really, is it? Just a gesture, old son, just a gesture. Gerry I don't have to spell it out to you, you were at the meeting. Louise has gone. Gone. I got pretty pissed, I admit it. What else was there to do, eh? And guess what, when I got home, Cathy had had a row with Bobby … I knew it couldn't last, and Bobby fled. Cathy said she'd gone to Mrs Cunningham's. I went round there straight away, but she wasn't there. She hadn't been there at all today, Mrs Cunningham said.

'Look, Aidan …'

'Gerry, what time is it? Time to start worrying yet?'

'It's just before nine. Have you any idea where she might have gone?'

'There's a couple of places, places of refuge … places of refuge from her mother … I've checked, but no result. And by the way, is she coming back?'

'I think you scared her a bit, Aidan. Brenda's suggested she sleep over with us for the night.'

'Hm, might be just as well for her to do that. I might just fucking well kill her if she came back. Anyway, I've rung the police; seemed the only option and for the present all I can do is wait. It will help, when we find her, if I can tell her Cathy's not going to be here. And Gerry, tell Cathy the police are involved now and they're going to want to talk to her.'

'Okay, mate. Hey, look, Aidan, just give me a ring if you need me.' They left the house together. Before turning to his car, Gerry gave Aidan a momentary hug. Aidan looked at Gerry with a grim smile and nodded.

Shutting the door, he went into the kitchen and primed the coffee machine. He made it extra strong. That'd better be his tipple for the present. While the machine was chuntering, he went over to the sink and irrigated his face, neck and much of his shirt, with cold water. He mopped himself up with a tea towel then went to the china cupboard for a cup and the medicine cupboard for aspirin. He lowered himself carefully into a kitchen chair and poured coffee. He placed his elbows on the table and, groaning, lowered his face into his hands, letting the coffee aroma take over his senses. When it was cool enough, he popped a couple of aspirins and washed them down with his first gulp, then quickly drained the cup. He looked at the kitchen clock; it was a quarter past nine and – he glanced out of the window – getting dark. He still felt drunk and in line for a monumental hangover. Good thing the whisky bottle was empty. Good thing he wasn't far enough down the slippery slope of alcoholism to go for the cooking sherry. But his normal apprehensions were returning.

He went back into the kitchen. More coffee. By the time the coffee machine had delivered, the doorbell was ringing. It was the police. Aidan put his cup down and went to through the hall to open the front door.

'Mr Hamilton?' Aidan nodded. 'Good evening, sir. I'm PC Evans and this ...' He indicated his companion, 'is WPC Dawson. I understand you've reported a missing person, sir.'

'Yes ... yes, I have. Please come in.' Aidan made to guide them into the sitting room. They seemed in no hurry. The constable had taken off his hat and looked briefly around him as he followed Aidan, allowing his eyes to dwell momentarily on the wreckage of the chair, visible, as Aidan now realised, through the open door to the dining room. Aidan offered them chairs. PC Evans produced a note book and pencil.

'Now, Mr Hamilton, can you fill us in on the details? Can you just give me your own details first, sir – let's see, name, address, yes and phone, contact number, home and workplace. And your wife, Mr Hamilton? Now the missing person?'

'It's my daughter, Bobby – Roberta, she's thirteen.'

CHAPTER 35

It was Saturday. Bobby had last been seen early evening Thursday. When she did not return and was not found on Thursday night – Aidan had sat up all through that night, seeing in Friday's dawn – it seemed then that a horrifying threshold had been crossed. It was one thing for her to be out late and worrying enough; but to be out overnight seemed almost to be the seal of doom. People are fragile, destructible – especially young ones – dependent in every detail of their lives on their fellow human beings and the night was dangerous. Night alone. Night was a time to be spent under a roof, protected by walls from the unseen menace in the dark. A time of elective withdrawal from the world into comfortable, secure, regenerative inactivity. What unimaginable horror could it be that had kept his thirteen-year-old daughter from the protection of her home?

Aidan and Cathy were facing each other in active non-communication across the breakfast table. There seemed to be nothing useful to be said. The local paper had been briefly scanned and discarded; an oily translucency had appeared where one corner had subsided into the butter dish. Since it was Saturday, neither of them had work to consider – nothing to offer even the remotest possibility of distraction from the horrifying reality they were facing

– that they were parents of a missing child. Through the first night, Aidan had run and rerun through his mind, the possible circumstances of his daughter's absence. She could be staying with a friend. That was least frightening and surely the most likely. But she could – he was remembering the episode before Roseberry – have gone somewhere quiet with the intention of harming herself; perhaps not to kill herself – but she could do that by accident and no one to help her. Or she could just have had a common-or-garden accident – fallen in the river and drowned or run over by a juggernaut. Or she could have accepted a lift offered by a sinister motorist, been abducted, raped, murdered ... oh God ... Friday had been lived through in a state of alternating hope and despair, awaiting the ring of the phone with a kind of desperate terror, wanting both to answer it in the hope of good news and afraid to, in despair of bad. By Friday night, the most innocuous possibilities had all been investigated and produced nothing. Aidan had, because it was one of the first things he thought of, contacted the hospital. The police had contacted Roseberry and through the staff there, Daisy Farrington, the girl Bobby had allied herself with while an inmate. Back in Swaleborough, she had only two friends Aidan could think of from school. He'd been able to find their parents in the phone book and they had been contacted – but with no useful result. So the police had immediately instigated a full-scale vulnerable missing person alert. Now only the unthinkable was left. And Aidan had to think it.

He looked again at the disassembled pages of the paper, imagining the next issue with Bobby's picture on the front page. Captions: MISSING SCHOOLGIRL or MISSING SCHOOLGIRL'S BODY FOUND. Every case of a missing child that he could remember passed through his mind. The radio announcement; Child last seen … Then next day, Police search continues for missing schoolgirl … Then, Missing schoolgirl found safe and well. Police said that … or Police report that the body of the schoolgirl who went missing on Thursday has been found … they would like to interview a man who was seen … He'd felt a shadow of the anguish of parents of missing children; my God, what could be worse? He supposed that all parents must feel the same and be thankful it was not them suffering, not their child missing. But now Aidan knew what it was really like; he was such a parent himself.

He got up from the table, went over to the coffee machine and poured himself another cup of coffee. His instinct, enhanced in the last few months, to blunt the cutting edge of a crisis with alcohol, was for this one, formidably blocked. This was not just a crisis, it was a looming tragedy. Sobriety was essential. A stoic was not a drunk; he must face the tragedy raw and unmitigated.

He turned and looked at Cathy. She was sitting motionless, staring apparently at nothing. She did not turn to engage with him. He wondered what was going on behind the impenetrable façade. Parents of missing children, he supposed generally found comfort and support in each other; tearful couples appealing on television for members of the public to help them to get their child back; appealing futilely for the possible abductor to return their child to their arms; for information – anyone seeing anything, any small thing. But he was alone; she was alone. He did not know if their feelings in any way corresponded, in the face of the tragedy he had warned her of, which had now arrived; which they were now living. It was a scenario he'd experienced in nightmares, but he knew he wasn't going to wake up in a wave of relief from this one.

He looked at her again. Had it sunk in? For Christ's sake, did she care? Did she care about the child she bore, nurtured and loved? Loved at any rate till that child was superseded. Had she just enough love for one? What was in her mind? Was there a pathology – a – what would it be – filiaphobia? A condition of daughter-fear – or daughter-hatred? Selective filiaphobia, of course. If that was it, once diagnosed, could it be treated – cured even – with drugs or psychotherapy, or cognitive therapy, or electric shocks, or a frontal lobotomy? Or was it in any case too late to matter?

There was no communication between them. There now seemed to be no shared channel, no common wavelength. Yesterday, they had agreed to go to work. Aidan decided that he at any rate would be better off trying to engage with something, something that would stave off complete collapse. And the police had workplace phone numbers. So Aidan had fumbled his way through the day somehow, listening, always listening for the ring of the phone, stopping, holding his breath at the distant sound, waiting in agony, in vain, for the summons. He'd appreciated the efforts of his friends and colleagues to help, but had to resist the lure of the pub at lunch time, the offers of companionship; he had to be there for the phone and companionship in this situation counted for nothing. There was nothing in his life, nothing at all but waiting.

So on the Saturday morning; they were confined to the house. After the attempt at breakfast, Aidan prowled, while Cathy seemed to busy herself or pretended to busy herself with school work. He prowled from room to room, upstairs, downstairs, into the garden, the garage, listening, always listening, unable to do anything, think anything but the now, the grim, the appalling now. Waiting in agony for the phone to ring.

He was in the garden, looking vaguely at the apple tree, when it did. Christ! He turned, jumped the small hedge at the edge of the lawn, crossed the lawn in a few paces, through the open French window, across the sitting room and into the hall, and stopped momentarily, his hand hovering over the ringing phone, his eyes shut. It was the nearest thing to a prayer. Cathy was standing in the dining room doorway when he picked the receiver up.

'Aidan Hamilton,' he said to it.

'Aidan, its Bella ...' Oh, for Christ's sake, what a time to phone.

'Bella, look, we've got an emergency here, I can't ...'

'Aidan, I know, I know. Listen, she's here, she's here ...'

'What? Say that again ...'

'Bobby. She's here. Turned up on the doorstep a quarter of an hour ago. She's here. She's safe – she's okay.'

Aidan's legs gave way and with a sob, he crumpled on to the stairs, dropping the phone and sat for moments while tears, held back for so long, overflowed. Cathy came towards him, panic in her eyes.

'Aidan ... for God's sake, what is it? What's happened?'

The voice from the phone came distantly, 'Aidan, Aidan, did you get that – are you okay?'

He picked up the phone again and took a breath, 'Okay, Bella ... just hold on a minute ...' He rested the phone on his knee, covered his eyes with the palms of his hands, his head tilted back, jaw sagging. He breathed deeply.

'Aidan,' It was Cathy. Terrified. 'For God's sake what is it?' Aidan looked up at her.

'It's Bobby; she's at Bella's. She's safe.' Wiping his eyes with the back of a hand, he picked up the receiver again.

'Bella, what happened? I mean how ... Look I'll get in the car and come straight over ...'

'Listen Aidan, I don't know anything yet. She was exhausted and famished. She's with Roger, he's helping her to cornflakes, toast and marmalade, and tea. That was first priority. Next, I'm going to give her a bath and some clean clothes. Maybe she'll want to sleep. After that we'll talk. But I think it would be a bad idea to come at the moment till we find out a bit more.'

'Oh ... well ... okay then Bella, perhaps you're right. The main thing is she's safe. Oh God, thanks, Bella. It's the most wonderful news. We were beginning to think the worst ...'

'Yeah, I know, I know. Now listen, why don't you ring in a couple of hours. Then we'll have more information; then we can make decisions.'

He put the phone down and looked up from his seat at the foot of the stairs, his face damp with tears. Cathy was looking down at him, biting her lip. Perhaps she had been suffering just as much as he had. Perhaps she was just better than him at concealing her feelings. Maybe, but only when she would be disadvantaged by showing them. He wondered what she would have felt if Bobby had come to some harm. She could hardly, surely not have felt remorse when it would have been too late to do anything. But then that was what remorse was. An unmitigatable wounding regret at the un-undo-able-ness of actions. It had not happened.

She put an arm around his shoulders. The first physical contact for months. He patted her arm and gave her a ghost of a smile. It would do instead of words.

'I need a drink,' he said. He had thought to replenish the whisky. He looked inquiringly at Cathy.

'Yes please,' she said. 'A celebration.' They drank together.

Next, Aidan rang the police and the search was called off. Then, he rang Gerry and Barbara and other friends and colleagues, to tell them, rejoicing.

Aidan rang Bella in the early afternoon. By then, she had a fairly complete picture of what had happened after Bobby fled the house. It seemed that on her return from Roseberry, finding little to reassure her that things were going to be any better than before, she had worked out an emergency plan. She had some money saved and had hidden it in the derelict shed in the allotments. So that afternoon, after she'd fled the house, she'd first of all gone to retrieve this. Then she'd gone into town and spent a while in a coffee bar. After it closed, she made for a well-known squat in a run-down terrace near the bus station and begged shelter for the night, no questions asked. There were kindred spirits there and she was received sympathetically. Next morning, she'd caught the first coach to Penrith, wandered round there for a bit, trying to work out how to get to Irethwaite. Eventually, she'd taken a bus to Cockermouth, tried to get another to Irethwaite, only to find that there wasn't one. So she'd set out to walk in the direction she thought Irethwaite was, but got overtaken by darkness and spent the night in a barn. Next morning, realising she was lost, she retraced her steps to Cockermouth and carefully counting out her remaining money, found a mini cab and asked the driver to take her as far along the road as her money would take her.

He'd taken pity on her and dropped her off on the doorstep of The Shippen.

CHAPTER 36

After the anguish of Bobby's disappearance had transmuted into an undirected overflow of gratitude over her finding, Aidan's anger at Cathy seemed to burn out, to be replaced by a numb indifference which made some sort of normalcy in the daily conduct of affairs possible. It also allowed the aching absence of Louise back into his life as a constant presence. In the intensity of the crisis he had been firmly resolved that when, if, Bobby was returned to him, he would immediately move out and set up in a flat with her, out of reach of her mother. Then ... and then, perhaps he would find Louise and she could come back to Swaleborough, she could join them and there – he had every confidence of this – they would become a new household, where peace and tranquillity would prevail.

But after his visit to Irethwaite and his reunion with Bobby, the discussion with her, Roger and Bella, they had suggested that Bobby stay with them for the present and it was all agreed, the move had seemed less urgent. Without the stimulus of Louise's presence and with the disappearance of their plans into some orbit in outer space, inertia again seemed to settle upon Aidan's shoulders. For the time being, he could avoid the disagreeable business of arranging the division of possessions, organising being a non-resident father, sharing the car and so forth, and so forth. So for the time being he stayed – less as a matter of conscious choice, than of a weary neglect to do anything positive and found himself de facto, still part of a family, albeit a twenty-five per cent depleted one.

However, one factor brought him consolation; Bobby was living a transformed life. Bella had been able to arrange a place for her in the school where she taught and Bobby accompanied her there every day. It was a pleasant, easy-going school and Bobby began to thrive there. She found life in a small village much to her liking and soon found friends who introduced her into a new world of cows, sheep, chickens, working dogs, farm cats, barns full of hay, ponds full of newts and sticklebacks, and woods full of rabbits and rooks where handy ropes hung from branches, for the adventurous to swing from. Aidan came for visits, sometimes bringing Dora with him and for the first time for some years he had hope for Bobby's future.

Gradually, his work with the students resumed a semblance of its previous effectiveness, but a pervading gloominess and abstractedness made his relationships with friends and colleagues problematic, for everything was shadowed by that gnawing lack, that absence of Louise, which followed him everywhere. It was only the daily bottle of whisky, which by easing the pain, made life tolerable. Well that and his painting. This was the kind of benumbed normalcy he slipped into.

When three months after her operation, Cathy's specialist appointment was due, Aidan expected he would be needed to drive her the thirty miles to the hospital, as on previous occasions. He had, in fact, made provision to cover his absence from college for that specific purpose and resisted, for once, the lure of the whisky bottle. But Cathy had other ideas.

The day of the appointment, the sky was tediously grey and Aidan, looking out of the kitchen window saw that it was treating the earth to intermittent showers of fine drizzle. No she didn't need a chauffeur, she said; she was going to drive herself. It was time, she said, that people stopped treating her as an invalid. It was ironic that for years she had, at any rate for Aidan's benefit, habitually played exactly that role, seeming to find it a rewarding strategy in her battle for attention in an atrophying marriage. But now, she was buoyed up by so many compliments on the speed of her recovery and the courage she had displayed in fighting her way back to health. Being courageous was a new and heady experience; she was determined now to live up to her new reputation and amaze everyone with the completeness of her recovery. She had gone back to work with the determination that she was not going to be any longer troubled by a trifling matter like cancer. She certainly didn't need him to drive her on a trivial sixty-mile round trip.

Dora was by now at the table in the kitchen, despatching her cornflakes, while her egg waited under its hen-shaped knitted cosy.

The Today programme was muttering in the background and Cathy was upstairs putting on her make-up, prior her departure. Aidan opened the front door and went out to get a closer look at the weather.

He didn't much like the look of it and when Cathy came downstairs with her keys in her hands, he said to her, 'Look Cathy, the weather doesn't look too good; don't you think you'd better let me drive you?' The look she gave him suggested that she took the very offer as an insult, and her reply was curt.

'No thank you,' she'd said, 'I'm perfectly capable of driving myself.' Aidan shrugged.

'Okay ... if you're sure ...'

'I am.'

She hadn't done that much driving since the operation ... but ... While she was putting the finishing touches to her appearance, Aidan opened the garage doors and reversed the car out onto the drive, leaving the engine running. Having bent to give Dora a kiss on the top of the head, she came out of the house, walked past Aidan to the car, slung her handbag inside, slipped into the driving seat and clipped on her seat belt, before turning and looking up at Aidan.

'Thanks for getting the car out,' she said. 'I should be back sometime around tea time.'

'Okay. Drive carefully.' She nodded briskly, put the car into gear and reversed into the road. Aidan waited, while she adjusted the driving mirror. She released the handbrake and pulled away without looking back. He stood watching till the Renault, trailing a cloud of vapour from its exhaust, disappeared up the hill and around the corner. Then he went back inside the house to see how Dora was getting on. It was a quarter of an hour before she need set off up the road to join Gudrun and Klara Svensen on the walk to school, so he picked up the Guardian from where it had dropped behind the front door, sat down on a kitchen stool to inform himself on the state of the world and size up the day's crossword. Dora had gone to the bathroom and he could hear singing through a mouthful of dental hygiene. This recital was followed by an animated conversation with several of her dolls.

Presently, he looked at his watch then called upstairs, 'Dora, come on. It's time you were off.'

'Okay, Dad … I'm coming.' She came downstairs, noisily, in twenty-one separate jumps the last one into his waiting arms. He whooshed her round and dropped her facing the door. He opened it, propelled her onto the doorstep. She turned round, looking up expectantly and he bent down to kiss her nose.

'Okay, love, get going, bye. See you at tea time.'

'Bye, Dad,' she said, skipping down the path. With one last look, he turned back into the house. He stood for some minutes, listening to the silence then walked through the house to where the French window overlooked the garden. He stared out morosely. Everything looked damp and miserable. Perfect for his mood. Thoughts of Louise were never far from his mind and now that he was alone, they flooded in with full force. Where was she now? Did she feel like he felt? Would he ever see her again? He stood, silent, for some minutes, before turning to the drinks cupboard. He opened the glass doors and took out the bottle of Laphroaig and a tumbler, and poured himself a stiff measure. He held it up to the light as he always did, to savour the pale amber glow, before deeply inhaling the fumes, then taking his first sip. Bliss. He wondered if he was becoming an alcoholic. He was pretty sure drinking whisky for breakfast was not a good sign, but he knew it would take the sting out of his reflections. It usually got him started on the day and on his way to the next staging post; but sometimes not. As he sipped, he was increasingly drawn to the prospect of slumping in an easy chair with the crossword and getting quietly rat-arsed.

It was touch and go, but making the effort to take charge of himself, when he had drained his glass, he replaced the cork firmly in the bottle and put it back in the cupboard. He had arranged for himself a day free of student commitments so he must use it. He must get himself to college, lock himself in his studio and force himself to his easel. It usually took a powerful act of will to fight his way through the seductive menu of displacement activities, but once he picked up a brush and dipped it into some paint, he knew he would be immediately hooked. Besides, there was his other bottle of Laphroaig in the cupboard in his studio.

He had become aware that outside, the drizzle which had been intermittent when he saw Cathy off, had now developed into a steady rain. Just what he needed, he thought. He liked rain, mostly; it seemed to offer a cleansing of the spirit. And his spirit was feeling particularly jaded. So yes, just what he needed. He got up, went into the hall, got his raincoat off the hallstand, wriggled into it, picked up his umbrella, let himself out of the front door. Before locking it behind him, he looked up at the sky. Pretty foul now, he thought, with a pang of anxiety. Perhaps he shouldn't have let Cathy drive herself. But she was determined, wasn't she? She was an adult, wasn't she? Capable of making her own decisions, wasn't she? He pushed the thought out of his mind. He'd got enough shit in his mind already; and he couldn't cope with any more. So he turned up his coat collar and hoisting his umbrella, he set out for college.

The weather continued to deteriorate. By now, the sky was a saturated, dirty grey blanket. It shed its rain with a slanting ferocity that animated the pavement with a million instant fountains, soon filling the gutters with fast-flowing cataracts that cut courses through the accumulated autumn leaves, washing them out towards the crown of the road, to lie there in sodden, treacherous lines, like seaweed cast up along a tidal shore. It was quite a broad road and though theoretically past the rush hour, cars were still shuffling along, hugging its central white line as though afraid to get their feet wet. Aidan tucked his briefcase more securely under his arm as he took both hands to the umbrella, which the gusting wind was trying to wrest from his grasp. Ducking behind it he battled blindly along the pavement, hoping not to collide with anyone coming the other way. The three side roads he'd already had to cross had, as the downpour intensified, acquired tributaries of progressively increasing width. At the last one, he'd had to make a perilous leap over the flooded gutter towards the crown of the road and another to reach the pavement at the other side. Neither leap had been quite adequate as now he was beginning to feel the water seeping into his shoes, adding to the discomfort of the trouser bottoms flapping wetly about his ankles.

He had always taken a perverse pleasure in outrageous weather and now that mankind was getting so cocky about its power to do what it would with the world, it pleased him – though he supposed it was a romantic idea – to think that nature would probably have the last word; and this was just one of those little reminders of its power. The last side road on his route to college brought him to a dripping halt. This one had no central refuge. The torrents in the gutters had risen until they merged, covering even the crown of the road with a thin, rippling, fast-flowing sheet of water. The side road was now a full-width tributary of the main road river. Water – everywhere. He raised the umbrella, risking the full onslaught of the driving rain, squinting through bleary eyes for a diversion, or an island, to take him across the road, but he could see none. Turning his head to see if a retreat would offer a safe detour, he did not notice the car swerving in towards the gutter, to give room for the oncoming bus with glaring lights that had pulled out over the centre of the road to avoid a parked car. It flung up a sheet of water that drenched Aidan's unprotected back from head to foot.

'God bugger it!' he yelled. He turned, clutching his umbrella and briefcase and howled his fury at the retreating rear lights of the offending car, mentally shaking his fist – and not noticing the following van, whose bow-wave splattered down his other side, completing his inundation. He was later to reflect that his discomfort was caused not just by one of nature's reminders, but by an unlikely alliance between nature and technology. But now, he stood for a few moments in impotent rage, as the wind and the rain attacked his umbrella. Then, 'Oh shit!' he muttered to himself through clenched teeth, 'Oh what the hell?' and plunged forward into the road, splashing into the fast-flowing, ankle-deep water, feeling it pour into his shoes. Once he was resigned to being wet, it no longer seemed to matter; no more need to pussyfoot around puddles. He thought suddenly of little Dora, allowed outside in the rain in her shiny mac and sou'wester and her little red wellies, stomping round in all that glorious water. Laughing to himself, he stomped off in the direction of college, making it his business to displace as much water as possible.

Having resigned himself to his wetness, plunging on towards college, he turned his mind towards the painting awaiting his attention. It was presenting him with problems. Well they always did, of course. He always had to bite on his tongue when enthusiastic amateurs in his evening 'leisure' classes told him they wanted to do painting 'for relaxation'. He always wanted to tell them that if they found it relaxing it must be lousy. But you can't say things like that to enthusiastic amateurs. You can't tell them that if it's going to be any good at all it's going to cause them grief. And that, that's something you have to grapple with.

Anyway, this current painting was causing him more than the usual amount of grief. It was again a parkscape. A parkscape? Was there any such word? Landscape, of course; seascape, yes; cloudscape, even. Well, then why not parkscape? Scape was a spare part hanging about in the language, just waiting to be picked up and hooked onto something else. So that's what he'd done. That's what his paintings were: parkscapes. They were paintings of the park he walked in almost every day. The park which when he had first discovered it, that day years ago, when he had first come to Swaleborough to be interviewed, had in an instant transported him into the world of Poussin; the world of classical antiquity seen through his seventeenth-century eyes, ordered by his stoic seventeenth-century mind. Since then, Aidan had drawn and painted it again and again, driven by the twin forces of the reality as he saw and understood it, and the mediated evocation of the remote past. He supposed he was presenting a twentieth-century view of a seventeenth-century view of the world of classical antiquity.

But his current painting was proving troublesome. It was almost complete, he knew that and yet there was something, something small, that left him deeply unsatisfied. It was a worry that had been nagging at the back of his consciousness for days, now. He had returned to it again and again, looked at it this way and that, turned it upside down, studied it back to front, through a mirror. He had stared at it for minutes on end, squinted at it then studied it painfully through one eye. He had attacked small areas with his palette knife, scraping, repainting, cursing then doing it all over again. Somehow the satisfactory resolution still eluded him and he was beginning to wonder if it was a painting too far. He was beginning to wonder if he had mined this vein to extinction. Had he said it all, all that was to be said about the park and his feelings about it?

Then suddenly, thinking of the park, he wondered about the state of the river. It must be spectacularly full. He had no teaching to do. He was intending to spend the day in his studio, working at the painting, but it could wait. On this impulse, he stopped and turned. Waiting for a gap in the traffic, he plunged back into the flooded road and adjusted his course in the direction of the park.

Ten minutes later, turning into Botany Road, he raised the umbrella to get a navigational fix and had to scrunch up his eyes against the rain – which seemed dedicated to washing them out of their sockets. He stopped and peered wetly ahead to the end of the road, where the Ionic portico marked the entrance to the park. The clouds were looming darker than ever and the portico he always thought of as the gateway to a small pastoral paradise, had today, in the stormy half-light, rain-lashed, its stones streaked wet, with its background of agitated trees, a Gothic presence which would have satisfied the most ardent lover of horror movies.

With the rain drumming savagely at his umbrella, he thought of that idyllic day in late summer, when, in the course of his teaching and without at the time realising it, he had fallen in love with Louise. It had been a day of Arcadian tranquillity. But then all days in Arcadia should be tranquil; tranquillity was the very essence of Arcadia – even if humans were, in inconspicuous corners, acting out their trivial tragedies – being attacked by snakes, clandestinely digging for their husbands' remains. Wait, though; does it ever rain in Arcadia? he asked himself.

Of course it does. It must. Otherwise, how is it so luscious and green? And think of poor Pyramus and Thysby; it was a day just like this when, like Romeo and Juliet, they killed themselves through misunderstanding. He adjusted his umbrella to maximise its protection from the onslaught and pressed on towards the portico, becoming increasingly aware of the crescendo of noise as he neared the swollen brook beyond it. Pausing in the temporary refuge of the portico, he could now see the first bridge. There was no space beneath it; the torrent was hurling itself at the upstream side, stacking up against the curving parapet a crazy sculpture of broken-off branches and waving leafy twigs, and bursting round its ends, to meet downstream in a brown, foaming maelstrom. Further into the park, he could see that that the brook had risen above its banks, taken a short cut across a meander and had set off across the path to inundate the playing field beyond. He stopped again, completely enchanted by the sheer, unmitigated, implacable wetness of the world. He suddenly knew; his current painting must be Wet Arcadia.

He stood, looking, just looking; his legs braced apart, his body swaying in the buffeting wind, both hands on the umbrella, which seemed to be fighting him for its freedom, his briefcase perilously jammed under his arm. Damn! He wished he didn't have his bloody briefcase. What he wished he did have was a sketchbook or a camera – just something to record it. All he could do was look and feel. So he looked, trying to fix the visual sensation in his mind, thinking of how he could paint the lavish wetness of Wet Arcadia, how he could, within the formalities of the painting, with nothing but paint, evoke the overwhelming penetrating, permeating sense of total inundation. He thought of Poussin, of Claude, of all those classical landscapists he loved and yes, they did paint rain.

Rain and storms didn't just come with the Romantics. They didn't invent that heightened awareness of capricious, dangerous, terrifying nature. He thought of John Martin: The Deluge. Okay, there was rain. After that, a feeble shower, or two, from the Impressionists then he thought with irritation, why the hell should I be thinking of them? He inwardly railed at the seeming impossibility of avoiding looking at the world through other artists' eyes; how impossible it seemed to disengage from one's learning, how difficult to withdraw oneself, to heave oneself out of the sedimented mire of one's knowledge, to look with detachment, with objectivity, to analyse a bit of the world and then approach the canvas, with eye and mind and paint, but without influence. Then his thoughts were interrupted.

He'd thought he was the only one in the park. Who, he asked himself would be daft enough to come to the park in weather like this? And then he saw the dog. He knew it of old, it was called Annie. He'd regularly seen it over the years, with its owner and, in the fellowship between habitual users of the park, they generally found a few minutes for a chat when their paths coincided. It must have been fourteen years since he first noticed the dog, tearing madly in and out of the trees in the enthusiastic, but fruitless, pursuit of squirrels. He didn't know much about dogs, except that they came in all shapes and sizes, and were often unwontedly and embarrassingly interested in genitalia; but there was something distinctive about this one. He'd decided it had set out to be a Jack Russell – white, with black and tan patches, but its legs must have gone on growing for a while after the rest of it had stopped. It had a fine pointy, probing nose, borrowed from some other breed and, improbably, a ridge down its back. A true, designed-by-a-committee dog, but with an awesome turn of speed.

Over the years, he had seen dog and owner age. She, the owner, he adjudged to be in late middle age when he first got to talk to her. They'd been having occasional chats for nearly three years before they got round to exchanging names. She was called Mrs Abrahams. Now she looked distinctly elderly, slow, stooped and dependent on a walking stick. Annie too looked of pensionable age. She no longer energetically ranged the woods or chased madly with the other dogs that made sport on the field while their owners chatted. She was no longer to be seen leaping over fallen tree trunks like impala on the Serengeti plains and endlessly pursuing squirrels. She was now, like many of the aged, hard of hearing and her eyesight was failing too. Never the brightest of dogs, she now seemed to find many things in the world confusing. To see a lifetime, from birth to senility, compressed into fourteen years gave Aidan cause for gloomy reflection; set him wondering how his own wrinkles were doing. Now Annie was most likely to be seen a few paces behind her owner, devoting herself to the simple pleasures of the fragrances she encountered as she probed with her pointed nose under bushes and round the roots of trees. Enjoying the smellscape, he supposed.

They must have been coming along the path towards the bridge just at the time when the water first leaked over the river bank and set off across the path, towards the playing field. Mrs Abrahams had stopped, but Annie hadn't. She had broken into a kind of arthritic parody of a gallop – stiff-legged, her back see-sawing, for all the world like a rocking horse. She had overtaken her owner and plunged on oblivious, into the deepening water spreading across the path.

Mrs Abrahams had stopped at the water's edge and holding on to her rain hat with one hand was calling, 'Annie! ... Annie!' trying to get her voice to carry across the sound of the wind in the trees and the roaring of the brook, but the dog, seemingly seized by some madness, carried on, slowed down now by the increasing depth of the water. Then Mrs Abrahams, almost hysterical now, caught sight of Aidan, 'Mr Hamilton ... Mr Hamilton.'

He could just make out the sound of her voice, as she gestured and pointed desperately. 'Stop her. Can you please try to catch her ...?'

Aidan waved. 'Okay ... I'll try ...' He sized up the situation, then dropping his briefcase, he veered to the right and set off as fast as his encumbering rainwear would allow, on a course to intercept the dog, hoping she would not blunder towards the fearsome waters round the bridge. Then she stopped. For a moment, she looked round puzzledly, then, turning sideways, to Aidan's relief, plodded, splashing to the edge of the flood water and onto the path. She turned to look for her mistress, now separated from her by a substantial stretch of water. It seemed that, with her failing eyes, she could make no sense of the situation. Aidan approached her with a rapid, but stealthy walk, hoping to reach her without provoking a panic.

'Annie! Annie!' he called. But she didn't hear him, didn't see him. Aidan was still twenty yards away, when, still unable to make sense of the situation, Annie decided to resume her gallop along the river bank. After all, it was the route she had walked every day for years. Mrs Abrahams had by now set off at right angles, onto the playing field, taking a muddy detour around the encroaching flood, casting desperate looks to where she hoped Aidan had been able to detain Annie. But he hadn't. He was following her as unobtrusively as he could, as she bumbled uncertainly along to where the river banks rose temporarily, to form a stone-faced cutting, ten feet above the roaring river, before giving way to a steep muddy slope from which grew clumps of straggly willow saplings and a substantial ash tree angled out over the river. Oh God, don't let her slip down there. Aidan winced at the thought. He was some way behind, thinking that if he made a sudden approach from the back, she might start, lose her footing and disappear over the edge.

He stood still and held his breath, as she unconcernedly, disregarding the pelting rain, sniffed her way along the narrow path along the edge of the cutting. He breathed a little easier when she got to the place where the vertical drop gave way to the steep muddy bank. He was now two or three yards behind her. In another ten yards or so, the muddy bank sloped down to where the river was separated

575

from the path by a low wall. If she made it there, it would be safe to dash forward and grab her. But she didn't. She stopped by the ash tree, seemed to think for a moment or two, then slithered down into the crook formed where the stout trunk curved outward from the sloping bank. She squatted to have a pee, looking with mild interest at the surging water below her.

No! No! Oh God ... Aidan was convinced that if she tried to scramble back onto the path, she'd more than likely lose her footing and slither down to her doom. So he would have to go for her – it was an instant decision. It had to be quick but stealthy; not to frighten her. Coming from behind, he got close, paused, then ... NOW. He made a grab at her collar. His feet slipped on the mud, he fumbled, missed the collar; she started and her back feet scrabbled in loose stones, before she slithered backwards down the bank. Aidan, with no time to think of what was down there, cast himself down the bank on the downstream side of the tree, tobogganing on his backside. As he hit the water, the current snatched at him and as his feet tried to find purchase on the smooth rocks in the bottom of the swollen stream, he grabbed with one arm at a straggly outgrowth of willow, in time to prevent himself being swept off his feet. With the other arm, he grabbed out at Annie, who, having, fallen through another clump of willow, still looking puzzled and paddling as fast as her arthritic limbs would permit, was about to depart downstream. This time, in a swift grab, he got her firmly by the collar and her back end swung round, like a boat settling to its anchor in an ebbing tide.

'Christ!' said Aidan, his mouth agape, rain trickling into his eyes, panting his relief. He was waist-deep, rushing water parting round his waist, forming a bow-wave in front and a wake behind him. Clutching the willows with one arm and Annie with the other, he clung on, trying to work out what to do next. There was no possibility of getting up the way he came down; the best bet seemed to be to carefully transfer his grip to the next clump of willow with his free arm, hanging firmly on to Annie with the other, to work his way downstream to where the bank became shallower. If he could avoid being swept away, it looked as though he might be able to scramble up there, dragging the bedraggled but acquiescent Annie after him.

By now, Mrs Abrahams, who had arrived on the bank above his head, was jabbering incomprehensible advice at him, as he worked his way along, trying to stay upright, stumbling precariously among the rocks in the bottom of the stream. At last, arriving where the bank became shallower, he wedged himself against the beginning of the wall and shouted to Mrs Abrahams to lower the end of the lead to him. He grabbed at it and clipped it to Annie's collar and Mrs Abrahams pulled while Annie scrabbled, and he pushed from behind.

Having successfully landed Annie, Aidan grabbed hold of the wall and, with feet slithering in the mud, managed to haul himself onto the bank. He stood there, open mouthed, panting, dripping, while

Mrs Abrahams, who seemed temporarily to have forgotten him, tearfully embraced Annie, who looked puzzled – as ever. Aidan, very wet, waited. Then Mrs Abrahams seemed to remember. She looked up.

'Oh thank you so much, Mr Hamilton. 'You're a hero,' she said.

'Yes, I'm going to make myself a cardboard medal,' he said.

No one was around when he got back to the department. Good. He looked at his watch. Coffee time. No time for that; anyway, felt anti-social; he'd give it a miss, today. He let himself into his studio and locked the door behind him. He looked at himself in the old wardrobe mirror that hung on the back of the door. Jesus, was there ever a drownder looking rat? He was dripping water on to the floor. He peeled off his clothes, layer by layer. Nothing could be saved. He stood naked in front of the mirror, grateful that his skin, at any rate was impermeable. He reached for the grubby towel – he should remember to change it sometimes – and rubbed his hair vigorously, creating an unruly thicket. For a few moments he looked at himself in the mirror. Hm, not bad for forty-five. Pity there's no one to appreciate it. In an instant, his mood sank. Louise, my Lulu, why aren't you here? Why aren't you here? He groaned, blinked at himself in the mirror and shook his head. Morbid reflection, he thought and smiled a bitterish smile at his cleverness.

He sighed now and took his naked self to the cupboard beneath the bookcase and got out the whisky bottle and a glass. Bugger the medal, he said to himself, this is the proper reward for heroism, he told himself, as he half-filled the tumbler. He draped his clothes on the radiator and anywhere else he could find space and unhooked from the back of the door the old boiler suit Wilf had given him for really dirty jobs. He climbed in and buttoned himself up, looking round for the beat-up tennis shoes that went with the boiler suit.

He took a good slurp of Laphroaig and selected from his cassette shelf Debussy piano music. He wanted wet music: Jardins sous la Pluie; Reflets dans L'eau; Le Cathedrale Englouti. None of them quite up to what he had in mind, though. He really needed the ferocity of the storm in An Alpine Symphony. But no; wrong landscape; over-the-top Romantic. Debussy would have to do. Then he went to the box in the corner by the radiator where he kept off-cuts of hardboard, ready, sized and primed dazzling white, ready for sketches and preliminary ideas. He picked up a few and took them over to his easel. He removed from it the painting whose finishing had been giving him so much trouble. It would have to wait. Probably a good thing anyway, he'd come back to it later. He put a small, primed board in its place, went over to the wall where his palette hung from a hook. 'Jesus Christ, what a mess,' he said to himself. Ever since his student days, he'd been meticulous about the craftsmanship of painting, but he had lately let things slip – discipline was out of favour. Cennino would not have been pleased – but getting the paint down on the canvas was what mattered now; life's too short … He reached for the glass and drank some more whisky. He'd not properly cleaned the palette for several days and it was polychromatically encrusted. Pleasing to look at though. God, I'm becoming a slob … a slob. Oh what the hell!

He took a palette knife, gave the palette a cursory scrape into the waste bin and put it down on the table. He'd got to being negligent with his brushes too and most of them had just been dropped into the paraffin bucket at the end of his last session. Slob. He swished them round in the paraffin, gave them a communal wipe on a rag, stuck them in the salt-glaze jar – a flower arrangement. From the scattering of tubes on his table, he selected, first, cobalt green and viridian, and squeezed almost half a tube of each on to the edge of the palette; then cobalt blue and ultramarine; lemon yellow; then black, glorious black. Finally, white. That'll do for starters, he thought. No, wait – an afterthought. Maybe Venetian red. He squeezed some on to the palette. Oh the contrast … the glorious sonorous contrast. Then from the bottle on the table, he sloshed some spirit of turpentine into a small jar. Ahh … the pungent fragrance took him straight back to his art school days. And now, it was Lissa, beautiful, ephemeral Lissa Dennison. Lissa Dennison, the red-headed Pre-Raphaelite beauty he'd spent one idyllic day with that summer at the end of his second year.

Suddenly … he wondered. The girl in the dream. He'd never been able to put a name to her – was it her? Had it been Lissa?

580

His glass was empty. Before picking up his palette, he half-filled it again and took a sip. Making a space among the tubes of paint, he put down the glass and took up the palette; with his thumb through the hole he nestled it comfortably against his arm. He switched on the tape deck – Images: Reflets dans L'eau: andantino molto – and picked up his biggest brush, dipped into the turps, then into the viridian and floated it in broad sweep across the top of the board, vivid and translucent, its horizontality supported by the verticality of the rivulets that descended from it. The horizontal and the vertical, that was the essence of it. Same with language – syntagma and paradigm; and music – melody and harmony. That structural grid in which all meaning was created. He knew now his painting was aspiring to the condition of music; it was form, tone, movement, above all, colour; and through these, atmosphere. The visible world evoked through the organisation, the manipulation of these elements. Debussy, manipulating them in the realm of sound, also evoking the visible world; the vocabulary shared.

Facilitated by the whisky, the audible and the visual interpenetrated in Aidan's consciousness: he had now got the massive, dark horizontality of the tree canopy and its reflex in the shadowed ground beneath; the swathe of luminous distance in between, portioned off by the measured verticality of the silhouetted trunks of the trees.

The music was wet alright; perhaps a little puny for what he'd just experienced and what he had in mind, but it served to get him started, to focus his whole self on this primal act of making an image. He lost himself in it. Disconnected from time.

He was on to the fifth sketch, four propped up against the bottom of the bookcase, awaiting later development. There was knocking at the door; someone trying the handle.

'Aidan, you in there?' It was Gerry. 'Hey, man, it's lunch time. You coming to the pub?'

'Ah, Gerry … z'at you?' Aidan's voice was slightly slurred.

'Course it's me. Who'd you bloody-well think? You okay?'

'Yeah, never better. Listen, Gerry … I'm in the middle of painting … can't stop. Going like a bomb. Anyway, it's still pissing down out … don't want to get my hair wet.' He gave a snorting laugh.

'Aidan, you should … Christ, never mind … You want me to bring you a sandwich or something?'

'Yeah, thanks …' Wet music swelled up discouraging further communication.

It was around three o'clock when, stopping to replenish his palette with cobalt green, he was suddenly overtaken by fatigue. He was on to the big one, now. Six feet by four. He'd been saving this canvas for something special and this was it. The six sketches, shiny and wet, were propped up against the bookcase and the door, where he could refer to them; he was pleased. The massed dark greens and blues of the foliage, moving in the wind and the shadowed grass sang out basso against the brilliance of reflecting water. The vertical intervals of the silhouetted tree trunks measured out the space, across and into the picture. And oh, wet, so wet. Aidan was pleased. He was also somewhat drunk. The whisky bottle was empty. Must get another tomorrow for the studio. Okay for tonight at home though. Had he time for coffee before going to meet Dora from school? He looked up at the clock above the door. Yes. He started up the coffee machine and while it was making coffee, he looked at his painting again. He scrunched up his eyes and squinted at it. He picked up a clean brush and loaded it up to the ferrule with Venetian red and painted a vivid oblong into the greeny-black of the shadows. He stepped back and studied the effect.

Wow! he thought, just what it needed. His thoughts were slurred. A voice inside him said, 'What's that?'

Complementary contrast. That was what was lacking. That's what's needed.

'But it's not there – not in the park.'

So?

'You can't do it. It's not true.'

Listen, get it into your head, I've stopped imitating the world. I'm now evoking it. And I'm having a sensual experience. Now, is that not wet Arcadia?

'Yeah … but …'

Look, it's like writing an autobiographical novel. It may be based on the real world, but man, it's a novel – you can invent, tell lies. There's nothing you can't do, nothing. Now bugger off.

Aidan went back to the painting and with the middle finger of his right hand carefully smeared one end of the Venetian red oblong.

He cleaned up his brushes. He felt good about that. Then he shifted the easel around till it was opposite to the easy chair. He relaxed into the chair with his coffee and appraised his day's work.

His clothes were still damp, but he had to put them on anyway. The rain had not stopped, but it had given way to the same depressing drizzle that the day had started with. He put up the umbrella and set off for the school. Now, for the first time since he saw her off that morning, he thought of Cathy. He wondered how she'd got on. He thought, in a drunken overflow of optimism, Perhaps they'll say she's cured. Then I can remind her I'm in love with another woman and, if she doesn't mind, I'm going to leave her – and it'll all be all right. Then, more doubtfully, I'd have to find Lulu and get her back. Maybe she wouldn't want me now. Maybe she's met someone else. The awfulness of this thought was cushioned by the alcohol. He tilted the umbrella and glanced up at the sky. Lousy weather for driving. He had offered to drive her. She should have been sensible and accepted. It was pride, sheer pride. She would show him whether or not he was indispensable. Suddenly, he was surrounded by kids and bumping into their parents. He was there; he'd hardly noticed; he was there, approaching the school gates.

He heard Dora's voice; didn't see her at first, but recognised her voice among all the other voices. Like a sheep can sort out its particular lamb from all the seemingly identical bleatings. Then her hand was in his. Looking up. Laughing. Happy. Lucky her.

'Hi, Dad ...'

'Hi love.' He looked down and ruffled her hair. She tugged at his arm, skipping sideways. Ordinary walking is no good to a six year old.

'D'you know what, Dad? Well today ...' She began a breathless rundown on the day's events, which took them all the way home. Once inside the house, she headed for the fridge and got herself a drink. After the first noisy gulp she asked, 'Dad, when will Mum be back?'

'Should be about six, love. We'll eat then, if you can last that long.'

'Okay, okay, okay,' she sang and set off upstairs to apprise her dolls of her return. Aidan thought he'd better get on with some cooking.

It was half past six and Cathy was not yet back. Held up by heavy traffic, Aidan supposed. Somehow traffic always seems worse when the weather is bad. Dora had come downstairs to watch television and to tell Aidan she was hungry now.

'Why's Mum late?' she asked Aidan.

'Oh, I expect it's the bad weather,' Aidan replied, dishing her out a helping of the Bolognese sauce he'd prepared for the evening meal and some pasta shells. He said no he wouldn't eat yet; he'd wait for Mum. Seeing her settled in front of the television with a tray on her knee, he thought, gin and tonic. He found alcohol a useful aid to waiting. He could wait any length of time if he had enough alcohol.

He sat down with the crossword. He'd got it half finished, then it was seven o'clock; seven o'clock. Still Cathy was not home. He got up from the chair and stood, looking, unfocused, out of the window. He was beginning to feel uneasy. He poured himself another gin and tonic, and asked himself why he should feel uneasy. Hadn't her absence, in recent years usually been a matter of relief? Those times when she'd stormed out after a row; when he'd not given a damn whether she came back or not; when he and his daughters had enjoyed a brief spell of tranquillity, while her absence lasted. Had he been worried then? Had he fuck. So what was different now? He didn't know the answer.

He took his gin and tonic to the front door, went out into the weather and looked up the road, as if his doing so would cause the blue Renault to appear round the corner at the top of the hill. At half past seven, he rang the hospital. The night staffs were in place. The staff nurse personally knew nothing about Mrs Hamilton, but she'd look in this afternoon's records and appointments. Oh yes, here it is; Mrs Hamilton's appointment was for four o'clock and yes, she'd been there and been seen. Well, she'd been allocated a half hour slot and the clinic had closed at five. So she must have left before that. Sorry we can't offer any further help.

Aidan put down the phone and stood by the telephone table, rubbing his chin. A bit worrying, her being this late. Shit, why was he worrying? He ran the possibilities through his mind; she could have had a breakdown, he supposed. At this moment, an RAC man could be stretched out under the car by the side of the road or stooped with his head in the bonnet. But wouldn't she have phoned to let him know? Or perhaps she might think it not a bad idea if he stewed for a while, just to keep him on his toes. Oh come on, she wouldn't do a thing like that, would she? Perhaps she just couldn't get to a phone. Or maybe she went to town, to do some shopping while she was up there and got blocked in. Or maybe she called on someone, on the way back and got involved in some way. But who? He didn't know.

'Mum's late, Dad, isn't she?' Dora's voice came from the lounge. He'd not noticed that the sound of the television had stopped and now there was just silence, occasionally broken by a familiar xylophonic clattering as Dora delved into her box of coloured pencils.

'Yes, she is a bit. Must have got held up somehow. She'll be back soon,' he said, reassuringly. He was not reassured. What should he do next? Oh, for God's sake stop worrying. He'd lived through plenty other occasions of unexplained lateness, inventing every possible disaster to account for it and it's all been unnecessary in the end.

When the doorbell rang and he saw, fragmented, through the hammered glass panel of the front door, the black and white check of police caps, he knew for certain that this was not one of those occasions.

'Good evening, sir. Mr Hamilton?'

Aidan stood swaying on the doorstep, trying to focus his mind.

'... blue Renault 16, registration ... very bad accident sir ... three-lane road just near ... almost head-on in the overtaking lane ...

My God, my God, my God ...

'My God ... how is she, do you know ...?'

'It was really bad, sir. The ambulance boys were right on the spot, got her straight into the Memorial Hospital, as soon as they got her out.'

'I've got no car ... I'm afraid I've had rather a lot of ... Can you ...?

'Of course, sir. If you get your coat, we can give you a lift straight away.' Dora had unobtrusively arrived behind Aidan and was looking on wide eyed.

'Dad, what's happened, what's happened?' she asked, looking in turn at Aidan and the policeman.

'Mum's been in a car accident, darling. They've taken her to the hospital.' From Dora, he looked appealingly at the constable.

'It's okay, Mr Hamilton, WPC Jacobs, here, she'll look after the little girl till you get back.' The young woman stepped forward. Aidan looked down at Dora again and for a moment, cradled her plump cheek in his hand.

'Okay, darling? I've got to go to the hospital. This lady's going to stay with you. Take her up … show her your room, your dolls. I'll get back as soon as I can.' Dora looked up into his eyes, wondering.

'Okay Dad.' Aidan took away with him the image of her anxious face. The WPC got down on one knee in front of Dora.

'Hello, love. I'm Liz. Now, what's your name?'

'Dora.'

'Dora, that's nice. Now, Dora, I'd really like to see those dolls your Dad mentioned.'

The constable escorted Aidan, struggling into his coat, to the waiting car.

* * *

When he arrived at the emergency ward, the curtains were drawn round the bed. He knew then that he was too late. The doctor who emerged from the cubicle was much younger than Aidan. His white coat looked as though it had seen him through a long day. He wore glasses. His hair was rumpled. His stethoscope was slung around his neck. He looked desperately weary. The nurse who followed him looked experienced, very experienced.

'Mr Hamilton … I'm Dr McRay, registrar. I'm afraid your wife is … we did everything we could, but we weren't able to save her … she had such severe injuries … head and chest … She didn't regain consciousness. I'm so sorry.' Aidan was silent, while he tried to take it in. They waited. Aidan closed his eyes and swayed, as though about to topple over. The nurse grabbed at his arm.

'Would you like …' she began.

'No, no, I'm alright, I'm alright. Can I see her?' The nurse looked for guidance to the doctor. The doctor breathed deeply and looking steadily into Aidan's eyes, said, 'Mr Hamilton, it was a bad smash. She's quite badly mutilated. We haven't had time to clean her up …'

'It doesn't matter. I need to see her.' The young doctor and the experienced nurse exchanged glances.

'Okay, if that's what you want …' Dr McRay led the way to the bedside; Aidan, with the nurse behind him, followed. Stopping at the bedhead, the doctor turned again to look into Aidan's eyes and Aidan nodded. The young doctor and the experienced nurse, synchronising, folded back the sheet that covered the body that had been Cathy and stood aside. Aidan stared, silent, unable to speak, for some moments. When he found voice, it was to utter for the umpteenth time that day, the words, 'Oh God,' in that helpless invocation of the non-existent, that will do equally as well for a spilt cup of coffee or a violent death.

CHAPTER 37

The undertaker had slipped away and drifted back to where the three large black cars were waiting. She looked at her watch and spoke briefly to the drivers. As they dispersed to their vehicles, she looked, with a faint trace of anxiety over towards the flower bunker, where Aidan and his daughters were still standing. Other mourners stood around irresolutely in twos and threes; some were now drifting back to their own vehicles. Aidan slowly raised his head sensing that the allotted time was up. He put his arms around their shoulders again.

'Come on, daughters,' he said, 'better get back to the cars. We can go back home now.'

* * *

It was agreed that notwithstanding the changed circumstances, it would make no sense at that time, to bring Bobby back to Swaleborough. She was happy and doing well in Cumbria, and Bella and Roger were happy to have her with them as long as necessary. So Aidan and Dora went back to the house in Oakdene Avenue, to make what they could of life as a single parent, single child family. Dora soon reshaped her life to accommodate the new circumstances. Her friends and their parents seemed to make special efforts to be helpful, in some way, to try to compensate for her loss. And Dora with her six-year-old's resilience was quick to respond. Aidan was particularly attentive to her needs; aware that the whole burden of parental responsibility was now his – and that awareness was to place the constraints on his life which prevented his disintegration into total drunken irresponsibility and decadence.

Nevertheless, in the following months, there had been times – many times in fact – when he just wanted to run away screaming or collapse into a helpless, blubbering heap of self-pity. But there were several resources he could draw upon, so he didn't do either. The fact was, he had friends and the best of them understood his plight. Those more distant, who understood less, thought it was the tragic death of Cathy which had shattered his life. To be sure, he had lost a companion of many years standing, a whole shared history. Even allowing for the turbulence and the agony of the recent years, which was not something that could be lightly dismissed. But his friends knew it was Louise he mourned.

Then, he began playing table tennis again. He played whenever he had time that might otherwise be spent in being actively miserable and he could find a ready opponent. He now played with a wild ferocity, which when successful, drove his opponents to duck under the table; when not, caused onlookers to run for cover. It was one of those activities, he knew, which, though not of cosmic significance, had the capacity to fully absorb the consciousness, leaving no room for morbidity.

As always, these last months, another resource was booze. He had, since being introduced to the pleasures of the hop in the early days at art school, been an enthusiastic beer drinker and lover of pubs. Since he was surrounded by like-minded friends, the opportunities were many – though, perhaps fortunately the number of occasions for taking them up were restricted by his domestic situation. He had never before drunk to get drunk. When he had got a bit pissed, it had always been a pleasurable by-product of the social situation. But now he saw no good reason to deny himself that solace. If life was so shitty, what the fuck did it matter if he was pissed half the time. He was convinced that it improved his table tennis and he even believed he taught better. As well as making sure of the whisky supply, he took now to storing consolatory cans of beer in various places in the house, in the garage, as well as ensuring that his room in college was well provisioned. He thought it was quite good for his painting too; for after his responsibility for Dora, that was perhaps his most valuable resource and he was determined that he was not going to fuck up on this chance he'd been waiting for so long.

Thus he managed a lot of the time to keep the pain of Louise at least partially at bay. He wondered if she now understood what an impossible situation she had allowed herself to be drawn into by messing with a married man. He would convince himself that she was trying to forget him and it would be sensible if he also strove for forgetfulness. Perhaps she rued ever meeting him. Well he was doing no ruing. She had changed his life, expanded it and enriched it. Whatever happened, nothing could change that.

Then a postcard arrived. It was posted in Florence. Poussin. Et in Arcadia Ego. How appropriate. It has been wonderful, this blissful world ... but ultimately, we all end up under a tombstone. No other message, no address, just Love, L. It rekindled his hope into a tiny spark for a while, but he quite quickly swamped that with alcohol.

A week or so before the exhibition, another card arrived. This one posted in Rome. Another Poussin. This time, The Martyrdom of Saint Erasmus, in which the eponymous saint is stretched backwards over a bench while his small intestine is being wound round a winch by the noblest-looking thugs you could ever hope to see. The message on the other side was again just Love, L. Despite himself, he laughed. Black, black, black. He knew what it was like to have your guts twisted. But it had to mean something and it was this thought which prompted him to go against her stated wishes and attempt to communicate. After all, he was free, now. A widower. How would she know? So he sent to her home address, asking for it to be forwarded, an invitation to the private view. He had written on it, please come. The possibility that she would was the other cause of his excitement, as the opening day approached.

CHAPTER 38

He went down to London two days before the exhibition was to open. Months ago, in one of the preliminary discussions, when Marcus and Helena had come up to Swaleborough, Helena had suggested that Aidan might take them to the park, to the area which had inspired so many of the paintings. Marcus thought that would be a good idea. So after lunch, Aidan took them there in a leisurely amble through the town. When they arrived at the end of Botany Road, he'd made them stop there, in the embrace of the Ionic portico, for them to share in his first vision of Arcadia. He'd thought wistfully of the day when he'd stood in that same spot and seen Louise standing there, alone, beautiful; and a wave of agony swept through him. He remembered his astonishment and delight when he'd found out that she'd not only heard of Poussin (most new students hadn't), but could talk about him knowledgeably and find evocations of his vision, as he himself did, in this park. It seemed an astonishing meeting of minds – though as he later discovered, it wasn't just coincidence. He knew now that that was when he'd fallen in love with her. How poignant the memory was.

'Oh yes, Aidan, I see what you mean about Poussin,' Marcus had said. Then, later, after an hour of wandering along the paths, through the trees and across the bridges, he'd said, 'As I see it, it's all so tightly themed … your show ought to have a title – you know, something a little more indicative than just 'Recent Paintings by Aidan Hamilton' … and it's obviously got to be something to do with Arcadia.' Aidan and Helena agreed, and after tossing a few ideas about, it was decided it would be 'EDGE of ARCADIA; Parkscapes by Aidan Hamilton'.

Aidan liked that; it was apt at so many levels. When he went down to London, two days before the opening, he actually saw it, EDGE of ARCADIA; Parkscapes by Aidan Hamilton, on the walls of the King's Cross Underground escalator among the advertisements for West End shows and Pretty Polly stockings. My God, he thought, that's me – I've made it; made it to London. After all these years! But by Jesus, it was a near thing … it was bloody touch and go, but I did it. Here I am in London, about to expose (if that's the right word) myself to the cognoscenti of the capital. He smiled to himself. He had arrived in London.

He reflected on his despair during the last six months. Yes he'd often been in despair, doubting that it would ever come off; times when he'd thought, Fuck it – what's the point? These were times when getting quietly – or rowdily – drunk seemed a hell of a lot more attractive than self-torment in front of an easel. But … but, there'd been other times when getting pissed and tormenting oneself in front of an easel had seemed an easy combination – and thank God for it or he'd never have got enough paintings together for the exhibition.

Hell, he'd just drunk and scrabbled his way through the mess in his head. That was the thing about booze; if you couldn't make a bad thing go away, a few pints of beer or a few treble shorts would slip a pair of mitigating spectacles between you and your unhappiness. Everything he'd read or been told by doctors labelled alcohol a depressant. Well, speak as you find; not for him, it wasn't.

And as to the paintings, it would show, in the exhibition, this instant when his life changed; the impact on his life of cancer. Ironic, that; not his cancer. It wasn't his but by God it had changed the course of his life and no doubt about it, it showed in the paintings. Arcadia? Oh yes, it rains in Arcadia. Poussin knew that all right. Poor Pyramus and Thysbe; he gave them lousy weather for the day of their destruction. Arcadia, crepuscular with storm clouds, the sky lightning-riven, trees bent before a raging wind. Well you couldn't have a double disembowelling on a balmy spring morning, could you? It was the day of Wet Arcadia when another double death occurred; the head-on collision which had carried off Cathy, with a complete stranger for company.

It would show. That had been the climax – some months after the initial shock of the diagnosis. The awesome power of just the word CANCER. He'd remembered, as a child, when his parents took him on a visit to Mrs Champion; her face, sallow, eyes darkened hollows, her thin arms extended over the neatly folded-back sheets, a sickly-sweet smell. Her husband solemn, starkly upright on a rush-seated, ladder-back chair. No one told him she had cancer; no one had told him there was such a thing. But somehow he knew. You couldn't say it though; you couldn't say the word – in case saying it gave it to you. Hah! – The omnipotence of thought. The dread disease was referred to by silent mouthing or by a gap in the sentence, a shake of the head and a meaningful look with pursed lips. Never the uttered word, for the very word carried contagion. He couldn't remember how he learned the word. But he remembered the dying Mrs Champion and his first inkling of the horror of the thing itself.

He'd learned, just before – it was at the beginning of the war – of what he then thought to be the incomparable awfulness of mustard gas. He could hardly believe that someone had invented this stuff; a liquid and a gas that would choke you, scorch out your lungs from the inside and on the outside, flay off your skin with blisters; he pictured the house painter with his blow lamp and scraping knife. You would die. Horribly. He'd looked down without much confidence at the cardboard box, slung by string around his neck, housing the gas mask the government had given him. Well mustard gas was invented by people and by then he knew people often did dreadful things to each other. But cancer, which could do all that mustard gas did and much, much more, that was invented by God. By GOD. Why would He want to do a thing like that? His Sunday School teacher didn't know. But she did say that God works in mysterious ways.

In time, as he'd learned more about life, he'd been able, to some extent, to slot the big C away in his compendium of life's nasties, to be dealt with as and when. It was out there ... but it wasn't something you expected; it wasn't something you allowed for. Yes he knew people got cancer, but that was people in the distance – people one knew of, but not people one knew; especially not one's nearest and dearest. Oh no? Before the war was over, he'd lost his father and two uncles. Cancer was stalking in the backyard.

Now in his middle age, he'd found it next to him in the marriage bed. She'd got it. His wife. His wife of twenty years, whom he'd known since school days. The wife whom possibly he had loved and was wrecking the life of their daughter, whom on that account, and because he had fallen in love with another woman, he'd been preparing to leave, had got CANCER. Oh, how that had changed his prospects.

It would be bad enough if someone you loved dearly was stricken. Bad enough? It would be horrendous. It is horrendous for those it's happening to all the time, everywhere. So is it worse when it happens to someone you're about to detach from your register of responsibilities? And suddenly, you can't, because those responsibilities have assumed a cast-iron irrevocability. You can't leave someone who's got cancer, can you?

He'd asked himself, would it be easier to bear if it was Louise who'd got it? He thought that was rather like being asked if you would rather die by having a red-hot poker stuck up your arse or having your intestines wound round the drum of a steam winch. But he rather thought it would. Then he'd be involved in a conventional kind of tragedy, in which a loved one dies and the survivor survives in totally legitimate abject misery, upon which, time, in the end, would effect a kind of healing and the possibility of a new start. All morally immaculate.

But, what was it called? The moral imperative ... that compelled you to do what was right. What was right? Well what was right and who said so? He was fucked if he knew. What he did know was he couldn't leave her. Not now that she had cancer. It may have been just pity, but for him it proved to be a force every bit as powerful as love. So for that present, he was trapped.

When could he have left her then? When she was cured? If she was cured. But if she was, when would she be? Could she be? He had foreseen a long period of indeterminacy in which he was kept hanging on by that sodding moral imperative. He'd known that his best hope for that future he'd been hoping for would be that she should die. He'd shocked himself with that thought and tried to file it away in that section of his mind reserved for the unthinkable. Anyway, if he did seriously wish it and it did happen, it would not be freedom he gained, not for him, anyway, but slow destruction by unassuageable guilt. He wondered if St Matthew had also written something along the lines of, Every man that looks upon his wife and wishes her dead, hath committed murder already in his heart. He had to be careful here. With him and Bobby both at it, the Almighty might have started getting ideas.

He and Louise had talked about it again and again. Even though Aidan had been swamped by guilt at the very thought of it, they had talked about the terminal condition, about its possibility and its consequences. After all, cancer was that kind of disease. They had talked about it without malice; just objectively, as one possible outcome by which their future might be determined. They'd known though that the odds in favour of survival, at least for some years were good and Aidan knew he could not keep Louise hanging about indefinitely. Whatever she'd felt when they'd begun their relationship (and she did say she had gone into it recklessly, with no long-term expectations), she did not now see her role as mistress, content to service the libido of a married man, for whatever rewards such a role might offer.

No, she was a wife in waiting, seeking in the end the conventionalities of commitment and exclusiveness. Aidan had known this and he'd wanted it too. But with Cathy's cancer his hopes for this future had shrunk, as through the wrong end of a telescope. In the situation as it was, he could not offer Louise the time and attention she needed, for God's sake he needed. Her patience had been stretched beyond all reasonable limits and she'd gone, leaving him in despair. Then he became a widower. Widowed not by the cancer, but by a head-on collision between two cars. He was a widower, now. Could Louise know that? Could the news of Aidan Hamilton's widowhood have percolated down through Europe to Florence, to Rome? He had an unreasoned hope that it might have.

That hope flickered into life when he arrived in London. Oh, excitement; he did not know when anything he'd done had filled him with such a feeling. Well, only one thing and despite his flickering hope, he was trying not to think too hard about that. No, it was the exhibition, this exhibition; something he'd wanted and worked towards for so many years. For so long it had occupied a place on the distant horizon and somehow, with each move he made towards it, it seemed to recede by an equivalent distance. In the end, though, he'd found out how to make it stand still and now he was approaching it; close proximity; it was within touching distance – a mere two days away.

Oh the excitement. Yet he knew the dangers of over-anticipating a singular event. Like the wedding day anticipated, planned for, longed for. Then it comes and it's gone. It's history. It's the afterwards. He had tried not to think of the afterwards – carpe diem – that had always been his strategy – but he couldn't help it. Would he get good reviews? Would he get any reviews? Would his paintings sell? If they didn't ... if they didn't and he had to ship them all back to Swaleborough, what then? Ignominy. The end of hope. He could hardly bear to think about that possibility. If it did though? A bonfire on the lawn, perhaps – yes and maybe himself on top. Perhaps he could allow himself to live, but just give up painting and stick to table tennis and booze – or take up something more fitted to middle-aged respectability, like golf. He cringed at the thought. No, that isn't going to happen. Think positive, Aidan. Here you are in London!

CHAPTER 39

There were a lot of people. The gallery must have done their publicity well. But did they only come to drink the wine? Aidan wondered and to exchange raucous chit-chat. The gallery, barefloored, resonated. The voices collided, interpenetrated and blended into an incredible continuous roaring sound, like the wind in winter trees; a complex counterpoint of streaming sentences. Sentences, as he pictured them, ejected at high velocity in every direction, dropping to the floor as impetus waned and accumulating in ever deepening drifts of words, in which they would all eventually drown. He wanted to stand in the middle of the gallery and shout, 'Why don't you shut up and look at my fucking paintings?' Yet some must be looking, he supposed, for there was a growing number of red spots to be seen in the bottom corners of the pictures.

So instead, he kept smiling over his wine glass, surveying the patrons. This is the art-loving public of the great metropolis, is it? For a time, he maintained anonymity. It was easy, for no one, apart from the gallery people, who were mainly occupied in welcoming and massaging the psyches of rich-looking patrons, knew him from Adam. He moved with his glass of wine, inconspicuously eavesdropping, wanting to hear people say nice things about this work, but was disappointed to hear little but last night's television, last week's theatre or a wonderful little restaurant discovered just off the Rue Martine.

Presently, Marcus disengaged himself from a Woodhousian archetype – stout, twin-setted, pearled, wielding a lorgnette – and launched her into the melee. His eyes swept over the heads of the crowd and located Aidan in his corner. Aidan surrendered himself and now found himself being launched. At last, he was in touch with his patrons, being passed from individual to individual, group to group. By now well lubricated, he began to rejoice in the limelight.

Sometime later, Helena detached herself from the group she'd been in animated conversation with and crossed the room to where Aidan was enjoying himself. He was amusing a very fetching young French woman, with his account of the origins of Wet Arcadia. Helena hung back, waiting for a gap in the conversation, trying to catch Aidan's eye. When he saw her waiting, Aidan, with only a little reluctance – for Helena too was extremely fetching – excused himself and went to her.

'Sorry to drag you away from the gorgeous Madame Simonet ...' Aidan smiled, turned his palms outwards and shrugged, in a kind of c'est la vie gesture. '... but we were just wondering if you'd mind giving the punters a short rundown on the work. As you can see from the number of red spots, you've got some real fans, already – and I know they'd like something from the horse's mouth.'

'Oh sure. No problem there. The horse will be delighted to oblige. There's nothing I like better than shooting my mouth off – especially about myself.'

'Great ... about an hour's time, I should think. I'll come and get you. Oh and by the way, we just had a phone call from Melissa. She should be here any time now. She's on her way, coming straight from the Airport.'

'Right, so I get to meet the fabled director at last.'

Helena nodded and said meaningfully, 'You sure do.'

Aidan set off on a leisurely itinerary around the gallery to pick out the pictures he might want to talk about, sipping wine, smiling, nodding and chatting to anyone who seemed to want smiling or nodding, or chatting to. He was peering meditatively over his glass of wine at Parkscape with Fleeing Dog, when behind him, against the background animated chatter and clinking glasses, a voice, a woman's voice said, 'Hello, Aidan.'

He'd been waiting, hoping, longing for a voice, but in the instant before he turned round he felt his hope dissolve – for this was not that voice. He turned slowly, to face her. She was smiling. Waiting.

'You don't remember me, do you?' Aidan was shocked into silence; his jaw sagged a little, as remembrance seeped into him, his mind winding rapidly back through the years. It was the same colour, the hair; no longer that disordered tumble about the shoulder. Now cut to a sharp line below the ears, curving symmetrically inwards to the chin, to frame the face, to give prominence to the sculpted cheek bones. But it was still that burning Titian red. She must be a year or two older than him. Her face had its share of those markers of passing time which women seem to dread, the slight wrinkling at the corners of the eyes, at the corners of the mouth. That was bright red. The eyes, a penetrating blue. She wore a slate-blue trench coat, collar turned up, open, over a white, polo-necked jersey. A marschallin, a mature beauty, sensual, experienced. He took her extended hand first in one, then, almost fiercely, in both. She waited. She waited for him to recover his power of speech.

Then he said, in almost a whisper, 'Oh I remember … I remember all right. How could I ever forget …? My God. Melissa Mierevelt … Melissa – Lissa Dennison … Melissa Mierevelt.' They fell together in a laughing embrace. Then hands on each other's shoulders, they pushed apart and drank each other in.

'You've matured well, Aidan. I like the beard. Distinguished …' It was a recent acquisition – he was, so far, quite pleased with it.

'And you, Melissa, after all this time … as Pre-Raphaelitely beautiful as ever. Just like you were on that day …'

'You remember it, then … that glorious day in Northumberland?'

'There's hardly been a day since when it hasn't drifted into my mind. It gave me a taste for heaven and I've been looking for more of it ever since.'

'And have you found much?' she asked, laughing, teasing.

'Hm, well some …' His mind slipped towards Louise. 'Oh I don't know …'

'It was a wonderful day, though, wasn't it?'

'It was – truly wonderful. But it was just a day. And then it was over. Afterwards, we never ever came close to each other again. It was as if it had never happened.'

'Well, you never tried. I sort of had the feeling that you had a girl in that smoky town you came from. What was it again … Blyth?'

'But I didn't think I could try. I didn't think I had the qualifications.'

Melissa laughed out aloud. 'Oh, Aidan … how absurd.'

'But it's true. You were at the end of your third year, doing marvellous paintings. I was just a first year, bewildered, awed, still just trying to get the hang of things.'

'Oh come on – you'd just won that first-year prize for life drawing, hadn't you?'

'Yes, I know … but that didn't make any difference. I was callow and spotty; you were beautiful and sophisticated. To me, it was as if a goddess had come down from Olympus for a day, to sample life among the mortals – and by sheer good fortune, she made rather a bad landing and fell into the seat I happened to be occupying.'

'Oh poor Aidan. How you must have suffered. I wish I'd understood. If you'd been a little more courageous … well anything could have happened.'

'It would have taken more than courage – a magic helper at the very least. It seemed to me that you'd gone back up to Olympus and were now surrounded by a pantheon of handsome, corduroy-jacketed gods smoking curly pipes. How could I have competed with that lot?'

'Oh Aidan, what can we do but sigh for opportunities lost? Then in a year, I'd got my degree and left, and we never saw each other again … until now.'

'And the years between?'

'Oh, I went to Amsterdam – worked in a gallery there, painted, exhibited. Met Hendryck – a conservator in the Rijksmuseum; we got married. Later we came to London. Hendryck had by then inherited quite a lot of money, so we were able to start this gallery.'

'And Hendryck?'

She allowed her eyes to drop. 'Four years ago … heart attack. Left me a widow.'

'I'm sorry.'

'Of course the gallery came to me and I decided to carry on. It's continued to do well and as you'll have realised, I get lots of lecturing and university teaching pushed my way. And so, here I am.'

'But when I first sent the slides … you must have known … why didn't you …?'

She looked down and tugged at her lower lip, as though it might help her to order her thoughts. 'Yes, of course I knew. I didn't suppose there would be another Aidan Hamilton – especially another

Aidan Hamilton who would paint like this.' She waved her arm around in gesture which encompassed all the paintings. 'I don't know … it was a bit naughty, I suppose, not to come clean and let you know who you were dealing with … but I was in the States most of the time, making the occasional dash back for business purposes. I kept thinking about it. I knew the nuts and bolts of the exhibition were in safe hands, with Marcus and Helena, and so I thought the revelation would keep – until I was in a position to savour it.'

Aidan grinned. 'Like now', he said.

'Yes. Like now,' she said, opening her arms and inviting him in. They embraced again, smiling.

'Aidan.' Helena was approaching. 'Are you ready to do your spiel? Come on, put him down, Melissa.' They separated.

'Yes okay. Any time.' He looked again at Melissa.

'Carry on, maestro,' she said. 'I'll see you later … and er … I think I'm probably going to invite you to dinner – that is if you're not doing anything else afterwards.'

'Oh …' Aidan's reply was lost, as Helena took him by the arm and whisked him off.

'Now, where would you like to start?' He was still in a state of shock, trying to get his head round what had just happened.

'Aidan?'

'Oh … yes, er, over there, I think, opposite the door. I'll start with Parkscape with Graffiti …' He tried hard to focus, '… er, okay … a few minutes of general introduction and then we'll do the tour. Then if anyone wants to ask questions …' Helena raised her voice above the gentle hubbub and assembled the audience of twenty or so; some brought chairs around, others stood. She introduced Aidan with a few brief words then handed him over.

He began, 'I was born and brought up in a small coastal town in the northeast, where they built ships, mined coal. They loaded the coal into the ships, sent it down the river to the sea. A lot of it came here, to London, to be burnt in Battersea Power Station, to make the electricity to light the shops of the West End. It was a hard, dirty business and the town was not very beautiful. At the end of the street where I lived – not more than a hundred yards away, there was a coal mine – a pit. Looking along the street, we could see the pit-head gear – the big wheels that lowered the cages with their cargo of human beings into the depths. Behind it was the pit heap. Every pit had its miniature mountain of smouldering refuse from the depths of the earth. Beyond the pit-heap were the rows of yellow brick colliery houses, with their little gardens and outdoor lavatories. The first of these rows, next to the pit-heap was called "Arcadia Terrace".'

There was a small stirring in the audience – a smile or two and Aidan went on to expand on his notion of Arcadia, which gave him the lead into his discussion of the actual paintings. He had turned sideways on to the audience to indicate a particular detail in the first of the paintings; as he turned to face them again, his eyes were drawn toward the vestibule, the door. The words he had prepared ... died on him. She was there, framed by the door. Almost silhouetted against the sunlit street. Black hair, red lips. Her eyes caught his. She smiled.

www.ingramcontent.com/pod-product-compliance
Lightning Source LLC
Chambersburg PA
CBHW072007020726
47501CB00006B/1718